I0692689

Coasts of Cape York

The Air Cadets

C.R. Cummings

Also By
CHRISTOPHER CUMMINGS

Kylie & Skip

The Boy and the Battleship

The Green Idol of Kanaka Creek

Ross River Fever

Train to Kuranda

The Mudskipper Cup

Davey Jones's Locker

Fourteen

Air Cadet

Below Bartle Frere

Bowling Green Bay

Airship Over Atherton

Cockatoo

The Cadet Corporal

Stannary Hills

Sugar & Spice

*Coast of Cape York

Kylie and the Kelly Gang

Beyond the Barrier Reef

Behind Mt. Baldy

The Cadet Sergeant Major

Cooktown Christmas

Secret in the Clouds

Mischief at Mingela

The Word of God

The Cadet Under-Officer

Through the Devil's Eye

Barbara in the Bush

The Smiley People

Barbara at her Best

Barbara's Bivouac

Coasts of Cape York

The Air Cadets

C.R. Cummings

DoctorZed
Publishing
www.doctorzed.com

Copyright © 2023 by Christopher Cummings

All rights reserved. No part of this book may be used or reproduced by any means, graphic, electronic, or mechanical, including photocopying, recording, taping or by any information storage retrieval system without the written permission of the publisher except in the case of brief quotations embodied in critical articles and reviews.

Third Edition published 2023 by DoctorZed Publishing

DoctorZed Publishing books may be ordered through booksellers or by contacting:

DoctorZed Publishing
10 Vista Ave
Skye, South Australia 5072
www.doctorzed.com

ISBN: 978-0-6458591-1-9 (sc)
ISBN: 978-0-6458591-2-6 (ebk)

A Cataloguing-in-Publication entry can be found at the National Library of Australia
www.nla.gov.au

This is a work of fiction. Names, characters, places, events, and dialogues are creations of the author or are used fictitiously. Any resemblance to any individuals, alive or dead, is purely coincidental. The views expressed in this work are solely those of the author and do not necessarily reflect the views of the publisher, and the publisher hereby disclaims any responsibility for them.

Cover design © Scott Zarcinas

Printed in Australia, UK & USA

DoctorZed Publishing rev. date: 12/12/2023

Dedication

This book, while a work of fiction, is respectfully dedicated to the air crew of the Royal Australian Air Force who flew the 'Black Cat' 'Catalinas' in the defence of Australia during the 2nd World War.

Especially the crew of 'Catalina' PB2B A24-204
Which was lost without trace over the Laoet Strait

During operations against the Japanese
27 January 1945

And all of whom are 'Missing in Action':

Flight Lieutenant J. A. Seage
Flying Officer P. Laney
Pilot Officer J. H. Brown
Warrant Officer M. V. M. Bowness
Flight Sergeant R. L. Warne
Sergeant A. S. R. Martin
Sergeant R. C. Preston
Sergeant J. K. Thomson

And in particular Warrant Officer Hector Wickham
Deeply loved younger brother of my late mother
Mrs Cynthia Cummings (nee Wickham).

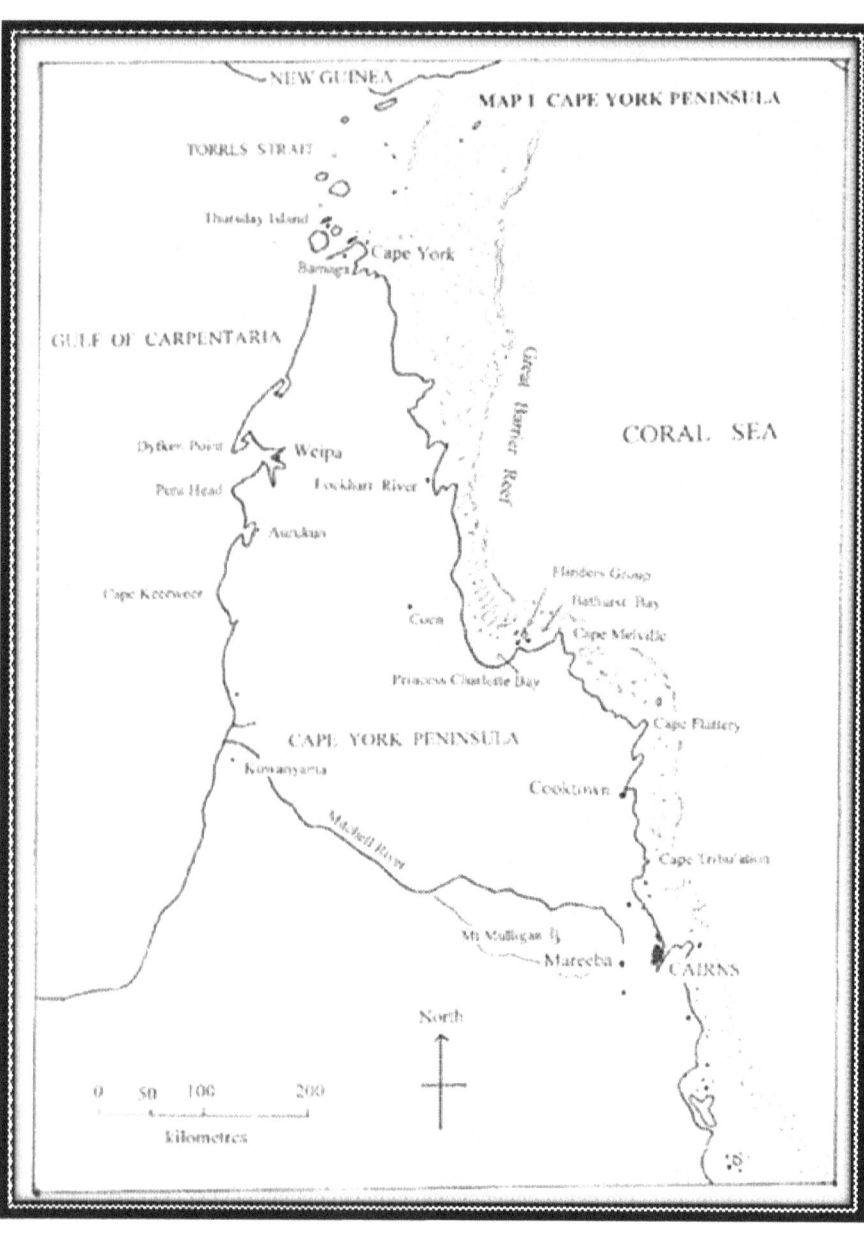

NEW GUINEA

MAP 1 CAPE YORK PENINSULA

TORRES STRAIT

Thursday Island

Cape York

Bamaga

GULF OF CARPENTARIA

Great Barrier Reef

CORAL SEA

Dyfken Point

Weipa

Pera Head

Lockhart River

Aurukun

Flinders Group

Bathurst Bay

Coen

Cape Melville

Cape Keerweer

Princess Charlotte Bay

Cape Flattery

CAPE YORK PENINSULA

Kowanyama

Cooktown

Mitchell River

Cape Tribulation

Mt Mulligan

Mareeba

CAIRNS

North

0   50   100   200

kilometres

Chapter 1

WHAT LUCK !

Willy Williams, 14 years old, a Leading Cadet in the Australian Air Force Cadets and mad keen on flying, looked out the window of the PBY5 Catalina Flying Boat and thought he was just the luckiest boy alive.

Everything seems to be going my way at the moment, he told himself.

He turned and looked along the interior of the fuselage. 'Cabin' seemed too grand a title for such a cramped and bare compartment. His friend, Leading Cadet 'Stick' Morton, met his eye and they both grinned.

"This is great!" Stick shouted above the bellow of the old Alison radial engines.

Even when Stick shouted Willy could hardly hear him as both wore ear protection to muffle the all but deafening roar. So did all of the other air cadets on the joyride. Only a few, mostly the adult instructors, had intercom attachments.

There were eight air cadets and two adult staff on board the restored PBY, along with a 'crew' of four. The aircraft was one of only half a dozen in the entire world that was still airworthy, and Willy appreciated just how lucky he had been to get the chance to have a flight in it. He had flown in a dozen other aircraft types over the years and made it a point of trying to fly in as many different types as possible. But all of them had been 'land' planes with wheels. This was the first time he had flown in a seaplane.

And an amphibian at that!

For a few seconds he pictured their take off from Cairns half an hour earlier and the memory made him smile. The unfamiliar buffeting as the hull struck the waves and the great curve of white bow wave and spray outside the cabin windows had added real novelty to a take-off.

I like it, he thought happily.

The girl beside him, also an air cadet, pressed herself against his arm. The pressure added to Willy's pleasure and he turned and smiled at her. The girl was Stick's sister and Willy's girlfriend. Marjorie was a year younger, 13, and a year behind at school, being in Year 8. She was very busty for her age and had a cheerful, freckled face and straw-coloured hair. She was very much in love with Willy and was very, very affectionate.

But Willy's mind was not on girls at that moment. *It isn't every day you get a chance to fly in a really historic aircraft,* he told himself.

It had indeed been by pure chance that the trip had been organised. One of their air cadet officers, Squadron Leader Sanderson, once their own CO but now a staff officer at Wing HQ, was an old school friend of the wealthy businessman who now owned the restored World War Two aircraft. When the plane had arrived for a 'Warbirds' air show Sqn Ldr Sanderson had requested a joy flight for the cadets. So many cadets had been interested that they had sold raffle tickets and then drawn the seats by lot. The owner and pilot, Mr Southall, had been planning a sightseeing flight up to Thursday Island in the Torres Strait and the cadets had been allowed to join it.

Willy also knew he was lucky to be crouched with Stick and Marjorie at the starboard side 'blister', one of two which had originally been fitted for gun mounts to protect above and behind. Being in the clear Perspex blister gave him a much better view than from in the cabin. In there the cadets had to take turns at peeking through the small circular portholes. Knowing that he had only another five minutes or so before it was the turn of another cadet to sit in the blister, he turned his attention to looking out.

For the next few minutes Willy's attention was taken up partly by looking at the scenery and partly by studying the details of the restored World War Two aircraft. *This plane is the real McCoy,* he thought happily, not being in the least concerned that parts of it were now over sixty years old. *This is one of the original 'Black Cats',* he told himself.

His eye travelled along the long, high-set wing, feasting on the lines of rivets and on the black paint work. The plane had been repainted in its original World War Two colours, after spending forty years painted bright yellow and red as a firefighting aircraft in Canada. Some of the black paint was now peeling off, revealing small patches of both bright colours and even some shiny bare metal but that did not dim Willy's appreciation. In his mind's eye it just made the aircraft look like it had done hard war service.

He began a daydream, imagining that he was the tail gunner and that the plane was on the last leg of a long overnight mission up into the Indonesian Archipelago. From his reading he knew that the Catalina squadrons of the RAAF had spent much of their time doing enormously long flights, up to 20 hours at a time, from Australian bases right up to the north of New Guinea and to the Moluccas and Sulawesi.

We have been laying mines in the harbour of Ambon, he decided, picturing the Japanese heavy cruiser that then hit one of the mines and sank. *And we have had to fight off Japanese fighters on the way back,* he added.

His eyes swept the sky, searching for the imaginary 'Zeros' and he pretended in his mind to fight them off, while warning the captain in time to take avoiding action.

A tremble of minor turbulence Willy just converted to the effect of flak bursting nearby. *From that Japanese destroyer that was hiding near that island,* he thought.

He looked down and noted several islands and a whole mass of coral reefs. At that moment the plane was just passing across Princess Charlotte Bay, that huge bight out of the east coast of Cape York Peninsula that is so conspicuous on the map of Queensland. Behind him he could see the brown smear of the coast in the vicinity of Cape Melville and just behind and 5,000 feet below, the large islands of the Flinders Group.

In fact the only vessel visible was a small white yacht, which showed as a tiny speck heading south near the most northerly island in the group. Willy had an Air Chart with him and moved his finger to identify it.

Stanley Island, he read.

It looked barren and rugged. Large coral reefs began to slide by below, very clear to see from above; dark blue water giving way to a fringe of brown which Willy knew as coral, with the inside area of the reef showing up as a pale blue, aquamarine and even a pale-yellow shade.

Stick leaned over to try to get a better view of the chart and then nudged him and shouted, "What reef is that?"

"Corbett Reef," Willy called back.

He prided himself in being good at navigation and was sure he was right. From the altitude they were flying at the shape of the whole reef could be seen and it matched the shape on the chart.

His eyes moved back to watch the ailerons moving slightly and he wondered if the aircraft was on autopilot, or whether the pilot or co-pilot were actually flying it.

What a great plane! he enthused, again sweeping his gaze over the starboard engine and the barely visible spinning disc of its propeller, then along the underside of the large high-set wing.

Then he looked down and resumed his daydreams. *No, we are flying north,* he told himself. *We couldn't be on our way back from the Dutch East Indies.*

It took him an effort to call Indonesia that, but he knew from his reading of history that back then the Dutch had owned most of the islands to the north of Australia.

No, he thought. *It is 1942 and we are on patrol out over the Coral Sea, searching for the Japanese invasion fleet.*

That wasn't hard to imagine as they actually were flying over the Coral Sea at that moment. *And plenty of coral too!* he thought, noting many more reefs, both under them and further off to the east.

Here a long, broken line of white surf and reefs was showing up. It was, he knew, the 'Outer' reef, the famous Great Barrier Reef which, as his Geography teacher Mr Conkey was always pointing out, was not a reef at all but actually thousands of reefs. Willy had seen parts of the Great Barrier Reef from the air near Cairns, but this was even better.

To keep a check on where the plane was Willy twisted around and looked out to the port side past the other blister. He actually wished he was in that one because from there he would have had a better view of the coastline and would have found it easier to identify the landmarks. As it was, he could see a fair bit, the east coast of Cape York Peninsula being only about 25 kilometres away. The main capes and bays were quite easily identified but he was also keen to note the smaller reefs and islands. He was quite surprised at how many small islands and reefs there.

And a lot of isolated rocks, he noted. *Bloody hell, look at that little one just poking out of the sea! What a nightmare for sailors in the old days!*

He then shifted his attention back to the sea below and to starboard. His mind shifted back to the WW2 daydream. He tried to imagine flying near a fleet of Japanese warships and he remembered reading an account of how 'Catalinas' had made some famous sightings of enemy ships, sightings that had been crucial in winning Allied victories.

The German battleship 'Bismarck', *she was found by a Cat. But that was the stormy North Atlantic, not this bright sunny day in the tropics. Was it a Cat that first sighted the Japanese aircraft carriers during the Battle of the Coral Sea?* he wondered.

He dimly remembered reading about a Catalina that had discovered an enemy fleet and had then gone in to attack an aircraft carrier with bombs while radioing back, 'Please inform Next-of-Kin.'

Was that at the Coral Sea? Or was it Midway? he thought. It niggled him that he could not remember.

The idea of trying to attack fast moving and heavily armed warships in such a large and relatively slow aircraft made him shake his head. *They must have had guts!* he thought with admiration.

Once again, he looked down, now pretending to search for enemy submarines rather than battleships. *The Cats did a lot of anti-sub work,* he told himself. And there was a sub! *No, it couldn't be,* he thought.

But it was something large and dark just under the water. Willy leaned forward. Whatever it was, it was almost right under them and almost out of sight. Then he saw a larger than normal splash of white among the many tiny white wave tops. More dark shapes seemed to shimmer under the water, and he wondered if his eyes were playing tricks on him.

No, I can see something, he thought.

Then it came to him, and he gasped with pleasure before calling out, "Whales! Look, whales!"

Jabbing down with his finger he attracted the attention of the others. Marjorie took the opportunity to lean right on him, pressing herself on his shoulder as she looked.

"Where? Oh yes! I see them!" she cried.

Willy attracted the attention of Flying Officer Turnbull, one of the officers on board, and he looked down and then spoke into his intercom. Willy felt the plane slow and then tilt. He saw the ailerons move and then the big rudder close behind him on his right. The Catalina went into a wide circle, slowly losing height. During the turn and descent Willy savoured the sensations of being pressed down against his seat by the centrifugal force and then of relative weightlessness as the nose was put down.

This is real flying, he thought happily.

Other cadets crowded into the blisters and at the portholes as they all tried to see the whales. By the time they came around again they had lost a couple of thousand feet and the whales were clearly visible. To Willy it was a revelation.

I can even see their tails, their flukes, he corrected.

They circled again, slowly so that all the passengers could see the whales clearly. Then the pilot straightened back on course and the nose tilted up slightly.

He's going to climb back to cruising altitude again, Willy deduced, this being confirmed when the engine note took on a deeper roar as power was increased.

"Time to swap places," Flying Officer Turnbull called pointing forward and indicating to them to move back into the cabin.

Willy did not want to go but knew it was only fair so he nodded and nudged Marjorie. She and Stick began moving forward. Willy got up from his uncomfortable crouching position and prepared to follow. As he did, he cast a last glance astern at the whales.

To his surprise, they were no longer visible, were in fact many miles astern. But his eye did pick up an odd shape in the waves below.

What is that? he wondered. He squinted against the sun's glare and peered down.

Flying Officer Turnbull called again and so did his personal rival, Leading Cadet Patricia Finlay. "Come on Williams, you've had your go," she shouted.

But Willy just shook his head and waved to wait. His eyes had suddenly made sense of the shape in a way that made his heart seem to stop. That tiny, ant-sized thing in the sea was a man! *A man,* he thought.

Or are my eyes playing tricks on me?

"Come on Cadet Williams, move forward," Flying Officer Turnbull ordered.

But now Willy did not want to lose sight of the almost microscopic shape. Was it a man, or just a trick of the light? Or maybe just blurred vision from staring out for so long?

No, they look like legs and that is an arm, he decided.

"Sir, come and look!" he called, gesturing urgently.

"What?" Flying Officer Turnbull called back irritably, but he moved to look. His gaze followed Willy's pointing finger.

By now Willy was getting anxious. The tiny shape was becoming very hard to see and he still wasn't sure it actually was man. "Sir, I can see a man swimming in the sea."

"Swimming in the sea!" Flying Officer Turnbull cried, half incredulously.

"Yes sir. A man. Back there." Willy pointed but now felt very anxious because he could no longer see the tiny shape. It was, he knew, slipping astern of them at a rate of about a mile and half a minute and was now at least three miles back and invisible to his eyes.

"Way out here? Are you sure?"

Willy was feeling torn and upset by this. The thought of a person being out there in the sea, that far from land, made him feel sick. *A person would only be there if something had gone badly wrong,* he thought. The coast was 15 miles away and the nearest island at least five.

"Yes sir. Oh please sir, tell the pilot. We must go back and look."

Flying Officer Turnbull frowned and hesitated. Willy felt so anxious that he overcame his normal reticence in the presence of an officer. "Please sir! I did see something. If I am wrong then we will only waste some petrol, but if it is a person and we leave them to drown I will never sleep again."

"Oh alright," Flying Officer Turnbull replied reluctantly.

He spoke into the intercom. The conversation seemed to take forever, and all the time Willy kept staring back trying to fix the point in his mind in relation to some big coral reefs he could see off astern to starboard.

After looking doubtfully at Willy and nodding, Flying Officer Turnbull turned to him and said, "The pilot said go to the cockpit."

"Yes sir," Willy replied, almost gasping his relief.

That meant he had to take his eyes off the area of now distant ocean, but he thought he could locate it again. As quickly as he could he scrambled past Finlay and the others who were waiting and made his way along the central aisle to the working part of the plane. The cadets and officers seated there all looked at him curiously, not knowing what was happening. Stick raised an eyebrow in query and Marjorie asked what was wrong, but he just shook his head and went on.

No time for explanations, Willy told himself.

As he made his way forward Willy began to have severe doubts about whether he actually had seen a person. Memories of how hard it had been to identify the whales rose to make him uncertain.

They are huge, he thought, *much larger than a human being.*

"But we must check," he muttered.

He made his way along the narrow corridor past the tiny space that was the crew's sleeping accommodation, galley and radio room and then up the short set of steps to the flight deck. As he reached a position just behind and between the two pilot's seats Willy paused. This was where he really wanted to be. His burning ambition was to be a pilot and for a few seconds his eyes ran over the controls and instruments, taking in the whole scene. Then his eyes met those of the pilot.

Mr Southall was in his sixties, short grey hair and a firm, tanned face with bright blue eyes. He lifted one earphone free of his right ear and leaned back. "Tell me what you saw," he said.

Willy swallowed out of nervousness. "Sir, I thought I saw a man in the sea."

"Are you sure?"

Willy wanted to say yes but shook his head. "No sir. It might not have been a man, but I thought I saw legs and arms."

For a few seconds Mr Southall looked thoughtful. "Okay, that's good enough for me. Take her back Frank."

Frank, Mr Lacey, the co-pilot, Willy remembered: middle-aged and black hair, nodded and at once set the aircraft into a descending turn.

As the plane came around, Willy felt even more relieved. But he was still scared, afraid they might not find the person in all that sea, and also anxious it might all be a wild goose chase.

Mr Southall held up his chart. "Any idea where you saw him?"

Willy nodded and moved closer, holding up his own chart on which his left thumb was firmly gripping the place. The navigator leaned over his right shoulder to look. Willy put his finger on the chart.

"Just west of this un-named reef between Hedge Reef and Lytton Reef," he said.

Mr Southall nodded and met the navigator's eyes. "Give us a fix George, and the magnetic reciprocal bearing," he said. Next, he turned to the co-pilot and said, "Take her down to a thousand feet Frank." He then began to push buttons on an instrument.

Willy thought this was a GPS but wasn't sure. The navigator did a quick calculation using a pencil on his chart and said, "Reciprocal is one five three degrees magnetic."

"Roger, one five three degrees magnetic," the co-pilot echoed.

As the pilot's hands moved the control column, Willy watched. He knew which instrument was the compass and he could see the figures moving around as the plane turned. Having been an air cadet for over a year he could also identify some of the other gauges and instruments. As the plane settled on a reciprocal bearing, he looked these over. Even with his limited experience he sensed that the instruments were a curious mix of old and new. It wasn't one of the new computerized 'glass cockpits' but there were a few little gadgets with quartz crystal displays that looked very modern.

Then he moved his gaze upwards and looked out through the front windows. At first he was disoriented and had to make a conscious effort to find things that he could identify on the chart. A couple of small islands helped.

That must be Fife Island, he decided. *And the one over to the south west of it is Hay Island.*

That got him looking in the right direction and he quickly made out the large brownish shape of Noddy Reef and then the even bigger Magpie Reef.

Willy was appalled at how far they had travelled since he first thought he had seen the man. *More than thirty kilometres!* he calculated. Then he shook his head. *I am in an aircraft, and old American one at that. I should be calculating distance in Nautical Miles. Let's see, that would be about… Hmm….about fifteen nautical miles.*

From that he worked out they would be back in the area in about seven minutes. *Not long,* he thought, until he remembered how hard it was to swim for any length of time. *I hope he's got a lifejacket,* he thought, before adding, *if I really did see a man!*

Even as he worked all this out the Catalina covered the distance from Noddy Reef to Magpie Reef and Willy clearly identified Lytton Reef ahead.

Not far now, he thought anxiously.

Mr Southall turned from scanning ahead with binoculars and said, "What's your name son?"

"Willy sir, Willy Williams, I mean Leading Cadet Williams."

"Williams, eh? Any relation to Group Captain Freddy Williams?" Mr Southall asked.

Willy shook his head. "Not that I know of sir. Both my parents are doctors," he replied. He found it hard to carry on polite talk when all he wanted to do was look outside. To his relief, Mr Southall nodded and also turned to look.

The Catalina flew quickly over Lytton Reef and then out over a stretch of open deep water about seven miles wide between it and the end of the odd shaped reef.

It was in this area, he thought as the western end of the odd shaped reef drew closer. He began to peer out anxiously, appalled at how much the surface of the sea was ruffled by tiny white wave tops. *Oh dear! This might be harder than I thought,* he realised. Now he regretted ever taking his eyes off the tiny shape.

They reached western end of the reef and the navigator passed over the bearings and timings for a square search pattern. The plane went into a gentle bank to starboard and then steadied on a run west. Willy moved to behind the pilot so that he had a clearer view.

Nothing. Mr Southall took the controls and turned the plane south for five minutes, then back east. Still nothing. Willy began to feel both anxious and very foolish. They turned north and headed back towards the western end of the odd-shaped reef. "This is the area where we saw the whales," Mr Southall said.

Willy stared down at the ripples and mottled blue surface of the ocean and felt slightly sick. There was no sign of the whales.

If we can't find a dozen huge whales, what chance do we have of finding anything as tiny as man? he wondered.

And then he saw him.

It was a man!

And he was waving at them.

"There!" Willy cried, pointing down off the port bow. "It is a man."

"Got him!" Mr Southall answered.

A huge wave of relief surged through Willy and he smiled. Then he went stiff with worry.

What is that in the water near him? he thought.

Just as his own mind registered the concern Mr Southall focused his binoculars on the tiny shape and said, "That's a bloody great shark in the water near him!"

Chapter 2

A GHASTLY MESS

Willy gasped in horror. "Oh! A shark! Quick! Land! We must save him!" he cried.

Mr Southall now had the Catalina in a steep bank. The plane slid down towards the water, and he stared out the window before easing the controls and levelling out a couple of hundred feet above the sea. As he took the aircraft around in a wide, gentle turn Mr Southall said, "There's a second man there."

The co-pilot nodded and said, "I see him."

Willy hadn't but the tone of the men's voices bothered him, and he peered anxiously out. Then his eyes detected the second man and he realised why he hadn't seen him earlier. The man was floating face down about fifty metres from the first and even at that height Willy felt sure he was dead. Worse still there was another shark there, and it appeared to be tearing at the man's left leg. Willy distinctly saw what looked like murky pink streamers trailing from the body.

The sight made him want to retch but it also made him cry out again. "Sir, quick! We must land and save that other man before those sharks attack him."

Mr Southall appeared not to hear him. He kept the plane turning so that he could see both men out the port window, but he made no attempt to land. Flying Officer Turnbull came and stood between him and the co-pilot and looked out.

"Sir!" pleaded Willy. "We must land. We have to save him!"

Mr Southall turned, his jaw set hard. He gave a slight shake of the head and said, "It's not just his life young Willy. There are fourteen lives in this plane and if I muck things up then they could be lost too."

Willy had known that, but now he recognised the terrible weight of responsibility thrust onto the pilot. Whatever he did risked peoples' lives.

"Can't we land sir?" he asked, swallowing to keep his stomach under control. He could still see the smaller shark gnawing and ripping at the floating corpse.

Mr Southall gestured with his left hand. "The sea is pretty rough. If we hit it hard or wrong the aircraft could plough under or, worse still, tip a wingtip and cartwheel. Even if we get down safely, we may not be able to get off again."

"But we could save that man if we did get down?" Willy pressed.

He felt very personally involved in saving the man's life and a sense of frustrated desperation was growing.

"Yes. But it's a real risk," Mr Southall answered.

Willy knew that he had once been a squadron leader in the air force and also a civil airline pilot who had flown the big 'Sandringham' flying boats from Sydney to Lord Howe Island and Norfolk Island back in the days when such planes were in service.

He has a lot of experience of flying seaplanes, and I don't, he thought ruefully. He could see that Mr Southall was torn and felt sorry for him.

Mr Southall kept the Catalina circling. Flying that low meant a fair amount of turbulence but Willy barely noticed. He was just aware that Mr Southall was flying the aircraft with unconscious skill. Willy saw that the big shark was also interested in the body of the dead man, but it wasn't far from the man in the water.

Poor bugger! he thought. *He can see us and thinks he is saved, and he must be able to see those sharks. He must be terrified!*

Flying Officer Turnbull spoke next. "We must think of the cadets and their safety first," he said.

That annoyed and sickened Willy. *Is he saying that because he is scared, or is he really concerned about us?* he thought unkindly.

Flying Officer Turnbull then said, "We can radio a ship and it can come and pick him up."

"Sir! That could take hours. That man hasn't got a life jacket, and anyway that big shark could attack him at any moment," Willy cried.

"Drop him a raft then," Flying Officer Turnbull suggested. "Do you have an inflatable raft, Mr Southall?"

"We have several and we will use one," Mr Southall replied.

That, to Willy, was a poor second, but better than nothing. He was now feeling almost nauseous with anxiety and apprehension. To be able to see the poor man and the huge shark and be aware that at any moment he might have to watch him being torn to bits!

Mr Southall then said to the navigator, "What is the wind?"

"From the southeast Ivan, varying from fifteen knots to twenty knots," the navigator replied.

"So, that gives a wave height of about a metre and half to two metres," Mr Southall answered.

The co-pilot answered. "Yes, but in the lee of the reef it should be a good deal less."

"That's what I thought," Mr Southall answered. He spoke into his microphone on the intercom and Willy realised he was talking to the flight engineer down in the cabin. Then he turned and said, "Okay we will try it. George, you radio the position and situation at once and then get the inflatable dinghy ready. Frank, go down and make sure all the cadets are securely strapped in and wearing life jackets."

At that Willy sighed with relief. "Oh hurry please!" he cried.

Mr Southall turned to him, "I will go as fast as it is safe to go, now get me a lifejacket and then you strap yourself into that dicky seat there behind me after you put a lifejacket on."

Willy nearly cried with relief. He reached down and extracted two lifejackets from under the seat. Before the flight they had been shown where the lifejackets were stowed and how to put them on as part of the safety brief. Now it thrilled him to watch as the pilot pulled his over his head. By then the co-pilot, navigator and Flying Officer Turnbull had all gone below. Willy tugged the lifejacket over his head and tied the straps around his waist. Doing that gave him a sick feeling of worry but it was nothing to the tense apprehension he felt as they yet again went round in a big circle.

Just behind the pilot was a small folding seat and he pushed it down until it locked into position. Then he seated himself and buckled on the seat belt. The co-pilot came back and pulled on a lifejacket, then took over the controls while Mr Southall did his jacket up. All this took more minutes and with every passing second Willy felt he would explode with anxiety.

Only when he was satisfied that all the cadets were securely seated and wearing life jackets and that the inflatable rafts were ready for instant use did Mr Southall take control again. Willy watched from close behind him with fascinated interest which partly over-rode the apprehension. Mr Southall took the aircraft well away to the northwest until they were several miles from the reef and the man. As he did, this he told Willy to make sure he kept the man in sight the whole time. Willy kept looking back as though his own life depended on it, until the man's head was just a tiny pinhead all but lost in the ripples and whitecaps. As the aircraft flew away from the area, the flaps were fully extended, and Willy saw the small floats on the port wingtip lowered ready for landing.

Mr Southall brought the aircraft around to the left in a curve so tight that it surprised Willy and pressed him into his seat with the G forces. Then the plane levelled out and Mr Southall said, "Okay Willy, where is he?"

"Almost dead ahead," Willy answered, then felt ill at the real meaning of those words.

"Got him! Good, okay here we go," Mr Southall answered. "Keep watching please, as we shall probably overshoot him."

Willy stared through the front as the aircraft slowly lost altitude. The changing view surprised and worried him. At the start the odd-shaped reef was plainly visible but as they came lower it was lost among the endless ripples of the waves. Then the horizon seemed to change, and he distinctly saw it become a jagged line of tiny wave tops. His intellect told him that was because as they came lower their range of visibility became shorter and shorter.

The horizon is about three nautical miles for a person standing on a beach? he thought, remembering something he had read.

But now it was confusing. All he was sure of was that the man's head kept vanishing in the wave troughs as they got lower. There was also an impression of things speeding up but that, he knew, was simply because they were much closer to the sea. A glance at the altimeter told him they were actually descending steadily from 200 feet to 100 feet.

Gosh! The waves do look big, Willy thought.

He could not see Mr Southall's face but a glance at the co-pilot showed a set jaw and lines of worry on his face.

The plane rocked and bumped through a layer of disturbed air and Mr Southall automatically corrected. Willy kept staring at the man's head and now saw a waving arm. They were close now and seemed to rush towards him. Willy even thought he glimpsed the dreaded triangular fin of the big shark but later wasn't sure if it hadn't just been a wave top. He noted that Mr Southall was aiming to land with the man just off the port bow.

Throttles were eased. The aircraft rocked and seemed to float as its nose was lifted slightly. Willy tensed and for the first time felt a prickle of concern that he might be in some danger himself. Then the man went by close underneath, his upturned face and open mouth clearly visible. That got Willy very anxious, and he leaned sideways and craned his head to look back through the small space available to him. Glances ahead showed the horizon looking even more jagged and closer and then he saw a distinct line of white in the distance and a sort of smear. He realised the white was the surf breaking on the far side of the odd-shaped reef.

Has Mr Southall miscalculated? Willy wondered.

Then he saw that he hadn't. The near edge of the reef was just visible a few hundred metres away. The nose of the aircraft went up and the keel hit the first wave top. It came as a solid thump which threw up a shower of spray behind, obscuring Willy's view. There was another hard thump and then more in rapid succession. Willy sensed that the nose was being held high to ensure the bow did not tilt and plough into the face of a wave. He also noted that they were running into much smaller waves and that the speed was coming down fast as the aircraft settled and the drag slowed it.

The aircraft suddenly slewed sideways and gave a slithering shudder. Willy saw that the port wingtip float had buried itself in a wave crest, the drag of the water pulling hard. For the first time awareness really sank in of how close they were to a crash, and how dangerous it actually was. A cold sweat instantly prickled his skin under the blue air cadet work uniform. But Mr Southall was ready for it and the aircraft yawed as he corrected. Then the wingtip float tore free of the water in a smother of foam and the plane straightened out again and thumped on over the wave tops, each thump being less solid and the speed quickly falling away.

And then they were safely down and turning on the surface of the sea. Willy felt relieved and then amazed at how much the aircraft rocked about as the wave motion took over. Mr Southall reached up and slid the port window open and then turned to look out to port as he swung the plane around back onto a reciprocal course. The engines roared, throwing up spray and making the motion slightly easier.

The navigator unstrapped himself and went down the steps into the cabin. Willy was able to lean his head half out the window to get a better view. That gave him a bit of a shock as he realised that the spinning propeller blades were close behind his head and seemed to be very close. To his relief, the man's head and waving arm were clearly visible. The plane began surging back with the waves, taxiing across the sea as fast as it could safely go.

Even that seemed agonisingly slow for Willy. *Oh hurry! Hurry!* he thought. Now his eyes were scanning for a sight of that dreaded fin. To his dismay, he could not see it anywhere. *Where is that damned shark?* he wondered.

The fuselage door was opened just back and below where Willy sat. He saw the flight engineer lean out to look. In his hands he had a boat hook and lifebuoy secured to a rope. The navigator's head appeared beside him. Willy watched with great interest as the wave tops caught at their wingtip float, the water surging and grabbing at it. Mr Southall had to use continual corrections of course to keep the plane taxiing in a straight line.

As they got closer to the swimming man Mr Southall turned away and then brought the Catalina around in a curve so that the wind and waves would drift the man down towards the plane.

"We don't want to run him over," Mr Southall explained.

The delay involved got Willy all anxious again. *If we aren't quick the shark will get him!* he fretted.

And there was the shark! Its fin broke the surface about fifty metres away. "Oh hurry!" Willy cried. "There's the shark!"

He looked down and saw the man was now close alongside and swimming with an awkward breaststroke towards them. What bothered Willy the most was seeing the man's legs so clearly in the water. The aircraft's engines went into reverse and the plane slowed right down, even as Willy feared they would run the man right over. Mr Southall now turned the aircraft, using the rudder and port propeller, so that the swimming man appeared to slide astern. In fact it placed him back under the wing and safely away from the spinning propeller blades, which Willy noted were coming dangerously close to the surface of the water as waves swept under the hull.

The flight engineer tossed the lifebuoy towards the man, a young man Willy now noted. The man splashed towards it, making Willy mutter, "Don't splash!"

The swimming man at last made it to the lifebuoy and grabbed it.

Willy could tell, by his face and the floundering strokes, that he was exhausted. *Oh hurry!* he kept thinking, very anxious about the sharks, both of which had now gone out of sight.

The flight engineer and navigator hauled slowly on the rope to draw the lifebuoy towards the aircraft. Willy understood that they were doing it slowly so that the exhausted swimmer did not lose his grip, but every second was nail-biting tension as he kept fretting about the sharks. Then the man was alongside. He reached up but they failed to grab his hand as the waves sucked him down and away. Then the man was washed hard against the hull by the next wave. To Willy's consternation the man went under.

For a few seconds Willy thought they had lost him, even wondered if the shark had pulled him under, but then his desperate, spluttering face appeared again. The swimmer still had a grip on the lifebuoy. Again he reached up, his eyes wide with fear. The flight engineer and navigator leaned out and reached down to grab the man's arms (He wore no shirt, Willy noted). As soon as they had a grip they hauled, dragging the man up inside.

As the man's legs vanished inside the doorway Willy sat back and almost cried with relief. *Oh got him! Safe!* he thought happily.

The navigator appeared at the top of the steps. "Got him skipper," he called.

"Good," Mr Southall answered. "Now we will try to collect what we can of that other poor bugger. Can you see where he is?"

The navigator shook his head and said, "No Ivan."

Willy craned his neck to look out and scanned the tossing wave tops. As he did, he tried to orientate himself. *The body was about fifty metres west of the swimmer,* he reasoned. But which way was that? He had heard the comment about the wind direction being from the southeast. The Catalina was rolling sharply in a quartering sea which came in under the starboard bow so he decided that west was back under the wing. He peered back through the spinning disc of the propeller in that direction.

It was a shark he saw, not the dead man. A swirl and splash in the waves caught his eye and a moment later he clearly glimpsed the long, pointed tail fin of one of the sharks.

"Back that way Mr Southall. I can see one of the sharks. I think the... the body is there," he called, pointing as he did. He actually thought that the shark was attacking it but did not say so. The idea made him nauseous.

"Good lad Willy," Mr Southall replied. "Now keep your eye on it while we taxi over."

He opened the throttle of the starboard engine slightly and the nose of the Catalina came around. When it was pointing directly at the area both engines were used to get the seaplane moving forward. The result was an uncomfortable slithering and pitching motion as it outran each wave and slid awkwardly down its face.

The navigator came up and stood between the pilots to look through the front. He chuckled. "There are a few customers getting a bit seasick back there," he said.

"They'll be even sicker if they see this bloke all mangled," Mr Southall replied grimly. "Try to stop them looking."

The navigator shook his head. "That will be difficult. There is a cadet at every port hole and the door is right in front of them."

Mr Southall shrugged. Willy wondered if he had forgotten he was there but did not say anything.

It was the co-pilot who spotted the shark again and a minute later the dark bobbing shape of the corpse became visible among the waves. Willy was now filled with morbid fears and wondered if he should look away rather than give himself nightmares, but he found he just had to look. As the seaplane edged down closer, he was able to look straight down on the dead body. What he saw made his stomach heave and it was only with an effort he kept the contents down, rather than spewing them all over Mr Southall and the flight deck.

The body had lost an arm, all of one leg and half of the other and its stomach had been ripped open. Revolting streamers of pink, purple and brown flesh, intestines and sinews waved in the moving water.

Not much blood, he observed.

For a few seconds he watched with ghastly fascination the way the limbs and head lolled loosely in the waves. Then his stomach heaved again.

As quickly as he could, Willy unbuckled his seat belt and struggled out into the passageway. Mr Southall turned and raised his eyebrows.

"Going to be sick sir," Willy managed to croak.

Then his stomach heaved. To stop it he clenched his teeth and held his mouth shut as he stumbled down the steps behind the navigator. It didn't work. Vomit squirted up into Willy's nostrils and began to trickle and drip out.

Worse still, as he reached the bottom of the steps he found Finlay standing at the toilet door. She also had her hand over her mouth and looked green and miserable. As Willy gestured to get out of the way she shook her head and kept a firm grip on the handle. Willy then noted Flight Sergeant Anderson and Corporal Francini standing behind her, also looking sick.

Again his stomach moved and there was only one place to go, rather than throw up all over the passageway in the cabin, the open door. It was only two steps away but the flight engineer and navigator were blocking it. Willy staggered over and tapped the flight engineer on the shoulder. The flight engineer turned a quizzical face to him but Willy could not speak. His mouth was now full of vomit and he was having trouble breathing. When he tried to suck air in chunky bits moved in the back of his nostrils and blocked the left one. The revolting stench and taste of bile burned at his throat and airways.

The flight engineer took one glance and grabbed him, then moved aside to hold him in the doorway. As soon as green water appeared below Willy opened his mouth and heaved. Then he spluttered, coughed again and saw the dead body directly below him. The horrible sight made him heave again. Lumps and sour liquid squirted and dribbled out and he felt hot tears of shame. He was aware that the flight engineer and navigator had a firm grip on him. They suddenly thrust him back inside and the navigator dragged Flight Sergeant Anderson to the door to throw up as well.

Feeling upset and bilious Willy stood back against the bulkhead to make room. Through eyes that were streaming he saw Anderson shoved back out of the way and then the two men knelt and reached outside. "Get out of the way you kids! And don't look!" shouted the navigator.

Willy tried to but he could only go back up the passageway towards the cockpit. Before his horrified and disgusted eyes he saw the dead body come slithering and flopping onto the deck at his feet, hauled in by the two crewmen. Finlay and Cpl Francini both stared at it in wide-eyed horror and then spewed. The vomit poured onto the deck and then began to swill around their feet and the body as the plane rocked about. The door to the toilet opened and a pale and drawn looking Cadet Todd looked down, plainly aghast. He then heaved again and fled back into the toilet.

"Back off kids!" the navigator shouted, pointing aft.

Finlay, Francini and Anderson all backed away, their eyes wide with fear and shock. Along the corridor Willy could see the horrified eyes of other cadets and officers staring towards the mess at his feet. He began to back up but the navigator looked at him and called, "Pass us those garbage bags please."

Willy was next to the cupboard of the tiny galley and saw some large green garbage bags there. He nodded, quite unable to speak and having trouble breathing. With shaking hands he passed the garbage bags quickly to the navigator. Unable to tear his eyes from the scene he watched with grisly fascination as the man began sliding the bag over the corpse's head.

As he did, Willy began to experience searing flashbacks. This was not the first time that he had seen a dead body. Seven months before his uncle had been murdered; mutilated by a chain saw. It had been Willy who had found the body. A few weeks later he had seen a man obliterated in a spray of blood and mince when he fell into a wood pulp machine. The man had been attempting to kill Willy, who had spent the previous night in terror as he faced his death. It had been a very dark period in his life and now it chilled him with redoubled force.

With an effort Willy snuffled and blew his nose into his handkerchief. A lump of something stuck in the back of his left nostril and he gagged and felt as though he would vomit again. His eyes watered and he clung to the door of the galley. A movement in front of him caused him to lift his eyes and through the mist of tears he saw the face of the man they had rescued.

The man looked to be about twenty and wore only shorts and a belt with some sort of zip-up bag on it. He had blond hair and startlingly blue eyes. These were fixed on the body of the dead man as the navigator and flight engineer struggled to wrap it up. The rescued man was also standing, clinging to the opposite doorpost, the entrance to the tiny crew's mess and bunk space.

The navigator turned to him and reached out a hand. "Pass me a blanket please mate," he said.

The man did so, then shook his head in obvious distress. Willy was also very upset. He met the man's eyes for a moment and said, "I'm sorry we weren't quicker. If I'd seen you earlier we might have saved your friend."

The man stared at him and then went wide eyed and shook his head. "No. No. You couldn't have saved him. He was dead already."

"Dead already!" Willy echoed. He swivelled his eyes to stare at the body.

"Yes," the man said. "He was shot."

Chapter 3

BETWEEN THE DEVIL AND THE DEEP BLUE SEA

"Shot!" Willy croaked.

The man nodded. He then pointed at the body and said, "In the chest, see."

Willy looked and now saw that the front of the man's shirt was stained and torn. "Who by? Why? When?" he asked, shocked by the information.

The man just shook his head and slumped against the door. The navigator called to Willy, "Help him! Put him on the bench."

Willy gripped the man around the chest under the arms and found he could hardly hold him up. With an effort he changed his grip and then struggled to half carry, half drag the man onto the empty seat at the side of the tiny compartment. This had a small fold-down table in the middle with a chart on it. The table was in the way and he banged himself a few times while he lifted the man onto the seat.

That done Willy turned to lift the table, which was hinged at the end. As he did, the man began to slide off the seat. Willy swore and grabbed at him while trying to hold the table up. It didn't work. Willy had to let the table drop on his back while he knelt to push the man back onto the seat.

The table was lifted, and Willy was aware that someone was helping him. He glanced up and saw it was Mr Southall. "You get up in the corner and hold him," Mr Southall said. He then clipped the table in the upright position against the forward bulkhead.

Willy was now able to get behind the man and lift him up onto the seat properly. He wanted to lie him down but there were four cadets sitting on the bench seat in the next compartment. He went to tell them to move when the man opened his eyes and croaked so Willy held him up.

"What did you say?" he asked.

"Water," the man croaked.

Mr Southall gestured to Willy. "You hold him up. I'll get the water."

Willy did as he was told, and Mr Southall quickly went to the tiny galley to get a cup of water. While he did this he spoke to the men in the doorway and then handed Willy the cup.

"Give him this while I help the others," he instructed.

Willy found it awkward to keep the man upright and hold the cup to his lips. The man put up his own hands to help and gulped greedily at the water, spilling half of it in his haste. Then he sighed and leaned back.

"Thanks," he croaked. After a minute or so he sat up. "Can I have some more please?"

"Will you be alright?" Willy asked, worried the man might slump off the seat again.

"Yes," the man replied.

Willy released his hold and made his way around to the galley, found the tap and filled the cup. As he did, Mr Southall came past with a blanket. When Willy recrossed the passageway, he glanced to his right and saw that the dead body was being wrapped up in the blanket. The sight made him shudder and feel very depressed.

He returned to the tiny cabin and handed the man the water, then sat opposite

him. The man drank the water greedily then smacked his lips with satisfaction. "Sorry," he said, "but I've been in the water since early last night and I'm a bit thirsty."

Willy did a quick calculation. It was only about 10am so he deduced the man had been in the water at least twelve hours. He wanted to ask what had happened but knew Mr Southall would ask that, so he said, "You were very lucky I saw you. We only came down low to have a look at some whales."

"You saw me? Thanks, I owe you," the man said. Then he managed a weak grin and held out his hand. "I'm Jacob van der Heyden. What's your name?"

Willy took the offered hand, blushing as he did. "Willy. Willy Williams," he replied.

After shaking hands, Jacob nodded and said, "When I saw the plane go over, I was full of hope but then it just flew off and I thought I was done for."

"I wasn't sure if it was a man I saw," Willy explained. "It took me a few minutes to convince the officers and the pilot."

"Officers?" Jacob queried, his eyes roving over Willy's blue uniform with its rank badges.

"I'm an air cadet," Willy explained.

Jacob nodded. "So this is an air force plane?"

"No, it's just painted this way for historical re-enactments," he said.

He began to explain the history of the Catalina. As he did, the men lifted the blanket shrouded body from the floor at the still open door and began carrying it into the nose compartment beyond the cockpit. Willy had his back to them, but he saw Jacob's face go pale, his freckles standing out very clearly.

Jacob then began to shiver and tremble. Willy realised he probably had hyperthermia from being in the cold water so long. "I'll get you a blanket," he said, standing up and moving to the oval doorway in the next bulkhead.

But that immediately led to another view of the body being stowed in the tiny storage space in under the flight deck. Mr Southall asked what he wanted and then came to get him a blanket from a small cupboard beside the galley.

"I'll make him a hot drink," he added. "You keep talking to him."

Willy took the blanket and wrapped it around the shoulders of the violently shaking Jacob. In fact he was shivering so badly that his teeth were clacking together, and Willy felt quite alarmed. He had read about people who had been rescued and had then just died.

To keep Jacob's mind busy Willy asked, "Where do you come from?"

"Sydney," Jacob replied.

Mr Southall came in a few minutes later carrying a cup of hot cocoa. While Jacob drank this Willy looked out of the porthole in the starboard side. From time to time he heard the engines roaring and he deduced that the co-pilot was keeping them facing into the weather.

When Jacob had warmed up and calmed down a bit Mr Southall, the navigator and flight engineer all crowded into the tiny cabin. Willy wasn't sure if he should leave but found he was blocked in the far corner so stayed. Mr Southall made no move to tell him to go. That suited Willy as he was curious about what had happened.

Mr Southall introduced himself and the other men and then pointed to Willy and said, "You owe your life to this young man. If he hadn't spotted you and then convinced me to turn back, we would have kept on flying."

Jacob looked at Willy and said thanks, making Willy blush and mumble that it was nothing.

Mr Southall then said, "Now, are you alright? Have you got any injuries? Do you need a doctor or anything like that?"

Jacob shook his head. "No. I'm not hurt. Just worn out and cold. I'll be right."

Mr Southall nodded and said, "So a few minutes more won't matter. So, who is the dead man?"

Jacob looked wretched. "His name is... was... Karl Renderman. He was my friend."

They were diverted from him telling his tale by the seaplane giving several very sharp rolls which sent them all bumping against the bulkheads. Willy heard the engines roar and again looked out the window. What he saw scared him. As far as he could see were tossing wave tops.

Mr Southall excused himself and went up to the flight deck. The awkward silence that followed was filled by helping Jacob to the toilet and then giving him another drink.

When Mr Southall came back, he said, "We have drifted out into a deeper bit of water away from the lee of the reef. Frank is taking us back in closer now. Time we were airborne I think."

Willy was now torn. He badly wanted to hear Jacob's story, but he also wanted to try to get back up onto the flight deck to watch the take-off. He was disappointed when Mr Southall said, "Willy, you stay here with young Jacob. I will get one of your officers to help."

All Willy could do was nod and hide his disappointment. He smiled at Jacob and then had to keep his features fixed when Flying Officer Turnbull appeared in the doorway. He came in and held up a lifejacket.

"Captain says to put this on while we take off," he said to Jacob.

Jacob took off the towel and stood up. Flying Officer Turnbull introduced himself, then pointed to the belt and zipped up wallet around Jacob's waist. "Would you like to take that off?"

Jacob shook his head vigorously. "No, that has my money and the... the... er a few things that are important," he replied.

He then allowed them to place the lifejacket over his head. While they did this, they were several times almost thrown off their feet by bigger waves slamming against the hull. Willy was glad to sit down and brace himself in the corner where he could see out of the porthole.

Willy heard the engines increase in revolutions and he looked out. *We are only taxiing,* he decided.

He also thought it was very rough, much rougher than when they had landed. The seaplane seemed to slam and buffet into the waves, and he saw sheets of spray flying past. The motion became so unpredictable and violent that he began to experience pricklings of unease. *Something wrong,* he decided.

He was right but got no explanation for nearly twenty minutes during which time the Catalina taxied back and forth in several directions, sometimes with the waves and sometimes across or against them. Looking out Willy saw that they were now very close to the edge of the reef, the foam of breaking waves being only about fifty metres away.

The engines were throttled back to idle, and Willy got another shock. He saw that the wind was blowing sideways across the reef to strike them almost beam on but that the Catalina was sliding crabwise along very quickly to port. Then his eyes noted the swirl of current along the edge of the reef.

"Something wrong?" asked Jacob anxiously.

"Not sure. Might be too rough to take off," Willy answered.

Jacob joined him at the porthole but only looked out for a few seconds before visibly shuddering and shaking his head before sitting down again.

He doesn't want to end up back in the sea, Willy thought.

Ten more minutes of engines throttling up followed, the Catalina buffeting across a confused set of waves. Then it turned in a welter of spray and big waves which tossed them hard against walls and bulkheads. Willy noted that he was now looking westwards. The Catalina began powering back against the current. After five more minutes of this the engines dropped to an idle and Mr Southall came down.

He poked his head in the door and said to Flying Officer Turnbull, "Too rough. I'm not going to risk it just yet. The tide is ebbing really fast and that is causing a strong current seawards. The wind is coming across the reef and meeting this and is churning up a very confused sea."

"Will we be able to get off?" Flying Officer Turnbull asked, anxiety clear in his voice.

"When the tide turns, or if the wind drops," Mr Southall replied.

"What if the current pushes us onto a reef?" Flying Officer Turnbull queried, voicing Willy's fear.

"We will use the engines to get clear," Mr Southall answered.

"How long can you do that for?" Flying Officer Turnbull asked.

Mr Southall gave a wry grin and said, "About another ten hours before we run out of fuel."

Willy felt another chill of fear. He asked, "Don't flying boats have anchors? Can't you anchor?" he asked.

Mr Southall nodded. "We do have an anchor. We thought of that but can't find anywhere safe to do it. The coral reef drops off into very deep water and we can't reach the bottom. We have been up and down looking for somewhere. And I don't want to secure ourselves to the reef. That would be too close, and it would only take a big wave or sudden wind shift to put us on the reef. That would be disastrous."

Willy glanced out at the churning whitecaps and imagined the thin aluminium hull grinding and tearing on the hard coral. *It rips the bottom out of big ships,* he thought. *An aircraft hull wouldn't stand a chance.* The idea of having to get out onto those waves in a small rubber dingy did not appeal to him at all. *Not with those sharks around!* he thought.

Flying Officer Turnbull then said, "So we are in trouble."

Mr Southall nodded and said, "Yes, serious trouble."

"Can't you radio for help, get a ship to come and pick us up or something?" Jacob cried, clearly very anxious.

"George is doing that right now," Mr Southall replied. "We have already been in contact with Cairns by radio, but radio reception isn't very good down here at sea level. They know there is a problem and our location but that doesn't mean they can do much to help us."

"But there must be ships!" Jacob cried.

"Calm down mister. If we have to we will try to taxi all the way to the coast. They might even be able to contact some yacht or launch. We are safe enough for the moment."

Jacob still looked very anxious. He said, "But what about helicopters or something?"

Mr Southall shook his head. "The nearest proper rescue chopper is at Cairns and will take about three hours to reach us at the earliest, and it will only be able to winch off three or four people. You will be one of them. The only other choppers in the area are tiny ones used for mustering cattle. They can only carry two people and I wouldn't want to be flying one of them this far out to sea."

Willy found all that very sobering. He knew they were about 20 nautical miles offshore but had left his chart up on the flight deck so could not check. Flying Officer Turnbull went out to brief the other cadets about what was going on. Mr Southall took Jacob to the toilet again and then got him another drink and some sandwiches. Flying Officer Turnbull then came back and sat down.

"Some very seasick cadets back there," he said. "It's a bit of a mess I'm afraid."

As the officer said this Willy realised that he had been able to smell the vomit for some time. Now the sour stench made his stomach turn over and he broke into a cold sweat. Mr Southall just nodded.

A moment later the navigator came back down and said, "No luck. The nearest trawler is down past Cooktown and couldn't get here before midnight and the nearest ship is a Panamanian bulk carrier just passing Thursday Island. It won't be in this area before tomorrow morning."

Willy experienced another spasm of what he grudgingly admitted was real fear. However he tried to keep his face calm, even as he tried to imagine what it must be like to float in the open ocean. To emphasise their situation, the engines increased their revolutions and the Catalina began butting across the waves again as the co-pilot moved them away from the edge of the reef again.

Mr Southall seated himself on the end of the bench nearest the door and looked at Jacob. "Well young Jacob, you may as well tell us your story while we wait."

Jacob nodded but did not answer. To Willy he seemed to shrink inside the blanket.

When he did not speak Mr Southall said, "Well, what happened? Who shot your friend, and how did you come to be in the water?"

For a few seconds Jacob appeared to hesitate and he shook his head before saying, "There was a fight on our boat and they shot Karl because... because... er, anyway, I had to jump overboard to save my own life."

"Who shot him?"

"'Gator' did. Gavin Smith's his name but his nickname is 'Gator'," Jacob replied.

"Why?"

"Because he wanted Karl to steal my... er... my er things. And Karl wouldn't be in it. He said he would tell me their plan so Corey, that's Gator's mate, tried to stop him. There was a fight and Corey drew a knife and Karl knocked him down and then ran up on deck. I was there and had heard them arguing. I was steering you see. Then Gator appeared in the companionway with a gun and Karl tried to jump him."

Jacob stopped and gave a little sob and then shook his head as though in disbelief. Then he went on, "Gator shot him. I couldn't believe it! Karl staggered backwards and as the boat rolled on a wave he just went over the side. It was my fault! I let go of the steering and the boat yawed. It... I... Oh!"

For a minute Jacob was too distressed to speak. Then he continued, "Anyway, Gator shouted at me to give him the... the... er my things... or he'd kill me too. He started up the companionway with the gun and I panicked and ran. But she is only a tiny little launch and there was nowhere to hide and no weapon handy so I dived overboard."

He shuddered, though whether from the recollection or the cold Willy could not tell. Then he said, "Just as well I did. Gator fired at me and I had to dive under."

"What time was this?" Mr Southall asked.

"About eleven o'clock last night," Jacob answered. "If it hadn't been so dark, he would have easily seen me and shot me. As it was, he and Corey got the boat under control and came back looking. They circled for half an hour, shining torches and calling out saying they wouldn't hurt me."

Mr Southall obviously did the same calculation Willy had as he said, "So you have been in the water for about eleven hours?"

"Yes," Jacob replied. He took a sip from his refilled cup.

Mr Southall shook his head. "You are lucky this is the Coral Sea and not the North Atlantic! You wouldn't have lasted eleven minutes in that."

The navigator spoke up, "You are bloody lucky it is October too. The average sea temperature at the moment is about twenty-three degrees."

Jacob swallowed another gulp and nodded, then said, "Yes, I know. The sea felt quite warm. It was my head that felt cold, with the wind chilling it."

Mr Southall again took out a notebook and pen and said, "What is the name of your boat?"

Jacob looked unhappy and said, "Not my boat. She's 'Gator's'. She is a motor launch called the *Saurian*. It means crocodile or alligator."

Mr Southall then looked at Jacob and said, "Your name is of Dutch origin, isn't it?"

Jacob nodded. "Yes, van der Heyden is Dutch. My grandfather was from the Netherlands."

Mr Southall said, "But from your accent you aren't Dutch. You are dinki-di Aussie."

"Yes," Jacob agreed. "My father was born in Australia and so was I but my mother is from Holland."

For a moment Mr Southall stared unseeingly out the porthole, then he said, "There was a Dutchman named van der Heyden on the first 'Sandringham' I ever flew on. Back in 1965 that was, flying from Rose Bay in Sydney to Lord Howe Island. He was our navigator. The 'Sandringham' was a large, four-engine flying boat."

Jacob's face at once lit up with interest. "My grandfather was a navigator on the big flying boats. He did that for about twenty years."

"What was his name?" Mr Southall asked.

"Cornelius, Cornelius van der Heyden," Jacob answered.

"That sounds like the name," Mr Southall said, nodding thoughtfully. "I was only a young second officer then, but I remember him. He flew in flying boats during the Second World War and settled in Australia after the war."

"That would be my grandfather," Jacob agreed. "He was an officer in the Royal Netherlands Navy back then. He flew from the East Indies to Australia in a Royal Netherlands Navy flying boat when the Japanese invaded."

"Is your grandfather still alive?" Mr Southall asked.

Jacob shook his head and Willy thought he saw tears form in the corners of his eyes. "No. he died a few months ago," he answered.

"Sorry. He was grand chap," Mr Southall answered. He then tapped his pencil on the notebook. "Okay, let's get a few facts. Can you give me your address so I can notify the authorities."

Jacob gave an address and phone number in Sydney. The house was in Manly and Willy could picture that, having been to Sydney a few times on holidays to see relatives.

Great beach. Lots of pretty girls, he thought.

Mr Southall then asked, "This boat, the *Saurian*, describe her please."

"A small launch, a cabin cruiser, ten metres long, white hull, the cabin taking up most of her length. Dinghy lashed on top. Hundred horsepower diesel engine. No funnel," Jacob answered.

"Not very big to be this far out to sea in," the navigator commented.

Jacob shrugged and did not answer. Mr Southall asked him for the details of registry and registration number. Jacob gave these. Mr Southall then said, "You'd better tell us all the details. I will have to radio the police about this."

Jacob sighed and nodded. "I suppose so." It was very obvious to Willy that he did not want to talk about what had happened.

Again he hesitated and Mr Southall frowned. "Go on. What were you doing up this way and how did you meet these characters?" he prompted.

Jacob sighed. "We were just... er... touring by boat. Karl and I were just hitching a ride."

Mr Southall looked hard at him and said, "So why should they shoot your friend and threaten to shoot you?"

"Just an argument."

"Rot! You mentioned that they wanted something from you," Mr Southall said. To Willy he sounded angry.

"Nothing important," Jacob answered lamely.

"Do they have it now?" Mr Southall answered.

"What do you mean?" Jacob said. Willy noticed his hand go to the zip-up wallet at his waist.

Mr Southall sighed. "Listen laddie, we have just risked our lives to rescue you and I don't like being given the run-around. You said they wanted something. If you don't have it on you then it must still be on their boat. Do you have it?"

Jacob blushed and bit his lip, then nodded. "I have it," he said.

When he didn't say any more the navigator said, "Is it a treasure map or something?"

"Why do you say that?" Jacob answered.

"Because mate," the navigator replied, "People don't usually shoot other people for nothing. If it's not some sort of domestic or family feud, then it must be over money."

Jacob looked sick. Mr Southall said, "Are you on a treasure hunt?"

Jacob licked his lips and nodded. "Sort of. We are looking for... for something. It isn't mine so I'm not at liberty to say what it is."

"And you have a map?" Mr Southall pressed.

"Only a tracing and some handwritten notes," Jacob answered. Again his hands fluttered near the zip-up wallet and this time he gave a wry grin and unzipped it. "If they are still any good after all that time in the water," he added miserably.

From out of the wallet he extracted a mushy pulp of paper and a wallet. Mr Southall unclipped the table and lowered it and Jacob placed the items on it. Then he tried to open them up and spread them out. It was instantly apparent to Willy that it was likely to be a hopeless task. Not only had most of the pages turned to mush but the ink had run. As Jacob tried to tease the wet sheets apart, they just tore or came apart.

The navigator laughed mirthlessly. "I hope you've got a copy of all that," he said.

Jacob did not answer but Willy noted a tiny nod. He thought that Jacob looked really sick and distressed.

A treasure! he thought excitedly. *What can it be?* He knew it couldn't be pirate treasure as found in other parts of the world as there was never piracy like that on the Queensland coast. *Gold perhaps, stolen during the gold rushes of the 19th Century? Or maybe pearls from when there was a huge pearling fleet operating up this way a hundred years ago?*

Chapter 4

CALCULATED RISK

While Jacob worked at the apparently hopeless task of retrieving his maps and notes Mr Southall continued questioning.

"So, this Gator character and his crony Corey, where did you meet up with them?"

"In Sydney. Karl knew them. We needed a boat and he knew them. I didn't like the idea, but I did not have enough money to hire my own boat. Also Gator and Corey know about boats and had been up to North Queensland before and neither Karl nor I had any experience of boats, so I said yes," Jacob explained.

"So whatever you are looking for is at sea or on an island?" the navigator commented.

Jacob looked surprised and then made his face go blank. "What makes you think that?" he replied.

The navigator smiled and said, "Because if it was on land, you could have driven there."

Willy saw Jacob's face twitch as he tried to control his expressions. Jacob made no reply.

Mr Southall looked puzzled. "Did they know what you were coming here to look for?" he queried.

Jacob frowned and said, "I don't know. Yes. I suppose they must have. Karl must have told them. The whole thing was his idea."

"Why?"

Jacob shook his head and looked uncomfortable. "I can't say. It really doesn't involve you and my family are involved. It is for them to decide."

"Fair enough," Mr Southall replied. "Okay, you look just about all in young Jacob so we will tuck you into bed. George, you look after him please. Young Willy, you'd better get back out with your mates and we will do something about making this ship smell a bit better."

Reluctantly Willy made his way aft through the bulkhead. He noted that the port door was now shut but all of the deck near it was awash with several centimetres of water and spew. The seaplane was rocking and pitching so much that he had to walk with both hands on the sides to stay on his feet. He saw that the deck all the way aft was sticky with a slush of vomit and water and the vile smell made his stomach turn. That more was liable to be added to it was plainly obvious from the miserable looks and peculiar colouring of some of the cadets.

It gave him a mild spurt of malicious satisfaction to see that Finlay was visibly green around the eyes and cheeks. Pilot Officer Lowe, a chubby female officer, looked a sort of pasty grey. Even Marjorie looked deathly white under her freckles and her eyes looked bigger than normal. The only spare seat on the temporary webbing seating was between her and Dodd so he squeezed himself in.

Marjorie at once gripped his arm and pressed against him. "Oh Willy, I'm glad you are back," she said.

"Why? What can I do?" he wondered aloud, a little annoyed at the public display of affection and the way others looked at them. Because 'fraternisation' was frowned on in the Air Cadets, he had no wish to have people suspect that he and Marjorie were more than just friends.

"Just because," she muttered, pressing closer.

She's scared! he thought, quite surprised at the idea.

Cadet Under-Officer Mathieson leaned across and said, "What's happening Cadet Williams?"

Willy really admired CUO Mathieson, and one of his strongest ambitions was to be promoted to be a CUO just like him. CUO Mathieson was in Year 12 and looked the very image of the sort of young officer Willy wanted to be. So he proceeded to tell him everything he knew, others nearby leaning over to listen.

It was uncomfortable though. The tail of the Catalina was swinging much more than the hull and from time to time it would go up and down with sickening swoops that even left Willy bathed in a cold sweat. Sometimes the undersides would smack into the surface of the sea and send a shudder through the aircraft. It was then that Willy understood how Marjorie was feeling, both mentally and physically, and he was ashamed to admit to himself that he was just a tiny bit afraid.

Marjorie pressed his right arm and whispered, "Wasn't it awful. I'm sorry we weren't able to save that other man before the sharks got him. I was sick when I saw what they had done to him."

Willy's mind swirled with horrific images of that corpse and of Uncle

Ted's mutilated body. He croaked, "Yes. I don't want to talk about it, thanks."

Marjorie, who had been at the farm the night Uncle Ted was murdered, gave him an understanding nod and squeezed his upper arm. Willy had to resist the temptation to put his arm around her and felt a surge of affection for her.

The talk died away after a while as the cadets began to succumb to exhaustion. Just bracing against the continual rocking and sudden movements was tiring. When the anxiety and morbid memories were included, the strain quickly added up. Willy badly wanted to be able to stretch out and sleep but there was nowhere he could.

For another hour the flying boat powered up and down to maintain a safe position clear of the reefs. Willy found he needed to go to the toilet. He waited till he saw Flight Sgt Anderson come out and then made his way forward. After visiting the toilet, which was a nauseous experience because it was full to overflowing, Willy found he was thirsty. He made the few steps across to the galley to get a drink. To get there he had to step around Jacob who was sleeping on bedding placed on the floor of the crew cabin.

The flight engineer was there and met his gaze. "Too rough for him to sleep on the bench seat," he explained.

"I'll buy that," Willy replied, bracing himself against another sudden lurch. "It's getting rougher, isn't it?"

"Yes, it is," the flight engineer answered. He looked grey with fatigue himself and that made Willy even more anxious.

At that moment the co-pilot came down the steps from the flight deck. He nodded to Willy and said to the flight engineer, "We are going to have to risk a take-off, Cyril. The wind is not only picking up but is changing direction. It is swinging around to the north and is starting to blow straight down this channel between the two reefs."

The flight engineer nodded and looked grim. "So the sea will get even choppier and more unpredictable then. How long before the tide turns?"

"It turned about twenty minutes ago, just after midday," the co-pilot answered, "But it will take a couple of hours to reverse its flow in any noticeable way. We can't afford to hang around that long."

The co-pilot now turned to Willy. "Can you get your officer son? I need to brief him."

Willy made his way aft to the port blister where Flying Officer Turnbull was seated with two sick cadets. "Sir, the co-pilot would like to speak to you," he said. From the blister he was able to see out over the miles of churned up sea and seeing that made him truly frightened. He realised he could no longer clearly see where the reefs were because the sea was so confused and there were so many whitecaps.

We are in trouble, he thought.

Flying Officer Turnbull made his way forward. A few minutes later, he made his way aft, stopping to speak to groups of cadets as he did. At each person he checked they had their lifejackets on and their seatbelt securely fastened. When he reached Willy and his group he said, "We are going to take off. The captain warns that it will be rough and that it might be dangerous. You need to be ready to evacuate if we crash."

"Crash!" Marjorie gasped.

Flight Sergeant Anderson gulped and looked scared. "Can't they just motor around behind the reef or an island or something?"

Flying Officer Turnbull shook his head. "I asked the captain that. He says that the problem is that the sea is becoming so confused that they can't see the reefs clearly and we could run onto one."

"Better to crash in the open sea," CUO Mathieson added.

Willy tried to imagine struggling out of a wrecked aircraft into the welter of surf on a coral reef. *We would just be ground to pulp,* he thought. *That's assuming we can even get out.*

Then another ghastly thought came to him. *If we are down in the sea, then the sharks might come!* That chilled him even more and he could only pray that things would go well.

To his dismay, he heard the aircraft's engines begin to bellow. He wanted to cry out that he wasn't ready, that they hadn't discussed this and needed more time to explore the options and to discuss the situation. Then he felt Marjorie gripping him tightly and he realised that he wasn't the only one who was scared. That helped. He smiled at her and put an arm around her.

The officers knowing that we are friends won't matter if we die, he thought.

Then he made a conscious effort to act calm and to help the others. It made his face feel like it was made of plastic, and it felt very stiff and unfeeling but he managed to pretend he was interested and enjoying the adventure. The Catalina began to bump and smack into the waves as it picked up speed and Willy began to try to remember what he had read about flying boats and safe sea states for take-off and landing.

Spray began showering back over the entire hull as the bow pounded harder and harder into each wave. From his vantage point Willy could see forward along the side of the hull and that was no help to his peace of mind. He watched with alarm as the bow drove hard into a big wave, sending a huge shower of water back over the aircraft. A lot of this was sucked into the engines or caught by the whirling propellers and then blasted back past him in a roaring mist which all but blotted out visibility for a few seconds.

Will all that water cause the engines to fail? he wondered.

He was very aware that the failure of even one engine in the middle of a take-off could have catastrophic effects on the aircraft's performance. As the bow slammed into yet another wave, causing the entire machine to buck and shudder, an icy clutch of real fear gripped Willy's heart.

The plane powered into an even bigger wave and seemed to lose all forward momentum to an alarming degree. *We will never get flying speed,* Willy thought. Now his face was a frozen mask, a grin fixed on it. But inside his heart was hammering and he knew he was afraid. *I will keep pretending I'm not so that Marjorie isn't too scared,* he rationalised.

The Catalina bounced and hammered across more waves, its progress all but hidden by the flying spray. Willy saw the starboard float dig deeply into a wave crest, causing the aircraft to yaw noticeably. Then the float dragged itself free and the engines kept bellowing. His sight of the propellers was lost in the sheer volume of spray and foam they lashed up and Willy could only hope that Mr Southall had a better view forward than he did.

As the bow dipped and the tail gave a sickening upwards swoop Willy feared that they were about to drive right under. Then the aircraft shuddered, shook, then powered on.

We aren't going to make this, he told himself. *The waves are too big for us to build up any real speed.*

But then Willy noted that the waves seemed to be getting smaller and as the spray thinned a bit he noted a huge area of churned up water a few hundred metres to starboard. That puzzled him for a second, even as his brain calculated that the maelstrom was getting closer with every second.

Then he gasped. *That is waves breaking on the reef! We are trying to take off in its lee.*

He now understood that Mr Southall had taken the Catalina out into the rougher water to start the take-off run and that they were now coming in to the relatively smoother water as they picked up speed.

Even as this realisation came to him, he worked out that the take-off course was diagonal to the edge of the reef. With every passing second the aircraft's course was converging with that welter of foam.

If we don't get off in the next few seconds we will run onto the coral! Willy thought.

Now the aircraft was hammering along rapidly over the smaller waves. Willy began to will Mr Southall to pull back, to try to take off.

Do it! Do it now! Rotate! he thought, gripping Marjorie tightly.

He noted that the spray was now coming from underneath in a solid curving wave. That told him that the Catalina had ridden up on its chine and was now aquaplaning on its 'First Step', the cut-away section of the hull. Clenching his teeth and staring anxiously out Willy saw that the starboard float was now almost over the breaking waves which marked the edge of the coral reef. He even got glimpses of dark objects in the white foam.

They are lumps of coral, he thought. *If the float hits one of them, we will rip a wing off!*

Suddenly the nose went up and the tail dipped so fast that the narrow fuselage under Willy kissed the waves, sending up more spray. The water was so close that Willy let out a gasp of pure fright. But before his scared mind could articulate thoughts about crashing the waves suddenly dropped away and he felt the zooming, soaring sensation of a take-off.

We are off! he thought as he saw the churning sea drop rapidly below.

Mr Southall held the angle of attack as steep as he dared for a few seconds to ensure that they were well clear of the biggest waves. Then he levelled out in a way that sent Willy's stomach up into his chest. The Catalina settled, bumped, then resumed rising.

Safe! thought Willy as the view opened up and he was able to see right across the reef and out to the far horizon. Only then did he realise he was gripping the seat and Marjorie so tightly that his knuckles were white and hurting.

Hoping that nobody had noticed Willy released his grip and gave a quiet sigh of relief. The Catalina went into a wide, sweeping bank to starboard and then continued to climb. As it did, Willy noted the distant coastline and a group of large islands ahead. The huge curve in the coast he recognised as the shore of Princess Charlotte Bay.

"We are going south," he said to Marjorie.

She gave him an anxious smile and nodded. "We are alright now, aren't we?" she replied.

Willy gave her hand a reassuring squeeze and then shook his head as Cadet Bull, who sat opposite, called back, "Unless a wing comes off."

As the aircraft settled into a steady climb Flying Officer Turnbull made his way aft, checking on each cadet in turn. Satisfied that no-one was hurt he said, "We are heading back to Cairns."

"So we aren't going to Thursday Island Sir?" Stick asked.

Flying Officer Turnbull shook his head. "Sorry. We need to get this fellow to hospital and there's a body to hand over to the police."

"So he really was shot sir?" CUO Mathieson asked.

That caused Willy to experience a sickening flashback to the torn corpse and he almost vomited again, except that his stomach was empty and felt very sore. He also felt a twinge of regret. Thursday Island was a place he had never been to and wanted to visit. It had an aura of mystique about it, one of those legendary places that are far away and exotic.

To distract himself from his horrible thoughts, Willy looked down. Just below him were a group of large rocky islands which he remembered were the Flinders Group. To help take his mind off death and horror he tried to remember the names of the islands, but he had left his chart in the crew compartment and knew it would not be wise to try to retrieve it at that moment.

A few minutes later, the aircraft flew across the coast in Bathurst Bay and all Willy could see below were vast tracts of bush and rough hills. These seemed to stretch as far as the eye could see before they were lost in the haze. Only a couple of tiny, wriggly scars indicated the route of dirt roads. There were no farms, no fields, and no other signs of civilisation for quite some time.

Later they flew directly over the small town of Cooktown. Looking down Willy could clearly see the grid pattern of streets and a number of tiny vessels moored in the Endeavour River. From then on, the Catalina flew just off the coast, allowing Willy a grandstand view of the beaches and jungle-covered mountains that lined that part of the Coral Sea. He was able to identify Cape Tribulation and the Daintree Rainforest. The Daintree River was very obvious to him, and from then on he was in home territory and could recognise most of the large coastal features: Low Isles off Port Douglas, Wangetti Beach, Buchans Point and Double Island, then the beaches just north of Cairns.

By then the Catalina was descending on its landing approach in to Cairns and, as always, Willy stared down with fascination at the all the tiny houses, roads and cars. *Just like a model,* he told himself, knowing that he said that every time he took off or landed. Seeing what looked like a tiny person on a tiny bicycle just added to the pleasure.

Going to land at the airport, he thought as the whirr of machinery made him look forward. The starboard landing wheel appeared in view, folding out and down. That did not surprise him. The Catalina was an amphibian. *Be easier to get an ambulance to the sick man,* he thought. Then he shuddered as he tried to suppress the next idea. But it came anyway. *Or a hearse.*

Sugar cane fields and mangrove swamps slid by below them, coming closer by the second. The road to Machans Beach swept underneath and then the Barron River and the mangroves along its banks.

We seem to be too low, Willy worried, staring ahead at the long stretch of bitumen with its white painted 'piano key' markings.

The flaps were fully extended and the aircraft rocked and wobbled as it encountered ground turbulence. Mr Southall quickly corrected, and they slid down to an almost faultless touch down.

As the wheels touched, Marjorie hugged Willy's arm and said, "Down! Thank heavens for that."

"Don't you like flying?" Willy asked, trying to pretend that he wasn't secretly relieved himself.

"Yeah, it's alright," Marjorie replied, "But I just wanted this trip over, you know, with the dead body on board and all that."

Willy could only agree. For once he was glad the flight was over. But he kept on acting as though nothing unusual was happening. As the Catalina taxied in off the main runway to the General Aviation side of the airport, he looked around and took in all the sights. This included noting all the types of aircraft parked there. That all helped to keep his thoughts off death.

Once the Catalina was parked and the engines switched off, the cadets were told to disembark, those in the tail section first. That meant that Willy was among the first off. As he climbed through the door and down the short flight of steps onto the tarmac, he was dimly conscious of the wave of tropical heat which engulfed him. But as he was a Cairns lad, born and bred, he barely noticed the 32-degree summer temperature. It was the last day of October, and he thought it perfectly normal. What he was very conscious of was the group of people waiting and the four vehicles parked nearby. Among them were the ambulance that he had expected, and a dark panel van which he suspected was an undertaker's vehicle to collect the body.

There were police, both State and Federal and both uniformed and plain clothes, plus several aviation officials and the paramedics. Mr Southall was there already, shaking hands and speaking to them. Flying Officer Turnbull directed the cadets to a nearby hangar to wait in the shade. Flying Officer Lowe led them across. Willy was reluctant to go with them. He badly wanted to learn more about what had happened to Jacob and why; and he also wanted his chart back.

However he judged that now was not the moment, so he walked with the others across the tarmac to the hangar. The sun was now almost overhead and was blazing down with tropical intensity, causing a heat shimmer off the bitumen so he was glad to reach the relative cool and shade of the hangar. The hangar contained a Cessna 172 undergoing maintenance, and the cadets were cautioned not to touch anything.

For the next few minutes they stood or sat and watched. Sweat trickled and Willy felt quite thirsty. But even though there was a toilet and washbasin in the back corner of the hangar he remained near the front. He was rewarded by seeing Jacob helped down from the Catalina by two paramedics. Jacob was then placed in the back of an ambulance, along with a uniformed police officer. Several other police then stood at the open rear door and appeared to be asking questions.

One of the policemen then detached himself from the group and came walking over towards the cadets. *I wonder what he wants?* Willy thought.

He soon found out. The policeman went to the officers and spoke to them and Willy saw them turn to look at him and then point. The policeman then came over to him.

"Cadet Williams? The survivor, Mr van... er... Mr van."

"Van der Heyden," Willy said.

"Yes. He would like to speak to you. Come with me please," the policeman said.

Willy was pleased at that. He walked back with the policeman, Flying Officer Turnbull joining them unbidden. As they walked across the tarmac, Willy saw two paramedics lift a stretcher out of the aircraft. On it was what he was sure was a body bag. The sight made him feel very sick and anxious. The stretcher was immediately placed in the rear of the dark van. The two paramedics climbed into the vehicle, and it drove off as Willy reached the ambulance and the semi-circle of adult faces.

Jacob was lying on a stretcher in the rear of the ambulance. A drip was stuck in his arm and he was all wrapped up. On seeing Willy he struggled into a sitting position and held out his hand.

"I just wanted to thank you for saving my life," he said.

That both pleased and embarrassed Willy. He had to climb into the back of the ambulance to reach Jacob's hand. He took it and they shook hands.

"It was nothing," Willy mumbled. "I just hope they catch the men who murdered your friend."

"So do I," Jacob said, his voice hoarse with passion and dehydration.

"And I hope you find whatever it is you are looking for," Willy added, letting go of Jacob's hand.

Jacob nodded. Willy went to move back and found his way blocked by more men who had just arrived. He turned and found himself staring into a TV camera. A man whom he recognised as one of the local TV news presenters thrust a microphone close to Jacob's face and asked, "And just what is it that you are searching for sir?"

Willy was both offended and amazed. He frowned and wondered why the police had not stopped the media people from pushing in. He was more annoyed to have his movements blocked.

"Excuse me," he said irritably as he went to climb back out.

Not at all fazed, the TV man turned to him, "And you are the cadet who spotted them down in the sea?"

"Yes, excuse me," Willy answered.

To his relief, Flying Officer Turnbull pushed forward and said firmly, "Please save your questions until the cadets have had a chance to refresh themselves."

Willy was allowed to climb down, and the police now moved to keep the news people away from the rear of the ambulance. The back door was closed and the vehicle drove off. Willy turned towards the aircraft, hoping to retrieve his chart. Mr Southall was standing there, so Willy went over to him and asked if he could get it.

Mr Southall nodded, "Sure thing son. Sorry about your trip to T.I."

"Thanks, sir," Willy replied. "It was a real adventure anyway. You are a great pilot."

He hurried away, embarrassed at having said that in public. He climbed up into the Catalina, again regretting that the flight had been cut short. His chart was still in the crew compartment, so he picked it up and said thanks to the Flight engineer, who was adjusting some hydraulic lines. Then he climbed back out.

Only to be confronted by the TV men again. One pointed the camera and the other said, "What is it that the man you saw in the ocean was searching for?"

"He didn't say," Willy answered, shortly.

"Is that a treasure map?" the TV man asked.

Willy was hot and irritated now and he shook his head and snapped back, "No. It is just an air navigation chart."

"Don't get shirty, kid," the TV man replied. "We are just trying to do our job. Can you show us where you picked the man up?"

Reluctantly Willy unfolded the map and showed them. The man took a photo with his mobile phone and made a couple of notes in a notebook. Then he again asked, "And you don't know what he and his friend were looking for?"

"No. That is his business. Ask him," Willy replied.

He then walked back towards the other cadets. But as he did, he could not help thinking the same thing: What is that Jacob was looking for that is so valuable that men will commit murder to get?

Chapter 5

A NEW INTEREST

That was also the question Willy's parents asked when they arrived an hour later in response to a phone call. Both Willy's father and mother were doctors so understood clearly what he had seen. They sat in with him while the police interviewed him. Thus they were also curious about Jacob's quest.

On coming out of the interview room at the Air Cadet depot Willy looked around for Marjorie. Since he and Marjorie had nearly 'done it' the previous month he had developed a lustful passion for her and right at that moment he felt the need for her physical presence, for her very animal aliveness, to offset the dark thoughts he was having. The memories of the torn and mangled corpse floating in the sea were mixed with darker images of Uncle Ted's mutilated body and Willy was terrified he would have nightmares because of it.

Maybe if Marjorie and I have a bit of a cuddle I will forget and not be so upset, he thought.

But she was nowhere to be seen so he could not organise this. Finlay told him she and Stick had gone home with their mother. That upset Willy but he hid his feelings and rejoined his parents, who were speaking to Flying Officer Turnbull.

Willy's home was a very well maintained, high-set 'Old Queenslander', made of timber and set up on concrete posts. The house stood in its own yard with a mixture of lawn and lush gardens. Upstairs was the kitchen, dining room and lounge, bathroom and toilet, and four bedrooms. Downstairs was enclosed and had a concrete floor. The downstairs area included a double car port, laundry, storeroom, and a workshop area. To Willy it really was a home in the emotional sense, and he was very glad to get there and to relax in the familiar surroundings.

That evening Willy saw himself briefly on the TV news. The images made him angry with the media but also roused his curiosity once more.

What was Jacob looking for? he wondered.

During the evening Willy had to tell the story to his big brother

Lloyd. He also got a phone call from his friend 'Noddy' Parker. Noddy was another air cadet and in his class at school. He had not been lucky enough to be picked for the flight but had seen the TV news.

"Was it horrible?" Noddy asked in his usual tactless style.

"Yes, it was. I don't want to talk about it thanks," Willy snapped back. His mind filled with horrible and morbid images, and he became worried that he would have bad dreams.

His fears were correct. That night he had a horrible nightmare full of grinning skulls and bleeding entrails floating in the water while a huge shark circled him. Then it dived and he could no longer see it. That raised the jeopardy to an unbearable level, and he cried out, waking himself and his parents.

His mother came to sit with him and to wipe his face. Willy was ashamed of himself and found that his pyjamas were soaked in perspiration.

"It was horrible, Mum," was all he could say.

She sat with him till his father brought him a cold drink. Then they left him but with the hallway light on. Willy gulped the drink down and then lay back, fearful of going back to sleep again. But he did drift off and managed the remainder of the night without another nightmare.

The next morning, being Monday, meant school. Willy briefly toyed with telling his mother he was sick but then changed his mind. His father helped by calling him to the kitchen and showing him the newspaper.

"You are in the paper son," Dr Williams said cheerfully. "It was very well done to spot that man."

Willy was both embarrassed and pleased. He saw that the rescue was the headline and that the colour cover photos included ones of the Catalina, of Jacob, and of himself. The article was so long it went over onto the next page and included a picture of Mr Southall and a map showing the location of the rescue.

I'd better go to school, Willy decided. *All my friends will want to know about it.*

Feeling tired and drained, Willy made his way to school. On arrival, the first people he met were his friends and rivals from the army cadets and navy cadets. Most were a year ahead, but the group had formed as a natural reaction to the negativity of most of the students to any sort of military association. The leader of the army cadet group was Graham

Kirk, a fit and handsome Year 10 and an acting sergeant. With him were his mates of the 'Hiking Team': Peter Bronksy and Stephen Bell, also Year 10s and corporals, and Roger Dunning, a lance corporal who was in Willy's class.

Stephen waved and called Willy over. "Hey Willy, tell us all about it," he said.

So Willy joined them and proceeded to tell his tale. While he talked three students who were also navy cadets joined them: Andrew Collins, Arthur Blake, and Luke Karaku. All were in Year 10 and Luke was a Torres Strait Islander.

By the time Willy had finished more students had joined the group. Among them was one who set Willy's heart a-flutter with frustrated desire: red-haired Barbara Brassington. Willy had suffered a futile crush on her earlier in the year, but she had rebuffed all his advances. Despite that, he still had secret hopes and yearnings. Barbara was everything he dreamed off: intelligent, strong-willed, beautiful, long-legged, slim-waisted, and with very prominent boobs.

Not like Marjorie's, he mused, noting Marjorie walking towards him.

Marjorie's breasts were big but hung down and wobbled a lot. Even so, the sight of them was enough to make Willy's mouth go dry with desire and for his hands to become sweaty.

On reaching the group, Marjorie pushed through and slid in to sit beside Willy, squashing her left boob hard against him as she did. Willy was filled with a mixture of conflicting emotions; wishing she would not be so possessive; regret that Barbara would think he was taken; and sheer lust.

As Willy finished his tale, Peter asked the question that was now nagging at Willy. "So what was this van der Heyden bloke looking for Willy? Is it a treasure?"

Willy shook his head. "Don't know," he replied. To divert the conversation Willy pointed to a magazine that Stephen had been reading when he arrived. "What's that, Steve?"

"A magazine about vintage aircraft," Stephen answered. "It's got some really interesting articles about old, restored planes and replicas, and there is a really good one about plane wrecks in North Queensland from World War Two."

"Oh yeah? Can I read it?" Willy asked, mildly interested. He noted that the title of the magazine was *Classic Wings*. Then he saw Graham looking around in a distracted way. "What's the matter, Graham, are you still wondering how we caught all you army cadets on that field exercise a few weeks ago?" he teased.

Graham scowled. It was obviously a sore point with the army cadets. They had been challenged by the air cadets to try to sneak up on a number of targets guarded by the air cadets and most had been detected and captured. Willy had played a prominent part in the Air Cadet's victory by setting up various electronic detection devices and by using one of his radio-controlled model aircraft as a reconnaissance UAV. Suddenly Graham stood up and pushed his way past Andrew and walked off.

Willy stared after him. "Sorry, Graham, I didn't mean to hurt your feelings," he called.

Graham appeared not to hear him and kept on walking. Willy looked around the group to check if any of the other army cadets was upset. None appeared to be.

"What's biting Graham?" he asked.

Stephen answered, "Just the latest true love in his life."

"Oh yeah? Who is she?" Willy asked.

"Carol Battersby. She's in Pete's class," Stephen answered.

"The skinny one with freckles and a haircut like a coconut?" Stick queried.

"That's her," Stephen replied. "He must need his eyes tested."

Barbara shook her head and said, "She is a very nice person; nicer than some people I know."

Stephen laughed but he blushed too. "They say beauty is only skin deep, but ugly goes right to the bone."

"Don't be horrible Stephen!" Marjorie cried. "She is a very kind girl."

The bell for morning classes rang at that moment so Willy stood up and shook himself free of Marjorie. She pouted and hinted she wanted to see lots of him at lunch time. That caused a ripple of laughter and good-natured teasing from those who heard. To Willy's embarrassment, Barbara looked from him to Marjorie and back again in a way that made his hopes fade.

To counterbalance that, Willy made a point of walking to class with Barbara and Roger. As they did, Willy glanced towards Marjorie and saw that she had an anxious look on her face.

She's worried I still like Barbara, he decided. That gave him a twinge of guilt because he and Marjorie were now so intimate.

Class was nothing special. Willy found schoolwork both easy and fairly boring. The only teacher to ask about the rescue was Mr Conkey, his Geography and History teacher. Mr Conkey was also the captain commanding the school's army cadet unit and that gave him extra status in Willy's eyes. The fact that Barbara had joined the army cadets a few months earlier was a small regret for Willy.

She should have joined the air cadets, he thought.

But he was glad she had joined something as it seemed to have steadied her down and helped her get her life back on the rails. Earlier in the year she had been developing a real reputation for bad behaviour and for going out with boys.

At morning break Willy sat with Noddy, Stick and Marjorie. It was an entirely routine 'little lunch' and that had a very depressing effect on Willy. *A man has died, and his murderers are still on the loose and nobody here cares,* he mused.

It was a very sobering lesson in the 'life goes on' aspect of life and of how focused on themselves most people were.

The middle session classes were just as routine and boring: Chemistry and Maths B. Willy just sat and did the work mechanically, then daydreamed. He tried to make the daydreams positive: always him as the hero and nearly always involving aircraft and flying and the rescue of a beautiful maiden, usually Barbara. Being able to see her from diagonally behind did not help. From that position he could admired the curve of her hip and thigh and the soft swelling of her right breast straining at the material of her shirt.

She is lovely! he sighed. *I wonder?*

At lunch time Willy met up with Marjorie in the library. They sat in a corner away from the prying eyes of teachers and others and held hands (Strictly against the school rules!). That got Willy all aroused and hopeful, but Marjorie ruined his hopes by reminding him that she had a part-time job babysitting after school.

When the pair emerged from behind the bookshelves after a solid 'pash' they found Stephen sitting on his own reading. He looked up and said, "Hi Willy. Hi Marjorie. Come up for air, have you?"

Marjorie giggled. Willy could only go red and snort, uncomfortably aware that he was very aroused. Hoping it wasn't noticeable he said, "What are you reading, Steve?"

"My aircraft magazine," Stephen replied. "You will find it very interesting Willy. It has a photo of a restored Catalina in it."

Willy was interested. At his request Stephen flicked over the pages and showed him the photo. He saw that it was a different Catalina, and earlier version which had no blisters on the rear of the fuselage. This one was painted red and yellow and had been used for aerial firefighting in Spain and was now being restored.

As he read the short article Willy's eyes also noted the next article. This showed a wrecked single-engine aircraft half covered in sand. Out of curiosity he quickly scanned the short article. It was an account of how a squadron of American 'Airacobra' fighters had come to grief on a ferry flight during World War Two.

"I've heard about this," he said. His eyes then took in some of the details: eleven Airacobras left Townsville on 26th April 1942 to fly to New Guinea. They refuelled at Cairns and Cooktown but then got lost and put down all along the east coast of Cape York Peninsula. The article stirred dim memories of stories he had heard.

Pointing to the photo he said, "This wreck is still there then?"

Stephen nodded. "Apparently. I think there are half a dozen others too."

"You'd think someone would have recovered them," Willy commented, bending down to study the photo in more detail.

"Not worth the effort maybe?" Stephen suggested. Then he added, "I did read somewhere that they recovered the machine guns and radios and so on at the time."

"Pity, I could do with a machine gun or two," Willy joked.

"It's not a very clear photo," Stephen said. "There was something odd about Airacobras wasn't there?"

Willy nodded. If there was one subject he knew about, it was types of aircraft. "Yes. They had the engine behind the pilot and a long drive shaft went forward to the propeller in the nose."

"Ah! Yeah. Now I've seen one of these. Where would it have been?" Stephen commented.

"Beck's Air Museum in Mareeba," Willy replied.

"That's right!" Stephen said. "It is a funny looking plane with a pointy nose. The one he has is restored but not flyable, right?"

"I think so," Willy answered.

"It belonged to some famous ace who shot down half a dozen Japanese planes didn't it?"

Willy shrugged. "Not sure. I think so. He could visualize the tiny Japanese flags painted on the fuselage but wasn't sure how many.

Stephen looked thoughtful. "Hmm. We are going up to Mareeba this weekend. I wonder if I can persuade Mum and Dad to visit Beck's?"

"Haven't you army cadets got your end-of-year Passing-out Parade on this weekend?" Willy asked. Then he grinned as he remembered the previous year's parade.

"Yes we have, on Saturday afternoon," Stephen answered. "Are you going to come and watch?"

"Wouldn't miss it for quids," Willy replied, grinning broadly.

Stephen looked at him suspiciously. "You aren't going to pull a stunt like you did last year are you?"

Willy shook his head and said, "No."

Then he laughed. During the parade the previous year his radio-controlled model aircraft, a large replica of the Red Baron's Fokker Triplane, had been flown by a jealous rival across the parade ground during the inspection by the visiting colonel. Unfortunately something had gone wrong with the controls and the plane had zoomed too low, forcing the VIPs to duck or throw themselves to the ground. The model had struck Graham, who had stood fast, and crashed. Willy had been in real trouble.

Stephen made a face. "You'd better not embarrass us this year."

Willy shook his head and said, "Don't worry, I won't. Are you going to come and watch our parade?"

"When is it?" Stephen asked.

"In a month's time, on a Friday night. It will be better than yours."

Stephen snorted derisively. "Oh piffle! Anyway, I can go to Mareeba on Sunday. I'd like to talk to Mr Beck about some of these old aircraft."

"Can I come?" asked Willy, whose interest was aroused.

"Sure, if you like?" Stephen answered.

Marjorie had been patiently listening. She said, "What about me?"

"Sure. We will make a party of it," Stephen said.

At that moment the bell went. As Stephen stood up Willy pointed to the magazine. "Can I borrow that magazine, Steve?"

Stephen handed it to him. "Sure. Just give it back to me tomorrow, and don't read it in class and get it confiscated by some grumpy teacher."

That caused Willy to laugh out loud as he had several grumpy teachers. "No, I don't have Mr Burgomeister or Miss Hackenmeyer after lunch, only Mad Max for Science."

It was not until he was at home after school that Willy got a chance to look at the aircraft magazine. He had seen it on the bookstands at newsagents but had never looked at one before. On reading through it he found it a fascinating revelation. The were numerous excellent colour photos of all types of planes, both old and new, plus articles on aircraft wrecks, restored aircraft, air museums, new replicas, historical accounts, air shows and advertisements. There was also a very interesting section devoted to reader's letters.

What particularly pleased Willy was that the centrefold was a great colour picture of a 'Black Cat' Catalina. It wasn't Mr Southall's but it was still a 'Cat' and Willy now had a great fondness for the type. He studied the photo minutely, noting that it also had no hull blisters.

Just as well we weren't flying in that one, he thought. *I would never have seen that Jacob then.*

For a few seconds he recreated the view from the blister in his mind, then shuddered as ghastly images of the mutilated body slid in.

Next, he read several of the articles. Two that he found particularly interesting dealt with the discovery of World War Two aircraft wrecks. One was a 'Liberator' four-engine bomber which had crashed in the New Guinea jungle. The other dealt with the discovery of the wreck of a flying boat named the *Corinthian* in Darwin Harbour. It had crashed in 1942 but the wreck had not been discovered for another 62 years.

Amazing! he thought as he read the details of what condition the various parts of the wrecks were in. There and then he decided to not only try to buy the same copy of the magazine but to subscribe to it.

That night he was in a slightly happier frame of mind when he went to bed. Now he was troubled more by the urgent desires of his fit young body. Having nearly made love to Marjorie a dozen times he felt the urge to be with her as often as possible.

And I think she feels the same way. I wonder if we will get a chance to be alone tomorrow? he mused as he drifted off to sleep.

Chapter 6

CADETS

Willy and Marjorie did not get a chance to sneak away on the Wednesday. That left them both feeling frustrated and Willy quite grumpy. He also felt quite guilty for thinking what he wanted to do as he knew that Marjorie was years underage.

Instead school ground on in its usual course, with the added tension of having end-of-year exams looming. That meant all the teachers were worrying and making the students revise and that irritated Willy even more. He was confident he would pass all the tests and exams easily and did not feel like studying.

During the breaks he discussed the articles in the aircraft magazine with Stephen. Stephen seemed to have been temporarily deserted by his mates so he was happy enough to talk. "Where are the others?" Willy asked.

"Pete's helping Mad Max do some chemistry experiment in the lab. Graham's off wooing his new girlfriend, and Roger's helping sort uniforms in the Cadet Q Store," Stephen answered.

"Are you still going to Beck's Museum on Sunday?" Willy asked. He had been there several times over the years, most recently in June with the Air Cadets, but now wanted to ask Mr Beck some specific questions.

Stephen nodded and took off his glasses to polish them. "Yes. Mum said she would drop us off just after lunch and pick us up a couple of hours later. You still want to come?"

"Yes please."

"And what about your snuggle bunny?"

"Marjorie? If I go she will want to be with me," Willy replied.

"What did you want to see?"

Willy pointed to the aircraft magazine that now lay on the table in front of them. "I'd like to find out about old aircraft wrecks in this area."

"So would I," Stephen replied. "There were lots apparently, and not all of them have ever been found."

"That would be great, to discover a missing plane," Willy said.

"Worth a try," Stephen agreed.

That afternoon as soon as classes finished Willy did not hurry home. Instead he and Stick both waited downstairs. The alleged reason was to talk to the army cadets before they started their weekly 'Home Training' parade but for Willy the real reason was to admire Barbara from afar. The school was one of the few in the region that still had an army cadet unit, mainly because Captain Conkey and his officers made the effort to keep it going. The Army Cadets, like the Air Cadets, was a part-time, voluntary organisation which got some government help.

The training did not begin until 3:45pm so there was half an hour to talk and tease. During that time the cadets changed out of school uniform and into their drab army camouflage uniforms. It also allowed cadets who went to other schools time to travel to the High School. When Willy saw Barbara appear in her uniform, he could only shake his head in admiration.

She even looks good in that shapeless camouflage stuff, he thought.

The Army Cadets followed a similar routine to the Air Cadets, starting the training session with a company parade. Willy watched this with interest, noting all the little differences in orders and procedures. The platoon sergeants lined their platoons up on the grass quadrangle and then the Company Sergeant Major called them 'on parade' and right dressed them. Next, the platoon sergeants marked their roll books. One of these was Graham and seeing him wearing the three stripes caused Willy a spurt of envy.

I want to be a sergeant, he thought.

From his friends he knew the story of how Graham came to be promoted above his peers at their annual camp a few weeks earlier,[1] but he still felt it was vaguely unfair.

Although Graham looks the part and can certainly do the job, he conceded.

He resented the fact that the army cadets seemed to get promoted much faster than air cadets and he doubted if he would reach sergeant for another two or three years.

Graham is only a 'Second Year' cadet, he thought. So was he but he had just reached Leading Cadet. *I hope I get selected for the Corporals Course in January,* he thought.

---

[1] Read *The Cadet Corporal* by C. R. Cummings

The sergeants gave their reports one by one to the CSM. He then handed the parade over to the OC, Captain Conkey. Captain Conkey fell the Cadet Under-Officers in and then stood the company at ease. After talking administration for a few minutes he reminded the cadets that the selection list for the December Promotion Courses would go up after the Passing-Out Parade that weekend.

"This is a test of loyalty. To make the parade look good we need numbers. If you don't turn up I will move your name to the bottom of the promotion list or off it," Capt Conkey said.

Willy could only agree with that sentiment. *If they could not be bothered to turn up for an important event like that they aren't worth promoting,* he thought. Then he chewed his lip with anxiety. *I hope I get selected to attend our Promotion Course in January,* he told himself.

That got him discussing with Stick how the army cadets did all their promotion courses at the same time in the last week of the school year but the air cadets did some courses in January and some in June.

For a few more minutes Willy stood there admiring Barbara, who even at a hundred paces, really stood out. Then, after the company marched away to do a parade rehearsal down on the oval Willy made his way to the bike racks with Stick. Willy then rode with him to his house. Marjorie was working again so Willy only stayed talking for a few minutes before riding off. He made his way to the newsagent his parents usually visited. There he was lucky enough to find a copy of the aircraft magazine he wanted. He also found a similar one by another company and on an impulse he bought that as well. Then he rode home.

That night Willy asked about going to Mareeba on Sunday. His mother and father had no objection and also thought it was a good idea. Willy suspected that was because they wanted him busy and not brooding about having seen another dead body, but he was grateful for their interest and consideration. They proposed to take him up and then visit Aunty Isabel at the farm.

"Can we take a couple of others?" he asked.

"Who?"

"Stick and his sister?"

"Young Marjorie? Certainly," replied his mother, smiling.

Willy then settled in his room to read the new magazine he had collected. From it he learned the outline stories of two B24 'Liberator' bomber crashes in North Queensland during World War Two. One was the sad story of an aircraft named the *Texas Terror*, which flew into the side of Mt Straloch on Hinchinbrook Island, in 1943, killing all on board. The other was, to Willy's way of thinking, even more tragic. It was the story of the B24 'Liberator' which got off course and ran out of fuel, then crash landed near Moonlight Creek in the Gulf Country west of Burketown. Of the ten men aboard only three survived. Four were killed in the crash. Two walked east and met the manager of 'Escott' Station, 15 kilometres west of Burketown. They had walked about 60 kilometres in 12 days. Four others walked west and three died of starvation, drowning and sickness. The lone survivor was found 150 kilometres from the wreck 5 months later.

"Poor buggers!" he muttered. "If only they had known about bush tucker."

That made him uncomfortably aware that he had very little idea of what plants to eat should his plane ever come down under similar circumstances.

Anyway, it won't happen nowadays, not with the EPIRBS and all the other electronic gadgets, he told himself.

Vintage, restored and replica aircraft were the main topic of conversation among Willy and his air cadet friends at school the next day. Stephen joined them, muttering that Peter was busy in the laboratory and Graham had gone off on his wild goose chase trying to woo Carol.

Stick then said, "How come Kirk was a sergeant yesterday. Wasn't he only a corporal?"

Stephen nodded. "Yeah, he was. Capt Conkey promoted him in the field to acting sergeant during camp."

Stick frowned. "Did he have to do a course or anything?" he asked.

Stephen shook his head. "No. Capt Conkey promoted him because he demoted one of the platoon sergeants for misbehaviour."

Noddy cut in. "Yeldham, for trying to chat up that Lucy chic," he said.

Stephen agreed and they discussed sergeants who had been demoted. The conversation then moved on to Lucy and girls.

Willy said, "Is it true that Graham has been picked to go on the warrant officers course in December and is to be your CSM next year?"

Stephen nodded. "Yes, that's right."

"That's a bit unfair," Stick said. "You have been in the cadets longer than him."

Stephen looked a bit uncomfortable then shrugged. "Graham will do a good job," he replied.

That comment raised him considerably in Willy's estimation. *Stephen is being very loyal to his friend,* he thought.

Noddy asked, "How come he is to be a warrant officer? What did he do to get that?"

"On annual camp he led the only patrol that was able to reach the objective during a field exercise against other cadet units," Stephen said.

Willy had heard the outline of that and said, "That was the raid by ten or twelve patrols against the Bunyip River Rail Bridge, wasn't it?"

"Yes, it was," Stephen replied.

"Did you lead a patrol?" Stick asked.

Stephen nodded. "Yes I did, but we ran into three lots of defenders and never made it."

"Still doesn't seem fair that Kirk should get promoted two ranks just for that," Noddy grumbled.

"It wasn't just for that," Stephen said. "He also did a great job leading a very difficult section, and he saved a kid from committing suicide."

"That was on the railway bridge at night, wasn't it?" Willy asked.

"That's right."

Willy frowned. "I heard that it was Peter who really saved the kid."

"Yeah, Pete was there. They both were," Stephen replied.

Willy could see that Stephen was looking uncomfortable defending his friend but respected him for trying. But the promotion still rankled. It obviously annoyed Noddy too because he said, "So Kirk goes from joining cadets in June last year to corporal at the start of this year, then to warrant officer by the end of the year?"

"Yeah, I suppose so," Stephen conceded.

"Not fair," Noddy grumbled.

"Why not?" Stephen challenged.

Noddy made a face and looked at the others for support. "Because in the Air Cadets you have to do a whole year as a recruit and then another as a leading cadet before you can even go on a corporals course. We won't go on ours till January next year and we have all been in longer than any of you army cadet types."

"Maybe you are all just slow learners," Stephen retorted.

This drew an outburst of derisive comments, to which Stephen just laughed. But it was an issue for Willy. Once again, he did his sums.

I will be a corporal next year, in Year 10. With luck I will make sergeant in Year 11. Then I have to be a flight sergeant and a warrant officer before I can even do my CUOs course. I will be very lucky to make CUO even by the end of Year 12.

He said this to Stephen who shrugged. "Don't pick on me," he replied. "I don't make the rules. Anyway, who is coming to Beck's Air Museum next Sunday? I need to telephone to let them know we are coming."

Willy said yes and explained that he could take Marjorie and Stick with him. While he was doing this a grumpy looking Graham appeared with Andrew Collins. As they sat down Graham asked, "Where are you all going on Sunday?"

"Mareeba," Stephen answered. "To Beck's Air Museum."

"I'm going to Mareeba on Sunday," Graham said. "To see my Gran."

"What time are we all meeting up then?" Stephen asked.

It was agreed that 2:00pm would be a suitable time. Andrew raised his eyebrows and asked, "What is this all about?"

"Steve's got as bee in his bonnet about old aircraft wrecks," Willy replied.

They discussed the B24 crashes and Willy provided what little details he knew. Stick then mentioned the Airacobras which crash-landed all over Cape York Peninsula in 1942. At that Graham sat up and said, "My Grandfather was involved in that. He was the captain of a small ship taking supplies to the airbases up in the cape and he told me he took several air force work parties to the wrecks to take out the guns, radios and instruments, and engines and so on. There are even some old photos he took somewhere at home."

Willy sat up, his interest aroused. "D'you think you could find them?"

"I suppose so. Grandad has been dead for five years, but Gran might still have them," Graham answered.

Noddy now said, "I heard there was the wreck of a B25 or something like that in the jungle near Babinda."

"See if you can find out more details, please," Stephen asked.

"I heard that a plane crashed up on Black Mountain back during World War Two," Stick added.

They discussed all the plane crashes they had heard about, and Willy realised he did not know very much. *I will start doing some research,* he decided.

Then it was in to class and another long, boring afternoon. It was only enlivened by Callum and Sean, the class clowns, getting into trouble for practical jokes. For Willy it was all just frustrating. He knew the work, didn't need the revision and itched to either be with Marjorie or be in the library.

After school he got to the library, but not to be with Marjorie. She had to go shopping with her mother. Willy began to wonder if Marjorie's mum knew more than he suspected.

Maybe she is making it hard for Marjorie and me to be together? he thought.

So he contented himself using the internet to research plane crashes. It came as something of a revelation to him. *I didn't realise there had been so many!* he thought, noting a 'Beaufighter' crash near Giru, south of Townsville; bombers laden with mustard gas bombs flying into the side of Mt Elliott, also near Townsville, 'Mitchells', 'Ansons' and P40 fighters going down in the sea or vanishing. He was particularly saddened to read an account of how a transport plane had crashed off Holloways Beach in 1944, killing all on board including Major General Vasey, the commander of the army's 7th Division.

Flying was a pretty risky business in those days, he mused.

That night Willy slept well for the first time since the rescue. He woke on the Friday feeling rested and fresh.

Oh! I hope Marjorie and I can get together today, he thought.

But it was not to be. She was kept in at lunch time for talking in class and not doing her homework. Then she had to go straight home to do her chores because she was not going to be home on Saturday afternoon or Sunday.

"We will make it up," she promised.

That sent Willy's hopes soaring but also made him think of a saying he had heard once that 'you never catch up on the ones you miss out!' He had to console himself by riding home and doing some of his own household tasks. He then busied himself with some work on one of the model aircraft he had under construction. Model making was one of his hobbies and he had a large collection. These ranged from 1:72 and 1:35

scale plastic kits to much larger flying models made of balsa or of plastic. These were powered by either petrol engines or electric motors and were radio controlled.

I haven't done much model making recently, he thought. But he knew why, too much time and energy taken up by Marjorie and by Air Cadets.

Friday night meant Air Cadets. Willy always looked forward to that. He put on his blue uniform with real pride, making sure it was well ironed and that his black boots shone with polish. His mother drove him to cadets. As usual, he got there half an hour early because he liked to help, and it gave him an opportunity to talk to other cadets from different schools. It also gave him a chance to speak to Marjorie, although he made very sure they never did anything at cadets that could be construed as 'fraternisation'.

As soon as his mother had dropped him off, Willy made his way across to the timber hut that was their depot and went inside. There were already a dozen people there. To Willy's disappointment, Marjorie was not there yet so he went over and saluted Flying Officer Turnbull and the CO, Flight Lieutenant Comstock, then went to talk to Joel Carpenter, another Leading Cadet, and Cpl Fazukis.

Inevitably the conversation turned to the Catalina flight and the rescue. Joel was obviously jealous at having missed out but still wanted to know the details. While Willy described the incident, they were joined by his section leader, Sgt Sarah Sleaford and by two other cadets. When Joel wanted to know all the gory details of the body in the water Willy shook his head and had to walk away.

He joined another group, only to be asked on arrival by John Soper, "Hey Willy, what happened to that bloke we rescued?"

Willy could only shake his head. "No idea," he answered. But the question made him think. "He went back to his home in Sydney, I suppose."

Jacob had certainly dropped out of the news quickly enough but that did not surprise Willy.

Nothing much stays in the news for more than a day or two, he told himself.

The arrival of Stick and Marjorie gave him the diversion he wanted. He hurried across to join them. With them was a blonde girl in civilian clothes. She looked the same age as Marjorie, and her face was familiar.

"Hello," Willy said politely, after giving Marjorie a big smile.

Marjorie smiled back and then indicated the girl with her. "You know Vicki? She is in my class at school. She has come along to have a look."

Willy nodded. Now he could place the girl. He had often seen Vicki around the school but had not known her name. They started talking cadets, trying to convince Vicki that she would enjoy it and that she should join.

The training then began. First there was a parade. The flight Willy was in, 16 Flight, went on parade behind the much older 104 Squadron. Willy enjoyed the parade and compared it to the army cadet parade he had watched on Wednesday afternoon. In outline it was similar: the Warrant Officer (Drill) (WOD) called markers and the flights then marched on from the side, did a left turn and stood at ease. He then ordered a right dress and eyes front then the Flight Sergeants called the roll. After that the WOD handed over to Flt Lt Comstock.

The cadets were then moved into the hall and seated for end-of-year theory exams. These were on the organisation of the RAAF, Theory of Flight and Aircraft Recognition. Willy really enjoyed these tests and was sure he got nearly every answer correct. After that there was a short canteen break, during which he talked to Marjorie and Vicki.

The squadron then did an hour's rehearsal for the passing-out parade. Willy enjoyed that, even though he was just one of the cadets in the ranks. The whole ritual and sequence interested him, and he was determined to do his best. He actually enjoyed drill and took pleasure in holding himself still and in the self-discipline of trying to make his muscles do exactly what he wanted.

After the dismissal parade Willy sought out Marjorie to check that she was attending the army cadet passing-out parade the next day. She looked deep into his eyes and said she was. The look in her eyes made Willy's heart beat faster and he went dry in the throat. "I wish we could get together tomorrow," he murmured, keeping his voice down so that no-one else could hear.

"We can tomorrow night," Marjorie said. "Come over and we will play board games or something."

"Or something," Willy hinted.

Marjorie giggled. Stick, who was walking towards them said, "Or something what? What are you two planning?"

"Oh, nothing," Marjorie replied, trying to look innocent.

"Nothing eh? Well that nothing might cost you a fair bit to buy my silence," Stick answered, giving them a wink and a leering grin.

Willy felt a rush of guilt and went red. Marjorie just poked her tongue. "You tell on me and I will tell on you," she retorted.

That silenced Stick at once and he changed the subject to the army cadet's passing-out parade. Arrangements were made to meet at the school oval. They had permission to wear their Number 1 uniform and Willy was looking forward to that. He often saw the army cadets in their uniforms, but he rarely got the chance to wear his where they could see him.

Willy walked with Marjorie and Stick to the car park and said goodnight, then went to his mother's car. He knew his mother approved of Marjorie, though would not approve of them being too naughty. That made him feel another surge of guilt for trying to deceive her.

At home he had supper, then a shower because it was the last day of October and the nighttime temperature still hovered around 23 degrees C. When this was coupled with a humidity level of 70 or 80 % it made it very sticky. As neither of his parents liked air conditioning, he had to lie under his fan with the window open to get cool.

But it was not the heat and humidity that kept Willy awake until well after midnight. It was hot thoughts about Marjorie. For several hours he lay and fantasized about having sex with her. Finally he drifted into a restless slumber.

Next morning he felt tired and hot but made himself get up at the normal time and have his shower and breakfast. Then he set to work on his Saturday chores of mowing, sweeping and tidying up. His father and mother both joined him in the garden, snipping, weeding and pruning. Sweat poured out of them in rivulets, necessitating frequent cold drinks and a good long morning tea break.

After lunch Willy ironed his uniform and polished his boots. His mother had insisted from the day he joined the air cadets that he do all these things himself and he now accepted it as part of his duties. When his uniform was ready, he lay down on his bed to read. Despite the 34-degree heat he drifted into a fitful sleep.

By 3:30pm he was up and having a cold shower. After that he dressed carefully in his uniform, then had another large cold drink. At 4:15pm he and his parents set off in the car for the High School. On arrival they parked the car and joined the crowd of spectators. By 4:40pm they were seated on a row of chairs under the trees beside the school oval.

While they waited one of the army Officers of Cadets, Lieutenant Hamilton, came walking along greeting people. When he got close Willy stood up and self-consciously saluted.

Lt Hamilton returned the salute then fixed Willy with an intense stare. "You aren't going to try any tricks like last year are you, Willy?" he queried.

Willy blushed and shook his head. "No sir," he replied.

"There had better not be or it will all end in tears," Lt Hamilton warned as he walked on.

Willy sat down embarrassed, perspiration from his anxiety adding to the trickle from the humid tropical heat. His blue shirt was soon soaked, and he felt quite put out. Both his parents gave him sympathetic but 'I-told-you-so' looks. Marjorie took his hand and squeezed it until he pulled it away.

"Not when we are in uniform Marjorie!" he hissed.

The army cadet's passing-out parade began a few minutes later. The VIPs: Capt Conkey, the Principal, Mr Crossland, an army Lieutenant Colonel, Squadron Leader English, and Flt Lt Comstock, two officers from the Navy Cadets, and a few other dignitaries moved to the front row of seats and the displays began. Captain Conkey then took over, speaking over the PA system to the parents.

As he did, Willy was reminded that in his youth Captain Conkey had been a regular soldier and had fought in the jungles of Southeast Asia. The row of bright medals hanging from their coloured ribbons pinned to the left side of his shirt showed that. Seeing his teacher wearing the army ceremonial uniform gave Willy a peculiar feeling of pride and satisfaction.

When the army cadets moved into position in front of the audience Willy was able to pick out his friends and rivals. Graham was the platoon sergeant of Number 3 Platoon. Roger, a lance corporal in Number 4 Section. Stephen commanded 6 Section and Peter was in charge of the HQ Signals Section. Willy was also able to pick out Barbara. She stood in a section behind a very attractive blonde female corporal.

Gwen someone or other in Year 10, Willy remembered.

He shifted his attention back to Barbara. Then he shook his head and muttered, "She is just so lovely!" But what to do about her? He could not decide.

The previous year the displays had included one showing piece by piece the organisation and rank structure of the company; a second one showing the types of training activities done, with each section doing a different short act; and a third showing some drill by the corporals. This year the three displays began with the organisation of the unit. This was followed by two that were races between the sections. The first race was to carry out First Aid on a 'snakebite' victim and get him on an improvised stretcher quickly (1minute and 15 seconds for the winners!). The second race was much more entertaining and involved the sections erecting a shelter using only two broom handles, some thin rope, 6 pegs and one Shelter Individual.

To Graham's obvious discomfiture, both races were won by 2 Section. The company then moved off for a drink (It was very hot and humid, even at 5:00pm) and to prepare for the formal ceremonial parade.

Willy really enjoyed watching the parade. He saw his friends trying their very best to do their drill. Graham in particular did an outstanding job. As a temporary sergeant he was the centre escort in the five strong cadet Flag Party. As such he marched between the two CUOs who were carrying the Australian flag and the school flag.

The three sergeants guarding the flags were of particular interest to Willy. All wore scarlet sashes over their right shoulders and carried old World War Two Lee Enfield .303 rifles. They did the old drill with these, the rifles at the 'slope' over their left shoulders. Added to the shimmer of the CUO's swords and the glitter of polished brass and badges it all looked very military to Willy. He even admitted to himself that it did look impressive and that he was just a little jealous!

After a march past and an 'advance in review order', there were speeches and the presentation of prizes. Graham got the award for Best Junior NCO, it being explained that he won the award while still a corporal.

Once again, Willy experienced a twinge of envy.

Chapter 7

AIR MUSEUM

Through all of the army cadet parade Marjorie sat close beside Willy, pressing her hip and leg against his. As Graham marched past she leaned over and whispered, "Gee, Graham is really handsome isn't he?"

Willy felt another spurt of jealousy but snapped back, "Well, you can have him if you like."

Marjorie shook her head. "No. I love you," she replied. "Besides, he is going out with Carol Battersby."

"Is he?" Willy asked doubtfully. "I heard rumours he wasn't doing very well."

"Well, she's here watching and giving him big smiles," Marjorie said.

Willy's gaze followed her pointing hand and he saw Carol sitting along to his right. He was surprised to see her, both because she lived near the Caster Sugar Mill, which was quite some distance away, and because he had never thought she would be interested in anything military.

After the parade, Willy went with Marjorie and Stick to talk to the army cadets after they had been dismissed. Willy made a point of congratulating Graham. While he did this, he had Marjorie's story confirmed. Carol was standing with Graham and had her hand on his arm. Graham looked extremely pleased.

And so he should, Willy mused.

They were joined by several Navy Cadets, resplendent in their dress whites. These included Andrew Collins, his big sister Carmen and Tina Babcock, Andrew's girlfriend. For a few minutes they discussed the differences between the drill done by each service.

Stephen joined them. "What are we doing tonight?" he asked.

To Willy's embarrassment, Marjorie giggled. That made the others all look from him to her, then grin. Willy blushed and knew it. Even Marjorie went red when she realised what she had done.

He said, "We are playing board games at Marjorie's."

"Board games, eh?" Stephen said in a suggestive voice.

"Yes," Marjorie said, trying to look indignant.

Stephen turned to Graham. "What about you Graham?"

Graham gestured to Carol and said, "We are going to the theatre."

Marjorie nudged Willy. *So Graham is starting to win,* he thought.

Stephen had no luck with Peter or Roger either so went away muttering. Graham made excuses and led Carol away. Stick stopped chatting to Andrew Collins and said, "Come on Marjorie. Teatime. Let's go home."

"Okay," Marjorie replied without enthusiasm. She squeezed Willy's arm and then whispered, "See you later."

After they had gone, Willy talked to Andrew and Carmen for a few minutes before going to find his mother. They went home and Willy got out of his uniform and had a shower while she prepared tea. Willy then dressed in shorts and casual shirt in preparation for the games night. It was a very sultry evening, the grumble of a distant thunderstorm hinting at the possibility of rain.

The games night at Marjorie's was attended by Stick, Noddy, Vicki, Tod, Soper and Katrina Ferguson from 2 Section. The games included 'Uno', 'Scrabble' and a couple of dice games they had made up themselves. Throughout the evening Willy sat with Marjorie beside him. She kept up the pressure, touching him and pressing her legs against his. That got him all aroused and he was careful not to stand up when anyone was liable to see his condition.

What he really wanted to do was get Marjorie outside, but no opportunity seemed to present itself, at least not without making it very obvious and attracting sniggers and lewd and embarrassing comments. It also seemed that Marjorie's mother was making sure they had no chance to get away. She kept coming in with drinks and cakes and stayed just in the next room watching TV.

During a change of games Willy leaned over and whispered in Marjorie's ear. "I don't think we are going to make it," he said.

"No," Marjorie replied. She sounded grumpy and made him even more frustrated by saying, "Ooh! Oooh! Oh bugger Mum!"

They did not make it. To put the lid on their chances Willy's parents arrived and sat talking to Marjorie's. At 10pm they took him home, saying he looked tired and that he had a big day next day. It was a very frustrated but also relieved boy who lay tossing restlessly in his bed far into the sultry night.

On Sunday morning Willy slept in and then had a slow start. He also clicked onto the internet to look up plane wrecks and restorations. One of these dealt with wrecks in the Darwin area and Willy did some reading about the Japanese air raids on that town back in 1942. He had been hoping to find more about the wreck of the flying boat, the *Corinthian*.

In this Willy was disappointed. In the past he had read accounts of the Japanese attacks on Darwin on 19ᵗʰ February 1942, but he now read the details with more interest. As he read, he tried to imagine what it must have been like, particularly for the aircrew.

Four American 'Kittyhawks' shot down in a few minutes and the fifth one managed to shoot down one fighter and two dive bombers. That was a great effort! he thought.

For a few minutes he daydreamed, placing himself in the cockpit of that hard pressed fighter plane. It made him particularly pleased when he learned that the lone 'Kittyhawk' had managed to land safely afterwards.

A few pages further on Willy read a short account of another raid he was vaguely aware of knowing about. This was the Japanese raid on Broome in Western Australia on 3ʳᵈ March 1942. When he read that flying boats were involved Willy concentrated more closely. What he now learned quite amazed him.

Sixteen flying boats destroyed on the water in one raid! Sixteen! How on earth did that happen? he wondered.

It particularly saddened him to read about Dutch civilian refugees, including women and children, who had been evacuated that day from Java, being killed while still in the seaplanes which were sitting on the harbour.

That scene he could imagine and vivid images of the dead body with its pink and purple entrails hanging out like obscene streamers made him feel upset and nauseous. *Oh, what a shame!* he thought, wishing the people in charge had either refuelled the planes and sent them on before the raid, or had moved the unfortunate people ashore. But 16 flying boats! He had no idea so many were in service at the time.

He also read that an American B24 'Liberator' with 33 people on board was shot out of the air during the raid, only one person surviving the crash into the sea. Again he had vivid images of seeing Jacob in the waves and he shuddered.

"And two B17s, a second 'Liberator', a Dutch transport plane and an

RAAF 'Hudson' also destroyed, all on the ground," he read aloud. Then he shook his head. "What a wipe out! We obviously weren't very well prepared."

His interest was also sparked when he read that the Dutch plane had been carrying diamonds and that they had vanished from the wreck when the rescue teams arrived at the beach where the plane lay in the shallow water.

Diamonds, eh? Could that be what Jacob was looking for? he thought. Then he shrugged and read on. *I wonder what type of flying boats they were?* he thought.

At the back of his mind was something he had read the previous year about the Imperial Airways flying boat routes from Britain to Australia that were set up in the 1920s and 1930s. He thought the route went via Broome but wasn't sure.

I must find out more about that, and about the Japanese raid, he decided.

That sent him to his reference library of aircraft types and he quickly dug up the flying boat he was interested in. *An 'Empire S30C', all metal, high-wing monoplane, four engines,* he noted.

It was obviously a predecessor of the famous 'Sunderland'. He read that they: 'carried passengers in style, with standards taken from the leisured and spacious days of the previous century'.

All those planes had names starting with 'C'. I wonder if that one they found in Darwin Harbour, the Corinthian, was one of that class?

Still pondering flying boats Willy joined his parents in the car after morning tea. His brother Lloyd declined to come, preferring to go to a friend's house. First, they drove to Marjorie's and collected her and Stick. They then drove up the Kuranda Range and southwest along the Kennedy Highway.

Lunch was taken at Aunty Isabel's farm near Davies Creek. That caused Willy some depressing flashbacks as both Stick and Marjorie had been at the farm the night Uncle Ted was murdered. In fact Willy had been in Marjorie's bedroom when Uncle Ted had got up to investigate engine noises down along the creek. Remembering those horrible events made Willy feel very sad and depressed.

At 1:30pm Willy's father drove him, plus Marjorie and Stick, to Beck's Air Museum. This is beside the Kennedy Highway 5km south of the town of Mareeba. It is set back from the highway, separated from it by a 100 metres wide belt of open savannah woodland. Parked outside the front gate is a yellow painted World War Two 'Matilda' tank. That didn't particularly interest Willy but seated on it, waiting for them, were Stephen and Graham.

Dr Williams drove in and parked in the bitumen car park. Graham and Stephen walked over to join them. As he got out of the car, Willy noted that Graham was smiling and looking very happy.

"G'day Graham. How'd your date go?" he asked.

Graham blushed but beamed. "Good," he replied.

"Well, what happened?" Stick queried.

Graham went even redder but was saved by Marjorie who snapped, "Don't you tell them anything, Graham."

Stick laughed. "Come on Graham, give us the juicy details."

Now Marjorie got angry. "It's awful the way you boys boast about your... er... your... er... what you claim you did," she said.

Stephen snorted and cried out, "Oh, and you girls *never* discuss the boys you went out with of course!"

"I... We... You..." Marjorie spluttered.

She was saved by Dr Williams who said mildly, "Enough of that. A gentleman never tells. Now let's go."

To the left of the small car park was the museum. This was housed in a huge shed with a rectangular base and semi-circular 'igloo' type roof. Attached to it is a smaller and newer concrete block shed which contains the office and a huge collection of models and other exhibits. The group made their way to the ticket office inside the front gate and were met by the owner, Mr Syd Beck, and his son Norman. Mr Beck, a red-faced elderly man, was expecting them and was very pleased to show them around.

"Is there anything in particular you want to see?" he asked, after being reminded they had all been there before.

"The 'Airacobra'," Willy answered.

Mr Beck led them out into the large semi-circular hangar and past other aircraft including a 'Neptune', a 'Sea Venom', and a 'Canberra' and also several armoured vehicles and lots of aircraft engines and propellers to the 'Airacobra'.

For nearly ten minutes Willy studied the plane and asked Mr Beck questions. Knowing that the aircraft was the 'real thing' impressed him and he drank in the details. The Airacobra was painted a drab olive green but what really took Willy's interest was seeing the small Japanese flags painted just below the cockpit.

This plane actually fought to defend Australia, he mused.

For a few seconds he wondered if he would ever be good enough to fly a fighter in his country's service.

If I have to I will, he determined, but not without niggling doubts about his ability and courage. *I hope I am good enough if I am put to the test,* he thought.

In his notebook he jotted down the main details: Bell P-39 Airacobra serial number AC 41-6951; armed with one 37mm cannon firing through the nose, plus 2 X .50 cal. machine guns and 4 X .30 cal. machine guns. Powered by a 1,325 hp Allison V12 engine; top speed about 380 mph.

Willy also noted the details of who flew the plane: an American 2LT named Charles Faletta had been the pilot when the plane 'did its stuff'. 2LT Faletta had belonged to the US 36th Squadron but had been on exchange with the RAAF 75th Squadron at Port Moresby when he had gone into action for the first time. He shot down three Japanese planes: two 'Betty' twin-engine bombers and one 'Zero' Fighter.

After studying the aircraft from all angles, Willy said, "Mr Beck, do you have any information on the others that crash landed on Cape York Peninsula?"

"I certainly do," Mr Beck answered helpfully. He led them back to the front office, which also housed a very large collection of extremely well put together models and a small library. The models were mostly plastic kits on 1:72 or 1:35 scale but they were so well done they really aroused Willy's interest and even jealousy.

They are much better done than most of mine, he thought, noting the care in assembling and the fine details in the painting and decals.

He found himself torn between wanting to look at all the models and the desire to learn about the crashed Airacobras.

"There are some of these still where they crashed aren't there?" he asked.

"Yes, there are," Mr Beck answered. He then named four places where he knew of wrecks.

Stephen looked up from a book he was leafing through. "There are a few other wrecks up there aren't there, like P40 'Kittyhawks' and some 'Beauforts' or 'Beaufighters'?"

"Yes. I know where there is a 'Kittyhawk' in quite good condition and also most of a 'Beaufighter'," Mr Beck answered.

Stephen frowned. "If you know where they are why don't you go and get them?" he asked.

Mr Beck laughed. "It's called money. And you need permission, permits and so on. They are in very inaccessible places, and you can't get a truck in to them. It means either hiring a big helicopter, or a barge of some sort."

"My dad owns a landing barge," Graham said.

"Does he now? And who is your dad?" Mr Beck asked, obviously interested.

"Bert Kirk, of NQ Marine Contractors," Graham answered. "He owns three ships and a big dumb lighter."

"Is that like a cigarette lighter?" Stephen quipped.

Graham obviously wasn't amused and gave him a look suggesting he was dumb. "No, a dumb lighter is a barge that has no engines. It has to be towed. Dad uses it to move oil drums and things like that," he explained.

Mr Beck nodded but then shook his head. "I can't really afford to hire ships. And anyway, I would also need men to help with the work."

"We could do that," Stephen offered. "The school holidays are only a few weeks away. We could go on a trip to help you find these things and then provide you with some volunteer labour."

Mr Beck looked interested but made a wry face. "You and who else?" he asked. "It would take half a dozen at least."

Stephen looked around at the group. "Us?" he suggested.

Willy found himself glowing with excitement at the idea. *What a great idea for the holidays!* he thought.

Up till now they had loomed as nothing much, except for the 9-day cadet promotion course at Garbutt RAAF base in late January. *And only if I am selected!* Now he liked this idea. He turned to his father. "Could I do that Dad?" he asked.

Willy's father rubbed his chin, then nodded. "I suppose so. It would depend on who else was going and how the expedition was organised."

Now that there was a glimmer of hope Willy turned to Graham. "Can you come Graham?"

Graham gave a wry smile. "I will be at sea on dad's ships anyway, at least after Christmas. It would depend on when and where."

"Would your dad help with the shipping?" Stephen asked. He was obviously keen on the idea.

"I don't know. I would have to ask," Graham answered.

Mr Beck now spoke. "I can cover some cost, but not a great deal. I might be able to pay freight and the cost of the day or so lost from a voyage while we load a plane."

"Whereabouts are these planes Mr Beck?" Graham asked.

Mr Beck shook his head. "Ah, that is secret."

"Why?" Stick asked.

Mr Beck laughed. "Because there are a dozen other collectors and museums in Australia, all thirsting to get their hands on some original aircraft, even on parts. And there are lots of overseas collectors. We are talking big money here."

That was a revelation to Willy. He said, "We won't tell."

Mr Beck looked thoughtful. "Well, I suppose if you are going to volunteer to help." He reluctantly reached down and pulled an air chart of Cape York Peninsula from under the counter. This was spread on the desk, and he pointed to two locations.

"There is a P40 'Kittyhawk' here," he said, "and a 'Beaufighter' further north, up here near Cape Sidmouth."

The friends bent to study the chart. Willy noted that the 'Beaufighter' was on the shore almost opposite where the Catalina had turned back to begin its search. Once again, he experienced vivid flashbacks of the rescue and the dead body.

Graham studied the chart and then nodded. "That is right beside the main shipping route. I might be able to persuade Dad to pull up for a few hours."

Mr Beck nodded. "Please try. I have the permits to remove the wrecks, and the permits to go onto Aboriginal land. The longer I leave this the more likely some rival collector will learn about them and snap them up."

"So we will organise an expedition during the holidays then," Willy stated, looking around at his friends for agreement. Now he was seized by the desire to find an aircraft wreck. He pointed on the chart and said, "Which wreck is the best one to try for first?"

Mr Beck pointed to the shore of Bathurst Bay, just west of Cape Melville. "This one, the 'Kittyhawk'. The only real snag is that it is almost two kilometres inland, with a lot of scrub between it and the sea. The 'Beaufighter' is right on the beach."

Stephen studied the map and then said, "If it is right on the beach, how come someone else hasn't found it?"

"Because it is in among some low sand dunes, and a few bushes have grown up to hide it. It was only luck that I found part of the tail poking out of the sand," Mr Beck replied.

"How did you know where to look?" Willy asked.

"I read the pilot's report. He wasn't sure where he had landed, and he walked along the coast for days before some Aborigines found him and took him to Coen. I worked out the general area and then hired a plane and flew over. That didn't show me anything, so Norman and I went walking with metal detectors. Took about two weeks," Mr Beck explained.

Stephen chuckled and took off his glasses to wipe them. "What if we shift tons of sand and find it is all rusted away? We would look silly then!"

Mr Beck smiled and shook his head. "It is all there, a complete 'Beaufighter'. We dug it out to check, then buried it again. Took us three whole days. But this time we covered it with canvas tarpaulins to help protect it from the sand and salt."

"So we need some fit people and three days of time," Willy suggested.

"And a ship or barge," Stephen added.

Graham now looked doubtful. "Even then it might not be possible. What is the shore like Mr Beck? How deep is the water offshore and are there any rocks or reefs?"

"I don't know. It looked like an ordinary beach to me," Mr Beck answered.

Graham added to Willy's concern by adding, "It would depend on the weather too. Any sort of surf and it might not be possible to get a landing craft onto the beach safely."

"Oh Graham! Stop being such a Gloomy Jimmy!" Stephen cried.

"Just trying to help by being realistic," Graham replied, adding, "And there is the tide too, don't forget. That would determine the best time to make the attempt."

Mr Beck looked very thoughtful, but Willy was now determined. He said, "We will look up the tide tables and you can work out a suitable time. Then we will go as soon as we can arrange a ship."

Willy agreed. "We will work it all out and then come up again next weekend for a planning conference to get things organised," he said.

"Now steady on young Willy," his father said. "There are adults to consult yet. Your mother might not approve."

"Aw Dad! If she doesn't then I will try to make another airship," Willy replied.

Dr Williams laughed, then said, "No emotional blackmail, thank you, and no underhand deviousness either. We will see."

Graham shook his head. "I might be busy next weekend," he said.

"Oh Graham give it a break!" Stephen snorted. "She can live without seeing you for one weekend."

Graham sniffed and muttered but went very red, confirming Willy's suspicions that Stephen was referring to Carol from Caster. They left it like that. Willy travelled home snuggled up with Marjorie in the back seat, his mind divided between her physical charms and the hope that they could organise an expedition to recover a real plane wreck.

Chapter 8

PLANS

The moment he arrived home, Willy put the idea of the expedition to his mother. She listened and then raised an eyebrow to her husband, who turned to Willy and said, "You trot along and do your homework while we talk it over."

Willy withdrew to his room, but he felt distinctly hopeful, if only from the tone of his father's voice. He was right. His mother said yes, as long as it was properly organised and supervised by responsible adults. It was agreed that both Mr Beck and Captain Kirk were responsible adults.

Now I hope Graham can persuade his dad, Willy thought.

He settled to his study. That night he slept well, except for a dream in which he and Marjorie were caught by Marjorie's mother just as they were about to be very naughty on a beach.

Monday morning found Willy back at school with plans to visit the town library that afternoon, the school library being almost bare of information on either World War Two in North Queensland or on aircraft wrecks. Once at school he sought out his friends. The one he really wanted to see was Graham and he was relieved to find him sitting with his mates of the Hiking Team in their usual place.

After the usual causal greetings, Willy asked if there was any chance that Graham's father could help. To his relief, Graham nodded and said, "Yeah. I spoke to dad last night on the radio. He said it would depend on the ship's schedules but he might be able to see his way clear to help. What really helps is that it won't take any ship far out of its normal route."

On hearing that Willy felt a stab of anxiety. "You didn't say where the wrecks are, not over the radio?" he asked.

"No. I'm not that silly Willy. We not only learn radio security in the Army Cadets, we actually practise it," Graham replied.

Willy laughed with relief, then could not resist a jibe. "So how come we were able to monitor all your radio traffic and track all your patrols on that last field exercise, the one that WE won?"

This brought a chorus of cries and denials from the army cadets. Willy could only chuckle. It was not often that he was able to get one up on them and he relished the small victory.

He asked, "So, who would like to come on this expedition? Can you come Graham?"

Graham gave a rueful smile. "If it is Dad's ship, I will probably be press-ganged into being aboard anyway," he answered.

"Does your mum agree?" Willy asked.

Graham laughed. "'Only the good die young,' she said. Anyway, it's normal for us kids to help out on the ships during school holidays."

"Pete?"

Peter shook his head. "I'd love to, but I have to go and spend this Christmas with my dad in South Australia."

There was a short, embarrassed silence. Willy knew that Peter's parents were separated and felt very sorry for him. Having his own two very loving parents in the same house seemed even more special to him. He muttered an answer and turned to Stephen. "What about you Steve?"

Stephen looked worried. "Mum says yes but dad is a bit undecided. But I reckon I can win him around. But it can't be until after 'Promo'."

"When is that?" Willy asked. He knew that the Army Cadets did their annual promotion courses before Christmas.

Peter answered, "In six weeks' time, starting on Saturday the fifth of December. That includes the last week of school. It ends on the fourteenth and we will be home the next day."

Willy pulled out a pocket notebook and a pencil and made some notes. As he did, they were joined by Andrew Collins and his three Navy Cadet friends. Andrew again congratulated the army cadets on their Passing-Out parade. "Well done," he said.

"Pity it won't be as good as ours," added Arthur Blake.

"Oh pull the other one!" cried Stephen. "You lot can't march for nuts." He stood up and called to an imaginary parade, "Ship's motley crew, Ho! Crew, swab the decks. Aye aye sir!" Then he swept his hand across to his waist and added, "That's a navel salute. Get it? A navel salute."

Willy saw Andrew pull a face, but he had to laugh at the play on the word 'naval'. Then he grinned again as Roger made a comment about the 'Belly button cadets in their belly bottom trousers'.

"Better than being Space Cadets," Blake retorted.

"Yeah, space between their ears!" Luke Karaku cried, his black face splitting into a huge grin.

Andrew turned to Willy and said, "Anyway, what are you doing here plotting with these troublemakers?"

Willy looked at Andrew and had a sudden idea. *Navy cadets. Sailors,* he thought. *They might be useful.*

So he outlined the idea, explaining he had to keep the location secret. Then he asked, "Would any of you be interested in joining us as voluntary unpaid labour?"

They were interested. Andrew nodded and said, "I wouldn't mind a trip up the east coast of Cape York Peninsula. I've never been up past Cape Tribulation. But you might have to allow my sister Carmen to come along."

"That's alright," Willy replied. "Marjorie will probably be with us, so she won't be the only girl."

The bell for classes ended further discussion but during the morning break and lunch time Willy also sounded out his other friends. He learned that both Marjorie and Stick could go, but only if Marjorie was not the only girl. The possibility of Carmen Collins being with the group made Marjorie whoop with delight, but not because she particularly liked Carmen.

"I will be able to be with you," she cried, jumping forward and putting her arms around Willy's neck and kissing him.

That got Willy into trouble from Mr Ritter, his Maths teacher, who happened to be passing at that moment.

"Stop that you two! It is against the school rules!" he snapped.

It was too, but Willy had enjoyed it and badly wanted more. He went to class wondering how and when he could get Marjorie away somewhere private for some more physical delights.

But it wasn't to be that afternoon or evening. Instead he went, as planned, to the city library and borrowed several books. At home that night he read them, learning a little more each time.

Tuesday and Wednesday were similar, except that one by one the friends reported whether they were allowed to join the expedition or not. Stephen was. So were Andrew and Carmen. Blake wasn't but Luke said 'maybe'. Roger confirmed he was not allowed. Because Carmen could go Marjorie was also allowed, but only for the first expedition.

"We have to go on a family holiday to visit relations in Brisbane after Christmas," Marjorie explained.

That afternoon Willy found many more details on the sinking of the flying boats at Broome in 1942. He found them in the Official History of the RAAF in World War Two. What he read both sadden and amazed him. What particularly annoyed him was reading that a Japanese reconnaissance plane had circled the harbour at 3pm the day before the raid. At that time there had been three flying boats moored in the bay but four more alighted at dusk and nine others during the night so that by dawn there were 16 flying boats anchored off the town.

Surely the people in charge could see the danger? he thought.

Shaking his head he read on. It angered him even more to read that the captains of the planes were warned to take off as soon as possible but that none had done so before the first Japanese fighters attacked at 9:20am.

All over in 15 minutes! Willy noted. *And 24 aircraft destroyed by only 6 enemy fighters!*

Sadly he read about Dutch civilians who had been refused permission to come ashore because they did not have the correct paperwork and who were then shot or drowned in the attacks. Reading the details of people swimming in the sea and of the battle caused Willy a severe flashback to the rescue of Jacob and of the mangled body. For a few minutes he had to stop reading while he trembled, sweated and gasped for air.

After recovering sufficiently Willy read on, noting with interest that the 16 flying boats had comprised two Empire flying boats, three Dutch Dorniers, two British and two American Catalinas and seven other flying boats.

Seven others? I wonder what types they were and what they were doing there? he thought.

Having read the account Willy was left feeling sad and angered. *We did not have our act together very well,* he decided. But it also made him more interested in finding out all he could about flying boats and about World War Two aircraft wrecks. What he read in a local history book that night gave him ideas.

Friday came around with Willy even more determined to find a plane wreck. During the lunch break he said to the assembled group, "We might even be able to find our own local plane wreck."

"Oh yeah?" Stephen commented. "Where?"

"In the Graham Range behind Caster," Willy replied.

Graham at once sat up. "Behind Caster? What type of plane? What happened?"

Willy knew exactly why Graham was suddenly interested but that just seemed like extra good bait to get him to join in. He explained, "I read about it last night in a local history story. It happened back in 1942. Apparently an American B25, a 'Mitchell' bomber, got lost during bad weather at night while returning from a raid on the Pacific Islands. Some local farmers said they saw a big explosion right up near the top of the mountain just before ten o'clock that night. But they never found any wreck. The Americans admitted they lost three planes out of a flight of five, so it could have been a plane crash."

"But if it was seen to crash why didn't the Americans send a search party?" Stick asked.

Willy shrugged. It was Peter who answered, "Probably short of men and with too many more pressing concerns with a war going on."

"We could look," Graham suggested.

Willy was pleased at that. He liked the idea of finding his own plane wreck. "When?" he asked.

"Next weekend?" Graham answered.

Willy shook his head. "Sorry, no chance. We are going back up to see Mr Beck on Sunday and we have exams starting on Monday."

Graham nodded and looked disappointed. Andrew added, "And we have our annual parade on Saturday afternoon. I was hoping you blokes might come and watch."

"We will," Willy replied. "It will cheer us up to see that we are much better."

"Better! Oh, piffle!" Andrew snorted. He then muttered about 'blue orchids' and 'show ponies'.

"So when can we go looking for this B25?" Stephen asked.

They discussed the calendar of events for the next few weeks. With the Navy Cadet's parade on this Saturday and the Air Force Cadet's parade on the Friday night a week later, and with two weeks of exams at school they agreed that the earliest they could plan on was the weekend after the exams finished.

"Ask your parents so we can do some planning," Willy requested.

This was agreed to, and Willy went home that afternoon feeling very hopeful. That evening he again went to Air Cadets for the usual Friday night parade. As he entered the squadron hut, he saw that there were at least twenty others already there. Most were cadets but standing with the officers was a middle-aged civilian, a thin man with short grey hair, and a trim grey moustache. He wore glasses and his neat clothes and polished shoes suggested he was well off.

As all the other cadets were bending over some sort of display on a table Willy made his way over to the adults, saluting the CO, Flight Lieutenant Comstock, as he arrived.

"Good evening, sir," Willy said.

"Ah! Leading Cadet Williams, how are you?" Flt Lt Comstock replied, returning the salute. He then half turned to the civilian and said, "This is the cadet who spotted the men in the water the other day during the Catalina flight."

The civilian nodded and said, "Oh yes, I read about that." He turned to Willy and smiled, then put out his hand. "Mr Jemmerling, Francis Jemmerling."

Willy took the offered hand and shook it. "Willy Williams sir. Nice to meet you."

Flt Lt Comstock then said, "Mr Jemmerling is a collector and has brought along a display to show us. We are also going to have a quick look through his aeroplane."

"Collector sir?" Willy replied, puzzled and wanting to get away to talk to his friends.

"Of aircraft," Mr Jemmerling replied. "You've heard of the Jemmerling Collection?"

Willy did not know what to say. He did not want to lie but equally he did not want to offend a guest by suggesting that he was quite unknown to him. *By the way he said that he thinks he is a big noise,* he thought.

So he said, "Aircraft, sir? That sounds like an expensive hobby."

Mr Jemmerling gave him a thin smile and his watery blue eyes seemed to go frosty. Then he remarked dryly, "Hardly a hobby, at two million dollars a year. But I manage."

That made Willy blush for sounding so ignorant. Feeling somewhat flustered he asked, "Do you own many aircraft sir?"

Mr Jemmerling nodded. "Yes actually. I have ten aircraft in my collection, plus two on the civil register. I have a 'Beaufort' bomber, almost completely restored and which should be ready to fly by next February. There is a non-flying 'Spitfire 111' and I am negotiating to purchase a flying 'Spitfire 1V'. I have a B25 'Mitchell' bomber that flies and a 'Tiger Moth', plus a 'Wirraway' trainer that is unfortunately not airworthy at the moment. As well I have Dragon 'Rapide'. That's a twin engine bi-plane."

Willy nodded. "Yes sir, I know."

"And I have several parts that I am trying to build up into complete aircraft. I have the front half of a B17 'Flying Fortress' with two engines and one wing. There is a P51 'Mustang' fighter minus an engine and propeller boss; the back half of a 'Hudson' bomber and various other bits and pieces. I also have a 'Cessna 180' and a De Havilland Otter that I use for both business and pleasure, but they are modern planes, and I don't consider them as part of the collection. My favourite is my P.B.Y. Catalina."

"That sounds like a really impressive collection sir," said Willy as politely as he could. His interest was sparked by the mention of the Catalina. "We had flight in a Catalina." He saw out of the corner of his eye both Stick and Marjorie come in the door and wanted to get away.

But Mr Jemmerling wasn't finished. "What I am really looking for are parts to complete a 'Kittyhawk' and a 'Beaufighter'."

Willy started in surprise. "A 'Kittyhawk'! Why, I just read that there are several wrecked ones lying on the beach up along the coast of Cape York. They crashed there back in 1942," he said, then remembered he shouldn't and felt a surge of guilt.

Mr Jemmerling nodded and said, "Yes, I know. That is one reason why I am in North Queensland."

Flt Lt Comstock now added, "Mr Jemmerling's collection is at Bogga Bogga in western New South Wales."

Mr Jemmerling nodded and then said to Willy, "So, it was your keen eye that saved that unfortunate young man from the sea the other day. I read about it in the paper. Very well done! Now, please tell me, how did it come about?"

Willy wanted to leave but felt compelled by good manners to stay and explain the rescue. He did this, being prodded to provide details such as wind speed and direction, the names of the reefs, and so on. When he named Mr Southall Mr Jemmerling nodded and said, "Yes, I've known Ivan for years. He did a magnificent restoration job on that Catalina of his."

He sounds just a tinge jealous, Willy thought. "Is your Catalina like his, sir?" he asked.

Mr Jemmerling smiled again and nodded. "It is a PBY 5 A, an earlier version than the one you flew in. Unlike Mr Southall's splendid machine it does not have hull blisters."

"Is yours a restored aircraft sir?"

"Yes. It was once a Royal Air Force machine and was then taken over by the French for Air-sea rescue work. Then it sat in a hangar for fifty years. I have only just had it completely restored and flown it back to Australia," Mr Jemmerling answered.

Willy nodded, wondering just how rich Mr Jemmerling was. He said, "I like the way Mr Southall's plane has been repainted in the 'Black Cat' wartime colours."

"Yes, so do I. In fact, my machine is also painted black, although she was never an RAAF or US Navy Black Cat. She's parked out on the apron right now and you can have a look at her later. Now, I am very interested in the rescue flight. Please tell me the details," Mr Jemmerling explained.

Willy described the visibility and weather, the whales, the speed and altitude changes and then the return and search and the landing. Then he began to get a bit upset as the horrible memories of the torn entrails and mangled body filled his mind.

"Sorry sir. It was pretty gruesome. I don't like to think about it," Willy admitted.

"Quite understandable," Mr Jemmerling said. "So you pulled this young fellow out of the water. What was his name again?"

"Jacob sir, Jacob van der Heyden."

"Van der Heyden? That sounds foreign, Dutch or something."

"Yes sir, Dutch. His grandfather was a Dutch naval officer during World War Two," Willy explained.

"Navy officer, eh? Would you know what ship he was on?" Mr Jemmerling queried.

"Not a ship sir. He was a navigator for navy flying boats. Mr Southall said he knew him, that he flew with him out of Sydney back in the

1960s," Willy explained. He had to think hard to remember the details of the conversations.

"Fascinating," Mr Jemmerling said. He looked thoughtful, then said, "This Jacob van der Heyden, he was searching for something wasn't he?"

"Yes sir."

"Do you know what?"

Willy shook his head and felt uncomfortable. "No sir."

To Willy's relief, Flt Lt Comstock now interrupted, pointing out that the cadets needed to be forming up for the admin parade to start the training. As he moved to join the cadets Willy saw the new recruit, Vicki, standing with several other young people in civilian clothes over at the side of the small bitumen parade ground.

After the parade the flight was marched inside and seated in rows of chairs in the lecture area. Flight Lt Comstock then introduced Mr Jemmerling. He spent the next 40 minutes describing his collection, illustrating his talk with photos projected by a Litepro data projector. Willy found it very interesting, and it made him aware of what a huge gap there had been in his knowledge about an entire area of aviation.

When Mr Jemmerling had finished speaking, he answered questions and the cadets were then allowed to look at the items on display on the side table. Much of this was in the form of literature and that got Willy's interest as well. He flicked through a dozen books and brochures, collecting any of the pamphlets that were free.

The flight was then told to move outside and form up in threes. They were then marched off by the WOD. He marched them through a gap between two hangars and out onto the apron fronting the 'General Aviation' hangars. A hundred metres to the left the Catalina was parked. Seeing the aircraft really sparked Willy's interest. For the next twenty minutes he happily explored the machine, touching it and enjoying the smell and feel of it. There were two crewmen inside and they took the cadets inside in groups of six.

The interior was different from Mr Southall's plane. There were two small cabins with bunks and an office as well as a tiny saloon-dining cabin. The whole thing was more comfortable. Because of the short time and the crowding Willy did not enjoy the tour as much as he would have liked but he savoured the couple of minutes on the flight deck, where he sat in the pilot's seat and lightly touched the controls.

I will be able to fly planes like this one day, he thought.

With so many cadets wanting to look in the flight deck Willy had to reluctantly give up the seat and move back outside. There he looked around the hull of the plane. On the side of the bow he found a name painted in white paint.

Pterodactyl it read. *They were pre-historic dinosaurs that could fly. What a good name!* he thought.

The cadets were then marched back to the hut and fallen out for a canteen break. During this Willy looked at more of Mr Jemmerling's display. As he did, he saw that Mr Jemmerling was now talking to Stick and Noddy. When Stick nodded his head to some question he was asked by Mr Jemmerling and then moved over to where a large air navigation chart of the whole of Queensland north of Cairns was pinned to the wall, a tiny niggle of concern crossed Willy's mind.

I hope he isn't going to tell that Jemmerling man where our wrecks are, he thought.

Feeling anxious about what their conversation might be about Willy hurried towards them. As he did, he was dismayed to see Stick's hand go up and his finger tap the chart in the Bathurst Bay area. *Oh no! He hasn't!* he thought, speeding up.

As he reached the group Willy distinctly heard Mr Jemmerling say, "And it is a 'Kittyhawk' is it?"

Willy was appalled and furious, but he tried to hide it. He pushed rudely in and said, "Stick, you are needed outside by the CO."

"Eh? What?" replied the puzzled Stick.

Willy did not wait to explain. He gripped Stick's arm and propelled him towards the door. As he did, he gave Mr Jemmerling a neutral look and said, "Excuse me sir, Air Cadet business. Come on Noddy, you are needed too."

By then they had moved four or five paces. Stick frowned and then complained, "Hey! What? Why does the CO want me?"

"He doesn't!" Willy hissed in his ear. "But you were showing that man where our wrecked plane is and we promised not to do that."

"But... but I only... I... er... He just asked if I knew of any," Stick replied. A look of understanding crossed his face and he glanced back at Mr Jemmerling.

"Don't look back, and don't look guilty," Willy grated angrily.

Then he spotted Marjorie and Vicki walking the other way. "Noddy, get Marjorie and Vicki to come with us," he ordered.

To his relief, Noddy obeyed without argument. Willy marched Stick outside and around the corner. "Now tell us what he said, and what you told him," he snapped.

"Oh, nothing much," Stick muttered. He now looked very crestfallen. "He just said he was looking for aircraft wrecks and Noddy said, 'So are we.' He then asked if I knew where there were any and I... er... Noddy... er... said we were going to get a 'Kittyhawk' in a few weeks' time after school finished."

"So you told Noddy as well?" Willy said accusingly.

Stick nodded and looked very unhappy. "Yeah, well. Yeah, but he's a mate and he knows we are going looking anyway."

"Yeah, but he didn't know where," Willy grated.

Marjorie, Noddy and Vicki joined them. Willy did not let up. "Keep going. What else did that man say?" he said.

"Well, he just asked where it was. He didn't sound very interested or anything," Stick replied defensively.

"But you showed him," Willy stated.

Stick hung his head. "I... I just didn't think. He seemed such a nice guy."

"He probably is," Willy answered, "But we promised not to tell anyone, so let's all make sure we keep our lips sealed."

Vicki looked puzzled so Willy said, "Sorry Vicki. We promised someone not to talk about something. Nothing against you but we can't explain."

"Fine by me," Vicki answered.

"Thanks," Willy said, giving her a reassuring smile. Then he turned to the others, "Now, be careful what you say please. Noddy, please promise not to tell anyone."

"Yeah, okay," Noddy replied.

"What if that man talks to us again?" Stick asked.

"Then be vague and point to somewhere hundreds of kilometres from where we plan to go," Willy answered.

At that moment the W.O.D. began calling the cadets to form up for Passing-Out Parade rehearsal. The drill then became Willy's dominant concern, but he did glimpse Mr Jemmerling watching from the sidelines and that bothered him. As the parade was the following weekend, he made a special effort to get the drill perfect.

Or those army and navy cadets will tease us something chronic, he thought.

When the rehearsal was finished Willy noted Mr Jemmerling shaking hands with the CO. Mr Jemmerling then climbed into a car and drove away. *Good!* thought Willy. *That is one less worry.*

The cadets were dismissed soon after. On the dismissal parade they were reminded of the invitation to go and watch the Navy Cadet parade the following afternoon. Quite a number of cadets put their hands up to indicate they intended going.

As they walked towards the car park afterwards Marjorie said, "Can we get a lift to the Navy Cadets with you Willy?"

"Let's ask my Mum," Willy replied. He knew that Marjorie's parents were not very well off and only had one old car for the family, while his parents both had their own new cars. Willy's mother was quite agreeable to this, so timings were agreed on. She then said, "In the car William."

"Yes Mum," Willy replied. He cast a 'meaningful' look at Marjorie and whispered, "Wish I was going home with you."

"Me too!" Marjorie whispered back, giving him a sad, big-eyed look in return.

It was obvious to Willy that she wanted to hug him and give him a kiss but there were other cadets and officers around so he gave a slight shake of the head and climbed quickly into the car. But that look of promised pleasures kept his imagination aflame and he spent hours lying in bed in a highly aroused state that night.

Chapter 9

PARADES AND PROBLEMS

W illy really enjoyed the Navy Cadet parade. It did not have the numbers or the marching spectacle of the Army Cadet parade, but he still found it impressive. Partly it was the setting and partly the uniforms. The navy cadets stood facing the setting sun. This shone on their white uniforms so that the cloth appeared to glow. The sunlight also shimmered on the blades of the swords and cutlasses held by the Cadet Midshipmen and petty officers.

A dozen air cadets in their best blue uniforms stood in a group behind the chairs occupied by the parents and guests. With them stood nine army cadets, including Graham, Peter, Stephen, and Roger. Beside them stood Barbara and the female corporal who was her section commander, Gwen. Among the guests was Captain Conkey and he gave Willy and his friends a welcome smile before he sat down. Flight Lt Comstock was there too but he merely returned Willy's salute and gave the group of air cadets a brief nod.

The reviewing officer was a navy captain, resplendent in dress whites and with a bright splash of colour made by his medals. Willy had to admire the officer's caps with their gleaming black brim and startling white top. The sun glinting on the gold leaves on the brim of the navy captain's cap added another touch to the spectacle.

This looks really good, Willy thought.

Obviously, some of his friends were not as impressed, or at least pretending not to be. Stick sneered and muttered, "Their drill isn't nearly as good as ours."

It probably isn't, Willy thought.

But despite that he enjoyed watching, and liked seeing the little differences in the way things were done. His gaze roved along the ranks of navy cadets while they were being inspected.

There is Andrew, he noted. *He looks very proud of himself. And there is his sister Carmen.* For a good few seconds he studied Carmen. She was in Year 11 and was the petty officer standing at the rear of the group on Willy's left. *She looks very attractive,* he thought. It was honest admiration, quite different from his hopeless adoration of Barbara.

After the first group had been inspected, the Cadet Midshipman commanding the second group, a very reliable looking youth, called them to attention.

"Port Watch... Ho!" he cried.

"Hoe what, the garden?" jibed Noddy.

"Hard a port!" said Stephen, just loudly enough to make a few parent's heads turn.

"Pass the port more likely, at least with that bunch," Stick added.

The army and navy cadets all chuckled and made more comments until Capt Conkey turned in his seat and frowned at them. That caused Willy to blush with embarrassment, knowing it was really just bad manners.

After the parade there was a barbeque. During it Willy sought out Andrew and his friends and congratulated him. He ended up talking to Andrew, Blake, Carmen and Andrew's girlfriend Tina.

Andrew drained a cup of orange cordial then said, "Willy, are you still planning this expedition to the Cape in a few weeks' time?"

"Yeah, why?"

"Because Carmen and I still want to come. But we might have to work to pay our way," Andrew answered.

"Work? What sort of work?" Willy asked.

"Graham's dad is going to put us on the payroll. We have to join the Seaman's Union. That costs a bit, so we need the money," Andrew explained.

It wasn't something Willy had ever thought about, but he could imagine it, having some familiarity with the numerous rules and regulations governing aircraft.

He said, "Mr Beck, the man who owns the Air Museum in Mareeba, is going to pay for most of it."

"I've heard of him. Is the museum very good?"

Willy nodded. "Yes. He has lots of interesting things. He even has three tanks and a couple of armoured cars, plus a lot of planes and things. They are all in a big old hangar. We are going up there tomorrow afternoon to talk to him."

"Can we come too?" Carmen asked.

"If you like," Willy replied, adding, "You might have to pay the museum entry fee though."

"That's alright," Andrew replied. "That is fair."

The conversation was interrupted by Willy's mother, insisting they go home. Willy had to agree. He badly wanted to be alone with Marjorie and suggested he be dropped off at her house for a few hours, but his mother shook her head. "Certainly not! You have a big day tomorrow and your exams start on Monday. You are not going to tire yourself out staying up late or... er... So that's it."

That was it. They dropped Stick and Marjorie off, arranging to pick them up at 11:00 the next morning. Then it was home to a quiet night of TV and study. This left Willy feeling very frustrated and as a result he slept badly, with more erotic dreams.

Next afternoon Andrew, Stick, and Marjorie were taken to Beck's Museum by Willy's father. Once again, Graham was there with Stephen. Graham was in a foul mood and Willy guessed it was because he wanted to be in Caster with Carol.

And I wish I was somewhere with Marjorie, he thought.

Andrew and Carmen arrived with their parents. They were introduced and taken on a tour of the museum. The others strolled along behind. Willy spent most of his time looking at the tanks. The one that really impressed him was the 'Centurion'.

Mr Beck pointed to the 50-tonne, green-painted monster and said, "This one and the 'Saracen' APC and the 'Ferret' scout car all still work."

"Oh! Can we see one drive around?" Stick asked.

Mr Beck shook his head. "No. Sorry. There are all sorts of legal reasons why not, insurance and that sort of thing," he explained.

That was a disappointment, but Willy could only accept it as one of those adult things he knew he would have to face up to one day. He strolled over to have another look at the 'Airacobra'. Stick and Marjorie joined him, then Mr Beck and the others.

Mr Beck explained the aircraft to the adults, then said, "We are hoping to add to the collection by adding a 'Kittyhawk' fighter and a 'Beaufighter'."

"These are the ones crashed up on Cape York that the kids want to help you find?" Mr Collins asked.

"Yes, that's right," Mr Beck answered.

Marjorie piped up to add, "We are not the only ones trying to get them either."

Mr Beck looked at her. "Aren't we? Who else is trying to get them?"

Marjorie screwed her face up in concentration and said, "I can't remember his name. A man who collects old aeroplanes. He has an aircraft collection too."

Willy broke in. "Mr Jemmerling."

To Willy's surprise, and dismay Mr Beck looked suddenly very anxious. "Mr Jemmerling!" he cried. "How do you know?"

"He visited the Air Cadets on Friday night," Willy explained. "He showed us slides of his collection and we looked through his restored Catalina."

"I hope you didn't mention our plans," Mr Beck asked, his anxiety plain.

That made Willy feel very guilty and he glanced at Stick, who blushed. Willy then said, "I'm afraid we did."

"I hope you didn't give away any details," Mr Beck replied.

Willy glanced at Stick who shifted uncomfortably from one foot to the other before admitting, "I told him. I'm sorry. I didn't think. We, that is Noddy and I, were talking about 'Kittyhawks' and that man must have overheard us. He then got us talking about 'Kittyhawk' wrecks and we told him we were going to look for one. He then asked where it was. I... I... er... I just didn't think. I pointed to Bathurst Bay on the air chart on the wall."

Mr Beck frowned and pressed his lips together.

Stephen cried, "Oh Stick, you bloody nong! I hope you didn't show him where the 'Beaufighter' is as well?"

Stick shook his head. "No, I didn't."

"Did you tell him we were looking for it too?" Stephen asked.

Stick swallowed and went red, then nodded. "Yeah, sorry. It just sort of slipped out."

Mr Beck shook his head. "Did you show him exactly where the 'Kittyhawk' is?"

Willy answered before Stick had time to. "Not exactly. He only pointed to the general area before I dragged him away."

Graham now asked Mr Beck, "Who is this Jemmerlane anyway?"

Mr Beck sighed. "Mr Francis Mortimer Jemmerling, millionaire. He is my greatest rival. We have been trying to beat each other to wrecks for twenty years. Unfortunately he has a lot more money and is doing much better than I am. Now it looks like he may beat me yet again."

Hearing that made Willy feel very guilty, even though it had not been him who had given away the secret.

He said, "We will do our best to help you find the planes first Mr Beck."

Mr Beck smiled. "That's fine young William. Let's hope we can, but he has a couple of planes he can use for aerial searches."

"He said a Cessna 180 and a PBY Catalina," Willy replied.

"That's right. The Catalina is painted black, and he calls it the *Pterodactyl*. I didn't know he was in North Queensland. I wonder what brought him up here?" Mr Beck replied.

"Maybe he was here for the same air show as Mr Southall?" Willy suggested.

Mr Beck shook his head. "No. I would have heard of that. No, I'm afraid Mr Mortimer Jemmerling has picked up some clue and is now sniffing around for more information."

"Then we must make sure he doesn't find any," Marjorie cried.

Mr Beck gave a short laugh, then said, "Easier said than done my dear. But I must ask you again not to speak to anyone, not even your friends."

"We won't," Willy promised.

Graham now mentioned the B25 that was rumoured to have crashed in the jungle up behind the sugar mill at Caster. Mr Beck nodded. "Yes, I've heard of that one but never had time to go and look. It is up in very thick jungle, and no-one has ever been able to find anything. Why do you ask?"

"We thought we might have a go," Graham answered.

"Good luck!" Mr Beck replied. "When are you doing that?"

"Two weeks' time, after exams are finished," Graham replied.

They settled to discussing expeditions and timings and Mr Beck made arrangements to meet with Graham's father when his ship docked in Cairns the following week. By then they had run out of time and began dispersing. Willy and his group were the last to leave, allowing Willy another chance to admire the superb collection of models.

His group were then driven by Dr Williams back to Aunty Isabel's farm to pick up Willy's mother. That meant some afternoon tea and scones and Willy had to tell Aunty Isabel all about his schoolwork. What he really wanted to do was get Marjorie around the back to give her a good pash. Just looking at her bouncing bosom was getting him aroused and frustrated.

But he was denied even that pleasure because Marjorie and her brother were dropped off first when they arrived back in Cairns. Then it was home, with an evening spent completing an English assignment that was due the next day.

That night Willy had some very mixed dreams. Two of them started with him trying to impress Barbara but Marjorie kept appearing and he ended up with her, being caught kissing by Barbara. The other was more of a nightmare. In that Mr Jemmerling kept appearing, gloating over their difficulties. His face then turned into a grinning skull and Willy found himself suddenly down in the ocean with sharks circling. He woke up in a lather of sweat and had to go and have a drink to calm down.

Monday was all study and revision for exams. Willy handed in his English assignment and worked hard. Being focused on becoming a pilot in the Air Force helped him work hard as he had heard just how competitive it was to get in. The only things that enlivened the day were watching Barbara during classes and having a quick cuddle with Marjorie when she cornered him in the library.

During the day Willy also thought frequently about their planned expeditions and that set him fretting about the possibility that Mr Jemmerling might even then be out searching.

Tuesday was two exams: English in the morning and Maths A in the afternoon. After school Willy went to the newsagents to see if there were any new magazines on vintage aircraft. That evening he did another assignment, history this time. That night he slept well.

Wednesday was just a day of revision and study. During the school day the only incident that stuck in Willy's mind was seeing Graham sitting with Carol. They both looked a bit tense.

I hope Graham does alright, he thought.

After school the Army Cadets had a training parade. This was to prepare those selected to go on the promotion courses. Willy talked to Stephen and Graham for a few minutes before they began, reminding them that the Air Cadets had their Passing-Out Parade that Friday night.

That parade was now starting to loom larger in Willy's thoughts. Mostly this was as a niggling anxiety that the parade go well so that the army cadets and navy cadets couldn't tease. There was also the worry that Mr Jemmerling might beat them to the plane wrecks.

Thursday was a Science exam (Physics) which Willy felt he had done very well at. He then studied hard for the next exams and also completed a Geography assignment. For interest sake he did this on the pattern of swamps and beach dunes on the east coast of Queensland, using the coastline from south of Cairns north to Buchans Point as the example. For this he used the military topographic maps and also a selection of photos, some from tourist brochures and some he had taken himself.

It got him thinking about the coast of Cape York Peninsula, which appeared to have the same pattern: a rocky headland with a swampy bay on the north side, then a sandy beach leading to another rocky headland. The prevailing southeast trade wind was a major factor in this because it caused the coastal current which moved sediment northwards. While working he often worried about Mr Jemmerling, picturing his Catalina flying over that coastline and landing in the shelter of a headland to search the beach.

Friday brought more anxiety and another exam. This was in the afternoon and was Maths B. Once again, Willy was sure he had done very well. Immediately school was over he hurried out to the bike racks. Here he found Stephen and Peter talking.

"Are you coming to our Passing-Out Parade this evening?" he asked.

Stephen nodded. "You bet," he replied. "It will be very entertaining."

Willy suspected that he was being teased but said thanks. He then hurried home and settled to polishing his parade boots. Next, he carefully ironed his uniform. After a shower and dinner he dressed with particular care, pulling the sides of his shirt around into small folds to make both front and back appear smooth. The small single-bladed propeller badge that proclaimed him to have done a full year of training was pinned to his right sleeve. That done he stood in front of the mirror and admired himself, adjusting the angle of his cloth cap to see which he liked best. Then he set it at the regulation angle and did a few practice salutes.

I hope nothing goes wrong, he thought, aware that he was feeling very nervous.

But it wasn't the worry that someone might muck up the drill that caused Willy the greatest anxiety when he arrived at the Air Cadet depot that evening. It was the presence of Mr Jemmerling. Willy saw him almost as soon as he arrived. Mr Jemmerling was standing over to one side with another man, a solid looking, middle-aged man with close cropped grey hair.

What is he doing here? Willy wondered as he made his way across to where the other cadets were forming up.

As he joined Stick and Noddy Stick pointed towards Mr Jemmerling and said, "There's that Jammything bloke. I wonder why he is here?"

"Don't know, but it is a worry," Willy replied. "I suppose he wants to pump us for more information, so we had better be careful what we say."

"Pump who for what?" Marjorie asked as she pushed through to stand beside Willy. She said it with a mischievous grin and the innuendo caused Willy's mind to immediately speculate on what he would like to be doing with her.

The loud voice of the WOD ended such thoughts. The cadets were formed up in one single line, tallest on the right and shortest on the left. They were then numbered and formed up in three ranks. This placed Willy in the front rank of the flight only three from the right marker. The cadets were then reminded of the sequence of the parade.

The parade was on the small bitumen parade ground in front of the hut. The guests were seated on chairs placed along the front of the hut. While standing in ranks waiting to march on from the side Willy scanned the crowd. He checked that Mr Jemmerling was still there but actually took comfort from his presence.

That means he hasn't got enough information yet, he thought.

But it was actually Barbara that Willy was looking for. He saw a number of army cadets but did not see any sign of her. Graham, Peter and Stephen he identified and that put him on his mettle.

We must do well, he told himself, *or they will criticise every little thing.*

White uniforms appeared in the lamplight and Willy saw Andrew and Carmen, plus several other navy cadets. One of their officers took his place among the seated VIPs in the front row, his white dress uniform a splash of brightness.

And there is Captain Conkey talking to the Mayor, Willy noted, seeing the portly shape of the army cadet OC in his ceremonial uniform.

Willy was curiously moved by knowing that the people from the other cadet forces were present. Somehow it made things more complete and gave him a pleasant feeling of tension.

We will show them how drill should be done, he vowed. But it was a pity that Barbara was not one of them.

His mother and father were both there, along with his brother Lloyd, but their presence did not have the same effect. That was just nice, making him feel they cared.

I am so lucky to have such great parents, he told himself.

At 1930 hours the parade began. It was a hot, sultry night but a breeze coming in from the sea and across the airport kept it reasonably cool. As far as Willy could tell the parade went without a single hitch. He stood tall and erect, chest out with pride, his eyes taking everything in. The marching on of the banner party caused him another bout of pride. *I will do that one day,* he vowed as he watched the banner carrier slow march across the front of the parade.

He also admired the superb drill of the CUOs and sergeants. Just watching the squadron command group all move in flawless unison as they turned and stood at ease made him glow with ambition. Seeing his hero, Cadet Under-Officer Mathieson, saluting with his sword filled Willy with a burning desire to reach that rank.

That will be me when I am in Year 12, Willy told himself.

The regional Wing Commander was the Inspecting Officer, and he was received with the appropriate salutes and then conducted the inspection. As he went past the wing commander briefly met Willy's eyes but did not stop to speak to him, instead selecting Marjorie, who stood in the centre of the front rank. The inspection over the squadron turned to the right to march past.

After the march past and advance in review order came the awards. To his own surprise Willy heard his name called out as the winner of the Service Knowledge prize for gaining the highest marks in the exams conducted a few weeks earlier. For a second he stood there, not quite sure that he had heard correctly. Then he stamped to attention and stepped smartly out of the ranks before marching across the bitumen. As he did, he concentrated on trying to make his marching as perfect as he could, haunted by the memories of seeing other cadets make a hash of that apparently simple skill. It made him very self-conscious and he felt very stiff and gawky but at least managed to keep his arms and legs synchronised.

To 'dodo' march with the army cadets watching will just be the greatest shame job! he thought.

And they were watching. Even as he stamped to a halt and flung his right arm up in salute he glimpsed their grinning faces at the rear of the crowd.

Mum and Dad are watching too, he thought.

The wing commander returned the salute, then shook his hand and handed him a small trophy, a shiny gold coloured aeroplane mounted on a small wooden base with an inscription on it. Camera flashes flickered and Willy was dimly aware of his mother standing to one side, camera in hand. Then he stepped back, saluted, turned left with his best turn at the halt, then marched over to hand the trophy to Pilot Officer Lowe. Then he marched proudly back to his place in the ranks while the crowd clapped.

When the parade was over Marjorie was the first person to congratulate him. She rushed up to him and flung her arms around his neck.

"Oh Willy! I am so proud of you!" she cried before kissing him.

That both worried and embarrassed Willy but nobody seemed to think it odd or even notice. Then it was his mother's turn, so he had an excuse to disentangle Marjorie's arms. His father shook his hand and then the army cadets arrived, smiling with apparently genuine pleasure to do the same.

It was a moment of real satisfaction for Willy, tempered only by the niggling anxiety of noting Mr Jemmerling watching him from a distance.

Why is he looking at me? he wondered. It was a worry.

Chapter 10

WORRY

On Saturday morning, Willy sat in his room carefully painting the pieces of a plastic kit model P40 fighter when he heard voices at the front door. As they sounded like his parents talking to an adult, he just went on with his painting. Footsteps in the corridor made him look around, paint brush poised.

It was his father. "A visitor for you, Willy," he said.

Mystified, Willy wiped the brush and placed it in the small bottle of thinner that he kept for cleaning paint brushes. After quickly placing the lid back on the small can of Humbrol paint he made his way out to the lounge room. As he reached the doorway he almost stopped in surprise, and he was sure his mouth fell open. Seated in a lounge chair talking to his mother was Mr Jemmerling!

As Willy crossed the room, Mr Jemmerling stood up and held out his hand. "Hello, young William," he said.

Being called William was something Willy did not like at the best of times, but to have 'young' added to it irritated him even more. Despite that, he managed to fix a smile to his face and held out his hand. Whatever he felt, he knew his parents expected good manners.

"Hello, Mr Jemmerling. This is a surprise," he replied.

Willy's father said, "Mr Jemmerling wanted to ask you about the aircraft wrecks you and your friends are looking for."

That statement almost made Willy gasp. He lowered himself into a chair, his mind racing at how to answer. After a moment he met Mr Jemmerling's eyes and shook his head, then said, "That is interesting, sir, but I am very sorry. I promised not to talk about them."

Mr Jemmerling nodded and kept on smiling but Willy saw his eyes harden. Mr Jemmerling then said, "That is a pity. I thought we might be able to help each other. You know where the wrecks are, and I have the means to find and recover them. I thought that could be a mutually advantageous arrangement."

Willy's heart was beating fast now. He wasn't scared, but he didn't want an embarrassing scene either. Again he shook his head before saying, "That is probably right, sir, but, as I said, I promised."

"Then you must keep your promise," Mr Jemmerling replied.

He said it so smoothly and with so little facial expression that Willy was unable to tell if he was sincere or not. By then his suspicious mind was asking how Mr Jemmerling knew his address. Then he shrugged.

He could have just looked it up in the phone book, if he knew that both Mum and Dad are doctors, that is. It did not seem all that hard to find out, but it bothered Willy that this stranger had made that effort. *Am I being spied on?* he wondered.

Another worrying thought came to Willy. He turned to his parents and said, "Mum, Dad, please don't tell him anything. He is Mr Beck's enemy."

Mr Jemmerling kept his smile but held his hands up in mock horror. "Oh, that's a bit harsh. A rival certainly, but not an enemy. I have great respect for Syd Beck."

Willy's mother looked anxious. "I'm sure Willy meant no offence."

There was an uncomfortable pause during which Mr Jemmerling nodded and kept smiling.

For something to say Willy deliberately changed the subject, saying to his parents, "Mr Jemmerling owns a Catalina amphibian too. We had a look through it at Air Cadets."

Mr Jemmerling smiled again and nodded. "I do indeed. It is a fully-restored PBY 5 A. It is my favourite." He described the aircraft to Willy's parents, mentioning how much it cost to have it restored to flyable condition.

Willy nodded, wondering just how rich Mr Jemmerling was and if he would offer him a bribe. He nerved himself to resist, just in case. For something to say he asked, "Where is it now?"

"Still parked at the airport. I use it for all my long trips," Mr Jemmerling replied.

"Are you a pilot sir?" Willy asked, pleased that the change of subject seemed to have worked.

"No. I employ my own, a chap named Johnson," Mr Jemmerling answered. Then he shook Willy by saying, "I spoke to Syd Beck on the telephone this afternoon and he said that you cadets were part of his team."

"Did he?" Willy replied, managing to keep the surprise out of his voice and off his face.

"He did," Mr Jemmerling said, his face breaking into another smile. "And he wouldn't tell me what he was looking for either. Well, never mind. I will keep looking and maybe, just maybe, I will beat you to it. It seems we are to be rivals, not partners."

"No offence meant sir," Willy replied.

"None taken. The world of vintage and replica aircraft is a cut-throat, dog-eat-dog place. I wish you luck but will do my best to beat you to it," Mr Jemmerling answered.

He said this with a smile, but Willy thought he detected more than a hint of irritation in his voice.

"How do you make money doing it, sir?" Willy asked.

Mr Jemmerling gave a short laugh, then said, "You don't mostly. I make my money in business. Aircraft are just my hobby."

The conversation then turned to the other aircraft in Mr Jemmerling's collection, and of his other rivals and their museums or collections. Willy's father and mother did most of the talking and Willy was able to sit back and recover. He felt distinct pangs of jealousy and even of regret, wondering if he had thrown away a really good opportunity to get more flights or to visit other places.

When Mr Jemmerling described how some unscrupulous collectors would just steal pieces off parked aircraft or just rip parts off wrecks that were war graves, with no regard for the spiritual, historical or heritage value of the site Willy felt quite angry.

There are certainly some greedy people in the world, he thought, shaking his head sadly.

Soon after that Mr Jemmerling made his farewells and left, amid much handshaking. As he drove off in a taxi Willy's mother said, "What a fascinating man. It must be nice to be that rich."

"Yes," Willy's father agreed, then added, "I was a bit worried he might offer to pay for information."

"I wouldn't have taken it Dad," Willy replied fiercely.

Willy's father grinned and clapped him on the shoulder. "I know that son. That's why I am so proud of you."

Hearing that made Willy glow with a deep sense of being valued and loved. But then his mother said, "But he might offer money to some of your friends and I'm not sure all of them are strong enough to resist temptation."

Just thinking about that made Willy feel very anxious. Into his mind sprang images of Stick, Noddy and Stephen. Just having such doubts about his friends made Willy feel bad and he considered ringing them all up to warn them. That, he decided, was a good plan, even at the risk of offending them.

For the next hour Willy was on the phone. He called all of the friends involved in the project and found that none had been approached by Mr Jemmerling. All assured him they would not tell Mr Jemmerling anything. This was the awkward bit as Willy made no mention of what they should do if Mr Jemmerling offered money, for fear his friends feel insulted and then do it out of pique.

Talking to Marjorie took most of the time and she suggested that they get together. That sounded like a good idea to Willy, so he said, "What did you have in mind?"

"The swimming pool? I could go with Vicki and Stick and that would keep Mum happy," Marjorie answered.

"That is a good idea," Willy agreed. Even as he said it he was aware that he was perspiring in the sultry tropical heat. A dip in the pool seemed very desirable. "I will ask my Mum and ring back," he added.

His mother said yes so Willy phoned back and arranged to meet Marjorie that afternoon at the Tobruk Pool. Having made the arrangements Willy became very horny in anticipation.

We will get a chance to sneak away together, he thought.

Imagining what he and Marjorie might then do got him even more aroused and he found he was so fidgety and restless he could not concentrate on anything very well. The plastic model was the only thing he could work on without too much distraction.

After lunch Willy packed bathers and towel in a bag and rode his bike to the Tobruk Pool. He had often met his friends there and they had a favourite place among the garden beds. As he entered the pool grounds Willy made straight for that place, hoping to find them there. To his disappointment, they were not. Worse still other people were sitting or lying there. Then Willy recognised one of them as Barbara and he was even more dismayed. She was wearing a red one-piece swimsuit and to Willy's eyes her body looked just perfect.

Barbara! Oh no! She will see me with Marjorie and that will end any chance I have of ever winning with her, he thought.

He turned to find another semi-private space among the garden beds but then saw Barbara looking at him. To his surprise, she waved to him. He waved back and managed a grin before a wave of jealous misery swept through him. She was sitting with two other girls and three of the Year 12 boys.

When he had selected a place about twenty metres away on the other side of a garden bed Willy seated himself side on so that he could watch Barbara without seeming to. For the next ten minutes he was filled with resentment and jealousy as he watched one of the Year12 boys rub sun cream onto Barbara's back and even on her legs. It was obvious she had asked him to and that she did not mind him touching her.

Marjorie arrived soon after that. With her were Vicki, Stick, Noddy, Stephen and Stephen's friend Betina, a Year 10 girl with freckles and glasses. They joined Willy, but not before Stephen had veered across to say hello to Barbara and Gwen Copeland. The casual way in which Stephen did this aroused more feelings of jealousy and unhappiness in Willy.

Willy's emotions received more of a battering as Marjorie at once rushed over to hug and kiss him. In the process she pressed her bosom hard against him and got him very aroused. It also got him anxious.

Barbara is watching, he noted. *She will think I don't like her.*

But he did enjoy Marjorie's touch and responded. She added to Willy's discomfiture by standing in front of him and peeling off her T-shirt and shorts. This revealed that she was wearing her white bikini with the red polka dots. She had often worn this before and he had been expecting it but now he felt quite disturbed. The bottom part was very small but the top was even smaller. It was just two triangles of cloth and four strings. The triangles were so small that most of her very ample breasts bulged out on all sides. To make things worse Willy noted that Marjorie was up to her usual tricks and had done up the cords so loosely that her breasts swayed and bobbled alarmingly.

Oh my God, they will fall out! he thought, casting anxious glances at Barbara as he did.

Marjorie did not seem to notice and bent down in front of him to adjust her towel, presenting his adolescent eyes with a vision of trembling, swaying bosoms that made his mouth go dry and lust to surge. It caused him both relief and regret when she at last lay down.

Even then her teasing was not over. She reached behind her and undid the bow holding the back straps. That would not have been so bad if she had then lain on her front but instead she rested on her elbows, facing Willy to talk to him. In that pose her breasts were partly revealed in a very provocative way. From time to time, as she spoke to the others or laughed, she moved and allowed tantalising glimpses, causing Willy to become even more aroused and also more concerned that Barbara might notice.

He noted that both Vicki and Betina kept casting glances at Marjorie. They weren't exactly disapproving looks and Willy wondered if they were jealous and would like to do the same thing but weren't game. The fact that all the other boys could also see was a further cause of mental turmoil and Willy had to concede that he was jealous.

Marjorie then increased the pressure by asking Willy to rub suncream on her back. There was no way Willy could refuse, so he moved at a crawl that hid his aroused state until he could crouch beside her. Then he began to smear the cream on her bare back. Acutely conscious of her femaleness, he gently spread the cream. Her skin felt very nice, even if it was pasty white and freckled.

Her back was easy. It was how far down each side to do that got him all hot and flustered. She made this worse by saying, "Don't miss any. I don't want to get any more freckles."

That got all the other boys leering and watching. Willy swallowed and summoned up the courage to reach down and rub the cream onto her skin, reaching around as far as he dared. In doing so he became filled with urgent desire. Embarrassment added to his discomfiture as he was acutely conscious of the other girls watching. But it was nice.

No sooner had he finished than Marjorie sat up, granting more tantalising glimpses. Without batting an eyelid she began to tie the tapes at the back and said, "It's hot. What about a swim?"

The others agreed and there was a general movement to stand up. Willy was reluctant to do so as he was hotly aware of his aroused state and did not want the others to know. But he also knew that to delay would draw attention to him. Feeling very self-conscious, he stood up and walked quickly towards the water.

Walking past Barbara and her friends was a bit embarrassing and he noted her glance and smile. As soon as he reached the edge of the pool, he jumped in. The water was a cool relief, but Marjorie now made another spectacle of it by standing on the edge and leaning forward to test how cold the water was.

"Is it cold?" she asked with apparent innocence.

Her brother Stick, who was already standing in the water, answered. "No, it's not. Now stop showing off and get in."

With that he began to splash her with water. Marjorie squealed and then jumped in, to hide behind Willy, clinging to him and pressing herself against his shoulder and back.

There was a general water fight and splashing till all were in and swimming around. Then Noddy suggested a game of tiggy, and they next ten minutes were spent swimming around the pool. At the end, Willy ended up standing in the shallow end with Marjorie still clinging to him, only this time in front. She smiled, held him tight and kissed him.

As Willy returned the kiss, he heard aero engines. The Tobruk Pool is almost directly under the flight path to the Cairns Airport so that in itself was no surprise. Willy being very interested in aircraft, always glanced up at passing planes anyway. But the sound of these motors was so unfamiliar that he was intrigued. He held Marjorie away and looked up.

What sort of plane is it? he wondered.

Across his line of sight slid a large black aeroplane, a twin-engine, high-wing monoplane. As soon as he saw it Willy recognised the type.

A Catalina! he told himself.

Stephen also watched it fly over. The Catalina was obviously coming down to land at the airport. Squinting because he did not have his glasses on in the water he said, "A 'Cat'. Is it the one you were in?"

Willy's gaze slid over the aircraft before it vanished from view behind the roof of the grandstand. *No blisters on the aft fuselage*, he noted.

"No," he replied. "I think it is the one owned by Mr Jemmerling."

"Mr Jemmerling? Who's he?" Betina asked.

Before Willy could explain Stick answered. "It is his plane alright. That was the *Pterydactyl*."

"How can you tell?" Stephen asked.

To Willy's surprise, Stick was able to describe how the *Pterodactyl* had no blisters. A wave of worry swept through him.

I didn't think Stick took that much notice. Has Mr Jemmerling made him an offer? he wondered.

For the next few minutes, while Stick explained to Stephen who Mr Jemmerling was, Willy pondered whether Stick was in Mr Jemmerling's pay.

Noddy spoke next. "I wonder where Jemmything has been?"

"Probably looking for our plane wrecks, I suppose, after you told him where to look," Stick replied.

"Oh I did not! That was you!" Noddy retorted.

While the two argued Willy had to admit that the same thought had occurred to him. *With a plane Mr Jemmerling has a much better chance of finding the wrecks before us.*

He also worried that perhaps Stick or Noddy had taken money from Mr Jemmerling and might be his spies. That caused him to feel uneasy as he did not like to think ill of his friends. Instead, he wondered where the Catalina had been and where it was now.

He said he parks it at the airport, he thought.

Looking around at the nearby slopes of Edge Hill and Lumleys Hill an idea came to Willy. Several times over the last few years he had walked up the walking tracks to the lookouts up on the mountain.

I would get a good view from up there. I should be able to see where it is parked, he thought. He wasn't sure why he wanted to know that but just felt an urgent desire to find out. *The more we know about the enemy the better,* he rationalised.

With that in mind he turned to Marjorie and said, "How would you like to go up to the lookout up there?"

Marjorie turned and looked at the scrub covered slopes. "What for?" she asked.

"To look at the planes landing," Willy replied.

"Oh, is that all. I thought you had something else in mind," Marjorie whispered back, her face dimpling into a mischievous grin.

That hadn't occurred to Willy, but he instantly seized on the idea. "That too," he answered.

"Okay then," Marjorie replied. She kissed him and pressed against him, to Willy's mixed embarrassment and delight.

"Come on then," Willy said. He moved to the nearest steps and heaved himself up.

As Marjorie went to climb out after him, Stick called, "Where are you two off to?"

Marjorie turned and poked her tongue at her brother, then giggled. Willy grunted, "Never you mind," and walked off.

A chorus of 'We know what ya doin'!' and 'Don't do anything we wouldn't do!' followed them across the lawn. That got Barbara's attention and she gave Willy a quizzical grin which made him even more embarrassed. But now that he had the idea he was determined.

Hotly aware that he was very aroused, and that lust was not helping him think straight, Willy got dressed. Marjorie pulled on a T-shirt and shorts. As they walked hand in hand towards the gate, Willy sensed that he and Marjorie could easily end up doing things they shouldn't, and that that could dramatically affect his life. But he was so hopeful he felt an intense desire to act.

But it didn't quite work out like that. To begin with, they had to get from the pool to the bottom of the walking tracks. These started at a car park beside 'The Tanks', old naval oil tanks converted into art and craft workshops. That meant a ten-minute ride along Collins Avenue. Between the tropical heat and busy traffic, Willy almost lost interest. Only after they had parked their bikes, as Marjorie took his hands and grinned at him, did he start to become excited again.

It was so hot and humid that both were perspiring, and within minutes of starting to walk up the hill the sweat began to pour out of them. Willy had forgotten just how big the hill actually was, and as he plodded up the 'Blue Track' he wondered if he had miscalculated. At the junction with the 'Red Track' on the edge of the Bamboo Patch he paused, unsure which track to take. In the end he took the right fork and led Marjorie up through the Bamboo Patch.

As they puffed and sweated up the slope with its many steps, Marjorie began to grumble and get sulky. "We don't have to go all the way up this hill, do we?" she complained.

Willy had no clear answer. As they plodded up through the bamboo, the breeze was cut off and he felt quite hemmed in by the thickets of bamboo. To make matters worse, mosquitoes began to buzz annoyingly. It was only when they came out on the more open eastern slope of the hill and got a view that he felt better.

Marjorie obviously wasn't happy. "I'm not enjoying this," she grumbled as they came to another section of the track which was even steeper and with hundreds of steps.

"Not far now," Willy replied while wiping sweat from his forehead.

"I'm thirsty," Marjorie whined as she came to a puffing halt on another set of steps.

Willy was too but he didn't want to admit that. Instead, he stood and waited till she had her breath back. The pair then resumed their upward climb. To make matters worse they were passed by lots of other people, mostly joggers doing fitness runs. Willy had thought they would have the place to themselves.

Marjorie wasn't impressed by them either. "There are a lot of people," she muttered.

"We will find somewhere private," Willy promised.

At length they arrived at the first lookout, but Willy at once decided it would not do. Not only was there another couple seated at the only seat, but the trees had grown up to obscure most of the view. He pointed to the next lookout 500 metres further up the hill.

"We will go there. The view will be better," he said.

"Oh bloody hell!" Marjorie grumbled. She looked hot and annoyed, and Willy knew he was not doing very well.

Reluctantly she followed him. He led the way along a short cross track to rejoin the main track. Then it was on up the slope. Once again, they passed groups of walkers and joggers and people who were obviously tourists. The path was not as steep and was bitumen and fairly easy going. Best of all it gave a view of the airport and as they plodded up Willy spotted the black shape of the *Pterodactyl*. The amphibian was parked in the general aviation area amid a couple of dozen smaller planes.

At length the pair arrived at the second lookout. To Willy's immense relief, there was no-one else there and they were able to slump down on the seat in the small shelter on the crest of the open ridge. From there they had a marvellous view out over Cairns, Trinity Bay, the Coral Sea, and the Airport.

That's better, he thought, placing his arm around Marjorie's shoulders.

But Marjorie wasn't interested in the view. She just wanted to snuggle up to him, regardless of their skin being slick with perspiration. Willy made himself ignore the sticky sensation and responded. As he did, he kept glancing past Marjorie to look at the airport. That did not help.

As he kissed her, his eyes noted tiny figures near the *Pterodactyl*.
That is Mr Jemmerling, he thought. *I wonder where he has been?*

Suddenly Marjorie's angry face filled his gaze. "Well if you aren't interested, we may as well go home!" she snapped.

I did say I wanted to look at the planes, Willy thought, but he had the good sense not to say it.

Instead, he muttered 'sorry' and turned to look at her. Then he gave her a good kiss and a hug before kissing her again. Willy would have tried to go a lot further, but a family group arrived and stood around the lookout. Annoyed, he sat up and released Marjorie. Then he looked at his watch and was surprised at the time.

"It's after four. We had better start back down soon," he said.

Marjorie was not happy, but grumpily agreed. Willy stood up to watch a commercial jet come in to land. As he did, he noted dark grey clouds billowing over the mountains across the inlet. Heavy showers of rain could be seen beneath them and there was the grumble of thunder.

"We had better get down quickly or we will get a wet bum," he added.

So they set off back down the track. It was a lot easier, except on the knees and calf muscles but the approaching storm increased the humidity so that sweat dripped and trickled off both of them. By the time they reached their bikes, the first drops of rain were starting to fall. That meant a quick ride along Collins Avenue to the shops to take shelter. They were then marooned for the next hour as lightning cracked down and rain fell in a genuine tropical deluge.

Marjorie was not amused. "I will be in trouble with my oldies now," she said unhappily. "They thought I was going swimming with Stick."

"I'll come with you and explain," Willy offered as they wheeled their bikes out into the last of the rain.

"Next time we will go to the movies and sit in the air conditioning," Marjorie muttered. "Or sneak off somewhere cool and comfortable."

At least there will be a next time, thought Willy.

Chapter 11

GRAHAM NOT INTERESTED

Sunday afternoon found Willy, his father, mother, and brother at Beck's Air Museum. Willy's mother had never been there before so had to be shown around. While this was being done Graham arrived with his father, mother, sister Kylie and big brother Alex. Willy had met them all before and secretly thought Kylie, who was a year younger than him, was just about the most beautiful girl he had ever seen.

Graham's father, Captain Kirk, was a solid, weather-beaten man with a serious face. Willy could clearly see that Graham would look just like him when he was older. He knew that Graham often wished his father would stay at sea more but also knew he respected him enormously. Willy found it easy to visualize him as the ship captain he was, even though he was dressed in casual civilian clothes.

The Kirks had been in Mareeba visiting Capt Kirk's mother so the meeting at the Beck's had been easy to arrange. Capt Kirk shook hands with Mr Beck and then said, "So you'd like to charter one of my ships to move some wrecked aircraft?"

Mr Beck nodded. "That's right, two World War Two wrecks."

"Are they easy to get to? Can a vehicle collect them and drive them on?" Capt Kirk asked.

"One is. It is right on the beach. But the other is in a fairly inaccessible place. We might need to take our own vehicle with us, and then think about winching or using a crane. There are no roads leading to either area," Mr Beck answered.

"Beaches, eh? Hmm. So we need to worry about the depth of water, the tides, and any underwater obstructions. Can you show me which beaches please?" Capt Kirk said.

As a chart of the East coast of Cape York Peninsula was spread on the bench top Willy had a stab of worry that Capt Kirk might steal their secret. Almost immediately he felt a stab of shame.

He has to know to plan the thing and I'm sure Graham's dad would never do anything like that, he thought.

Capt Kirk was shown the approximate locations and bent to study the chart. After a few minutes he straightened up and said, "No obvious problems. It depends on the weather and the tide. When are you planning to do this?"

"Four weeks' time, after the Year Tens have finished school," Dr Williams answered.

A calendar was consulted and then Capt Kirk opened a book of tide tables and studied them. "Should be alright," he commented. "Depending on the weather of course. You can get a lot of northerlies at that time of the year and they could build up a dangerous surf in Bathurst Bay. It is also the cyclone season," Capt Kirk said.

"Cyclones? Are they likely?" Mr Beck asked.

Capt Kirk looked thoughtful and nodded. "December to March is the cyclone season, but they are very rare up in that part of the coast. They usually come in much further south, Bowen and the Whitsunday Islands for example. But the weather people will give us plenty of warning so it shouldn't be a problem. I still have to sail anyway."

"So you think our scheme is feasible?" Mr Beck asked.

"Certainly. We can use the *Wewak*. She is our old Landing Craft Tank. We could drop you off with some vehicles and supplies on our way north to Thursday Island. We always do a run with Christmas supplies at that time, and could pick you and your wreck up on the return trip a week later," Capt Kirk said.

Mr Beck looked anxious. "Wouldn't that be a bit unsafe, not having any transport if we had an accident?"

"Not really," Capt Kirk replied. "If you had a good radio or a satellite phone you could just call the Emergency Services helicopter from Cairns. It would be there in an hour or so."

"I will be there as well," Dr Williams added, "So you will have a doctor on the spot."

"So, what date are we looking at?" Capt Kirk asked.

Friday the eleventh or Saturday the twelfth of December," Mr Beck answered.

Graham groaned. "Aww! That means Steve and I will miss out."

"Why is that?" Capt Kirk asked.

"Because our army cadet promotion course doesn't end till Tuesday the fifteenth," Graham explained.

Capt Kirk shrugged. "Stiff! Life is going to be full of those sorts of choices. You must choose. Which do you want the most; promotion in the army cadets or a trip on the landing craft?"

Willy saw Graham grimace and knew he had often been made to do trips on the ships during the holidays. Graham then said, "Couldn't the trip be put off a few days?"

"It probably could be, but the ships are trying to run to a schedule. Other people are involved. They are depending on those vessels being available. I have another contract with a mineral exploration party in that area about then. If you like you can pay to hire the ship for five days and we will wait."

"No thanks," Graham hurriedly answered.

The discussion now moved on to what vehicles and cranes might be needed, and how the various parts they might salvage would be moved, protected, and stowed.

Mr Beck pointed out the far end of the big hangar. "I am building a new shed to restore and then display them in."

Willy looked and saw a concrete slab and a steel framework with a few sheets of corrugated sheet metal fastened to it. "It isn't finished," he commented.

"No," Mr Beck replied. "Norman and his friend Jeff are working on the roof and hope to have that done by next weekend. Then they will start on the walls."

Norman now spoke up. "It would go a lot faster if we had a few more workers."

"What about a working bee?" Willy's father suggested.

"That would be a great help," Norman answered. "Even if they just held things or passed tools and so on. It would speed it up a lot."

"We could do that," Willy offered.

"When?" Norman asked.

"Can't be next weekend," Willy answered. "We are searching the jungle near Caster then. It would have to be the weekend after."

"That will do," Norman replied.

Timings were then agreed on. Marjorie also volunteered and so, reluctantly, did Stick. There was then a discussion about who was going. Capt Kirk was concerned as he explained that none of his vessels were registered to carry paying passengers.

"I understand there are a few who might come as non-paying passengers," he commented.

"That's right," Mr Beck answered. He looked at Willy who said, "There are myself and Dad, and Andrew Collins and his big sister Carmen. They are navy cadets so should be useful. Then there might be Stick and his sister Marjorie."

"Girls, eh? And who is going to chaperone them?" Capt Kirk asked.

It took Willy a few seconds to work out what the old-fashioned word 'chaperone' meant. Then he blushed and said, "Oh, they are all big girls. They don't need anyone to look after them."

Capt Kirk smiled and said, "Maybe not, but I don't want the responsibility of looking after two or three teenage girls. We need an adult female."

"Mum might come," Kylie suggested.

Capt Kirk looked at her in surprise. "I doubt it! Are you planning on joining this expedition 'Hickety Boo'?"

Having her family nickname used in public caused Kylie to blush deep red. She vigorously shook her head. "No. I am going to Port Douglas with Sally. Besides, we all have to do the trip just before Christmas, don't we?"

"Yes, you do," Capt Kirk agreed.

Dr Williams now said, "I will ask Helen if she will go."

Capt Kirk nodded, then turned back to Mr Beck. "Which of these two jobs do you wish to do first Mr Beck?" he asked.

Mr Beck hesitated. Willy had no doubts. "We must go to Bathurst Bay first," he said.

Mr Beck nodded. "Yes, you are right. If we are to beat the opposition that is. Bathurst Bay Captain."

Capt Kirk nodded. "That suits me fine. I have to take the mineral exploration people to Bathurst Bay at about that time. Maybe we can fit the two trips together to keep down the costs."

They left it at that and the meeting broke up. Willy was now very keen to go on the expedition. He wasn't quite so sure about Stick and quite undecided over Marjorie.

She could be trouble, he thought, then he blushed at the lewd thoughts that flitted across his mind.

Back in Cairns that evening Willy's father asked his mother if she would go. She was not happy at the idea, replying that she had been planning various charity events during that time, but she reluctantly agreed. That pleased Willy even more. The next hour he spent on the phone, updating his friends on what had been decided. This included talking to Marjorie for half an hour. Knowing how she liked to talk he made this the last call. That done he settled to studying for the exams with a much easier mind.

The week seemed to drag by, punctuated by three major exams: Geography, Chemistry and History. There was also the added excitement of preparing for their own little expedition to search for the crashed B25 in the jungle in the mountains behind the Caster Mill.

To Willy's surprise, Graham was not very keen. "I might join you for a little while," he said.

"Why? Where will you go then?" Stick asked as the friends sat under the school at lunchtime.

Graham looked uncomfortable and then shrugged. "Down to Caster."

"Oh yeah? What's on there?" Stick asked.

"The sugar mill is putting on its annual Christmas Party," Graham explained.

"Oh, I see," Stick commented, obviously not seeing at all.

Willy understood though. *Carol's father is the Chief Engineer of the mill. She will be there,* he thought.

But Graham's defection bothered him. He had been counting on Graham's jungle experience to help with the expedition.

He said, "So who is going? Are you going, Steve?"

To Willy's surprise, Stephen shook his head. "No. I'm going to the party with Graham."

"Why?" Willy asked in astonishment. Then he shook his head. "No, don't tell me. I can guess. So what about you Pete?"

Peter nodded. "Yes, and young Roger here. And Andrew and his team say they are still interested."

"That's good," Willy replied. "How are we getting there and back?"

Details of transport were discussed and then timings. While they discussed these details, the sound of radial aero engines came to them and Willy looked out. He was just in time to see a black-painted Catalina climbing off out towards the Coral Sea.

Mr Jemmerling's plane. I wonder where he is off to? he worried.

He worried some more when he saw the *Pterodactyl* in the distance the next afternoon. It was obviously coming in to land and Once again, he wondered where it had been.

I wish we had a plane, he thought.

Each day Willy met with Marjorie. Usually this was in the library. That offered a few hidden corners where they could sneak a few kisses and the odd fondle and fumble. But it was all more frustration than satisfaction. There was no help for it. During exam time Marjorie's mum would not allow her to play after school, or to go out at night.

"Are you still allowed to come on the trip this weekend?" Willy asked. He was hoping they might manage something once they were out camping in the jungle.

"Mum's not very keen on it," Marjorie replied. "I can only go if I share a tent with Carmen Collins. If she doesn't go, then nor do I."

That was a worry for Willy, so he sought out Carmen to check. She assured him that she and Andrew were still going.

"And Tina Babcock," Carmen added.

"Andrew's new girlfriend?" Willy replied.

"She wishes, and so do I," Carmen responded with a sigh. "Tina is just so nice, but Andrew is besotted by Jennifer Jervis."

"The Pommy sheila who goes to Trinity Anglican?" Willy asked, picturing the pretty blonde and half agreeing with Andrew. For himself he still wished that Barbara would notice him.

If only...

Friday night was Air Cadets. Even though the unit had conducted its Passing-Out Parade there was still training. This was mainly to prepare candidates selected to attend the annual promotion courses to be held the following January. These courses were to be conducted at RAAF Base Garbutt, in Townsville. Willy now learned that his name was on the 'panel' for the Corporals Course. It was what he had been hoping for and seeing it in print made him feel even better. Noting that people like Finlay were on it as well did not dampen his enthusiasm.

I will show her who is best! he told himself.

At home that night Willy found he could hardly sleep for excitement. Exams were over, he was on the corporals course, the big expedition was now only three weeks away, their own little expedition was the next morning, and tomorrow night he might just get to be with Marjorie. That thought came to dominate, resulting in him becoming very horny. For an hour or so he lay and fantasized about what they might do, the fantasies tinged with irritating images of Barbara.

Saturday morning dawned clear but hot and humid. Willy was woken by his mother at 6am and he at once set about his morning routine and packing. By 7:30am he had eaten breakfast, dressed and packed. For the expedition he wore a pair of jeans, an old, long-sleeved, dark blue air cadet shirt (without any badges), and a baseball cap. On his feet he wore gym boots. He would have liked to wear his cadet boots, but knew that to use them for anything but official parades was against regulations so he did not.

When he was ready his mother bundled him and his pack and webbing into the car and they set off driving. By 0800 they were at Marjorie's. She and Stick joined him in the car, their assorted camping gear being stowed wherever it would fit. Both wore jeans and short sleeved shirts. In Marjorie's case this was only a yellow T-shirt which was too tight, so that her boobs strained at the thin material. Willy looked at it and wondered if he should hint at more appropriate dress, but in the end he only shook his head.

Once the gear was loaded, Marjorie squeezed in beside Willy in the back while Stick sat in the front. That suited Willy and he allowed himself to relax and enjoy her touch while they drove south out of Cairns. Caster was a small sugar mill town set in the 'Coastal Corridor'. For many kilometres south of Cairns there is a series of flat river plains, bounded on both side by rugged, jungle-covered mountains. The mountains to the east line the coast, with the Coral Sea beyond them. Those to the west form part of the tangle of ranges on the eastern edge of the Atherton Tablelands.

In this area the main North-South railway (The Sunshine Route) and highway (Bruce Highway) from Cairns to Brisbane run along the floor of the valley. Most of the level country is sugar cane fields with patches of swamp and tropical rain forest on the hills. Small towns and numerous farms dot the valley. It was a very pretty drive which Willy had done many times before and always enjoyed. This journey, with Marjorie cuddling up to him, he found particularly enjoyable.

The town of Caster began as a scatter of buildings on the left of the highway, a hotel, and some shops and a petrol station and mechanics workshop. A bitumen side road led west for half a kilometre with more buildings along the left side. On the right were sidings for the light railways used to transport the sugar cane and then fields of sugar cane. The buildings were all old, late 19th and early 20th Century designs made of timber or corrugated iron. These included several shops, another hotel, and more houses. Near the end of the road they crossed the main railway and came to a large park through which ran a ring road. The park was dotted with very large trees and had for its centre piece an old steam locomotive. Buildings made up the other three sides of the ring road. On the southern side stood four very large and gracious 'Old Colonial' style houses provided by the mill for the senior staff: the manager, chief engineer, etc. These residences were set in beautiful gardens. Opposite them on the north side of the park were a dozen much smaller low wooden houses for the permanent specialist workers. Between the two, but still outside the ring road, were the mill offices. The huge buildings of the sugar mill stood behind them to the west.

As planned, Willy's mother dropped them off near the steam locomotive. She then waited until more members of the expedition arrived. These were Peter and Roger, driven by Peter's mother. The two mothers sat on a nearby park bench to talk while the teenagers all climbed onto the old 2' gauge steam loco. Both Peter and Roger wore their calf-length army boots and army camouflage trousers and cloth hats but had long-sleeved work shirts. For the hike they had brought their army basic webbing and packs. They were obviously better prepared for the conditions but Willy had expected that.

After all, they are the 'Hiking Team' and have a lot more experience, he told himself, while still wishing he had worn his cadet boots.

Andrew and his sister were the next to arrive. Willy was pleased to see Carmel because then Marjorie could stay. He was also interested to see that Tina Babcock had come. All three wore dark blue long trousers and long-sleeved shirts. These had the appearance of being navy cadet issue, as did the black boots and dark blue baseball caps they wore.

While talking to Tina Willy studied her carefully. *She seems nice enough,* he decided, noting a very pleasant but freckled face and liking her friendly style.

While they waited for Graham and Stephen two teenage girls dressed in shorts and cotton tops appeared from one of the manager's houses, which were set in well-tended gardens. As they got closer Willy noted that one of them was Carol Battersby.

Carol greeted Carmen and Marjorie and said, "Graham not here yet?"

"Not yet," Carmen said. "He says he is going to some party here."

"Yes, the mill Christmas party," Carol replied. "The mill puts it on for all the workers and their families. There are usually hundreds of people there; kids everywhere."

"I hear there have been some terrible accidents at the mill recently," Stick commented, gesturing to the sugar mill, which was in full production and spurting clouds of smoke and steam from the huge steel chimneys.

Carol looked upset. "Yes, it's been horrible. There have been four men killed and a lot of trouble with the workers. It is the worst year in the mill's history, and that is more than a hundred years."

Willy remembered hearing about some of this on the TV News and from Graham. So had Stick, who, in his usual tactless style, said, "I heard they were real gruesome, that one guy fell off the chimney up there and hit the steel ladders so hard his head flew off."

Carol looked sick. "That's right. We saw it. I'd rather not talk about it thank you." She looked away, then muttered, "Oh no, here comes that little tease, Betty Morrow!"

Willy looked and saw three more girls approaching but this time from along the 'main street'. One was a busty teenager of about 12 or 13 while the other two were at least a year younger and had a primary school look about them. One was obviously a little sister.

"What's wrong with her?" Willy asked, eyeing the named Betty with curiosity.

"She's a real little pain," Carol replied. "She is always butting in where she isn't wanted and keeps flirting with Graham and Steve."

Willy now studied Betty with more interest, noting that she had a round, fairly plain face with a cheeky grin on it. But her main attributes were a pair of very prominent boobs which stuck out and bobbled inside a very short T-shirt which was cut off to reveal her midriff and navel. Her breasts looked to be twice the size a girl of her age should have.

Yes, he thought, *they would get Graham's attention, and Steve's!*

As the three girls arrived so did the Kirk's car, driven by Mrs Kirk. Out of it climbed Graham and Stephen. Both wore the same army boots, camouflage trousers and hats as Peter and Roger and both had long-sleeved shirts. In Graham's case it was an old jungle green one and Stephen's was khaki. They also had army packs and webbing.

Willy was then entertained by watching how Carol and Betty went into almost open competition to get the attention of the two boys. Carmen watched this and said, "No love lost between those two girls. I can see why Carol calls her a pain."

Tina pursed her lips and muttered, "If I was that Betty's mother, I'd smack her behind and tell her to dress decently."

Willy did think that Betty's top was a bit revealing but he had been enjoying the sight. Now he was careful not to openly ogle. He also wondered how Tina and Andrew might get on.

Tina might be bit of a prude, he decided.

Graham and Stephen greeted the girls and then their friends before unloading their gear. This included two bags which were handed to Carol and her friend. Mrs Kirk cast a frowning glance at Betty before going to chat to the other mothers.

Peter now took charge. Indicating his watch he said, "Let's get moving. It is after half past nine and we have a long way to go."

"Where are you going?" Carol asked.

Peter had both a map and a book. He orientated the map, an army 1:50 000 scale topographic map, and then pointed to the jungle covered mountain a kilometre to the west.

"The book says that the local farmers saw a big flash up near the top of Mt Graham there, and then a glow from a big fire. They said it was just on the other side of the peak," he explained.

Roger looked at the map and then at what could be seen of the mountain through the trees and mill buildings. "We could go up this ridge that runs up directly behind the mill," he suggested.

"That's what I thought," agreed Peter. "What do you think, Graham?"

Graham was not even looking. Willy saw he was busy chatting to Betty, who was smirking up at him and wiggling her bottom from side to side. A look of annoyance crossed Peter's face while Roger made a wry face. Carol blushed and looked unhappy while Stephen just grinned.

When asked again Graham merely shrugged and said, "Whichever way you think best."

Peter pursed his lips and shook his head before saying, "Fine, I will lead. Packs on and let's go!"

As he moved to hoist on his pack, Willy was very aware of the undercurrent of tension. It was obvious that Graham did not want to go and that both Carol and Betty were giving each other hostile glares.

This is not a happy group, he thought.

Marjorie nudged Willy and whispered, "If Graham doesn't stop flirting with that Betty then I don't think his affair with Carol is going to last very long."

Willy glanced again at Graham and noted he was smiling at something Betty had just said. Carol was looking quite peeved, and Graham seemed to be quite unaware of this.

"You are right," he replied. He then bent to pick up Marjorie's pack.

After helping Marjorie to pull on her pack, Willy started walking, following Peter and Roger, neither of whom waited for Graham and Stephen. Stick, Andrew, Tina and Carmen all set off after them. Peter detoured across to say goodbye to his mother and the mothers then waved and called the usual 'Take care' and 'Don't do anything silly,' and 'Watch out for snakes'. Peter's mother asked him to check that the mobile phone he was carrying was working and Peter did so, then resumed walking.

Fifty paces along the ring road Peter looked back and then shook his head. Willy turned to look back and saw that both Graham and Stephen were still standing talking to the girls.

Graham isn't very keen on this expedition, he thought.

When he said this to Marjorie, who was now walking along beside him, she snorted and replied, "He's not thinking with his brain!"

Nor am I, Willy thought, glancing out of the corner of his eye at the way Marjorie's shirt front bobbled provocatively. *Maybe…?*

Chapter 12

JUNGLE SEARCH

For the first few hundred metres the group walked along the bitumen ring road to the right. After passing the last house a side road went off to the right. Palm trees and brilliant clumps of Bougainvillea gave the place a very tropical appearance. The hot sun and humid air added to this, causing them all to perspire freely. As they turned right at the last house, Willy looked back and saw that Graham and Stephen were at last pulling on their gear and preparing to follow.

On the side road they had a cane field on their right, and an even bigger and much busier light railway marshalling yard on their left. Several loaded cane trains stood on sidings waiting to be unloaded and another came rattling in behind a small, yellow painted, diesel locomotive. The driver gave them a cheerful wave as it passed.

The side road curved slowly to the left, crossed two narrow gauge railways that came in at different angles from across the cane fields and then curved sharply back to the left under a line of mango trees. These grew along the bank of a large creek. Another branch of the light rail network went off under the trees and across the creek on a high timber trestle bridge.

The creek was significantly larger than Willy had expected with quite a deep pool along the side nearest them. The water was at least 50 metres wide and was flowing. On the other bank was a series of small beaches and thick patches of guinea grass. The bridge was a dual purpose one with a timber deck for road transport and with rails laid down the middle for the cane trains.

After checking there were no trains coming, the group walked across the bridge. As they did, Willy looked down and saw small fish flit through the shadows in the deeper water.

"It looks like a nice place to swim," he commented.

Peter pointed back along the creek to the bank they had just left. Fifty metres downstream was a small beach with a muddy track leading up the bank under the trees. A rope hung from the overhanging branches.

"I'd say that is the local kid's swimming hole," he suggested.

"Here come Graham and Stephen," Roger added, pointing back the way they had come.

"They can catch up," Peter said, obviously a bit put out by their attitude.

He turned and led the way on to the far end of the bridge. Once there he consulted his map and then led the way along a dirt vehicle track between the creek and a cane field. The cane field had been harvested, so Willy was given a clear view across it to the mountains.

"They look pretty big," Willy commented, his gaze roaming over the steep, jungle-covered slopes that now loomed high above them.

"Only about seven hundred metres the one we are going up," Peter answered, holding up the map as proof.

"Is that the ridge we are going up?" Willy asked, indicating the nearest spur of the mountain.

Peter nodded. "Yes. That should be the easiest way up. Usually the ridges have more open vegetation on them and there might even be an old timber road running up it."

That seemed sensible to Willy, so he accepted Peter's judgment and continued walking. As he did, he kept glancing at the mountain and had to admit to himself that he was actually a bit scared. He had never been in the rainforest, other than to stroll along a National Park walking track for a few hundred metres. That was why he was glad that the army cadets were with them. He knew they had done several expeditions in really thick jungle, and he was counting on their experience. In fact he doubted if he would have been allowed by his parents to come on the expedition if they had not been coming.

At 10:30 the leaders reached the edge of the rainforest and stopped. Willy studied the green tangle in front of him with something close to dismay. *Bloody hell! This looks pretty thick,* he thought.

There was no obvious sign of any sort of track and a dense thicket of bushes and long grass formed a barrier on the side of the cane field.

Peter did not hesitate. He took out a pair of garden secateurs and began to trample and cut a track through the wall of vegetation.

"It's always thickest just on the edge," he explained. "It's because the sunlight can get at it and all the weeds grow well."

Roger followed Peter into the scrub. Willy looked at the others, noting looks of positive dismay on the faces of the three navy cadets. Rather than admit he was even apprehensive he followed Roger. Marjorie and the others came along behind. Within ten paces Willy saw that what Peter had said was correct. As they moved into the shade of the uncleared rainforest it thinned out and he was able to see for 25 metres instead of five or ten.

After another ten paces, just at the point where the slope really became steep, Willy made another painful and dismaying discovery. A vine snagged his arm with vicious little barbs. It hurt so much he stopped and cried out in pain.

Peter and Roger both turned to look, and Peter said, "Wait-a-while. Sorry, we didn't think to warn you."

Roger helped Willy to ease the barbs of the vine out of his shirt. "You have to back up and roll away from it," Roger explained.

Willy nodded and then studied the dots of blood that had sprung up where the barbs had hooked into his flesh. He had heard the army cadets talk about wait-a-while, but he never experienced it. Peter now explained it to them. Willy saw that it grew off a palm that grew in clumps. Thick 'lawyer' vines coiled away from it, some of which had coverings of spines near the plant. But the real problems were the thin tendrils hanging down from the ends of the palm fronds.

Peter held a tendril between finger and thumb and said, "See how the barbs are curved backwards? If you keep pulling they just dig in deeper. And there is no way you can break them. The tendrils are stronger than a human being."

Roger pointed to a nearby plant. "See those thin green tendrils? They are just as bad. And they are harder to see than the older, thicker ones."

Willy now saw that there were tendrils of all types near him. Some were dark green and as thin as fishing line. Most were as thick as string and had obvious yellow and brown barbs on them. A few older tendrils were at least five millimetres thick and had gone brown and dry. They all looked unpleasant, and Willy now saw that there seemed to be wait-a-while plants in all directions.

Trampling noises heralded the arrival of Graham and Stephen. "What's up?" Graham asked as he reached the rear of the group.

"Just explaining wait-a-while to the 'Blue Orchids' and 'Matelots'," Peter answered.

Stephen snorted and said, "If that's all they are worried about they will be lucky."

Willy looked back at him, amazed that he was hidden by the vegetation and was hard to see even ten paces back. He knew, from stories the others had told, that Stephen had once spent a day and a night alone in the jungle.

Roger confirmed this by saying, "Steve doesn't like the jungle, not since he got lost at Kanaka Creek a couple of years ago."

"I wasn't lost!" Stephen snapped back, giving Roger a glare. "I was being chased by those crooks."

"Yeah, whatever," Roger answered.

Willy noted the animosity between the two and sensed that Roger had just taken the chance to get a bit of his own back. He knew that Steve could be a bit harsh with his tongue and suspected that Roger had been the victim of it on more than a few occasions.

Graham now said, "I suppose we should have warned them it wouldn't be a stroll in the park."

"That's right," Roger agreed, adding, "There are lots of little nasties to watch out for."

"Like what?" Andrew asked.

"Stinging tree, ticks, snakes, spiky bushes, leeches," replied Roger with a wide grin.

"Leeches!" Marjorie shrieked, looking around her.

"Yes, leeches," Roger agreed. "Big, fat ones that suck your blood. They wriggle in where the skin is softest and juiciest and start sucking."

Marjorie went pale and glanced around again. "Do they hurt?"

Roger chuckled but Peter cut in to say, "Not a bit. They spit some sort of anaesthetic on your skin, so you don't feel them bite. It contains an anti-coagulant too, so the blood flows more freely."

"Are they poisonous?" Marjorie asked.

Peter shook his head. "No. They just fill up with blood and drop off. In the old days doctors used to put them on patients to draw blood out of them."

"Yerk!" Marjorie cried in disgust.

"The ticks and mites are the real danger," Peter went on. "Some ticks are really poisonous and can even kill you; and there are mites that bite you and can give you scrub typhus and that can be fatal."

Willy felt quite uneasy on hearing this and noted his friends looking anxiously around. He said, "How do we stop getting bitten?"

"You should have put mite/tick repellent on," Peter answered. "My fault, I should have checked you had some. We had better do it now."

He swung off his webbing and dug in the backpack to extract a small grey plastic bottle. After unscrewing the lid he squirted a small amount of liquid into the palm of his hand. Rubbing both hands together he smeared the liquid on the tops of his boots and around the bottom of his trouser, which were tucked into the tops of the boots.

"You only need a thin smear," he explained. "If you can see splotches on the cloth then you have put on too much. You must not get it on the more sensitive parts of your skin. It burns if you do."

"That's right," Stephen added. "Don't use the repellent and then go and have a pee. You don't want it on your 'willy' Willy."

Willy was both concerned and embarrassed. Carmen was not amused. "Don't talk like that please Stephen," she reproved.

"Sorry, just giving fair warning," Stephen replied.

"The army repellent melts plastic too, so make sure there is none left on your hands before you touch a compass, or the face of your watch," Graham added.

"Or the lenses of your glasses," Stephen said.

"Or in your mouth," Roger said. "It burns your lips and tongue, and it tastes horrible. And keep it away from your eyes."

Andrew let out a short laugh and said, "Are you trying to put us off?"

"Just making sure you know what you are letting yourself in for," Peter replied.

Ten minutes were spent applying mite/tick repellent before the journey was resumed. When it did Roger led the way, secateurs in hand, while Peter followed. He had secateurs as well but also held a compass. That surprised Willy who thought they just had to walk uphill but it also reassured him.

Pete knows what he is doing, and is careful, he told himself.

The course Peter chose led them away from the creek line. As they angled slowly up the slope, dodging around clumps of wait-a-while, they got further and further from the creek until Willy could no longer hear the water gushing down over the stones.

It was all a lot harder than he had expected. At almost every step they got caught up by something: a vine which hooked their equipment; or a tree root which tripped them, or a rock or tree they had to detour around. There was wait-a-while everywhere and it was so thick in places that Peter and Roger did not try to detour but slowly snipped a path through it, with much muttering and under-the-breath swearing as they did.

Even when a path was cut there were always tendrils they missed and these snagged those behind, causing cries of dismay and pain. It was slow going and also very hot. Perspiration trickled and soaked clothing so that shirts clung to them. It was quickly apparent to Willy that Marjorie was not enjoying herself and was sure she wished she had not come. For himself there was no way he was going to admit it was hard, not with the army cadets there to note any weakness on the part of the air cadets and navy cadets!

I'm not going to give them any ammunition for later put-downs, Willy resolved.

For the next hour they struggled up the ridge. At 11:45 they came to a panting, sweating halt on a small ledge. Marjorie wiped her face and groaned, then said, "Are we nearly there yet?"

For an answer Peter laughed. "Not even a third of the way up I reckon," he said.

Hearing that dismayed Willy but he tried not to show it. In an attempt to check whether what Peter had said was correct he looked around, attempting to get a view out through the thick vegetation. But everywhere he looked was a tangle of growing things: leaves, vines, ferns, and trees. There wasn't a single gap large enough to allow him a glimpse of any of the farmland he knew was out there.

Until then he had never really appreciated that what he had been told about the jungle being a claustrophobic environment was true. Now he knew it was. He shook his head. "The vegetation is too dense," he commented.

"We are the ones who are dense," Andrew replied, wiping his face with his sleeve.

Willy looked at Marjorie to check how she was coping. He saw that she looked tired and unhappy. Her hair was a rat's nest and her clothes torn and dirty. She had scratches on her arms and... and...

What is that? Willy wondered.

He pointed to Marjorie's arm. "Marjorie, what's that?"

Marjorie looked, then used her other hand to touch the black object the size of her finger that was on her upper arm. Suddenly her eyes went wide, and she began to shriek in fright and jump up and down.

"Eeek! Eeek! Oh, take it off! Take it off! Get it off me!"

Willy now saw that it was a leech. Her frantic efforts scraped the thing off but left a smear of blood and a very clear wound from which more blood trickled. Marjorie continued to cry out while Stephen sneered and said, "Bloody hell! It's only a bloody leech, not the end of the world!"

Willy stepped across and put his arms around her. After a minute or so she calmed down and snuggled into his embrace.

"It's alright," he said soothingly, ignoring the looks on the faces of the army cadets.

Suddenly Marjorie jerked back and began to shriek again, her eyes wide with alarm. "Oh! Oooh, lookout! Oh, there's one on you too!"

She pointed to Willy's neck, her face a mask of horror. Willy put his hand up and felt a slimy thing. Amid a mild attack of panic he scraped at it, ignoring Peter and Graham who cried not to pull it off. The leech came loose and he flicked it away, shuddering with disgust at the feel of it. Then he saw the blood all over his fingers and was amazed.

Worse was to come. Marjorie pulled out her handkerchief and pressed it to the bite and then wiped at it. Willy was astonished at how much blood there seemed to be, although none of the army cadets seemed to be impressed.

"It's only a little bite," Graham said. "You won't die."

They all now checked themselves for leeches, and all found at least one or two. Most were thin and small, only a millimetre or two in thickness and a centimetre or so long but a couple had gorged themselves and were slick, fat slugs which Willy found repulsive. There were more shrieks and cries of horror and disgust. Trouser legs were pulled up and a dozen at least were plucked from around the tops of socks and one even from the inside of Andrew's thigh.

Stephen laughed. "You don't want them any higher up," he joked.

Carmen wasn't amused. "Don't be disgusting Stephen!" she snapped.

"Just trying to warn you," Stephen replied.

To Willy's annoyance the army cadets seemed to have hardly any on them and only one or two in the top of their boots. He began to really appreciate why they always tucked the legs of their trousers into the tops of their boots, or secured the bottoms of the trousers to the boots by elastic ties. They all took the opportunity to apply more repellent and Willy noted that Graham even smeared it around his collar and seams and around the brim of his hat.

That done they found rocks or tree roots to sit on and settled to eat their lunch. While they did Willy kept glancing down to try to spot more leeches before they could get on him. He spotted one moving with its head-tail-head-tail movement onto Marjorie's shoe.

"Look out!" he said, pointing.

Marjorie again almost had hysterics. She hit at it and tried to flick it off. Laughing, Graham reached down and plucked it off with his fingers, then rolled it in a ball and flicked it away.

"You can't squash them," he explained. "You can try to mash them but only repellent, fire or salt kills them."

"And that is supposed to be an agonising death for the poor little things," Peter added.

"Poor little things! What about poor little me," Carmen retorted.

That caused a burst of laughter and morale began to pick up. That pleased Willy because he had been starting to wonder if any aircraft wreck was worth this much effort. Still wondering if they would find anything he munched away at the sandwiches his mother had provided him with.

Then it began to rain.

As the heavy drops dripped from the leaves Willy was amazed at how cold they felt. He took out his raincoat and pulled it on, as did Marjorie, Stick and the three navy cadets. Not so the four army cadets. They laughed the idea to scorn. "It's summer, in the tropics," Peter said.

Roger nodded. "In the steaming tropical jungle," he added with a grin.

Graham laughed. "The raincoat will make you twice as wet. You will sweat like pigs in it. Better to just let the rain cool you."

Willy wasn't amused and did his raincoat up. *I don't think I am enjoying my day in the rainforest,* he thought. He even began to wonder if they shouldn't turn back. Then he got all stubborn. *I'm not going to give the army cadets the satisfaction of seeing me give up,* he vowed.

So he was the first to stand up and say, "Well, come on. Let's go and find this plane wreck."

As before Roger led, followed by Peter. The route was still up the ridge and as they struggled slowly up this became an ever-narrower spur with steep slopes on either side. There were stretches with no wait-a-while, but they were few and the narrowness of the spur meant they had to cut a path.

After ten minutes of sweating and panting as he hauled himself up from tree-to-tree, Willy had to admit that wearing the raincoat was like being in a sauna but not for anything would he take it off until the rain stopped. Then he casually unbuttoned it and at a convenient stop peeled it off and stuffed it back in his pack. The others did likewise, and Willy was sure they felt just as relieved as he did.

But they were obviously progressing. Several times Willy got glimpses back through the canopy of open fields and even of a distant farmhouse. That allowed him to judge their height. A view upwards that showed a ridge top almost at the same level cheered him even more. With experience they all began to find it easier, if not more enjoyable. They even dealt with the leeches more effectively.

Another heavy shower of rain swept across, the rain drops hammering on the leaves so loudly they had to almost shout to make themselves heard. This time Willy left his raincoat off.

I'm soaked from sweat anyway, he rationalised.

To his relief, none of the others made any comment and only Tina put hers on again. The upward slog was resumed. 1:00pm came and went, then 2:00pm. By then Peter announced them to be more than two thirds of the way to the top.

Graham looked up the slope. "I was hoping we would have been at the top by now," he grumbled.

Stephen took off his glasses and wiped them with a handkerchief he had kept dry in a plastic bag. "We would have been if it was just us," he said.

The implication that it was the air cadets and navy cadets that had slowed them down annoyed Willy but before he could reply Carmen snapped angrily, "I hope you aren't suggesting it was because we are girls that we took so long?"

Stephen did not reply but gave a lopsided grin. This annoyed Carmen even more. "I don't know why you even came," she said. She looked hot and annoyed.

"Neither do I," Graham replied. He looked at his watch and said, "Time we started back anyway Steve."

"Well, goodbye then!" Carmen cried.

"I hope you regret it when we find the plane wreck," Stick added.

Graham looked embarrassed but Stephen scowled. The pair muttered goodbye and turned to make their way back down the mountain. Marjorie then made things worse by calling after them.

"And you'd better work out which girl it is you like or you will both end up with none!"

Stephen's response was to shake his head, but Graham just hunched his shoulders and hurried on down the slope. Within seconds they were both lost to sight and before a minute had elapsed Willy could no longer hear them either. For a few moments the friends looked at each other as though unsure what to do or say. Peter ended this by taking control.

"Come on Roger, get up that hill," he said.

Roger nodded and started up the slope. The others followed. As they did, another heavy shower of rain swept across the valley and then deluged the mountain. Willy heard it coming, the rain falling so hard on the tree canopy that it was a roar.

"I hope their party gets washed out," Marjorie said.

Carmen shook her head. "Don't say that. It is a party for all the people at the mill. It will disappoint all the little kids if it is wet."

Andrew mopped sweat from his face. "I wouldn't want to be dressed as Santa Claus in this weather," he added.

"My word no!" Stick agreed. "It is certainly tropical."

For half an hour the rain poured down, but it did not seem to cool them much. Peter kept them moving and that kept them hot and sweaty. By then Willy agreed with the army cadets: a raincoat would just make it even worse.

At least this way the sweat gets rinsed out of my shirt, he mused.

After the rain came the sun. The clouds went away as though a giant had rolled them up and the afternoon sun struck down with tropical force. So hot did it become that the jungle did begin to 'steam'. Through gaps in the trees Willy saw wisps of condensing cloud drifting upwards from the damp jungle. Perversely he realised he was thirsty. After another big drink he noted that he had now emptied the two water bottles on his belt.

I only have the two-litre container in my pack, he thought, vaguely aware that shortage of water might become a problem.

In fact it developed into a crisis fairly quickly as Marjorie announced that she had drunk the last of her water. Peter looked at her in astonishment.

"Haven't you got more in your pack like we told you to have?" he asked.

"Sorry, no," Marjorie answered. She looked fed up and ready to burst into tears.

Peter looked exasperated but just shook his head. "We will organise to get some," he said. How he did not say. Instead he resumed climbing the mountain. Willy gave Marjorie a drink from his supply, then followed. He was now having strong doubts about the expedition being a good idea.

Another hour went by. Several times they came to a panting halt and Willy gave Marjorie more of his water. He studied her anxiously, concerned that she might give up or throw a tantrum. But she managed weak smiles and forced herself on. The three navy cadets were tight-lipped but determined and made no complaints.

Just after 4:00pm they reached a more level area, studded here and there with quite large rocks. Peter stopped and shrugged off his pack.

"I reckon we are on top," he said.

Willy looked around and noted that there was light showing through the jungle in all directions at or below the level he was at.

I hope so! he thought.

Chapter 13

NIGHT IN THE JUNGLE

Peter suddenly bent down to open his pack, calling to Roger as he did, "Quick Roger. Get your hutchie out."

Roger did as he was told, quickly dropping his pack and opening it to extract the camouflaged plastic shelter the army cadets called a hoochy or hutchie. As Peter unrolled the nylon cords wrapped around his he said, "You others get yours out as well. Select some flat areas between four trees and put them up as quickly as you can."

Willy, Stick, and Marjorie all had 'Shelters Individual' and had been on bivouacs where they had put them up so knew what to do. They took off their packs and began taking them out. The navy cadets only had a small plastic tent, each one carrying part of it. They also set to work.

But Peter worked with what appeared to Willy to be frantic speed and had his tied up by its four corners to four trees within what seemed like seconds but was actually a bit over a minute. He tied it up so high he could stand underneath it. That done he dragged his pack and webbing underneath and called out, "Too late. Get your gear under here, quick, and get your water bottles out."

Willy suddenly understood why they had been in such a hurry. He became conscious, by the sound and by the progressive darkening, that another shower of rain was coming. He lifted his pack under the shelter and then helped Marjorie with hers. By then the first spits were hitting the treetops. Within a minute, heavy drops were splatting on the plastic sheet. Peter held an open water bottle under the lowest point and a trickle began flowing into it.

As the rain got heavier the trickle became a gush and Peter soon had his water bottle full. Willy was ready and immediately replaced his with Marjorie's. By then Roger had his shelter up as well and Carmen, Andrew and Tina crowded under it with him and also began refilling water bottles.

By the time the rain eased off half an hour later all of the water containers had been refilled, some of them twice, as Peter had insisted they all drink their fill then refill the water bottles. Knowing that they now had enough water for the night greatly eased some of Willy's apprehension, but he was still very conscious that they were very much on their own. Even though it was only 2 kilometres to the nearest house on the map he understood it was very much more than that.

Once the rain had gone Peter instructed them to set up camp. He indicated suitable flat areas among the trees, ferns, and vines. They were able to set up the shelters in a rough semi-circle. Willy shared with Stick, despite Marjorie's wistful looks. He knew that she had promised her mother she would sleep with the girls, and he was determined to help her keep it. The three girls shared the small tent and Andrew joined Peter.

Following Peter's guide they did not set up the shelters in a low 'A' shape but tied them higher up as a flat roof.

"In the jungle you don't need it low," Peter explained. "You need to be able to sit under it out of the rain so you can do cooking and so on."

Roger agreed. "Captain Conkey also says that from a tactical point of view a flat hutchie is harder to see for an attacking enemy running through the jungle than a low one pegged down at the sides," he added.

Willy had never thought about it, the Air Cadet instructors insisting they make them low and pegged down. He suspected that maybe they did that because that was how they were taught but that they did not really have much practical experience and so just always did it that way. He was starting to really admire Peter and grudgingly (but secretly) began to admire the army cadets methods.

They do know what they are about, he told himself.

Peter next instructed them to eat. They sat in a circle on their packs or groundsheets to cook. The army and air cadets all had small folding stoves that burnt hexamine. They heated their water and food in their mess tins over the flames. The navy cadets had a much larger spirit stove and a variety of metal bowls and plates.

As he spooned hot 'Steak and Onions' into his mouth, Roger said, "I wonder if Graham and Steve got to their party on time?"

"Bugger their party!" Peter snapped.

Willy glanced at Peter and realised that he was really peeved that his friend had left them.

Carmen swallowed a mouthful and then said, "Graham's normally really keen on hiking, isn't he?"

Even though she was looking at Peter, it was Roger who answered. "Yes, he is. It's just that he's got his mind on other things."

"He's in love," Marjorie said.

"Love!" Stick snorted. "The way he was looking at that Betty broad I don't think it was love that was on his mind!"

Carmen frowned at this. Tina spoke and said, "I think he is wasting his time. From the look of it, Carol has realised he isn't the man for her but hasn't worked out how to tell him."

"Never mind Graham's love life. I hope he misses out," Stick added.

"Stick! That's not very nice," Marjorie chided.

"Yeah well, if we have to get soaked and eaten by leeches in this bloody jungle, then at least he could be here. It was his idea, wasn't it?"

Willy could not remember who had suggested the expedition but to change the subject he dug out the photocopied pages of the book in which he had read the account of the crash and asked Peter what the plan was the next morning. Peter gestured to the surrounding jungle.

"We search the top end of the re-entrants, starting with the northern side. That's where any wreck should be."

"Do we split up?" Marjorie asked, slipping in to sit beside Willy as she did.

"No. Too risky," Peter answered. "We can't afford to have people lost."

Andrew now asked the question that had been nagging at Willy. He said, "Why would any aircraft be flying so low if they knew there were mountains around?"

"Maybe they didn't know there were mountains. I think there was cloud," Peter replied.

Willy answered that after checking the printed account. "Yes, there was."

"Maybe they thought they were somewhere else, a navigational error?" Carmen suggested.

Stick scoffed, "Oh, fair go! They must have known where they were."

"I wouldn't bet on that," Willy said. "I read that the 'Liberator' bomber that crashed during World War Two near Moonlight Creek over in the Gulf Country near Burketown was way off course. They had been bombing Japanese ships north of Buna in Papua New Guinea and were on their way back to a place called Iron Range up in the Cape. After the crash two of the crew, the captain and navigator I think, set out walking east believing they would soon come to the east coast of Cape York."

Carmen was still incredulous. "But... but to get to the Gulf Country near Burketown they must have flown right across Cape York Peninsula. How could they do that?"

Willy shrugged. "I read that they ran into bad storms, and it might have been dark by then," he said.

"But... but... but that is a thousand kilometres off course!" gasped Carmen.

Willy nodded. "That's right."

Stick snorted and said, "Oh, I don't believe that! Nobody could be that bad."

"Oh yes they could," Peter said.

Roger nodded. "The navigator might have put his protractor sideways on the map and gone off at ninety degrees to the way he meant," he said.

Peter gave a short laugh and Willy saw a sly grin spread across his face. "Just like someone I know did on a cadet navigation exercise you mean?" Peter said.

Roger went red. "Bite your bum!" he snapped.

"Sorry," Peter said. "But that is a good theory Rog.."

Roger appeared mollified by this. Carmen now spoke. "They might have got their magnetic variation wrong too, added it when they meant to subtract or something like that."

That made sense to Willy. He had done just enough navigation training to know that the magnetic compass did not line up with the grid lines on maps, or the lines of longitude on charts. He said, "The magnetic variation in this part of the world is about seven degrees east, isn't it?"

Peter answered: "Nearly eight now. Would have been seven then. It slowly changes. That is possible too."

"Seven degrees isn't enough to put a plane that far off course," Roger objected.

"No, but it would be enough for a plane flying down the east coast of Cape York to think he was out over the sea when in fact he was over land. It would be more than enough to cause a crash into a mountain in cloud," Peter said.

"Particularly if he added when he should have subtracted. That would give a fourteen-degree error wouldn't it?" Carmen suggested.

'She's a bright girl!' Willy thought admiringly, trying to work out in his own mind what would have happened.

Peter gave the answer, further confirming Willy's belief that Peter was the real 'brains' of the Hiking Team. "That's right. Let's say they were flying south, and the grid bearing was one hundred and fifty degrees. In that case the Magnetic Bearing should have been one fifty minus seven, which is one forty-three degrees. That is using a magnetic variation east of north. If the navigator added instead, he would have told the pilot to fly on one-fifty-seven. That would bring the plane on a converging course with the coast and then on over land."

Tina looked horrified. "That's an awful thought, that all those men could die just because someone made a mistake in their maths."

"I think it happened a lot, in the age before GPS and computers," Peter said.

"Even so, I think I will pay more attention to my mathematics at school," Tina replied.

It was a sentiment that Willy agreed with. The idea of killing other people by making such a simple mistake appalled him.

More rain pattered and dripped, forcing them all to huddle in under their shelters. By then it was getting dark, and Willy began to experience quite unfamiliar feelings of anxiety. The dark jungle seemed to wall him in, and he felt very isolated. Marjorie snuggled closer and he put his arm around her and held her tight.

By 7:30pm it was fully dark. Stick suggested they light a fire, but Roger vetoed that. "Not worth the effort," he explained. "The wood is all wet and this rain forest wood is all so rotten it burns to ash in a few minutes. You'd spend more time out in the jungle looking for more."

"It's dark!" Andrew commented.

Peter chuckled. "Yes. It gets really dark in the jungle. You can't see your hand in front of your face."

Willy had heard this so now he tried it. To his surprise, he found it was true. Even when held only centimetres from his eyes he could not see his hand!

Tina suddenly cried out. "Oh! What is that stuff that is glowing?"

Willy looked and noted a strange pattern of ghostly glow on the floor of the jungle. Stick turned his torch on and the glow instantly vanished. In the beam of the torch all Willy could see were dead leaves and sticks.

"Turn the torch off Stick," Peter instructed. "It is only phosphorescence, natural luminous."

Stick did as he was asked, and as Willy's eyes adjusted to the dark he again saw the faint glow. Peter and Roger both reached out and scooped up dead sticks which had the whitish luminosity on them and passed them around. Again Willy was amazed. There was more to come. A firefly flickered through the camp, but they had no chance to catch it. Willy found the sight truly fascinating.

"There are even little luminous bugs," Roger explained. "Once on a scout camp we caught a dozen of them and put them all in a bottle and you could read by it."

Willy didn't know if he believed that or not, but Peter assured him it was true. "It's how they attract their mates," he explained.

At that Marjorie gave Willy a squeeze that got him all aroused and he wished they could get away somewhere private. But that was not to be. Roger suggested supper so stoves were dug out and lit and warm drinks were prepared: Milo, coffee and cocoa. Willy enjoyed a cup of hot Milo and was surprised to find he was getting cold.

Later in the night, Willy was glad he had the sleeping bag Peter had insisted they all bring. *I wish I had Marjorie with me to warm me up,* he thought.

But she had (reluctantly) rejoined the girls in their tent at 9:30pm when it was voted they get to sleep so as to make an early start in the morning.

But Willy found it hard to sleep. He kept waking and staring at the blackness that enveloped the camp. All he could hear were the breathing of his friends and the drip of water. Occasionally some bush animal would scuttle, causing alarm. After being woken several times, Peter got grumpy.

"Listen, if it scuttles it is just a rat or something. You will hear a pig or cassowary long before it arrives."

"What do we do if one does?" Stick asked, a noticeable quaver in his voice.

"Pull your head into your sleeping bag and go to sleep!" Peter replied sharply.

Willy wasn't sure if that was an order or the policy to adopt but found he had trouble staying calm. Not being able to see began to wear down his nerves. So did the thought of things crawling or slithering in out of the night.

Snakes and centipedes, for example, he thought anxiously.

He found he was breathing hard and knew he was scared. Sleeping in the open with no protective walls he found freaky but both Peter and Roger said it was the best way.

"You can see what is coming and you can get out quickly if you need to," Peter said.

"See!" Willy retorted sarcastically.

Peter's laughed. "Use your torch," he replied. "Now go to sleep."

All in all Willy did not enjoy his night in the jungle. Nor did most of the others, judging by the number of times they sat up or shone torches around or grumbled. It was with genuine relief that Willy checked his watch (for the fiftieth time) and saw it was 5:00am. From then on he lay awake, willing the daylight to hurry up and arrive.

Feeling distinctly washed-out, Willy got up and stretched as soon as it was light enough to see. He was not the only one awake. Andrew and Stick both sat up. Stick rubbed his eyes and said, "What a horrible night! I didn't enjoy that."

Andrew nodded. "Give me a ship anytime," he added.

Peter stuck his head out of his sleeping bag and looked at his watch. "Go to sleep you mob!" he growled.

"Can't. Anyway, it's daylight," Stick answered.

"Bloody hell!" Peter said, sitting up and stretching. "What a crew! I won't take you lot camping again. You are a mob of scaredy cats."

The girls woke up as well and joined in the discussion of all the things they had heard during the night. Marjorie crawled out of the tent in her pyjamas and the sight made Willy shudder. Her hair had a 'bird's nest' appearance, and her face was all puffy, with dark rings under her eyes.

Dad said you need to see them first thing in the morning to help you decide if they are the one for you, Willy thought.

Then he had a vivid image of Barbara and wished it was her, not Marjorie, who was his girlfriend. That was followed by almost instant guilt as Marjorie greeted him lovingly, much to the amusement of everyone else.

Marjorie's response was to poke her tongue at them. "You are all just jealous," she commented, drawing a chorus of laughing denials.

Peter insisted they pack up their bedding. "And your tents," he added.
"What if it rains?" Carmen queried.

Peter looked up. "It hasn't rained for most of the night. There isn't even any cloud. It will be alright."

So they packed up and then sat on their packs to have breakfast. That cheered Willy a bit, but he still felt tired and stiff. For breakfast he had a muesli bar, followed by a can of spaghetti and meatballs which he heated in a mess tin. These were washed down by coffee sweetened with condensed milk from a tube.

By 7:00am they were ready to explore. Peter instructed them to leave their packs at the campsite, saying, "No point in lugging them up and down the mountainside. It will be hard enough as it is."

He wasn't wrong. From almost the first minute of searching it was sweaty work. Peter led them north, using his compass. This put them on another ridgeline. When they were a hundred metres down the slope, he turned them left and explained how they were to search in 'extended line', side by side and ten metres apart.

"We will sweep right around the mountain at this level," he explained. "Now make sure you can always see the person on either side of you. If the line breaks, then call out and we will stop and reform."

It was fine in theory, but in practice it was extremely difficult. Not only was the jungle very thick it was full of wait-a-while. As only Peter and Roger had secateurs, the others had to make big detours to get around the masses of thorny tendrils. Worse still, once they got off the spine of the spur into the re-entrant, the slope became very steep. In places it was too steep to stand and the only way to progress was by moving from tree to tree. In doing so there were numerous slips and falls and a lot of sweaty grumbling.

Everyone got bruised and scratched by constant bumping into trees, vines, and spiky bushes. Willy became hot and frustrated and several of the others began to complain and had obviously lost interest. Marjorie gamely kept going but was plainly unhappy. Stick was the most vociferous about how hard it was and within half an hour he was loudly grumbling that they were just wasting their time.

As he struggled slowly along Willy tried to imagine what it must have been like for the people in the plane. One moment they would have been just flying along. The next they would have been dead.

I wonder if they had a second's warning? he thought, picturing the front of the plane suddenly smashing in.

The image made him shudder at the horror and tragedy of it. He had seen photos in the aircraft magazines of wrecks found in rainforest, so he had some idea of what they were looking for.

There should be bits of mangled metal wrapped around trees and half buried in the leaf mould, he told himself.

Stick had asked about what to look for and had suggested broken trees, but Roger had said no, pointing out that any broken vegetation would have long since rotted and new growth taken its place. Despite this, Willy had several moments of hope when he came across recently fallen trees. Then his rational mind dismissed the notion that a crashing plane from seventy years before might have caused it.

Obviously blown down in a recent storm, he thought, noting that the tangle of vines festooning the fallen tree were still green.

Worse still, fallen trees presented a formidable obstacle that took a lot of effort to detour around, particularly on such a steep slope.

It took over an hour to move just 300 metres. The searchers clawed their way up onto the next ridge, arriving in three straggling groups rather than in a line. As they came together Stick voiced his thoughts. "This is bloody hopeless. It will take weeks to search the whole top of this mountain," he cried.

Willy wiped sweat from his face and mentally agreed. It was obvious to him that most of the others were quickly losing interest. Andrew shook his head and said, "This was only a rumour anyway, wasn't it?"

"Yes, it was," Peter agreed.

"I am nearly out of water again," Tina added.

That was the nub of the matter. Despite refilling their water bottles from the rain they had all used much of it during the night. Willy checked his own supply and noted he had only two bottles left and was feeling thirsty. Despite that, he stubbornly wanted to continue the search around into the next re-entrant. To check he walk a few paces and looked down the slope.

One glance made his hopes slump. The slope looked even steeper, almost vertical, and it appeared to be just one huge tangle of wait-a-while. Peter joined him. "I don't like the look of that," he commented.

"Real 'tiger country'," added Roger.

Peter shook his head. "I think we had better be safe rather than sorry. Most of us are short of water so we had better give this up and start down. I don't want to have to call the rescue helicopter on the mobile phone when someone has heat exhaustion," he said.

Willy felt simultaneously relieved and disappointed. He was glad that Peter had taken the decision and agreed with him. None of the others disagreed and most even looked relieved. As there was no argument, Peter turned and led the way up the spur. Even though they were only fifty metres below the top it still took ten sweaty minutes to make their way back to their camp site.

Once there, Peter did not allow them time to linger. He just hoisted on his pack, ordered the others to do likewise, then set off down the spur they had come up. His only comment, after checking the time on his watch, was to say, "We had to start back by ten o'clock at the latest anyway."

Willy glanced at his own watch and saw it was nearly 9:00am. That made him feel better. *We are only losing about an hour of search time,* he told himself.

But as he trudged down the slope behind Roger, he had the nagging suspicion that he would never be back and would spend the rest of his life wondering if there really was an aircraft wreck somewhere in the jungle up on the mountain.

The climb back down took nearly four hours, one longer than they had planned on. It was almost as hard as going up as they frequently lost the track they had cut on the way up and had to battle through the wait-a-while and vines nearly all the way. They all ran out of water and got very hot, sweaty, and thirsty. Willy began worrying that one of them might get heat exhaustion.

Peter obviously had the same concern because he led them down off the spine of the spur and into the re-entrant to the north until they came to the headwaters of the creek. He made them all drink the creek water, over-ruling any objections about it not being safe.

"There is no pollution upstream, and it is clear and flowing," he said, adding, "Besides, an upset stomach later is better than heat exhaustion now."

Carmen strongly supported him, so they all drank. Willy actually found the crystal-clear water both cold and refreshing. He drank his fill and then filled two water bottles. Peter then led them back around to the ridge and on down.

Sweating heavily and feeling quite wrung out Willy stepped out of the jungle into the open track beside the cane field at 1:20pm. The group stood for a minute to get their breath and to drink before continuing to walk. Now they were out of the rainforest the sun struck down with vicious force, seeming to burn through clothing. Willy sweated even more.

Peter urged them to keep walking. Half an hour of plodding in the heat had them back at the big creek near the sugar mill. They crossed the bridge and trudged on around past the railway sidings to the park inside the ring road. At the old steam locomotive they dropped their packs, all with sighs of relief.

Roger pointed along the 'main' street. "I wonder if that shop there is open?" he said.

"A cold soft drink would be nice," Carmen agreed.

It was at least 300 metres to the shop, and both Stick and Marjorie grumbled that it was too far to walk on the off-chance that a shop might be open on a hot Sunday afternoon.

"I'll bring you a drink," Willy answered.

Leaving Stick and Marjorie to mind the gear the others strolled across the park and then along the footpath. The street was lined with a mixture of low-set 'Old Queenslander' houses set in their own gardens, and shops. Several shops and the hotel halfway along the street had awnings or rooms which overhung the footpath.

From out of the door of the shop near the hotel appeared two young girls. Willy immediately recognised them as Betty and her little sister. The two girls saw the group and at once turned and hurried towards them.

"Here comes Betty the Flirt," Carmen murmured.

"She looks a bit upset," Tina replied.

She did. As she reached them, Willy saw that she was crying and that her face was very red. Peter called to her, "Hi Betty, have you seen Graham and Stephen?"

At that Betty's face crumpled and more tears flooded out. "Yes... Oh! Oh, boo hoo!" she sobbed. "It's awful! They've both been taken away by the police."

"By the police! Why?" cried Peter.

Chapter 14

TROUBLE

"Taken away by the police!" Peter cried. "Why?"

Betty sobbed for a moment, then wiped her tears. "Be... be... b... because (sob). Because Graham and Stephen have been accused of bashing Declin Riley," she explained.[2]

Peter shook his head in disbelief and dismay. "Declin Riley? Who the hell is he?" he asked.

"H... h... he (sob) is a bloke who works at the (sob) mill," Betty answered.

"But... but why would Graham and Stephen beat this Declin guy up?" Peter asked.

Betty sniffled, then wiped her nose on her sleeve, causing Willy to inwardly cringe. Then she said, "Because Declin likes Carol Battersby."

Peter looked at Roger, disbelief written all over his face. Roger shook his head and said, "I don't believe it. Graham is not like that. He's been in a few fights at school, but he has never started one."

Carmen backed him up. "I agree. The only time I have heard of Graham getting into a fight it has been against a bully or as a knight in shining armour to help someone else."

Peter nodded and turned back to Betty. "This Declin, tell us about him."

"He's a tall, skinny joker, seventeen or eighteen. He works in the office. He's a real boring pain, a computer geek."

"A real nerd," Betty's little sister added, wrinkling her nose to emphasise her dislike.

"So what does this Declin say happened?" Peter demanded to know.

"Don't know. He was found bashed unconscious this morning and an ambulance took him off to hospital. They reckon he might die from head injuries," Betty explained.

Willy felt a wave of shock. The story seemed to go from bad to worse. "So why did the police pick on Graham and Stephen?" he asked.

---

[2] Read *Sugar and Spice* by C. R. Cummings

"Because they had some sort of a fight with Declin last night at the Christmas party," Betty answered.

"What over?" Peter demanded to know.

Betty went silent for a moment, then said, "Over me and Carol. Declin said to Graham to make his mind up and not to do anything to hurt Carol."

"I still don't believe that would be any reason for Graham to beat this bloke up," Roger said.

"Nor do I," Peter agreed. Willy nodded and noted Tina giving Betty a hostile look.

She thinks that Betty has caused this, he thought.

Peter asked, "So the police came and took Graham and Stephen away?"

"Yes," Betty replied.

"At about nine o'clock," her little sister added.

"What about their gear?" Peter asked.

"They took it with them," Betty answered.

At that moment a red-faced, middle-aged man in shorts and singlet stepped out of the shop doorway and then yelled loudly, "You girls get back inside, and stop talking to strangers."

"That's our dad," Betty explained. She and her sister turned and hurried home, obviously afraid of their father.

They left the group shocked and upset. All thought of going to any shop had been driven from their mind and they walked back to the park discussing the bad news.

As they arrived back Marjorie called, "What's wrong? Where is Graham?"

"In trouble," Willy answered. "The police have arrested him for bashing some guy."

"Oh no!" Marjorie cried.

Stick asked, "What about Stephen?"

"Him too," Willy added.

"Good!" Marjorie snapped.

That really hurt Willy. Earlier in the year Stephen had taken Marjorie out and he had always been jealous and suspected that Stephen had done something Marjorie hadn't liked. The comment seemed to confirm that but also added to his jealousy.

He could also see that Tina was really upset and that this was bothering Andrew. Then he remembered that Tina had gone on several dates with Graham a few months before.

She must still like him, he thought, again noting Andrew's anxiety.

The news set the whole group in a depressed mood. Willy found he just did not believe that Graham could have done it. The others all agreed. Tina said, "Well, the truth will come out when this Declin fellow gives his side of the story."

"If he doesn't die," Peter said, his voice bitter and laden with anxiety.

That was a shocking prospect. Willy shook his head in dismay, *Graham could go to jail, or to one of those juvenile detention places,* he thought sadly. *I might never see him again!*

From that followed the thought that neither Graham nor Stephen might be available for any of the expeditions to recover plane wrecks. It was a depressing and very sobering thought.

The friends sat in the shade and discussed the situation, the failure of their own little expedition quite forgotten. It was a very subdued group who were collected by parents at 3:00pm for transport back to Cairns.

During the trip home Willy described the events of the weekend to his mother and father. His father then asked if he planned to have another go at finding the crashed plane.

Willy shook his head and looked at Marjorie and Stick. "I don't think so. I'm not sure that the story is true anyway."

"And this terrible business about Graham and Stephen," Willy's mother said. "I thought they were spending the weekend with you, searching for the plane crash."

"So did I," Willy agreed.

"I hope they haven't been deceiving their parents," Willy's mother added.

That was an unpleasant thought. It gnawed at Willy until he was home. Once he had unpacked and had a shower he went to the phone and tapped in Graham's number. Graham's mother answered the phone and from the tone of her voice Willy could tell that she was not happy.

"This is Willy Williams Mrs Kirk. Is Graham there?" he asked.

"I'm sorry, Willy, Graham can't talk to you right now," Mrs Kirk said.

Willy had half expected that but it also worried him. *I hope Graham isn't really in trouble,* he thought.

For something to say, he said, "Thank you Mrs Kirk. Please tell him we didn't find the plane."

After hanging up he considered phoning Stephen but, in the end, did not. He did not like Stephen that much and still hadn't forgiven him for whatever it was he had done to Marjorie.

Worn out by the exertion of searching the jungle, the poor sleep the previous night, and worry about his friends, Willy went to bed early and slept soundly. On Monday he hurried to school, hoping to get the details on what had happened to Graham and Stephen. In this he was disappointed. Neither came to school.

Nor was Marjorie there. "She says she is sick," Stick explained. "She's just fat and unfit really."

"She's not fat!" Willy snapped, feeling his own ego to be under attack by his choice of girlfriend.

Then it was time for classes. There were still three weeks of school to go for the Year 9s and Willy was not looking forward to them at all.

Complete waste of time! he thought. *We have done our exams, and all the teachers will do is go over all our mistakes in the tests and carry on about how we need to do better next year.*

In this he was not wrong, the situation made worse by the fact that the Year 12s would finish at the end of that week and the Year 10s and 11s at the end of the following. That would leave only the Year 8s and 9s at school during the last week, unless they were part of some school trip. One of the approved school trips covered the army cadets attending the annual promotion courses.

With exams over the school reverted to its normal timetable of 6 periods each day. During the day Willy was informed of his exam results in English and, as he had predicted, the class then began to laboriously dissect the test questions, plus do similar questions to ensure they now got the message and understood.

The main fly in the ointment though wasn't the schoolwork but not knowing what had happened to Graham and Stephen. Salt was rubbed in Willy's jealous wounds by Barbara who asked him what had happened. Willy had to admit he did not know. Nor did Roger, who said that Graham was at home but not allowed to speak to anyone.

"Graham's dad gets back tomorrow afternoon," Roger added. "I reckon skin and hair will fly then."

"I hope that it doesn't mean Captain Kirk won't support our expedition," Willy said.

Peter, who had been listening, shook his head. "I doubt it. Captain Kirk made the arrangement with Mr Beck, and I can't see him breaking that contract. Besides, Graham wasn't going on your first trip anyway. He is going to promo with us."

"Will he still be allowed to go?" Willy asked.

Peter shrugged. "Don't know. Hope so."

Stick asked, "You are going aren't you, Pete?"

"Yes. I am doing the sergeants course."

"And I'm doing the corporals course," Roger added proudly.

"So am I," Willy said, not wanting to be upstaged.

The conversation drifted onto the differences between the promotion courses run by the army cadets and air cadets, each group convinced theirs was the better system. The bell for classes ended the debate, which was, as usual, unresolved.

Tuesday followed a similar pattern except that both Graham and Stephen were at school. "What happened? Tell us the story," Peter demanded as soon as they arrived.

Graham looked miserable and shook his head. "Sorry. We are not allowed to talk about it to anyone. Please don't ask."

"Who said?" Stick asked.

"The police. Drop the subject please," Graham replied.

To change the subject Peter described the search for the aircraft wreck, with the others adding details. This included a lot of moaning about the rain, the leeches, the wait-a-while and so on.

"Are you going to go up there and have another look?" Graham asked.

Peter looked doubtful and shook his head. When Graham looked at Willy, he gave an emphatic shake of the head.

"No thanks. I've had enough jungle to last me for quite a while."

That at least caused some laughing and the mood slowly improved. The conversation shifted to rumours about what the Year 12s were planning to do on their last day at school. Over the last few years a tradition had grown up of the 'Seniors' doing something unusual on their last day. This time the rumour was that they would be setting electric wires to all the urinals so that when boys went to do a pee they would get an electric shock.

Peter dismissed the story as not being technically feasible. Willy knew that Peter usually got top marks in subjects like science but he still wasn't convinced it could not be done. Stick thought it was a great rumour and went off to spread it by telling some of the Year 8s.

During the day Willy learned that he had achieved a Very High in Maths A. That pleased him but he had been reasonably sure he would get a good result so wasn't surprised.

I need VHs in all my subjects right through school to be sure of being accepted by the Air Force as a pilot, he reminded himself.

He knew that many hundreds applied to be pilots but that only a select dozen or so were chosen each year.

Marjorie was very proud of him and gave him a little hug and kiss on the cheek when he told her, despite the presence of two teachers. They just told her to stop doing that but in such a mild tone it made Willy sure that all the staff thought of him and Marjorie as an old married couple and therefore not worth worrying about.

I hope Barbara doesn't think that, he thought.

Marjorie had only achieved 'Sound' levels in most of her results, whereas Barbara's results were either Very High or High. *Barbara is just so talented,* Willy thought, a feeling of wistful adoration and regret surging through him.

Wednesday was similar. The only new things were Graham telling them that his father had returned and was still planning to take Mr Beck's expedition to Cape York; and the bad news that Declin was still in a coma in hospital and was on 'Life Support'.

This bothered Willy a lot, so he sought out Graham and asked if there was any change to Declin's condition. Graham shook his head and muttered 'no', before turning and walking away. Willy was sure that was to hide the tears that he had seen spring to the corners of Graham's eyes. Graham's appearance worried him too. He looked exhausted and had dark rings under his eyes.

The strain must be wearing him down, Willy mused.

He found Peter and Roger and asked if they had any news. Peter shook his head and said, "No. I'm really worrying about Graham. If he doesn't get to go on the warrant officers course in two weeks' time I am scared he might... might do something."

The implication struck a chilling chord in Willy. This was turned to deep apprehension when Andrew, who had been listening, added, "So am I. He is having a real fit of the dejections. I am worried he might try to commit suicide."

That really shocked Willy and the others listening. "He wouldn't, would he?" he asked.

Andrew looked grim and bit his lip, then said, "He might. Two years ago, when he learned that he could never be a naval officer because of his eyesight he tried to."

"Did he really? What did he do?" Stick asked.

"We were diving at Green Island and he told me he didn't want to live anymore and that he was going to end it all. He was just going to swim out and let himself drown. I talked him out of it. Then we were in that plane crash on the way home and we ended up in the sea for eighteen hours."

Willy nodded. "I remember that. It was a float plane, wasn't it?"

"Yes, it was," Andrew answered. "Anyway we had to keep the pilot afloat, and also Graham's paraplegic friend Ken. Several times Graham said he wanted to give up and didn't see what it mattered but then he changed his mind and decided he had to stay alive to save his friend. So he did."

"Is it possible that he might miss out on the warrant officers course?" Willy asked.

"If he is in trouble with the police, probably," Peter answered.

Another worrying thought then came to Willy. "I suppose this isn't doing Graham's romance with Carol much good," he said.

Carmen, who had been listening in, answered, "You can say that again. She won't even speak to him. I think that romance is dead."

That word 'dead' sent another chill through Willy. *What can I do to help?* he wondered.

But no particular strategy came to mind. It was all very worrying information and Willy felt upset and frustrated at not knowing what to do. It quite spoiled the news of learning that he had achieved VHs in both Maths B and Physics.

Later in the day, during the break between two periods when classes were moving from one room to another, Willy saw direct confirmation of Carmen's words. He was walking with his class across the pathway beside the quadrangle. Graham's class was ahead of them, straggling as was usual. From the other direction came a Year 10 class, Carol's. Willy saw Carol hurrying towards them, a bundle of books clutched tightly across her front. Suddenly she saw Graham. Her face appeared to freeze, and she turned abruptly and almost scurried back the way she had come. Within seconds she vanished through the ground floor doorway.

Willy got only a glimpse of Graham's face, enough to know that Graham had seen Carol, and long enough to allow the concept of bleak despair to form.

Graham is certainly upset over it all, he thought.

But still no plan of how to help came to Willy's mind. To him, Graham's situation seemed worse and his physical appearance showed he was under great strain. When Willy saw him during the lunch break, he shook his head.

I hope he doesn't snap and do something, he thought.

That afternoon when Willy got home the problem gnawed at Willy's conscience. For a while he considered phoning Graham to talk things over, but Willy was very wary of phoning Graham's house and did not want to talk to Stephen.

I will try Peter and see what he suggests, he thought. So he phoned Peter.

Peter's mother answered and called him to the phone. "Hello, Peter speaking," he said.

"This is Willy Williams, Pete. I was wondering if there was anything we could do to help Graham," Willy said.

"Graham! Oh hell, you don't know. He's gone missing," Peter said.

"Missing!" Willy was shocked and at once apprehensive. "You don't think he... that he..."

"Has done himself in?" Peter finished. "No, I don't. He just left school during the afternoon, and nobody knows where he has gone. I think he is having a fit of the dejections and I'm really worried."

"You don't think he might have gone to Caster to see Carol?" Willy suggested.

"Don't think so. He was told not to go anywhere near her," Peter said.

Feeling really anxious Willy hung up and went to tell his parents. That took some explaining as they did not know the background. Both adults just shook their heads sadly.

"I don't see what we can do," Willy's father said.

Nor did Willy and that made him feel even worse. As a result, the remainder of the afternoon was a worrying time. Willy moped around the house, did his share of the chores, and then lay on his bed and fretted. Even a visit in mid-afternoon by Stick, Marjorie and Vicki did nothing to cheer him up. He told them the tale and the girls became so upset that Willy was first astonished, then jealous, then annoyed.

I didn't know Marjorie liked Graham so much! he thought.

At that moment, the phone rang. Willy picked it up. It was Peter.

"Good news!" he almost shouted. "Graham is safe."

"Where is he?" Willy asked.

"At the police station," Peter replied.

"The police station! Is he in trouble? What did he do?" Willy asked.

"I don't know," Peter said. "I just got a call to say he was safe. We will have to wait till tomorrow to find out."

What really got Willy and his friends speculating were the news headlines that evening that mentioned another suspicious death at the Caster Mill.

Graham suggested that there was something fishy was going on there. I wonder what it was? Willy thought.

When Willy got to school the next day, he walked around looking for Graham. He found Peter, Roger, and Stephen but all they knew was that Graham was safe but not at school.

It was not until Willy found Graham sitting with his friends at lunchtime that he finally got the story. The main fact was that Declin Riley had recovered in time to save Graham's life and to tell the police that both he and Stephen were innocent. Two other men had bashed him.[3]

When Graham had finished his tale, Peter asked, "Have you spoken to Captain Conkey yet, Graham?"

Graham nodded. "Yes, first thing this morning," he replied.

"Can you still go on the promotion course?" Peter asked.

"Yes."

The whole group seemed to sigh with relief. Stephen mentioned that he was allowed to go as well but it did not have the same emotional impact. From then on, the mood lightened and they began to joke and laugh. Willy could see that Graham was still upset and guessed it was from a broken heart.

---

[3] For the full story, read *Sugar and Spice.*

He will be okay. He will soon fall in love with some other girl, he thought.

Friday came around. The only good news for Willy was that he had achieved a VH in Geography. Captain Conkey commented that his assignment on coastal landforms on the coast of Cape York Peninsula was excellent work.

But schoolwork and expeditions were not Willy's only worries. After school he spent two hours scouring the shops looking for inspiration to buy Christmas presents. It brought home to Willy just how confusing life could be.

So what do I buy my dad? he wondered.

His mother was a bit easier and big brother Lloyd could have some new golf balls, and some music and video CDs.

While he was at the Newsagents Willy also collected the latest edition of his aircraft magazine. He quickly flicked through it and was interested to note that there was an article on the wreck of a Japanese 'Zero' fighter which had been shot down in New Guinea in 1943 and only found a few months previously. There was also one on Dutch Navy 'Dornier' flying boats in the East Indies and Australia during World War Two.

Seeing that reminded him of Jacob van der Heyden and made him want to sit and read the article there and then but by then he was late and had to ride quickly home. Once there he had to rush through the shower and then get dressed in uniform and then have his dinner. After cleaning his teeth and checking his appearance in the mirror he saw that he had a few minutes to wait. To fill them in he picked up the magazine and flicked through the pages. By chance the magazine flicked open at a page with photos of the crashed Japanese fighter. Automatically his eye read the caption under a photo.

'The paintwork on the underside was in such good condition that it looked as though it had just come from the factory,' it read. That made him shake his head.

That couldn't be possible, he thought.

To check he quickly read the page, finding the author's description. It confirmed the caption. Even after more than sixty years the paint on the surfaces that were protected from the sun and the rain looked as though it had just come from the factory. The author expressed the same surprise and disbelief as Willy had felt but the photos seemed to bear him out. Very clear to see was the blood red roundel of Japan with its white surround and the dark green colour of the wing it was on. Several letters and numbers were also clearly visible.

The idea that there might be more aircraft wrecks in similar condition got Willy's hopes and imagination going but at that moment his mother called him. He placed the magazine on his bedside table, ready for reading as soon as he got time. His mother then drove him to Air Cadets.

Cadets was all preparation for promotion course in January with drill and lessons on how to navigate, signals and RAAF 'General Service Knowledge'. Willy enjoyed it all and knew he was feeling well and that he should be happy. During the canteen break he was asked about the search for the plane wreck and then ribbed for not finding it. He joined in the general chatter but without much enthusiasm. Most of the talking he left to Stick and Marjorie.

"So you didn't find this bomber then?" Noddy sneered.

"No," Willy admitted.

"Are you lot still going to look for that 'Beaufighter' up the Cape during the holidays then?" Noddy asked.

"Yes," Willy answered.

He was then careful not to say more as he didn't trust Noddy. *Someone told Mr Jemmerling our plans and I think it was Noddy,* he thought.

But that made him feel guilty at the injustice of being suspicious without any real proof to back it up.

Noddy now annoyed him further by saying, "I don't know why you are bothering. There won't be much left of any wreck after that long."

"There might be," Willy retorted. He then described the wreck of the Japanese 'Zero' and the photos. Noddy looked very sceptical and said he did not believe it. That needled Willy some more. "Then all I can do is show you the magazine article," he retorted.

They bickered a bit longer but had to leave the argument unresolved as it was time for the next lesson. But Willy did not forget about it and decided to do some research on the topic. It made him glad they had agreed to help Mr Beck prepare the shed where they were to restore any wrecks they might recover.

That was what he, Stick, Marjorie, Vicki and Noddy did on Saturday. As arranged, they drove to Mareeba, clad in work clothes, and were set to work, under the supervision of Norman. The task was to finish erecting a large shed on a concrete slab. Most of the heavy work had been done and Mr Beck would not allow any of them to climb up to do roofing work, or let them use any power tools, so it was mostly carrying, holding things, or cleaning that they were engaged in.

Willy did not really mind, and as he worked he plied Norman and Mr Beck with questions about the condition wrecks might be in after lying in jungle, swamp or beach sand for long periods. He learned that World War Two aircraft wrecks were still being recovered from lakes in North Russia and Finland and that these were often in very good condition.

"Because of the cold and the lack of oxygen in the lake bottom," Norman explained.

"What about in a mangrove swamp in the tropics?" Willy asked.

Norman shook his head. "Not so good. The heat and salt both cause rotting and corrosion. We helped get an 'Airacobra' out of a mangrove swamp up in the Cape a few years ago and the whole bottom was rotted away and the steel parts like the engine were just a mass of rust flakes. Here, pass me that drill," he said.

Willy went to hand him the drill when he saw two men walk in through the open door of the shed, along with Mrs Beck. His mouth fell open with surprise.

"Mr Jemmerling!" he muttered. "Now what is he doing here?"

Chapter 15

UNEXPECTED OFFER

Mr Jemmerling saw Willy and smiled.

"Hello young William, would you introduce me please."

That really surprised Willy. He glanced anxiously at Mr Beck and saw that he was looking at Mr Jemmerling with a look of puzzlement. *He doesn't know who he is,* he deduced.

Swallowing to moisten his suddenly dry throat and unsure Willy said, "Mr Beck, this is Mr Jemmerling."

Mr Beck's face registered shock and then anger. "Jemmerling! What brings you here, sir?" he barked, ignoring Mr Jemmerling's out-thrust hand.

Mr Jemmerling ignored the insult and casually dropped his hand. "I could say that I am just visiting. I have never seen your collection before, sir, but I have heard good reports of it. But actually I also came to make you an offer."

"An offer?" Mr Beck asked in a voice laden with suspicion.

"Yes, but first I would appreciate a look around if I may," Mr Jemmerling replied. He held up his hand. "We have paid for our tickets."

Mr Beck looked a bit baffled and suspicious, but then nodded. "Yes, alright. I will show you around myself."

"Thank you," Mr Jemmerling replied, adding, "I think it is a good idea to see what others in the business are doing."

Mr Beck nodded and grunted what could have been agreement. The three men and Mrs Beck then moved away to the main hangar. Norman watched this, then shook his head in amazement.

"Jemmerling! Here! As bold as brass."

"Shouldn't he be?" Stick asked.

Norman shook his head but said, "He and Dad have had a few disagreements in the past, but apart from that, no."

"Has he ever been here before?" Willy asked.

Norman shook his head. "No. Never seen him in my life," he answered.

"Your father didn't seem to recognise him," Willy commented.

"No. Even though they've been rivals for years, he's never met him before. Well I never, Jemmerling here! I wonder what his offer is?" Norman said.

They did not find this out for nearly another hour. The whole group gathered on chairs in the shade for morning tea. Only after drinking a cup of tea and nibbling a biscuit did Mr Jemmerling start to reveal his offer. First, he introduced Mr Hobbs, his 'man'. Then he praised Mr Beck's collection and, in particular how well the 'Airacobra' had been restored and maintained.

Willy sat at the back and observed, noting that Mr Beck was accepting the praise with grudging acceptance mingled with caution. Mr Jemmerling then drained his cup and brushed crumbs off his white shirt.

After looking around at the group, he said, "The offer is this. I need a local guide who can show me where the aircraft wrecks in North Queensland are. The ones that are known about that is, and I wondered if you would accept the task. In return I will give you a weekend flight up to Thursday Island and back, visiting some of the wrecks along the way."

"A weekend?" Mr Beck queried, obviously unsure of how to react.

"Yes. We would go in my restored Catalina *Pterodactyl*. It is possible to go up and back in one day but that leaves no time for sightseeing, so I thought an overnight trip next weekend. What do you say?" Mr Jemmerling asked.

Mr Beck still looked wary. "Why me?"

Mr Jemmerling smiled disarmingly. "Because I have been flying around looking and haven't had much luck. My enquiries inform me that you are the expert in this area, so I thought we could do something of mutual benefit," he explained.

"What exactly is your offer?" Mr Beck asked.

"That I provide the aircraft and the fuel and pay any landing fees and so on; and that you and your team provide the local knowledge to show me the known aircraft wrecks and sites in Cape York Peninsula. I will even provide the food and accommodation if that helps," Mr Jemmerling answered.

Willy had been listening with great interest and deep suspicion. He felt sure it must be some sort of trick to reveal to Mr Jemmerling where their own aircraft wrecks were.

He wants to beat us to them, he thought.

But it was a very tempting offer, and he was gripped by a strong desire to go for another Catalina flight. Seeing that Mr Beck was deep in thought Willy asked, "Exactly who are you offering to take on this flight, Mr Jemmerling?"

Mr Jemmerling turned to look at him and again smiled his very charming smile. "I said the whole team, didn't I?"

"All of us?" Willy gasped, his hopes and fears both soaring.

"Who are we talking about?" Mr Jemmerling asked, looking around.

Mr Beck indicated the others with a sweep of his hand. "These are my workers."

Mr Jemmerling looked at Willy's father. "You too, Dr Williams?"

"It is always a good idea to have a doctor along on expeditions," Willy's father replied with a grin.

"And a girl?" Mr Jemmerling asked, indicating Marjorie.

Willy answered, seizing the chance to put in for his friends. "Three girls. There are three navy cadets in our team," he said.

"And my wife as the adult female to look after the girls," Willy's father added.

Mr Jemmerling did not show any surprise. He did a quick mental calculation and said, "That is seventeen people, about four thousand pounds weight. That is if you are coming too, Mrs Beck?"

Mrs Beck looked horrified. "Oh dear me no! Count me out. I'm happy to stay at home."

"Can the Catalina carry that many?" Willy asked.

Mr Jemmerling nodded. "Oh yes. It has seats for four in the cockpit and nose, plus eight more in the cabin and we can fit in a couple of extras in the saloon. The plane can lift seventeen thousand pounds but that includes fuel. If it was carrying guns and bombs these would typically have weighed in at about three thousand pounds."

"When are we going on this jaunt, you mentioned next weekend?" Mr Beck asked.

"Yes, that is the most convenient time for me. I do have businesses to run so can't stay on holiday swanning around for ever," Mr Jemmerling replied.

Willy's father now asked, "Can you be more specific; times and places and so on?"

Mr Jemmerling nodded. "Yes. I can pick you up here at Mareeba at nine next Saturday morning and we can then fly north, overnight on Horn Island or Thursday Island and then fly back on Sunday to be back by about lunch time," Mr Jemmerling answered.

"Why Mareeba, isn't your plane at Cairns?" Willy's father asked.

Mr Jemmerling shook his head and replied, "No, not anymore. I have just moved it up to Mareeba. The airport fees here are much less and there is a lot less traffic, so not as many flying problems," he explained.

A few more details were discussed, and Mr Jemmerling then gave the adults his telephone number to co-ordinate. He then thanked them and excused himself, leaving with Mr Hobbs.

As the two men vanished from view, Stick burst out, saying, "I wonder what his devious plan is? I'll bet he just wants to trick us into showing where our planes are."

"He seemed too nice and too friendly," Norman agreed.

"It could be a trick," Willy added.

Marjorie shook her head. "Well, I thought he was a really charming gentleman, and I would love to fly in his aeroplane."

"So did I," Willy's father said. "And even if he does hope to pick up clues, I don't see why we shouldn't take advantage of his offer."

"You mean we can go, Dad?" Willy cried, thrilled by the opportunity.

Dr Williams nodded and said, "If your mother agrees."

They left it at that and went back to their various jobs. Willy spent the afternoon carefully cleaning the interior of the 'Neptune' and was instructed in more of the arts of maintaining vintage and replica aircraft by Norman, who was a skilled expert.

As soon as they picked up his mother from Aunty Isabel's, Willy explained the proposal to her and asked if they could go. His mother looked at Willy's father and raised her eyebrows, to which he nodded.

"Yes, alright," she replied. "Lloyd must come too, if he wishes," she added.

But Lloyd wasn't interested. He had already made arrangements for a party with his Year 11 mates at Darren's house. That pleased Willy who did not want his big brother along. Next, he phoned Andrew to see if he and Carmen were interested.

Andrew replied, "Yes, but I will have to ask Carmen and then Mum and Dad. I will also call Tina. Wait and I will call you back."

Willy did. He lay on his bed and read the magazine article on the Dutch 'Dornier' flying boats. What he read both amazed and fascinated him. 'I didn't know the Dutch had so many planes in the Far East,' he thought. He now learned that the aircraft were German designed Dornier Do 24s; all-metal, high-wing monoplanes with three engines and with the impressive maximum range of nearly 3,000 nautical miles.

'Wingspan 27 metres, length 22 metres, wights: empty 13,500 kg; loaded 18,400 kg; maximum speed 340 kilometres/h; service ceiling 19,360 feet. And a pretty impressive armament for a flying boat: three gun positions with one 7.92 millimetre MG in the nose, another in the tail and a dorsal turret with either a 20 millimetre or 30 millimetre cannon.'

That got him studying the illustrations and photos. It took him a few seconds to find the tail gun turret. At last he found it, perched right up on the tailplane between and slightly aft of the twin tail fins. 'I wonder if the gunner could get back into the main fuselage from back there,' he mused. They were, he decided, quite impressive aircraft.

Next, he read that they carried underwing bombs or depth charges. 'They were naval aircraft,' he read. 'Used for maritime reconnaissance and anti-submarine duties. Usually they carried a crew of six: Pilot, co-pilot, navigator/radio operator, and three air gunners. First flew in 1937, last flew (in Spain) in 1967.'

There were details of their manufacture. The article read:

'An excellent tri-motor flying boat, it was one of the few aircraft to be designed and sold by the Nazi government to a foreign country, in this case to the Netherlands. A total of 11 were manufactured by Weserflugzeugbau. In addition 26 more were manufactured under licence by the Dutch de Schelde and Aviolanda companies. All were deployed to the Netherlands East Indies (now Indonesia). The Dutch aircraft were designated the Do 24K-2.

That Jacob van der Heyden we rescued said that his father was an officer in the Dutch navy and that he had been a navigator on flying boats. I wonder if he was on these planes? Willy thought.

For a few moments he wondered what had become of Jacob. Then he shrugged and went back to his reading.

Willy read that after the Netherlands were conquered by the Germans in 1940 the Dutch factories, plus the French Potez-CAMS plant were used to make more, the aircraft being used by the German Luftwaffe. 170 were manufactured in the Netherlands and another 48 in France. What surprised Willy even more was to read that, after the war, the French made another 20 for their own use and that they had as many as 60 in service until 1955. Others were sold to Spain.

What he found most interesting were the short paragraphs mentioning that when the war with Japan began the Dutch Dorniers did magnificent service in reconnaissance, bombing attacks and laying mines as part of the allied defence. They were crucial in providing early warning of several approaching Japanese fleets, including the one that took part in the Battle of the Java Sea.

Here another big gap in Willy's historical knowledge was exposed and he only gained a glimmer of it by reading that a combined Dutch, British, Australian, and American fleet, all commanded by the Dutch Admiral Karel Dorman took part in the battle. Willy was saddened to learn that the allies lost badly and that one of the ships which took part, and which was sunk two nights later in the Sunda Strait, was the Australian light cruiser HMAS *Perth*.

I must read more about that, he decided, feeling a strong desire to know his own country's history.

Then he read the paragraph which mentioned that the Dutch Dorniers were also very extensively used to evacuate important senior officers and political leaders, diamonds, gold and money, and Dutch and British civilians from the Netherlands East Indies to safety in Australia as the Japanese invasion progressed.

That reminded him of the tragic story of the flying boats sunk at Broome by the Japanese air raid when many civilians were killed because they were still on board the anchored flying boats out in the bay.

Some of those flying boats were Dutch, he remembered.

He went to look up the details of this but was interrupted by Andrew phoning back. "Sorry Willy, but I am the only one," Andrew said. "Carmen and Tina have both already made commitments to go to some birthday party and they don't feel they can let their friend down."

"So it is just you?" Willy asked.

"Yes. Look, if you need more, why don't you ask Graham or Stephen?" Andrew suggested.

Willy thought for a moment but then shook his head. "No go. They will both be on their army cadet promotion course then," he replied, feeling silly at having shaken his head in reply.

They had to leave it at that but anxiety about the upcoming flight and expeditions caused him more anxiety. As a result, he slept very badly, with bad dreams full of death and grinning skulls. Several times he woke up in a cold sweat and then tried not to go back to sleep.

As a result, Sunday was not a good day. Willy moped around the house, did his share of the chores and then lay on his bed and worried. Even a visit in mid-afternoon by Stick, Marjorie and Vicki did little to cheer him up.

The good news was that Stick and Marjorie were allowed to go on the Catalina flight. "Even if you are the only girl?" Willy queried.

"Yes. Your Mum is going, isn't she?" Marjorie answered.

The remainder of the day passed slowly. Then it was school again.

For the whole of that week the atmosphere became a mixture of boredom and excitement. As the Year 10s and 11s were finishing that Friday they had no interest in schoolwork and a holiday and party mood gripped them. Willy and the other Year 9s were infected by this but also mildly resentful that they still had another week still to endure.

"The whole system is a bloody farce," Stephen said. "All year levels should finish on the same day and save all this waste of time and effort."

"It's so that the teachers can mark all our assignments and exams," Stick said.

Stephen snorted. "Oh piffle! They did that weeks ago. Now we are just wasting time. We could be out searching to get the plane wrecks before that Jemmerling beats us to it," he said.

That made Willy feel quite anxious, again being tormented by suspicions that Mr Jemmerling's offer of a flight over Cape York might be just a trick.

We will just have to be careful what we do or say, he decided.

Both Graham and Stephen assured Willy that they were still interested in taking part in an expedition up the Cape after Christmas. They both expressed some mild resentment that there was to be an expedition before then, but as both were going on the army cadet promotion course the next day this was not very strong. When told of the proposed flight that weekend Stephen was quite obviously annoyed and jealous.

"You could have asked us!" he said.

"I knew you were leaving for your promotion course on Saturday," Willy answered.

Graham shook his head. "Good luck then. But if you are going in that Mr Jemmerling's Catalina you will need to be very careful in case he manages to get information out of you about our plane wrecks."

"I've thought of that," Willy answered. "We will be careful, won't we Marjorie?"

Marjorie nodded. Stephen guffawed and cried, "That's what they say; if you can't be good then be careful!"

It took Willy a few seconds to realise what Stephen meant. Then he got annoyed. Marjorie sniffed and turned away from him while Vicki, once the innuendo had been explained to her, said, "Don't be horrible Stephen!"

That afternoon at the school gate Willy said goodbye to Graham. "I hope you do well on your promotion course," he said.

"I'll try my best," Graham promised. "Now you watch out for that Jemmerling character."

"I will. You have a happy Christmas. See you in the new year," Willy replied.

The two boys parted with cries of 'Merry Christmas'. As he rode home Willy was quite emotional. He found it hard to realise that another year of school was almost over. Was over for Graham and his friends.

Now we can really start searching for these plane wrecks, he told himself, excitement bubbling up with the thought that tomorrow he was going flying again.

And in a Catalina!

Chapter 16

CAPE YORK FROM THE AIR

Friday night meant Air Cadets. For Willy there was more excited anticipation as the permission forms and administrative instructions for the January promotion course were issued, along with more items of uniform and kit. Willy found it impossible not to boast about the Catalina flight the next day and that aroused a fair bit of jealousy and a few barbed comments, particularly from people like Finlay and Morrow.

That night, before he went to bed, Willy carefully packed everything needed for the weekend, the hardest part being to stop his mother doing it for him.

"It's alright, Mum. You don't have to fuss! I know what I need. I've been on cadet camps and trips before," he said.

Willy had a restless night. Dreams kept him on the edge of waking for much of the time, but he woke feeling eager and fresh despite that. The family was all up at 5:00am and on the road by 6:00am. There was a detour to collect Andrew, Marjorie, and Stick. By 8:00am they were at the Mareeba airfield.

As they turned off the Kennedy Highway, Willy scanned the aircraft that were visible but did not see the Catalina. Clearly visible were some of the vintage aircraft of the North Queensland 'Warbirds' Club but no flying boat. Willy had several times watched the NQ 'Warbirds' perform at air shows, and he thought they were very good. As he was driven past them, he admired the club's 'Winjeels', 'Nanchangs', DC3 and 'Harvard'. But it was the seaplane he really wanted to see. It was only as they pulled into the bitumen car park near the office buildings that he spotted the black wing of the *Pterodactyl* poking out from behind a hangar.

The wing tip floats are folded up, he noted with interest.

Standing outside were the Becks, Mr Jemmerling and Mr Hobbs. The car was parked, and they climbed out to a chorus of cheerful and friendly greetings. Willy was still intensely suspicious of Mr Jemmerling but had trouble remembering that when the man was so friendly.

A man came around the side of the building and was introduced as

Harvey. He was the flight engineer and looked to be in his sixties. He gestured in the direction of the aircraft and said, "Bring your gear. We are ready to start up."

As Willy picked up his kitbag he felt another surge of excitement, and just a twinge of apprehension. At the back of his mind lurked the knowledge that the Catalina was nearly seventy years old and things might go wrong.

But it wouldn't be allowed to fly if it was unsafe. It must have been certified as airworthy by the Civil Aviation Department, he reassured himself.

When the Catalina came into view Willy stopped and studied it. Even though he had seen it before he was half lost in admiration. It was freshly painted, a dull, matt black, and it looked better than Mr Southall's machine. His eyes picked out the name painted in small white running writing on the side of the nose: *Pterodactyl.* Willy studied the lines of the black painted machine and nodded.

Yes, in the dark it would look like the pre-historic flying dinosaur.

"Mr Jemmerling, did you choose the name?" he asked.

Mr Jemmerling shook his head. "No. But I think it suits her, don't you?"

Willy did. "It's a great name."

"I gather that all the aircraft in the flight had names starting with 'P'," Mr Jemmerling explained, *"Pterodactyl, Peregrine, Predator, Panther* and so on."

Willy now noted that the *Pterodactyl* had the registration letters VH-PTY on the fuselage, plus the World War Two RAAF roundels used in the Pacific: a blue ring with a white centre, the red dot having been painted out to remove any possibility of confusion in the heat of combat. He had read that in the early stages of the war with Japan, there had been a number of tragic mistakes when pilots or anti-aircraft gunners had seen the red and fired, thinking it was the red roundel of the Japanese.

Willy took a photo, then walked forward to rejoin the others who were being introduced to the pilot and co-pilot. The pilot was an elderly man with white hair and a straggly moustache. His name was Mr Johnson. The co-pilot was a young man in his twenties with dark hair and a ready grin. He was called 'Hec', but Willy did not catch the rest of his name.

From the short discussion that followed Willy understood that the members of the crew were permanent employees of Mr Jemmerling and that they usually worked at his museum and airfield in New South Wales. Hec was gaining experience on the Catalina and was keen to qualify on all the old 'Warbird' types.

The bags were loaded in and then they climbed aboard and were shown to their seats. As he climbed aboard Willy experienced a small thrill and imagined himself back in the war, about to take off on a desperate mission. Having toured the plane he was familiar with the interior layout. A short corridor led off on his left to the steps leading up to the flight deck. On the left of the corridor were a galley and a toilet. Directly opposite was a table for the navigator & radio operator and aft of that two bench seats. Aft, on the right, was a small cabin with bunk. This was built around the machinery for operating the retractable undercarriage. The cabin had a large square window. Beyond that a ladder led up to the wing. A tunnel in the upright part of the fuselage which connected with the wing had small windows on either side and there appeared to be a small hatch in the upper surface of the wing. That intrigued Willy and he determined to ask about it at the first convenient opportunity.

Behind the sleeping cabin was a larger cabin with two rows of seats, eight in all. Each had a porthole next to it. Behind that the fuselage stepped up to the aft section where there were rectangular hatches in lieu of Perspex blisters. This time Willy made sure he was seated on the port side.

The sun will be shining on what I am looking at, he thought, having been on the starboard side on the previous Catalina flight.

Marjorie seated herself across the aisle from him and Stick behind her, next to Andrew. Mr Beck was invited to sit up on the flight deck with Mr Jemmerling. Willy's parents sat in front of him, and Mr Hobbs and Norman sat at the rear. Harvey acted as loadmaster and went along checking they had their seatbelts done up. He then gave them a safety brief, making each one put on their lifejacket and then re-stow it. He also showed them how to open the rear hatches and where the inflatable life rafts were stowed.

Once that was done, he went forward to the flight deck, then climbed out to remove the wheel chocks and to check that the motors were running properly. As the motors kicked into life Willy experienced another spurt of excitement. Once the motors were going and after the usual pre-flight checks (Willy could see the flaps and ailerons being moved) Harvey climbed back aboard and closed the door. He then went forward into the saloon.

The Catalina began to move. Through his porthole (which he wished was much larger) Willy could see the undercarriage legs and wheels. It fascinated him to watch the tyres bulge on the bumps and how the undercarriage legs moved up and down as the plane rolled across minor irregularities in the bitumen. These movements became even more pronounced as the aircraft began its take-off run. There was the usual bouncing and swaying and attendant anxiety as they roared along the strip. Then they 'rotated' and suddenly lifted off.

As the ground dropped away below him, Willy watched with interest as the undercarriage was retracted out of sight into the wheel wells on the side of the fuselage. It confirmed him in his opinion that amphibians were just the most useful type of aircraft, even though his rational mind told him they paid a penalty in terms of fuel and payload because of the weight of the extra machinery.

It was a beautiful clear morning, as it usually is around Mareeba, except in the 'wet'. The Catalina climbed away to the east, then banked to the left., Willy now took out his Air Navigation Chart and folded it to the correct area before looking out again. He was able to see the town of Mareeba off to the left and then got an excellent view of the Kennedy Highway and Aunty Isabel's farm.

He pointed this out to his mother and said, "I hope she's watching."

"She is. I can see her," Willy's mother replied. Willy looked more carefully and just made out a tiny figure standing beside the farmhouse. Even from a couple of thousand feet he saw her arms waving. He lifted his hand to wave back, then felt silly.

She won't see my hand from that distance, he thought.

The farm slid away underneath. The Catalina flew across a range of hills covered with savannah woodland. The railway from Cairns to Mareeba was easy to detect. So was the Barron River. The aircraft's course then took them northeast across forested hills and areas of plantation pine trees. The bulk of a large, conical mountain covered with jungle slid by on the port side. Willy decided that it must be Black Mountain.

Also called Mt Harris, he noted. He looked at the massive bulk of it and shook his head. *I wouldn't like to be flying this close to it if there was any cloud,* he thought. Then he remembered the rumour of a plane crash on it back in World War Two. *I wonder if that story is true?* he thought. After his recent experience near Caster he wasn't keen to go looking in the jungle.

The Catalina came out over the Coral Sea just south of the town of Port Douglas. Before take-off it had been explained that they would only fly at a couple of thousand feet, accepting the turbulence as part of the price to be paid for a better view. This early in the day there was virtually no air movement, so the flight was nice and smooth.

Willy now tracked their route on his chart, naming places as they went. The mouth of the Daintree River was very obvious, and he was able to look back along its winding course to locate the small town of that name. Then huge jungle-covered mountains reared up to port. The massive bulk of Thorntons Peak was easy to identify and just looking at it made Willy shudder. On the south side of the mountain was the wreck of an aircraft, the result of a tragic crash years before. Even though he knew roughly where to look he was unable to detect any sign of it.

This is a dangerous part of the world to fly in, he thought. *Or at least in bad weather.* That crash had been in daylight but with thick clouds. *When I am a pilot, I will be very careful,* he told himself.

More mountains slid by, then the very prominent Cape Tribulation. Willy undid his seat belt and leaned over Marjorie to see if he could spot the reef on which Captain Cook's ship HMS *Endeavour* had nearly come to grief in 1770 but he was unsure which of the isolated reefs that he could see was the one. Out to starboard the Great Barrier Reef was now clearly visible. Beyond the reefs was the dark blue of the ocean, marking the deep water beyond the Australian continental shelf. Willy found it fascinating to actually see the things he learned about in Geography at school.

He now ticked off the recognizable features as they slid by: Bloomfield River, Cedar Bay, Weary Bay, the Endeavour River and town of Cooktown.

Traveling at nearly 300kph certainly makes the landscape slide by quickly, he mused.

The Catalina turned slightly to starboard and the rugged shape of Cape Bedford slid by. Next came the seemingly endless white beach and sand dunes leading up to Cape Flattery. Willy knew they were almost pure silica sands and remembered Capt Conkey saying that many were hundreds of metres high. He also noted that the geography teacher had been right about another thing: the dunes that were not fully stabilised by vegetation had 'blow outs' with main central part of the dune moving ahead of the ends.

Crescent dunes in deserts, barchans I think Captain Conkey called them, are the opposite, the ends leading as they blow downwind, he thought.

The Catalina banked to the left around the rugged shape of Cape Flattery and then tracked north past a whole series of rocky capes and sandy beaches. As they did, Willy saw his Geography assignment appear in real life: a rocky cape, then a swampy creek mouth, then a sandy beach. The mouths of any creeks further north all ended in a sharp curve to the left with a sand spit on their southern, seaward side.

How interesting! he thought, his camera clicking frequently.

The whole time they flew over numerous detached reefs and small islands, some rocky and others flat and covered with scrub. The outer edge of the main Barrier Reef was also a constant sight to the east.

As they passed Barrow Point, Willy felt himself becoming tense. *Cape Melville and Bathurst Bay are next. That is where out 'Kittyhawk' is. I hope no-one lets slip any clue.*

As they rounded Cape Melville in a sharp turn to the west another worrying thought came to Willy: what if the wreck of the 'Kittyhawk' was visible from the air?

The wind might have blown the sand off it, he thought.

To his relief, the Catalina did not follow the curve of the bay but cut straight across. Willy took a couple of photos and stared very hard at the area where he thought the wreck lay hidden, but the distance and vegetation revealed no sign of it.

His father pointed down and said, "That is Bathurst Bay. Did you know it is the site of the worst cyclone disaster in Australian history?"

"No. What happened?" Willy dutifully asked.

"Back in 1899 or thereabouts, a fleet of pearling luggers and schooners; more than a hundred vessels in all, took shelter there. This was before the days of radios of course so they had no warning that a very severe cyclone was heading for them. Most cyclones hit the Queensland coast much further south. It is rare for them to come in north of Cooktown, but this one did and it swept into the bay, driving the ships ashore and killing about 300 people," his father replied.

Even though he had been born and bred in North Queensland, Willy had never experienced a real cyclone, only been on the fringes of them. The worst one had been the previous January when a particularly powerful cyclone had moved south past Cairns to make landfall south of Townsville. Looking down at the shallow bay, he tried to imagine what it might have been like but could not really picture it.

"Did any of them survive?" he asked.

"A few," his father answered. "I think about five ships. Some of the crews of schooners driven ashore made it to the beach, but most were drowned in the surf."

Andrew, who had been silent during this, now said, "The reports said there was a storm surge. A mounted policeman and his black troopers were camped half a mile, that's about eight hundred metres, inland. He wrote that the surge was at least forty feet; about fifteen metres, high. That means that survivors of the shipwrecks would have had to contend with ten metre waves moving at fifty or sixty kilometres per hour in among the trees and bush. It was the highest storm surge ever recorded in Australia and washed up to five kilometres inland in places."

Marjorie was horrified. "That's awful! You couldn't swim in that," she said.

"No, you couldn't," Andrew replied.

Willy noted the grim look on Andrew's face and the almost haunted look in his eyes and then remembered that Andrew and Carmen had been caught in the cyclone the previous year.

"Is that what happened to you at that Cape Bowling Ball last January?" he asked.

"Cape Bowling Green," Andrew corrected. "Yes, it was. We had to tie ourselves to the tops of trees. The surge went right over the cape and even carried a fishing trawler across and into the mangrove swamps."

He then explained how, in the age of the radio, satellite cameras and mobile phones, they had come to be caught in the storm.[4]

Stick, who had been listening, then asked, "Is that the same cyclone that Kirk and his mates got caught in when they were looking for that lost gold mine in the Mulgrave Valley?"

---

[4] Read *Bowling Green Bay* by C. R. Cummings

"Yes, it was," Andrew agreed.[5]

"I hope I never have to go through a cyclone," Willy said.

Andrew gave a short laugh and nodded. "I don't ever want to be in another either," he agreed.

Willy's mother now interrupted by asking, "Willy, what are those islands down there?"

Willy looked out, then quickly checked his chart. A group of five large, rocky islands was almost below them. "They are Flinders Croup," he answered. "The big one in the middle is Flinders Island. The teardrop shaped one on its left is Denham Island and the long skinny one is Blackwood Island."

"Flinders? Did he come here too?" Stick queried.

Marjorie cried out, then said, "Oh brother! You should pay more attention in school. Even I know that one. Flinders sailed right around Australia. He circumcised it."

Willy's father stifled a guffaw and said, "The word is circumnavigated."

There was an embarrassed silence. Willy saw Marjorie go bright red and knew it was because his parents were there. Their eyes met and she had to stifle a giggle.

Stick then asked, "But isn't Flinders Island down in Bass Strait?"

Andrew answered him, "Yes. There is more than one."

Willy pointed out to port. "That great big curve in the coast is Princess Charlotte Bay," he explained.

He was now aware that the Catalina had turned to starboard and was not following the coast but instead cutting northwest across the chord of the semi-circular bay.

We are following almost the same track as when we rescued Jacob van der Heyden, he thought.

That got him both excited and anxious. Irrational fears that he was about to re-live that horrible incident mingled with ghastly memories of the mangled corpse they had retrieved.

Willy tried to stay calm, but a ghoulish fascination seemed to take hold and he found he had to continually check their position. To do this he had to leave his seat to lean over and look past Marjorie to see the reefs to starboard. He identified Corbett Reef and then Grub Reef.

Won't be long now, he thought.

---

[5] Read *Below Bartle Frere* by C. R. Cummings

Willy's mother noticed his behaviour and asked, "Is everything alright Willy?"

"Yes Mum. It's just that…just that this is where I saw that man in the sea."

His mother nodded and his father turned and met his eyes and said, "That was very well done, Willy."

"Very scary," Stick added. "Particularly that take-off in the big waves."

"It was all horrible," Marjorie said.

Willy could only nod and resume his seat as the western end of Hedge Reef slid into view. *Down there,* he thought. *That is where we landed and then had to cruise up and down waiting for the tide and wind. It looks much calmer today.*

In spite of himself, he strained his eyes to see if he could spot anyone in the water.

Andrew stared down as well, then asked, "What happened to the young bloke you rescued, do you know?"

"Jacob van der Heyden? No idea. Went back to Sydney I suppose," Willy replied.

"They never did find the blokes who murdered his mate did they?" Stick asked.

"No."

"What was he looking for?" Andrew asked.

Willy shook his head. "No idea."

"Treasure, I'll bet," Stick suggested.

"Oh treasure! Baloney!" Norman called from the back.

But the word lingered in Willy's mind as they flew on over the rescue area.

Was it treasure? he wondered.

Chapter 17

TO THE POINTY BIT

Willy's interest now focused on the coastline to his left. While the aircraft had been cutting diagonally across Princess Charlotte Bay the coastline had at first been so far away as to be just a vague line, half lost in the haze. Now, as they drew slowly closer, the details began to emerge and Willy was able to identify places and name them.

We are approaching the place where the 'Beaufighter' wreck is located, he thought. He took out his pencil and placed the point of it on the chart at the location of the wreck, then looked out to check their exact location. *Down there somewhere,* he thought, staring hard at the bush and scrub in from a long, sandy beach.

A movement beside Willy made him look up. Standing in the aisle and leaning over him to look through the porthole was Hobbs, Mr Jemmerling's Man.

"Where are we?" he asked.

Willy felt an instant surge of anxiety mixed with suspicion. *Did he wait until now and then sneak over to see where I was looking?* he wondered.

For a second or so Willy flustered inside, his mind churning with options. Then he quickly but 'casually' moved the pencil point and placed it on the nearest major coastal feature that he could identify.

"There," he said.

"Thanks," Mr Hobbs replied, leaning across to look through the porthole after glancing at the chart. He then said, "I just came to ask if you'd like some afternoon tea?"

Even though he really would have liked some Willy shook his head. "No thanks."

"If you change your mind there are refreshments in the galley," Mr Hobbs replied.

To Willy's relief, Mr Hobbs moved along to speak to Andrew. *Creepy sod!* Willy thought.

Then he leaned across to stare out of the porthole again. He was sure he was looking at the right stretch of coast but could see no sign of any aircraft wreck.

This one is in among the beach dunes, he told himself.

After looking around to check that Mr Hobbs had moved away and was not looking, he lifted his camera and took two photos.

A short while later the aircraft passed Cape Direction and the intercom crackled. Mr Jemmerling's voice boomed out. "Good morning, ladies and gentlemen. In a few minutes we will fly over the Aboriginal community of Lockhart River. We are then going to fly around a bit so that I can see what is left of the World War Two airfields in the area. As we do, I will give a bit of a running commentary and history, assisted by Mr Beck. Now, if you look out the port side of the aircraft, you will see the buildings of the community and beyond them to the west the airstrip."

Willy looked out and clearly saw the long bitumen runway. A couple of dirt roads snaked off into the hazy interior or off northwards through jungle covered hills. It looked to be a very isolated place.

Mr Jemmerling came on the intercom with an explanation of what they were looking at. He said, "This is the Iron Range area and during World War Two a number of airfields were built here. They were built by the United States Army engineers of the Forty Sixth Engineer Battalion. They were transported to Portland Roads, which is just north of us, by the SS *Wandana* and the MV *Islander* in June 1942."

"After constructing a road from Portland Roads the engineers built a short, three-thousand-foot airstrip to use for admin and medical evacuation. Then they constructed two large airstrips: No 1, named 'Gordon'; and No2, named 'Claudie'. No 1 strip was completed by mid-August. The first operational use was in September when a squadron of B-26 'Marauders' of the U.S. Twenty Second Bomb Group landed to refuel on the tenth, then flew on to attack Japanese targets in Rabaul. They refuelled at Port Moresby and then came back to refuel at Iron Range on the thirteenth. Unfortunately one of these aircraft crashed while landing."

Mr Jemmerling paused to clear his throat while the Catalina did a wide circle over the airfield. He went on, "Remember that the American strategy was to base all their bombers in Western Queensland, around Cloncurry and Julia Creek, so far inland that there was no possibility of any Japanese raid finding them. The planes were prepared for the missions there, then flew north and refuelled here or at one of the strips further up, then went on to New Guinea to do their job, often refuelling at Port Moresby on the way. They then flew back, hopping from airfield to airfield. The same planes could just as easily fly from Cloncurry to the Darwin area, refuel and bomb up, go on to strike at the East Indies, then come back. It gave great flexibility and made the bombers almost completely safe from any form of attack. That meant they could just be parked in the open with minimal guards."

"So the big planes weren't based here, at least not until the war had moved so far north that this was a safe rear area," Mr Jemmerling explained.

Willy found this fascinating, and he realised he had never thought about the strategy of air warfare in such a way. Until then his focus had been on the individuals flying the planes and on air tactics.

I need to study things a bit more, he thought.

The Catalina went round again, further to the north and west and Mr Jemmerling went on to detail how the RAAF No 26 Operational Base Unit was deployed to run the airfields, and to list more tragic crashes. The worst was on the 16th of November 1942 when a B-24 'Liberator' named *Bombs for Nippon* crashed on take-off, striking two other 'Liberators' with its wing tip before crashing into the trees where it caught fire and its bombs exploded, destroying it and a B-17 'Flying Fortress'. The total loss was four aircraft and eleven lives, plus two B-24s damaged.

Just thinking about that caused Willy to shudder in horror. He listened with sadness as Mr Jemmerling read more information, detailing another bad aircraft accident which occurred in December 1942 when another 'Liberator' crashed on take-off from Gordon. Its load of bombs exploded, killing all ten in the crew.

Mr Jemmerling went on to say that in that month the American engineers were moved and civilian workers from the Allied Works Council took over construction.

"That means that the Japanese had been pushed back to northern New Guinea. The Americans then based three squadrons of 'Liberators' of the 90th Bomb Group here: Numbers 319, 320 and 321 Squadrons USAAF, plus the 'Marauders' of Number 33 Squadron of the 22nd Bomb Group and also the 400th Bomb Squadron and 28th Service Squadron."

"By then this area had been developed into a large complex with roads, camps, taxiways, bomb, and fuel dumps. There was an Australian

Radar Station, No. 43, on the coast near Portland Roads, and there were Australian Anti-Aircraft units defending the strip, though they never fired a shot in anger as no Japanese plane ever came near the place."

"Gordon was closed in January 1943 for sealing and Claudie became operational but was never satisfactory because of cross-winds and flooding. A second 'Claudie' strip was then commenced. In February 1943, as the war moved even further from Australia, the American squadrons redeployed north to Port Moresby. The Iron Range strips were then downgraded from an operational base to a transit complex for refuelling."

"There were, unfortunately, more crashes. On the 15th of June 1943 Flying Officer N. P. Randall, of Dalby, Queensland, a member of the famous No 76 Squadron RAAF, lost his life when he crash landed his P-40 'Kittyhawk' fighter on a beach two miles from Portland Roads. An American pilot was killed in 1944 when a P-47 'Thunderbolt' which was landing crashed into his P-40, which was on the ground. In 1946 an RAAF 'Norseman' transport aircraft doing a ration run crashed in bad weather, killing the three on board, including the pilot, Flying Officer C. W. Law of Blackall in Queensland."

"In 1944 the area was so safe that the anti-aircraft units and coastal artillery were removed and the airfield handed over to the RAAF. Later it was handed to the Department of Civil Aviation. By then the war was over. But that isn't the end of the story. Part of the old Gordon strip was sealed and that is the airfield you can see now. It can handle most twin-engine aircraft and RAAF types such as 'Spartan' transports.

"The reason for that was a unique experiment carried out in 1964. To try to ascertain the effects of nuclear weapons on troops fighting in the tropics the army placed vehicles, guns and dummies in trenches in the jungle near here and then exploded hundreds of tons of conventional explosives. These were on a steel tower above the tree tops. It was called 'Operation Blowdown' and I was hoping to see some sign of it. We will now just circle the area and look."

Willy found all this fascinating and for the next fifteen minutes he stared eagerly down, but was quite unable to detect any sign of where a huge explosion might once have taken place. Nor could anyone else. As his father said, "I guess that the jungle has had time to grow back in forty years."

"They would never be allowed to do it nowadays," Willy's mother commented. "The environmentalists would stop it."

There was then another sad story. They circled over a jungle covered ridge to the northwest and looked down at the site where a civilian 'Metroliner' crashed when trying to land in bad weather in 2005. Once again, Willy wondered how such a tragedy could happen and hoped he would never be involved in such a terrible event.

The next place the plane flew over was the tiny jetty at Portland Roads. As they did, Mr Jemmerling added that he was reliably informed that there were no remains of aircraft wrecks in the Iron Range area. Mr Beck confirmed this. On hearing this Willy thought, 'That makes our wrecks even more important.'

Mr Jemmerling then added, "Nor are there any of the mythical aircraft allegedly left behind by the Americans when they left, so we are not landing to look. We are now flying on to the tip of Cape York."

The Catalina straightened up on a northerly course across Weymouth Bay, allowing Willy to identify the winding Pascoe River. He mentioned this to Andrew who nodded and said that he knew where they were. Willy twisted to look and saw that Andrew held a hydrographic chart. Andrew then said that back in 1848 the explorer Edmund Kennedy had experienced trouble with thick jungle in that area and that the Pascoe River was notorious for saltwater crocodiles.

"How on earth do you know that?" Willy joked.

"Because I pay attention in school; and because I am very interested in the history of exploration, particularly the sea explorers," Andrew replied.

That figures, Willy thought. Out of politeness he said, "Good, keep me informed."

The next area of interest had nothing to do with aircraft. It was another huge area of massive, scrub-covered sand dunes inland from Cape Grenville. After staring at the tangle for several minutes Willy shook his head.

I'd hate to have to try to cross that sort of place on foot, he thought.

The country from then on seemed to be one vast, trackless wilderness to Willy. The coast was the same alternating sequence of rocky headlands (mostly red in this part of the country), each with a swamp area in its lee, and then a long stretch of sandy beach. The beaches were almost pure white sand and he learned this was because they were largely composed of coral sand, rather than the grains of granite found in the Cairns area. Inland was a vast area of low hills and flat plains covered with what looked to be a tangle of some sort of scrub.

That doesn't look very pleasant either, he thought.

Mr Beck came on the intercom to announce that they were now flying over the area where the Airacobras had all crash landed back in 1942. "And over near the other side of the Peninsula in the swamps at the mouth of the Jardine River," he added. That got Willy staring down at the stretches of beach with great interest but there was no sign of any wrecks at all. "All taken away years ago, or lost in the sea and sand," Mr Beck explained.

They flew low over the extensive areas of mangrove swamps around the mouths of the Escape River and Jacky Jacky Creek.

Andrew said, "That is where Edmund Kennedy was speared by the Aborigines back in 1848. I read that if he and Jacky Jacky had been able to safely cross the Escape River, they would have been safe."

"Who was Jacky Jacky?" Stick asked.

"Kennedy's Aboriginal guide," Andrew replied.

Willy was puzzled. "Why would they have been safe?"

"I read that the tribe who inhabited the land on the other side of the river was friendly," Andrew answered.

"Wouldn't this Jacky Jacky person have been safe anyway, being an Aborigine?" Marjorie queried.

Willy's father answered that. "I was told, but it may not be true, that in the old days any Aborigine found in another tribe's area without good reason was usually killed."

Andrew agreed and added, "Jacky Jacky came from New South Wales. He was way out of his area."

"He wouldn't have even been able to speak the local language," Willy's father said.

Marjorie looked surprised. "Did the Aborigines have more than one language?"

"Yes, they did," Willy's father answered.

The Catalina went into a sharp bank to the right. Willy felt a twinge of alarm, then Mr Jemmerling said over the intercom, "Crocodile."

Willy had to leave his seat and look through Marjorie's porthole, but he clearly saw the huge saurian swimming along in what looked to be open sea. Then, as the aircraft continued to turn, he saw the mangroves of the river estuary.

"It looks like a gecko on the ceiling from up here," he observed.

"You wouldn't think so if you were down in the water with him!" Stick said with a laugh.

Once again, Willy had an almost overpowering flashback, with ghastly images of the shark tearing at the corpse. He shook his head and tried to look away.

Marjorie said, "It's a long way from the shore."

Willy's father said, "They swim in the sea. I have heard accounts of crocodiles swimming from Australia to New Guinea. They certainly often swim from one river mouth to another near Cairns."

"Wouldn't the sharks eat them?" Stick asked.

Willy's father smiled and shook his head. "I think they would win in any fight with a shark, with their teeth, claws and armoured hide."

Once again, images of sharks swamped Willy's consciousness and he shuddered. But then they spotted more crocodiles. These were basking on mud banks and went scurrying into the water as the aircraft roared low overhead.

The aircraft then levelled out and climbed higher, for which even Willy was thankful as the air had now heated up and there was a fair bit of turbulence.

Mr Jemmerling came on again to say, "We are now flying over Albany Sound and on your left are the remains of the first permanent European settlement, a place called 'Somerset'. It was settled by the Jardine family in 1864. The two sons drove a herd of beef cattle from near Bowen to here in an epic journey."

Willy looked down on a stretch of bright blue water and saw a small bay on his left with a sandy beach backed by a scrub covered slope. On top of the slope was a road, some ruined buildings all overgrown with vines and weeds and, to Willy's surprise, three old fashioned cannons and a memorial.

"I can see three guns," he cried.

"There was a Royal Marine garrison here for a few years," his father said.

"It was to be a new Singapore," Andrew added.

Willy watched the place slip astern, to be lost in a wilderness of rocky, scrub-covered hills, mangrove swamps and savanna woodland. To him I did not look a very promising site, but he did concede he knew very little about such things.

Mr Jemmerling then announced that soon they would fly over the very tip of Cape York, the most northerly bit of the Australian mainland.

Stick came and looked out of Willy's porthole. Then he pointed and said, "There it is, the pointy bit!"

Willy smiled, picturing maps of Australia. Seeing that small rocky cape gave him an odd feeling. *I have never been this far north before,* he told himself.

He found he felt both excited and uneasy, sensing that beyond the cape it was all 'foreign', that vast world of New Guinea and Asia.

The Catalina banked and did a wide circle around Cape York so that everyone got a good look. As it did, Willy noted numerous rocks, and rocky islands. Andrew drew his attention to the swirls of a vicious tide rip between the tip of the cape and two rocky islands just beyond.

"That would be a deadly place for a sailing ship," he said.

Willy agreed. Then he pointed out a line of tiny figures. They were tourists.

I must go there one day, he thought.

After circling once more Mr Jemmerling said, "Right people, that was the 'Pointy Bit'. Now let's see some crashed aircraft."

The Catalina now headed southwest down the 'Gulf' coast. On the way they flew past Possession Island 'Where Captain Cook claimed New South Wales, he meant all of Eastern Australia, for King George the third of England'. Ten minutes later they flew past Seisia and the small port in the Red Island passage. From there they turned inland and flew over the settlements that made up the Bamaga community. Willy had often heard about Bamaga but was quite surprised at how big it was and how well developed it appeared to be.

Mr Jemmerling said, "We are approaching the Bamaga airstrip. It was built by American Army engineers during World War Two and the airfield was called Henderson Field or, more commonly, Jack Jacky airstrip. Now it is called the Injinu Airport. We are going to fly past at a thousand feet, then come down to five hundred for a second circuit. As we do, we will hopefully see three aircraft wrecks."

There was a pause and then Mr Jemmerling went on, "My local map tells me there are the wrecks of a D.C. 3, a 'Kittyhawk', and a 'Beaufort' bomber."

It was midday by this time and the land had heated up so that the turbulence was very noticeable. As the Catalina bumped and swooped through the thermals Willy tightened his seat belt and looked out. Clearly in view was the bitumen road from Bamaga town to the airstrip. Following instructions over the intercom from Mr Beck he had no trouble in locating the DC3 wreck just after they flew over the gravel road that went off to the south.

The bitumen runway came into view and then slid astern. As he looked out, Willy realised he could see right across Australia at that point.

That is the Coral Sea I can see out to port and the Gulf of Carpentaria to starboard, the Pacific Ocean on one side and the Indian Ocean on the other.

That realisation gave him a definite thrill and sense of adventure. Then his attention was taken up by the buffeting of the aircraft as it banked around to port across the mudflats and mangrove swamps along Jacky Jacky Creek.

Bit bumpy, he thought, but it did not bother him and he was able to focus his eyes on the areas where Mr Beck was now saying the other wrecks were.

Because the country was covered in savannah woodland and not scrub or jungle, and using a couple of dirt roads as references, Willy was able to locate the wreck of the 'Beaufort'. He saw it was in a clearing with a ring road around the pieces of wreckage.

Of the 'Kittyhawk' wreck he saw nothing. The Catalina kept on, flying a big oval course; north towards Bamaga, then coming around to do a southerly run, coming lower as it did. This increased the turbulence and Willy noted Marjorie looking a bit pale and tense.

On this 'pass' Willy noted that the DC3 wreck was directly in line with the runway.

Crashed while landing? he wondered.

They flew on over the airport and its one building terminal. Outside on the bitumen apron were two small twin-engine aircraft. Several vehicles, including a white mini-bus stood in a car park. At least twenty people stood out in the open, staring up and waving.

The Catalina flew past them and then turned and went around the end of the runway back to the location of the 'Beaufort'. As it did, the turbulence became so rough that Willy at last began to become concerned. At the 'Beaufort' wreck the aircraft was taken around in a tight circle, left wing down. This allowed Willy a really good view and he was able to take some photos.

"I wonder why it crashed?" he said to no-one in particular.

Andrew answered, his voice sounding quite anxious, "Probably doing the same thing we are."

"Don't you like it Andrew?" Stick asked.

"No. It's bloody rough. I've never been seasick but this is getting at me," Andrew replied.

Marjorie added, "I will be sick if we keep doing this."

Luckily for her they didn't. The Catalina banked and then straightened up, to make a landing circuit. Once again, the turbulence was bad and Willy felt a few uneasy twinges as the machine sank and swooped in the heated air.

One particularly sickening lurch even had him mutter and say to himself, "Bloody hell, we will join the DC3 if we aren't careful!"

The buffeting continued, Willy very conscious of the way his seat belt kept pulling at him as the plane dropped and then felt loose as it was lifted abruptly on a thermal. He watched the wings wobble as the pilot tried to hold the aircraft steady.

Stick looked down. "We are just passing over that wrecked D.C. 3."

A very anxious looking Marjorie said, "There are an awful lot of aircraft wrecks around here. I hope it is safe."

Willy reassured her. "This is a good aeroplane, tried and tested."

"Yeah, seventy bloody years tried. That is old and worn out," Stick said as another updraught sent them into a sickening swoop.

"It has been fully reconditioned," Willy said, but as he did the aircraft dropped suddenly, sending his stomach into his throat.

A niggling little worry about pieces of wire being repeatedly bent caused him to think that perhaps something could go wrong with such an old aircraft.

Landing and taking off are the most dangerous times, he reminded himself.

Then the plane lurched, slewed, and dropped.

Chapter 18

TORRES STRAIT

Just as Willy felt a rush of fear the pilot regained control. Willy heard the engines roar and saw that the flaps were fully extended. To his relief, he saw the boundary of the airstrip slip past underneath. He badly wished he could see out the front and that he was in control.

I'm not a good passenger, he thought.

By then the landing gear had been extended and Willy watched with interest as the wheel on his side came closer and closer to the dry, brown grass. This was suddenly replaced by bitumen and Willy felt easier. Then the rubber tyre made contact and there was the usual puff of smoke and screeching noise and then they were down, the tyre spinning and rolling easily.

The Catalina was taxied in and parked beside a 'Metro'. Once the propellers had stopped Harvey came through and told them they could all get out and move to the terminal building. They did this, Andrew loudly saying how glad he was to be on the ground again. "I think I'll stick to ships in future," he said.

There was quite a welcoming group there. At first Willy just thought they were people who were waiting for an aircraft but then he realised that they were gathered to see the Catalina. Mr Jemmerling stepped off to a greeting by local leaders and even a news reporter with a camera. Mr Hobbs and Harvey moved Willy and the other the passengers to one side once that was all done.

It was very hot out in the sun and Willy gladly moved to the shade of the terminal, a shed with a small office at one end and toilets on the side. It was stifling inside but still cooler than outside. While there, Willy saw a group of school children being led forward to look at the aircraft. To add to Willy's sense of being in a 'foreign' place, he noted that nearly all the school children were indigenous. Mr Jemmerling spoke to them for a few minutes, then left the crew to look after the visitors while he walked over to the terminal.

For the next half hour the group enjoyed a picnic lunch. Willy sat with Marjorie and his parents, and they discussed what they had seen during the flight.

"There is a lot of wild country in Cape York Peninsula," Willy commented.

"Certainly a lot of nothing much," his father agreed.

When the school group had inspected the aircraft, the aircrew joined them for lunch. Willy enjoyed a bottle of cold lemonade and was able to relax and even daydream a bit. He found it all quite different, especially being outnumbered by black people. He had seen plenty in Cairns. There were at least fifty at his high school, but in the normal course of his life he rarely met one, other than Torres Strait Islanders like Luke. Here the indigenous people were the majority and on their 'home ground'.

A cheerful white man in shorts, and open shirt and thongs arrived and announced he was their driver. The group, including the aircrew, was ushered out to where the mini-bus waited. Willy climbed in and allowed Marjorie to sit beside him. When all were aboard the bus drove out of the car park and along a bitumen road in savannah woodland.

Five minutes later they reached the junction of the road to 'The South'– to Weipa and Cairns. They turned left and then almost immediately turned left again onto a dirt track through the trees. A minute later they parked near the DC3 wreck.

Willy found the visit to the wreck disturbing and saddening. He noted that the machine must have come down among trees, ripping its wings off and then smashing in its nose and breaking the fuselage in two. When he read that it was a civilian airliner, belonging to Australian National Airways, and flown by a civilian pilot he was surprised. He had assumed it was a military aircraft. Then when he read that the plane had flown all night from Archerfield near Brisbane to Bamaga, with refuelling stops at Cairns and Cooktown he shook his head.

The pilots must have been exhausted, he mused, picturing them trying to do a night landing on an unfamiliar strip. *This area is up on a sort of ridge, much higher than the actual runway,* he noted. *Perhaps they just miscalculated how high above the ground they were?* Whatever the cause, he felt it was an avoidable tragedy. *When I am a pilot, I will try to be more careful,* he thought.

What also surprised him was what good condition much of the wreck was in. The aluminium skin and spars mostly looked to be in reasonable condition, only a bit tarnished. Even some of the rubber was still not completely perished. Several parts looked so shiny and new it was hard to believe they had been lying out in the weather for seventy years.

As he studied the mangled and torn wreckage, Willy tried to imagine what those last seconds might have been like.

Did the passengers have any warning? he wondered, *or did it all just happen in a few horrible seconds?*

Reading the memorial plaque with the details and the names of the victims made Willy feel even sadder and he could only shake his head. He moved away from the others, not wanting them to see his emotion. It was sweltering hot and he was sweating profusely but he ignored this and moved slowly around, taking photos from several directions.

Then it was back into the mini-bus and they drove back to the main bitumen road and turned right, heading back towards the airport. At the bend which was in line with the end of the cleared strip, the bus turned left onto a dirt track. This went east across the end of the airfield and then into the forest. This was real savannah woodland of eucalypts, mostly iron barks, but with thick patches of cycads and an undergrowth of smaller trees.

All the way along this track Willy saw hundreds of rusting 44-gallon drums, obviously left from the war. There were so many he was astonished.

"Surely they would have been worth collecting?" he said.

"I think all the good ones were," Mr Beck answered.

The next site they came to was labelled on the tourist map Mr Jemmerling had as the 'Kittyhawk' site. But, to complicate matters, the RACQ road map that Willy's father had named the site as being that of a crashed 'Hurricane'.

"I didn't know there were any 'Hurricanes' in this part of the world," Willy commented. "They had three squadrons of 'Spitfires' at Darwin, but I have never heard of the RAAF having 'Hurricanes' in Australia."

None of the others had any answer to that but Mr Beck said, "It may not have been, but in any case, whatever it was, there is almost nothing left to see."

He was right. In a dusty little clearing among the cycads and gum trees lay a few torn sheets of metal and some unidentifiable pieces of machinery and the remains of a small cairn that had been smashed by vandals. Seeing the broken memorial really angered Willy.

What sort of low, cowardly mongrels would do a thing like that? he wondered.

As they stared at the bare earth and paltry remains Stick said, "Not much left alright."

Mr Johnson, the pilot, said, "Maybe it nosedived in and burst into flames. That wouldn't leave much."

"Maybe," Stick answered. Then he said, "Gawd, I hope there's a bit more left of the 'Kittyhawk' we are going to recover."

At that Willy felt a stab of anxiety. He noted how Mr Jemmerling and Mr Hobbs both looked at Stick with great interest. "Stick!" he hissed, wishing he could warn him not to say more without being too obvious. Marjorie glared at Stick, who only then realised what he had done. "Oops!" he muttered, making it worse.

As soon as he was able to do so without Mr Jemmerling or Hobbs noticing Willy nudged Stick and hissed, "Stick, be careful what you say."

"Sorry. I'll try," Stick promised.

The next site, the 'Beaufort' bomber wreck, was a few kilometres further along on a sandy side track. This wreck had no nose or cockpit section but the tail section and the middle part of the fuselage, including the mid-upper gun turret were plain to see. So was the central portion of the wings, complete with what remained of the two motors and the undercarriage. This section was upside down and Mr Beck explained that the wreck had originally been strewn over a large area, but the pieces had been moved to one location.

Once again, Willy found it sobering and saddening. He looked at the broken and empty mid-upper gun position and tried to imagine what it must have felt like for the gunner.

He would have had no control over what happened, he mused. *Those last few seconds when it was obvious they were going to crash must have been awful,* he thought.

Stick studied the wreck from all angles while Willy and most of the others took photos. Willy's father got him to pose in front of the wreck and then said, "Still want to be a pilot, Willy?"

"Yes Dad," Willy replied firmly.

Mr Johnson, the pilot, gave a short chuckle, then said, "Just remember the old saying young fella: 'There are old pilots, and there are bold pilots, but there are no old and bold pilots'."

Willy had heard the saying before but smiled and nodded. "I will," he replied.

He went back to studying the wreckage. As with the DC3 he was amazed that some of the machine parts in the undercarriage were still a shiny silver and there were even intact panels of Perspex in places. Because the fuselage section lay open to his view, he was able to study in detail how the aircraft had been constructed.

Stick commented on how some of the aluminium was rotten. "Weathered or oxidized," Willy corrected. Then he saw Stick poke at the skin of the wing with a stick, punching a hole in it. "Stick! Don't damage it any more," he snapped, instant anger welling up.

"Sorry!" Stick retorted in a sarcastic tone. "So what? The bloody thing is already all smashed up."

"Because it's... it's a war grave, I mean a war memorial. Men died in this plane while serving Australia. It doesn't show respect," Willy replied hotly. 'Sacrilege' was the word that came to mind but he did not use it. Stick had the good grace to blush but Willy didn't think he was convinced so he added, "If everyone breaks a bit there will be nothing left in a few years."

As he said this Willy noted nods of approval from both Mr Beck and Mr Jemmerling.

It was nearly 3:00pm by then and sweltering hot so Willy was glad to climb back into the relative comfort of the air-conditioned min-bus. He drank another bottle of cold softdrink and wiped perspiration from his face. They were then driven back to the airport. Here there was a half hour wait in the terminal building while the aircraft was refuelled. Once the pre-flight checks were done, they were told to get aboard.

By this time it was so hot the metal burnt the skin and Willy could see a heat haze shimmering across the airstrip. *This could be a bit bumpy,* he thought. He noted that Marjorie looked quite pale and that Andrew was obviously anxious.

The engines were started and the checks of the controls done, then Harvey climbed aboard and waved the airport attendant away with the wheel chocks. When he was clear and had given the thumbs up to the pilot the Catalina began to move, turning and rolling out to the runway. There was no taxiway, so they had to taxi along the runway to the end, facing the same way that they had landed. As the Catalina pivoted on its port wheel Willy got a clear view along the strip and saw that the heat shimmer seemed to be even worse.

I hope this old crate is up to it, he thought.

Next the engines roared on full power with the brakes applied and Willy tightened his seatbelt. Harvey came along and checked they were all securely strapped in, then reported to the flight deck. Almost at once the motors roared again and the plane began to roll. Willy was both amazed and concerned at how much it seemed to bounce on the bitumen surface. He saw the undercarriage flexing and the wing tip bending up and down.

This is going to be rough, he thought.

It was. The Catalina roared along the runway and then lifted off alright, despite the bouncing and shuddering, but as soon as it was airborne it began to bump and drop. Willy held on and tried to stay interested but realised he felt scared. As the aircraft clawed its way up into the heated air Willy tried to locate the wreck of the 'Beaufort', which he knew was somewhere out in the bush to port, but he was quite unable to. That irritated him and also hurt his pride.

I know just where it is. I should be able to spot it, he thought.

Once the Catalina had gained about a thousand feet it swung around to port and headed northwest. The turn took them out over the twisting course of Jacky Jacky Creek and its maze of waterways and mangroves. Willy looked for crocodiles but saw none. All he could detect back to port was the clearing of the airstrip and the smoke of a small bushfire off near the west coast. This showed as a hazy grey line.

Their route took them back over the town of Bamaga and on across the west coast. Once again, Willy was struck by how empty of settlement the whole region was, the few dirt roads snaking off through vast areas of bush. Then the west coast of the cape slid by underneath, resulting in much improved flying conditions. Willy looked out with interest and consulted his map. He was able to identify large mass of Prince of Wales Island.

As he stared at this, Mr Jemmerling came on the intercom and said, "If you look out to starboard you will be able to see Cape York and Possession Island."

Willy undid his seat belt and moved to look through Marjorie's porthole. He identified the tip of the cape and also Possession Island. He was also surprised at how many islands he could see, and at how dry and brown they looked.

As they flew over a small island west of Possession Island, he noted that it was almost bare of trees. The sea was very shallow in many places, sand bars and rocky reefs being very evident.

"That is the Endeavour Strait," he said to Marjorie.

"I thought it was the Torres Strait," she replied.

That stumped Willy a bit. "It is, but the narrow bit between that island and the mainland is named after Captain Cook's ship."

He returned to his seat and looked out to port. As he did, the eastern coast of Horn Island slid beneath them. Again Willy was surprised. "It is really brown and dry," he commented, "It looks just like the area near Townsville Airport."

Now he noted several concrete structures and then whitish circles which he knew to be concrete gun tubs made in World War Two for anti-aircraft guns. He was aware that there had been an airfield constructed here during the war and was interested to see what physical remains there might be.

The Catalina flew right across the island in a few minutes. As it did, Willy got a good view of the airport, noting two main runways at right angles to each other. He also saw that the airport was set in an extensive area of dry scrub and that, apart from the cluster of buildings beside the runways the country around it was almost empty of any settlements. A single bitumen road led away to the west to where a town nestled on the coast at the other end of the island. A few dirt vehicle tracks wound through the bush.

Into view came an area of ocean and then another island. Willy knew instantly that this was the fabled Thursday Island, the 'T.I.' of legend. By then the Catalina had descended to about 500 feet but the turbulence was not too bad. Through his porthole Willy saw that they were going to do a complete circuit of the island. Mr Jemmerling informed them of this, and Marjorie came over to look through his window, leaning over so that her bosom rested on his shoulder and half-filled his vision.

Thursday Island was hillier than he had expected. On the eastern end he saw huge wind turbines rotating, generating electricity. Further around, on the north coast, there were water reservoirs and a scattering of houses. The much larger Hammond Island lay close to starboard. The northwest corner had another suburb and then he glimpsed the Green Hill Fort.

That is a place I would like to visit, he thought, when Mr Jemmerling read from the guidebook, telling them that the fort was built before World War One. The hospital and then the main town and wharves came into view. Willy noted numerous small boats on the beach and at anchor, plus a few larger launches, but no ships. He also noted that there were quite a large number of people along the foreshore and out on the wharves.

"They know we are coming, and we are going to put on a short display for them and then open the aircraft up for inspection," Mr Jemmerling explained. "But first we will drop you off on Horn Island where we are staying tonight."

The Catalina then flew the length of the roadstead before banking sharply and coming back even lower and closer to the water. This put Thursday Island on the starboard side. Willy remained in his seat and heard Andrew muttering about seeing a Customs launch and then a navy patrol boat. After flying almost across to Prince of Wales Island the plane swung around and came back on a landing approach. As Harvey came along to check they were all strapped in Willy watched the wing tip float swing down and then the flaps extend.

It was a good landing, much smoother than Willy expected, and he thoroughly enjoyed it.

I love the way the spray flies up past the windows, he told himself.

For five minutes the Catalina taxied along close to the waterfront of Thursday Island. Willy saw hundreds of people waving and watching so he waved back.

Mr Jemmerling is doing a good thing, he thought, *even if he is going to charge these people money to visit the plane.*

The Catalina then swung to starboard and buffeted its way into a metre high chop across the two kilometres or so of water between Thursday Island and Horn Island. This took another ten minutes, and they came to a bobbing standstill close to the jetty and slipways at Wasaga. The Catalina was driven up onto the bottom end of a wide, gently sloping concrete ramp. "This was the hard and slipway used by the Ansett Airways Flying Boats in the Nineteen forties and Nineteen fifties," Mr Jemmerling explained as he joined them in the cabin after the motors were switched off.

"What type of flying boats were they sir?" Willy asked. He thought he knew but did not want to appear a 'know-all'.

"They were mostly converted 'Sunderlands', and a civilian version called the 'Sandringham'," Mr Jemmerling answered.

Willy nodded. *I was right,* he thought, picturing RAAF 'Sunderlands' on patrol, searching for German U-boats.

The group was then told to collect their gear and disembark. One by one they passed out their bags to Harvey and Mr Hobbs and then climbed down the short ladder. As soon as he was on the wet concrete ramp Willy was directed up past the bow to where a white min-bus waited. Here he joined the others and met the driver, a very pleasant and attractive lady.

"Please hop into the bus and I will take you to the resort," she said.

"May we watch the Catalina leave?" Willy asked.

"Certainly," she answered.

They climbed in and sat watching. Willy noted that Mr Jemmerling did not join them, but that Mr Hobbs did. Harvey folded up the steps and climbed back into the aircraft. As it was sweltering in the small bus the driver turned on the engine and the air conditioning while they waited. The Catalinas' brakes were released and it rolled slowly back into the water. A bow rope was thrown to a big Torres Strait Islander in an aluminium dinghy with an outboard motor. This then acted as a tow rope to spin the aircraft around. Once it was facing away from the shore the tow rope was cast off, the dinghy motored out of the way and the aircraft's engines were started. The Catalina then taxied off towards Thursday Island, the slipstream showering the waiting bus with a misty spray.

The bus was quickly driven away from the sea. The route was along the streets of the small town of Wasaga. To Willy it all looked fairly ordinary, but very dry. A few blocks away the bus parked at the 'Gateway Torres Strait Resort'. This was where they were staying for the night, and they unloaded their bags and went inside to register. They were then shown to their rooms. The resort was all one story with a large dining room and a bar and cabins and a swimming pool beyond the courtyard. It was all very pleasant and looked comfortable and clean. Of more interest to Willy was the discovery that the fourth side of the courtyard was taken up by a large hall that housed a museum.

TORRES STRAIT HERITAGE MUSEUM and ART GALLERY read the sign. This also listed the times and admission prices.

I must have a look in there, Willy told himself.

He was shown to a room which he was to share with Stick. As soon as he had placed his bags in the room, Willy went back out and asked if he could visit the museum. The driver, now acting as the receptionist, smiled, and nodded.

"It is paid for as part of your accommodation package," she explained.

Willy made his way to the museum and went in, followed by the others. Inside he found it was a large hall. Nearest the door on the left was an audio-visual display. All of one side was devoted to Horn Island during World War Two with hundreds of photos and signs explaining them. The other side included a Melanesian cultural display, models of pearling luggers, historical photos of Thursday Island and Horn Island; and an art gallery of paintings depicting Torres Strait myths and legends. There were also numerous artifacts such as drums, masks, spears, models of outrigger canoes and the headdresses called Dharis.

After a quick walk around to sample the range of items on display, Willy started at the beginning of the World War Two section. There were not only numerous photos but also a lot to read. These included signs, memoirs, books, and pamphlets. It was all very well set out and easy to follow. The first fact that he learned which surprised him was that Horn Island was the first place in Queensland to come under Japanese air attack during the war.

"I didn't know that," he commented to Marjorie.

Willy picked up a pamphlet and read the details, noting that the first raid was on the 14th of March 1942. The first Japanese raid comprised eight 'Zero' fighters and 12 'Betty' bombers. They were met by American 'Kittyhawk' fighters of the 7th Squadron, 49th Fighter Group and were led by Captain Bob Morrissey.

A painting nearby illustrated a critical moment in the resulting air battle when one of the American pilots, Lt House, having used his ammunition in shooting down one enemy plane then used his starboard wing tip to slice through the cockpit of another Zero which was on Captain Morrissey's tail.

That was a gutsy thing to do, Willy thought. It got him wondering if he would ever have the skill to do something like that, or even if he could. *Could I fire at another aircraft, knowing that I might kill a person?* he wondered.

It was one of those niggling doubts and moral dilemmas he was starting to consider more and more.

Then Willy picked up a pamphlet which instantly gripped his interest. It was the photo of the three-engine flying boat that caught this eye first. Then he read the caption. It read: 'Dutch Dornier flying boats at Horn Island after evacuating civilians from Makassang, 18th Feb 1942.'

"Dutch flying boats!" Willy muttered. "I didn't know they ever came to this part of the world."

Chapter 19

GULF THUNDER

Willy bent to study the small black and white photo more closely. *Dutch 'Dorniers' for sure,* he told himself.

He read the snippet of information beside the photo. It read:

As the Japanese over-ran the Dutch East Indies the flying boats of the Dutch Naval Air Service were used not only for reconnaissance and bombing raids but also to evacuate people to safety. The two aircraft shown had just landed at Horn Island after rescuing VIPs, Senior Dutch Officers, and civilians from Makassang. They had been attacked and chased by Japanese fighters but managed to escape.

The story fascinated Willy and he felt a strong wish to learn more. It also appealed to his imagination.

That would have been a really worthwhile thing to do, to save those people from under the noses of the enemy, he mused.

Andrew interrupted him by saying, "Willy, come and look at this fabulous model of a pearl lugger."

Not wishing to be rude Willy did so. It was certainly an excellent model but did not really interest him. But he did learn that there had once been a great pearling industry centred on Thursday island, hundreds of small sailing ships: schooners and luggers, which took divers out to the shallow areas where pearl shell lay on the bottom. He had heard a bit about it but now learned a lot more and felt quite ashamed of his ignorance.

Stick gave him another insight into the pearl divers by trying on the old-fashioned brass diver's helmet that was suspended by chains from the rafters. "Try this Willy," he called.

Willy walked over and ducked down to place his head in the helmet. The instant impression was one of claustrophobia. He felt quite anxious and realised he could hear his own breathing.

You can't see much through these tiny little portholes, he thought.

He knew the portholes had to be small so that the glass would not crack under the pressure when deep down.

Stick added to the awful images by saying, "You wouldn't have got me down in one of these, having to depend on some joker up in the boat to keep the air supply going."

Willy knew the old-fashioned divers had been supplied by air through a rubber air hose from a pump up in the lugger.

Nor me! he thought, imagining the air hose getting cut or broken.

Stick called to Andrew, "Hey Andrew, stick this on. You are a diver, aren't you?"

Andrew looked and then shook his head. "Not for me thanks."

"Why, ya scared?" Stick sneered.

To Willy's surprise, Andrew nodded. "Yes, I am. I'm a diver, so I know how dangerous it was. My Grandfather died diving in a helmet like that," he said. He then looked quite upset and turned away, walking off.

Marjorie at once snapped at her brother, "Oh Stick! How could you be so insensitive? Don't you remember that horrible business last year when Andrew discovered his grandfather's remains in that old shipwreck?"[6]

"Yeah well! He'll be alright," Stick muttered, but he didn't look sorry.

Willy decided the best thing to do was allow Andrew to recover in private, so he went back to studying the war records. These included accounts of air raids by the Japanese, aircraft accidents, engineering works to improve the base, and details of the various air force and army units based at Horn Island. The number and variety of these astonished and interested Willy. 'The RAAF had three squadrons based here: 32 Squadron with 'Hudson' bombers, 75 Squadron with 'Kittyhawks' and 7 Squadron with 'Beauforts',' he noted. There were pictures and plastic kit models of each type and he studied these.

He noted that American aircraft of the 19th Bomb Group and 49th Fighter Group were based there, plus an American anti-aircraft unit, the 104th. The Australian army had engineers (17th Field Coy RAE), heavy coastal artillery and two batteries of anti-aircraft guns (the 34th Heavy AA Bty and the 157th Light AA Bty).

"There were also the 5th Machine Gun Battalion, 26th Infantry Battalion and the Torres Strait Light Infantry Battalion," Willy read.

[6] Read *Davey Jones's Locker* by C. R. Cummings

The photos of Torres Strait Light Infantry particularly held his interest. *They look very 'colonial' to start with,* he thought, seeing photos of strapping big black men in shorts, boots, and slouch hats but no shirts in 1942.

This was followed by one taken in 1943 in which they were all dressed in the standard khaki long trousers and shirts that the army wore at that time.

Mr Beck and Norman joined him. "Anything interesting, Willy?" Mr Beck asked.

"Here is a plane crash," Willy said, pointing to a photo of the wreck of a P-47 'Thunderbolt'. He read the caption, which told him that on the 19th of March 1944 the aircraft, flown by Wing Commander Lambert, had clipped the propeller of a parked 'Kittyhawk' with its undercarriage, then the tail fin of another 'Kittyhawk', causing them to collide with yet another 'Kittyhawk' that was parked in the stand-by area. 'All the 'Kittyhawks' belonged to No 86 Squadron but were empty,' it said.

Then Willy read aloud the last sentence which said, "The remains of the aircraft sits on the spot where she landed in 1944, the pilot having escaped with minor injuries." He turned to Mr Beck. "Maybe we could go and see that wreck if it is still there?"

"Possibly," Mr Beck replied. "Depends on my friend Mr Jemmerling."

"Friend?"

Mr Beck laughed. "Oh, he's been nice enough but there is no doubt we are in competition, and he is continually trying to trick me into giving away clues."

Norman laughed as well, then said, "Here's another aircraft crash, a B-17 this time."

Willy studied the photos and read the caption and felt sick. The plane had been a bomber named *Tojo Jinx* and had been carrying five members of a salvage crew who had been sent to retrieve what they could from another B-17 that had crashed a few days earlier. 'The aircraft, No.41-2421, flown by Major McPherson and with Lt Penick as co-pilot crashed on landing. The cause of the accident seemed to be the scraping of the large wing on the ground. All 10 crew and the five passengers were killed,' he read.

The image of the bomber exploding and burning the people to death appalled Willy, and he felt momentarily queasy.

Norman pointed to a photo which showed one of the B-17's engines lying where the plane crashed.

"We could see that," he suggested.

Willy shook his head. "I'd rather not," he answered. He moved on, to read about the work of the engineers and to look at a display to the 1st Australian Camp Hospital. Marjorie joined him and snuggled in. "What are you looking at?" she asked.

"Just seeing if any of these nurses are as pretty as you," he replied.

"Oh get away with you!" Marjorie squeaked in delight. She snuggled closer and hugged him.

"Stop that you two! This is a museum, not a playground," called Norman, grinning from ear to ear.

"Oh poo to you!" Marjorie called back, poking her tongue at him, then giving Willy a kiss on his cheek.

As she did, Willy's father and mother came in. She at once let go and Willy blushed fiercely. His parents made no comment, but he was sure that was the reason they made very sure that he and Marjorie got no opportunity to be alone that evening.

Willy's mother said, "It is nearly dinner time. You children go and have a wash and change and then join us in the dining room by seven."

"Mum! We aren't children," Willy protested.

"No, maybe not," Willy's mother replied, giving Marjorie a cautionary glance.

Willy again blushed. "But we haven't seen half of this museum yet," he protested.

"Doesn't matter. You will have time in the morning, now go!" his mother said firmly. Willy knew that tone of voice, so he went and did what he was told without further argument.

A shower, change of clothes then dinner in the restaurant followed. Willy enjoyed the food and was happy to discuss all they had seen during the day but found he was yawning by 8:00pm. Unable to think of any plausible reason that might allow him and Marjorie get away on their own, he had to sit with increasing frustration and then made excuses and went early to bed. He knew there was no chance of seeing Marjorie during the night as she was sharing a room with his mother, while his father shared with Norman.

During the night Willy had two bad dreams. When he woke, he could only remember snippets but the one that stuck in his mind was of him being in a large propeller driven aeroplane which kept losing altitude towards an ocean full of sharks. Finally it crashed, and as Willy struggled to get out of the door he saw below him in the sea the floating corpse being savaged by a huge shark.

Stick, who had shared the room, was not amused. "Gawd Willy, you tossed and bloody turned and kept groaning and carrying on. I wish you'd stop dreaming about Marjorie," he complained.

"I wish I had been," Willy replied, rubbing sleep from dry and tired eyes.

By 7:00am they were packed and ready. Ten minutes later they were in the dining room having breakfast. Willy pretended he was fine though in truth he felt awful and more anxious than he could justify. By 8:00am they were all back in the museum. Mr Jemmerling and the aircrew had not had the opportunity to visit the previous day so another hour was spent there.

This time Willy concentrated on the cultural side of the museum, studying the paintings of local legends and scenes and reading their stories. He found it all very interesting and decided that he particularly liked the rhythmic music of the Torres Strait. Several times a cheerful and chatty Mr Jemmerling spoke to him, and Willy was even more confused. Was Mr Jemmerling really the deadly rival or not?

He seems so open and nice, Willy thought.

By 9:30am the whole group was standing outside the resort, loading gear into the mini-bus. The aircrew were driven to the Catalina with the gear. Twenty minutes later the bus came back and the others climbed aboard. A short bus ride took them through open, dry bush to the remains of a B17 that had crashed. All that remained were the rusting remains of the engines and a few pieces of aluminium. After a few minutes for photos, they got back on the bus and travelled on to the airport, but they only drove around for a few minutes, then travelled back to the town. This time the mini-bus took them to the hard.

The Catalina was ready for take-off by then, having been refuelled and had its pre-flight checks mostly done. The group climbed aboard and settled in the same seats as the previous day. As he did, up his seat belt Willy experienced a sudden feeling of dread and wondered if it was a premonition.

Are we going to crash on this flight? he wondered. As he usually really enjoyed flying the vague feelings of apprehension bothered him. *I'm being silly,* he told himself. *We are mostly flying over land, or near it, on this flight.*

Some lunches in cardboard boxes were passed up to Harvey and Mr Hobbs. Then the door was closed the Catalina rolled back into the water. Willy watched with interest as it was towed away from the shore and turned around. Being so low to the water that some of the spray swept over his porthole gave him a peculiar feeling of sinking, but the flying boat bobbed about easily on the small waves. The motors were started and run-up, then the aircraft taxied out into the open water.

Despite Willy's irrational misgivings the take-off was uneventful. Once airborne the aircraft turned to starboard and flew over Horn Island and then over Prince of Wales Island. As it did, Willy glimpsed several large, ocean-going ships to the north of the islands.

They are in the main shipping channel through the Torres Strait, he noted.

The aircraft continued to climb, going up to 1,000 feet according to Mr Johnson. Through his porthole Willy could see east over the Endeavour Strait and was just able to pick out the coastal settlements near Bamaga: Seisia and Injinoo. He noted with interest that he could just make out the other side of the peninsula.

That is the Coral Sea in the distance, he told himself.

Their course then was southwards over the waters of the Gulf of Carpentaria, with the western coast of Cape York Peninsula a kilometre to port. Willy knew that this coast was very different from the east coast, but even so it made him shake his head. Below him slid mile after mile of shallow water full of sandbars and mudflats, seemingly endless beaches backed by low scrub and dry bush and huge tracts of mangrove swamps intersected by twisting creeks and inlets. And in all that vast expanse there was barely a hint of any sort of human settlement or development.

Half an hour's flying brought them to the Aboriginal community of Mapoon. This was easy to identify, located as it is on a narrow peninsula on the seaward side to the large estuary of Port Musgrave. Willy ticked it off on his map and returned to staring out at another fairly boring looking strip of sandy beach backed by swamp and scrub.

Andrew came and stood looking through the porthole in front of him.

Willy noted his continual glances from a chart he held to the coastline outside. "What are you looking for Andrew?" he asked.

"A place called 'Flinders Camp'," Andrew replied. "I presume it was used by Matthew Flinders back in 1800 or 1801 during his circumnavigation of Australia."

Stick, chortled with laughter and called, "You hear that, Marjorie? Another circumcision of Australia!"

Willy glanced at Marjorie, who blushed but giggled. His mother then called, "No more talk like that thank you!"

That caused Willy to blush and pretend he had not heard. Instead he looked down, hoping to see some sign of the camp. But he saw nothing.

Andrew shook his head and said, "No sign of anything. That must be the Pennyfather River down there and that means we are past it. Never mind, we will be passing Dyfken Point soon and I want to see that."

"Why?" Willy asked.

"Because this is the first piece of Australia's coast that we know for sure the name of the sea explorer who charted it," Andrew replied.

"Who was he?" Stick asked.

"A Dutchman named Willem Jansz or Jantzoon, back in 1606," Andrew replied. "He was the captain of a Dutch ship named the *Dyfken*. Dyfken means 'Little Dove'. He is credited with being the first European to discover Australia."

"I thought that was Captain Cook," Stick said.

"Captain Cook! Fair go Stick. He wasn't even the first Englishman to visit Australia. All he did was chart the east coast. He is important because he gave a good report, which was something Jansz did not do for this part of the coast," Andrew replied.

"I can see why," Norman commented. "Nothing down there but sandbars and swamp."

Willy could only agree. As they discussed this the beach ended in a very obvious cape, a very large bay opening up to port. *Albatross Bay,* he noted after studying his map. As they passed the end of the point Mr Jemmerling came on the intercom to inform them that they were detouring to overfly the bauxite mines and port of Weipa.

For the next fifteen minutes Willy was given a bird's eye view of the huge open cut bauxite mines and the rail system that hauled the red ore to the bulk loading facilities at Weipa. The Catalina then did a wide circle, allowing Andrew a good look at the huge bulk ore carriers moored in the Embley River and Willy a clear view of the Weipa Airport. Further inland he could just make out the runways, taxiways and buildings of the huge Scherger RAAF Base.

We aren't allowed to fly near it, he thought.

Then it was on down the west coast, the turbulence slowly getting worse as the air heated up. Mr Johnson took the Catalina up to 2,000 feet to ease the bumps a bit. The beaches began to alternate with low cliffs of red rocks.

"Bauxite," Willy's father explained. "That is the ore they use to make into aluminium."

"That is Pera Head, that rocky cape," Andrew said, adding, "The *Pera* was another Dutch ship that sailed past about 1623. She was with another ship called the *Arnhem.* The captain was Jan Carstenz."

"Arnhem!" Stick said. "Does that have anything to do with Arnhem Land in the Northern Territory?"

"Yes it does," Andrew answered. "Arnhem Land was named after the Dutch ship, which is named after a Dutch town."

"I thought Arnhem was an Aboriginal name," Stick commented.

"No, it is Dutch," Andrew assured him.

Norman now added, "Arnhem is the town in the Netherlands where the British paratroopers tried to capture a big bridge over the river Rhine during World War Two."

"The 'Bridge Too Far'," Willy said. "I saw the movie."

"That's the one."

The next place of interest, after many more miles of boring sandy beaches and uninhabited scrub, was the Aboriginal community of Arukun at the mouth of the Archer River.

As they flew off southwards across a vast area of mangroves and melaleuca swamps, Andrew said, "That is one of the places where Jansz had some of his crew killed by the Aborigines. He wrote in his report that it was all just a huge swamp full of black savages, mosquitoes and crocodiles, so the Dutch were never interested in setting up colonies or trading bases in this part of the world."

Willy could only agree with his assessment. *Even now it doesn't look very hospitable,* he thought. *Certainly no place to crash.*

A few minutes later, they passed another cape, this time a wide, bulge in the flat coastline with yet another twisting, swampy river pushing through sandy shallows into the sea.

Andrew pointed and said, "That is Cape Keer-Weer. That is Dutch and means 'Turn back', or 'Turn again'. It is where Jansz stopped exploring and went back to Batavia."

Dutch again! Willy thought. *I wonder what happened to Jacob van der Heyden? And what was he looking for?*

There followed another half hour of flying over vast stretches of sandy beaches and swampy flats. A cut lunch was served by Harvey and Mr Hobbs: sandwiches with cold fruit juice. As he nibbled at the 'ham, cheese and tomato' Willy kept looking out. Inland the savannah woodland stretched away unbroken until lost in the misty haze of the interior.

"We are moving into that vague area where 'The Peninsula' becomes 'The Gulf Country'," Norman explained. Over the years he had travelled extensively through the vast area of flat plains. "In 'The Wet' this whole area just becomes one gigantic, muddy lake, for hundreds of kilometres," he explained.

They flew over the very isolated Aboriginal community of Pormpuraaw. Willy noted and airfield and a collection of buildings and a lonely dirt road that wound off eastwards through the bush. His map told him that it connected with the Peninsula Development Road at Musgrave Station over 200 kilometres away.

Then there was more lonely scrub, mudflats, saltpan and swamp until they reached the mouths of the Mitchell River. Here Willy spotted several more large crocodiles. The saurians were basking on mudflats and slithered quickly into the brown, muddy water when the aircraft approached.

Saurians, Willy told himself. *Big, slimy reptiles.*

Then he remembered that the missing motor launch with 'Gator' Smith and his crony on it had been named the *Saurian*.

I wonder where those murderers have got to? he mused.

It was now 1:30pm and the course was changed to fly inland to follow the Mitchell River. As they crossed the coast the turbulence increased quite dramatically. Mr Johnson called to inform them they were climbing to 5,000 feet. Willy thought that a good idea.

Nothing much to see anyway, he decided.

He noted that the area below seemed to be just more winding river channels in mangroves, backed by huge swamps and areas of flat heathland or claypans.

He also noted that clouds were starting to appear; fluffy balls of cumulus, mostly at about 2,000 feet. The Catalina flew over the Aboriginal community of Kowanyama, significant because, unlike all the others, it was not on the coast. There was a spider web of dirt roads there and more signs of human settlement. Willy noted that there was a road all the way from now on, winding across the swampy flats and crossing dozens of winding creek lines. The homestead of 'Rutland Plains' station slid by underneath, a twinkle of iron roofs in a vast sea of hazy green.

Then it was on to 'Dunbar' Station. Willy began to get bored because of the sameness of the country. He also found it much harder to keep track of progress on the map because the features were so numerous and so similar.

"You could easily get lost flying out here," he observed.

He noted that the clouds were thickening. The number of cumulous clouds grew significantly in a very short time. They also showed signs of vertical development; the tops billowing and growing upwards as thermals pushed from within.

The aircraft began to buck and swoop quite noticeably. "Ten thousand feet," Mr Johnson called.

Up they went again, and Willy found it hard to pick out details on the ground. He lost track of where they were in the vast sameness of it all, just flat bush and winding, braided river channels and hundreds of dry creeks. The only thing he was sure of was that the Mitchell had very little water in it, its bed now mostly white sand studded with millions of trees.

An hour droned by, Willy half nodding off. The turbulence prevented this, but he found that he was becoming heartily sick of the loud roar of the radial engines. Marjorie was looking very pale again and Stick went off to the toilet several times. Willy thought this was to be sick as he came out looking very green and drawn. He went once himself and enjoyed stretching his legs and looking at different parts of the aircraft.

As he came out of the toilet Willy met Mr Jemmerling, who was coming down from the flight deck. Mr Jemmerling smiled but looked quite haggard to Willy. The aircraft was buffeted so badly by the turbulence that both had trouble staying on their feet and had to brace themselves against the sides of the corridor.

"Hello young Willy. Would you like to go up to the flight deck for a while?" he asked.

"I'd love to," Willy replied. "That is if you don't want your seat."

Mr Jemmerling shook his head. "No. I'm feeling a bit worn out and am going to have a little lie down for half an hour. You can take my place."

"Thank you, sir," Willy said.

After Mr Jemmerling had made his way into his sleeping cabin Willy walked forward. As he did, the plane dropped suddenly and he experienced that peculiar sensation of weightlessness, to be almost immediately replaced by the need to brace his muscles to hold him up as the aircraft was lifted just as quickly. With some difficulty he hauled himself up the narrow stairway to the flight deck.

Getting a bit rough, he thought.

As he climbed up onto the flight deck Willy looked out through the front windshield, and got a shock. Seemingly filling the whole windscreen and directly in their path was a gigantic cumulonimbus storm cloud!

Chapter 20

A NASTY SURPRISE

As his mind registered the massive size of the storm cloud, Willy experienced a spasm of what he was ashamed to admit was fear.

Holy Mackerel! he thought. *Surely we aren't going to fly through that?*

Before he could open his mouth to ask the question the aircraft dropped so suddenly he had to cling to the arms of the seats on either side. Willy felt himself go cold and saw that the co-pilot, young Hec, was wrestling with the controls. He steadied the machine, just before an updraught pushed it up again. The pilot, Mr Johnson, saw Willy and turned to him.

"Hello, are you a navy cadet or an air cadet?" he asked.

"Air cadet. I'm going to be a pilot," Willy replied, his eyes scanning the instruments and noting that they were still only at about 9,000 feet.

Young Hec laughed. "Good for you! This will be good practice for you then." He then turned to Mr Johnson and said, "Okay now?"

"Yes, don't get too close," Mr Johnson answered, turning to look at the massive cloud, then back at Willy. "You buckle up young fella. This could get a bit bumpy."

Willy lowered himself into the seat behind Hec and did up the seat belt. This took a bit of doing as the aircraft was now pitching quite alarmingly. Once again, he wondered if they intended to fly into the storm cloud but even as he did the Catalina began a gentle turn to starboard.

From up on the flight deck Willy had a much better view and saw that the massive cloud they were turning to avoid was only one of a whole line of similar storms. These extended in a rough north-south line as far as he could see in either direction. He noted that they had formed over a change of terrain. Below the clouds, half hidden in rain, were the beginnings of hill country.

Another vicious bump sent Willy's stomach into his mouth, and he gave Mr Beck an anxious grin. Mr Beck looked tired but managed a smile back. Then Willy studied the massive storm cloud. It was, he knew from Geography lessons, a cumulonimbus, a thunderstorm cloud. This one even had the classic 'anvil head' shape at the top. High above him Willy could see the top of the cloud billowing up and then spreading out as it met a layer of different air. Wispy streaks of cloud were starting to stream away from the very top.

He estimated that the top was at least 30,000 feet high. It towered up so high he had to bend his neck right back to look at it. The bottom was so low it looked to be dragging along the jumble of small, rugged hills in the savannah. He knew this was an illusion, that the usual height of the cloud base was between 1,000 and 2,000 feet. The base looked flat, and he knew strong winds were being sucked into it. The ferocious updraught was clearly visible, the middle of the cloud a seething, tumbling mass of billows.

From the direction they were approaching, with the sun shining directly on the cloud, it was a brilliant white, reflecting so much glare Willy wished he had his sunglasses on. There were only hints of grey and purple at the sides and base. Higher up there were touches of yellow and orange which made the monster amazingly pretty. Right up in the wisps streaming from the anvil head Willy noted a tinge of green.

Ice or snow, he thought.

Snow never reached the ground in tropical North Queensland. Instead it melted on the way down. Sometimes, at this time of year at the end of the dry season, the rain from high up did not reach the ground either but evaporated on the way down. Lightning flickered inside the cloud, and even as Willy looked he saw a bolt stab down from the base. He knew that aircraft flying into storms like that could experience such violent turbulence that they could suffer structural failure. Light aircraft even have wings torn off. So he was relieved that they were turning to avoid the threat.

The whole storm was only about 10 kilometres wide, but it was overlapping more storms behind it. No clear path to the east was visible. That got Willy staring anxiously out, seeking for a safe gap. Both the pilots were doing the same.

Mr Johnson saw Willy's anxious face and said, "Don't worry son, we aren't going to fly into that. If we can't find an easy way through the gaps, we will turn back and land."

Hec wrestled to restore the plane to an even keel as it shuddered and swooped. Then he laughed and said, "You remember young fella, when you are a pilot; in the tropics never fly into something you can't see through."

"I'll remember," Willy replied. He smiled, knowing he was scared but also enjoying the thrill of it.

As they flew around the side of the storm, Willy saw that there was a gap several kilometres wide between it and the one echeloned behind it. The Catalina kept on slowly turning, circling around behind the storm. As they did, Willy was enthralled by the spectacular changes of colour. Seen from the back the thunderstorm became a mix of grey, purple, and black, shot through with streaks of lighting. Up near the top and on the sides there were patches of brilliant white, orange and yellow and right at the top the whole anvil was shredding away, torn off by strong winds in long streamers of dark grey.

To starboard the next storm cloud was half in shadow from its giant neighbour, but the right half was white and grey. To Willy it was awe inspiring. The sheer scale to the storms made him uncomfortably aware that aircraft and modern technology still had definite limits.

Once clear of the second cloud, a course to the east was resumed. Willy noted that there were a few scattered clouds in the distance but otherwise the sky was clear. The air became smoother and flying became pleasant once more. He also noted how the shadows of the huge thunderstorms stretched for many kilometres to the east. Between the shadows were long strips of country that were brightly lit by the afternoon sun, giving a wonderful light and shade effect on the ranges of hills.

The country they were now flying over was a particularly rugged area. From the air it gave the impression of being chopped up into rugged squares like a giant block of chocolate, except that the hills were a bright yellowish green dotted with the darker green specs of trees. It made him wish he had his map with him. Out of curiosity he asked Mr Johnson what range it was.

"Those hills are called the Featherbed Range," Mr Johnson replied. "I suppose it was just the old pioneer's idea of a joke. They are the roughest lot of hills I know. You wouldn't want to have to try a forced landing down in there."

Willy could only agree. It was truly awful country. Out to his right he could see the course of the Walsh River winding through this rocky jumble. The valley of the Mitchell was in gloomy shade to the left. Ahead a peculiar, flat-topped mountain came into view. It was not very high but stretched right across their front and was fringed with steep cliffs which glowed like molten gold in the afternoon sun.

"What mountain is that sir?" he asked.

"Mt Mulligan," Mr Johnson replied.

Willy had heard of Mt Mulligan but never been there. "It was an old mining area, wasn't it?" he queried.

Mr Beck answered that. "Yes, coal. First there was gold mining nearby in the valley of the Hodgkinson. There was a town connected by a railway to the Cairns Railway at Dimbulah. It is the site of the worst coal mine disaster in Queensland's history. Back in 1921 that was. The mine exploded, coal gas, and killed everyone in the mine. About ninety men I think."

Willy stared down at the spectacular mountain with renewed interest. As they flew over the eastern escarpment of the plateau, he glimpsed a couple of buildings and a scatter of ruins, roads and tracks down in the valley beyond.

I must explore that one day, he resolved, thinking that from a light aircraft, lower and slower, would be ideal to start with.

They flew over the dry bed of the Hodgkinson, which, when it had water in it, flowed northwest to join the Mitchell. Mr Beck pointed out the scatter of buildings and ruins that marked the old gold mining towns of Thornborough and Kingsborough. As Willy tried to see these clearly, Mr Jemmerling re-appeared beside him. "Thank you, young Willy, but I'd like my seat back now."

Willy at once unbuckled his seat belt and stood up, moving to one side. Mr Jemmerling squeezed past and into the seat. Willy lingered for another minute or so, looking out and taking in everything that was occurring on the flight deck and on the instrument panel. In the distance, beyond another very rugged range of mountains he saw a long line of clouds right on the curve of the earth. Some were huge white piles and others in layers. The impression they made caused Willy to think of pictures he had seen of the icebergs in the Arctic.

I hope we don't have to fly through that lot, he thought, knowing that there were more big mountains ahead.

They didn't have to. By the time Willy had resumed his seat in the cabin they were over the next range of mountains and the town of

Mareeba was visible in the middle distance. He now saw that the cloud masses were piled on the mountains beyond. A few minutes later, they began their landing approach, wheels being lowered and flaps extended.

The rugged conical shape of Mt Abbott slid by to port and then they were low over open bush which abruptly gave way to ploughed fields and flat country. The airport boundary fence slid below and then they were down. It was a smooth and uneventful landing and they rolled to a stop outside the hangar where the journey had begun the previous day.

Feeling stiff, hungry and deafened, Willy climbed thankfully out of the Catalina. It had been a great experience. He was glad he had been given the opportunity, but he had also had enough for the time being.

When all were out and their gear unloaded, Mr Jemmerling thanked them for coming. "I hope you enjoyed it," he said.

"It was great. Thank you, sir," Willy said.

The others said thanks as well and Willy noted that there was a wary tenseness when Mr Beck and Norman said their thanks.

The competition begins again, Willy thought.

"Good luck with your prospecting," Mr Jemmerling called as they walked towards their vehicles.

"Thank you, same to you," Mr Beck replied.

As they reached their parked car, Willy said, "I didn't like the sound of that. He sounds very sure of himself."

"I wonder what he knows that we don't know that he knows," Stick said.

"Not much I hope," Mr Beck said. He then turned to Mrs Beck, who was waiting with their car. "Hello mother. All well?"

"Yes. Now, do you all want to come home for some afternoon tea before you start driving back to Cairns?"

Willy's mother and father looked at each other, obviously reluctant but Mr Beck said, "I would appreciate it. There are a couple of details about next weekend's trip that we need to pin down."

"Alright, but not for long," Willy's mother replied. "We want to drop in on Aunty Isabel for a few minutes as well."

They stowed their bags in the boots of the two vehicles and then climbed into them. Willy went in the back between Marjorie and Andrew. As they drove away from the airport he cast one last affectionate look at the Catalina.

Good plane Pterodactyl! he thought. He noted that Mr Jemmerling and his crew had gone inside the nearby building, so he did not wave.

It was only a short drive, 5 kilometres, all along a good straight bitumen road. The Becks led the way. After only a few minutes' drive they reached the turn-off, easy to identify because of the signs and the yellow painted 'Matilda' tank. As they slowed and turned in past the tank Willy noted a man sitting astride a motorcycle which was parked behind the tank. The man had his helmet on so his face was not visible. He appeared to be studying the tank.

The two cars drove into the car park, the Becks parking near the front gate of their new house, which is to the right of the museum. Willy's father parked on the left of the Beck's car. They all climbed out, chattering happily.

Mr Beck stretched and groaned, "Oh, it's good to be home! I'm getting a bit too old for jaunts like that. I... Hey! Who is that?"

Willy looked up and his eyes followed Mr Beck's pointing hand. He saw a man walking across the side yard of the Beck's, having obviously just come out of the back door. The man was dressed in grey overalls and looked to be about thirty, with brown hair. In his hand he carried a grey carry bag with a shoulder strap.

Mr Beck started forward, yelling, "Hey! You! Who are you? What are you doing in my yard?"

The man immediately broke into a run. "Burglar!" Norman cried. He opened the front gate and started running after him.

Mrs Beck cried out in horror, then called, "Oh Norman, be careful!"

Willy saw instantly that the man would be over the side fence before Norman could reach him.

That crook is heading for the highway, he noted.

Without further thought he started running diagonally across the car park, ignoring his mother's cry to stop.

Andrew and Stick set off after him, all shouting at the man to stop. Willy saw the man jump over the fence and sprint off into the belt of open savannah that grew between the house and the highway. As the man ran, he slung the carry bag over his shoulder, casting frequent glances back at his pursuers. Norman reached the fence and scrambled over it, jumping down twenty metres to Willy's left.

Willy raced into the bush in hot pursuit. The savannah was mostly ironbarks with almost no undergrowth and only knee-high grass. It was no obstacle to running and Willy pushed thoughts of snakes aside.

I can catch this guy, he decided as he began to close on the man.

The man was only fifty paces ahead and obviously made the same deduction. Up till then he had been running directly towards the highway, with Willy angling in on his right rear. Now the man turned and ran off at an angle, directly ahead of Willy. Norman, Andrew, and Stick, all came dashing along behind.

Willy began nerving himself to try to tackle the man, aware that it could lead to a violent struggle. As he ran he was dimly conscious of others yelling and of vehicles whizzing past at high speed out on the highway. An engine burst into life and roared. Sweat began to trickle into Willy's eyes and he blinked. Now he had run a hundred metres and was starting to gasp for breath. He was no athlete and knew it but he kept pushing himself as hard as he could.

As they ran, they drew closer and closer to the highway. *He might try to stop a car,* Willy thought.

But now he was only about 25 metres behind and was sure the man would not have time to do that.

The man broke out of the bush and began running away along the mowed verge of the highway. Willy reached the cleared lane and turned to follow. As he did, a motorcycle came racing up from behind him.

Whack!

Willy felt the blow without understanding it. The next thing he knew he was rolling on the dry grass and rough gravel beside the bitumen. Half stunned and wondering what was happening he looked up. He saw that the motorcycle had screeched to a stop just ahead of the running man. The man immediately leapt onto the pillion seat. As soon as he was on the motorcycle's engine roared and it sped off, spraying dust and gravel into the faces of Willy's friends. To Willy's chagrin the motorcycle accelerated and sped away towards Atherton.

Stick helped Willy to his feet. "You okay, Willy?" he asked.

"Yeah, what happened?" Willy asked angrily.

"The guy on the bike hit you under the ear as he went past," Stick said.

Willy watched with frustrated anger as the motorcycle vanished from view, racing away at full speed.

"Bugger! We need a car. Quick, back to the cars!" he cried.

He turned and was about to start running back to the car park when his father's car pulled up. It was driven by his father, who switched off and got out. Willy ran over to it.

"Dad, don't stop! After him! They will get away!"

Willy's father shook his head. "No. I am not going to try chasing a motorcycle all over the Atherton Tablelands. That is a job for the police. Now, are you hurt? I saw that brute knock you down."

"I'm fine!" Willy cried in angry frustration.

He was aware that his head did hurt a bit and that he had some gravel rash but he ignored it. His father pulled out a mobile phone and called the police, then said, "You lot quickly write down any details, descriptions of what those men looked like, their clothes and so on, and their motorbike type and number."

That made Willy feel foolish. He hadn't thought to note the registration number of the motorcycle. He wasn't even sure what colour it was. Luckily Andrew had got that information. Stick knew his motorbikes and was able to provide the details of brand name and colours.

"Right, back to the house and we will wait for the police," Willy's father ordered.

He waited for them to climb in and then started the car and swung it around. A minute later he parked it back in the car park. They were met by Willy's mother, who at once began to fuss over the blood trickling down from his right knee. She hustled him into the house and Marjorie and Mrs Beck joined in worrying.

"Never mind me," Willy cried in exasperation. "It's only a scratch. What happened? What did the burglar take?"

Mr Beck came through from his study and Willy could tell by the expression on his face that it was bad news.

Mr Beck said, "He's taken all my information on the plane wrecks. All of it."

Willy was stunned. He shook his head in disbelief, then said, "Does that mean we can't find them?"

"Mr Beck shook his head. "No, but it will be a lot harder, and it means someone else wants them very badly and they might be trying to beat us to them."

"Oh no! We must hurry! We can't let those crooks get there first!" Willy cried.

Chapter 21

WILLY IS IMPATIENT

As the implications of the theft sank in Willy was aghast. "We must do something. We can't just wait and let those crooks find our wrecks."

"Not much we can do. We don't have a ship until next Saturday," Willy's father pointed out.

"Can't we see if Captain Kirk can start earlier?" Willy asked. His impatience was rapidly rising.

Mr Beck shook his head. "I believe he has another contract until then."

"There must be other boats!" Willy cried.

"Then you find one and hire it," his father said. "Now calm down and let your mother wash that gravel rash."

His mother nodded and bent to dab antiseptic on the scratches. "You have another week of school too," she pointed out.

"School! Oh piffle!" Willy snorted. "All the exams are done. We are just filling in time."

Stick now said, "There must have been two of them. That bloke on the motorcycle must have been watching."

"He was," Willy agreed. "I saw him looking at the yellow tank but thought nothing of it. I would have caught that bloke but for him."

"And probably had more than a few scratches to show for it!" his mother snapped. "Now sit still. Marjorie, pass me that bandage."

Willy looked up at Mr Beck as his mother began bandaging. "The crooks must have been waiting until there was no-one home so they could break in and steal your maps Mr Beck," he said.

Mr Beck nodded and aid, "Looks like it."

"But how would they know we were away?" Willy asked.

Norman answered. "It was no secret. We told plenty of people we were going."

Willy thought about that but was puzzled. "But if they go to the wrecks we might catch them there, or we will know who ends up with them. I don't see how they think they can get away with it."

"They might sell them to someone else who will deny it," Norman said.

"Jemmerling," Stick cried. "I'll bet he paid them to do it."

"Be fair Stick," Mr Beck replied. "You have no proof that Mr Jemmerling had anything to do with it."

"Yeah, but it looks mighty convenient to me. He hires the crooks, then takes us all away for the whole weekend to give them a chance to steal the maps," Stick replied.

To Willy that sounded plausible, but he felt quite uneasy about it. "Mr Jemmerling has just given us a real treat. I don't believe he is like that."

"I've heard he is a really unscrupulous character," Mr Beck said. "There have been stories for years about how the Jemmerling Collection was put together. But I still don't like to think ill of a man who has just done me a favour."

They left it at that because the police had arrived. For the next hour they were all busy being interviewed. The police examined the back of the house and reported that the back door had in fact been broken open. The whole incident left a bad taste in Willy's mouth and threatened to destroy his satisfaction over the weekend flights. Already he sensed that it would linger in his memory as one of the great flights of his life.

It was well after 5:00pm before they left. This necessitated phone calls to Andrew's and Stick's parents to warn them that they were all safe but would be late. On the way they stopped for a few minutes at Aunty Isabel's. It was nearly 7:00pm before they dropped Andrew at his home and by the time they had dropped Marjorie and Stick and driven home it was just before 8:00pm.

During the whole evening Willy puzzled and fretted over the robbery. *Who did it, and why?* he wondered. He found it hard to believe that Mr Jemmerling might have been behind the theft. *I like him,* he thought.

Besides, Willy felt grateful for the Catalina flight. So all he could do was carry on with his normal life while feeling irritable and wish they could move faster.

Monday came, starting the last week of school. Willy found that very irritating. With Captain Conkey away at the Army Cadet Promotion Course and half the students absent, for all sorts of vague reasons, there was no real study to be done. During History and Geography the rump of the class was joined to another and supervised by the Chemistry teacher, who had no interest in teaching anything. So Willy just sat and fretted.

After school he made his way to the city and purchased a couple of 1:50 000 scale topographic maps of the Bathurst Bay area, just in case. He also went to the library and borrowed some books on the early sea explorers of Australia. These at least kept his mind occupied. The on-going arguments between the historians who claimed that the Chinese charted the coasts of Australia in 1421; those who gave the credit to the Portuguese under Cristovao de Mendonca exploring the east coast in 1520 or 1521; and those who clung to the more traditional views that it was the Dutch, Jansz and so on, all kept him interested.

Willy also began packing and preparing for the expedition. To him the time seemed to drag, and he continually imagined the men locating the wrecks and hauling them away, although how and where to he could not decide. He became so short tempered and irritable his mother snapped at him to stop being impatient,

"And if you are bored, help by doing some weed pulling in the garden."

Each night his father phoned Mr Beck and they discussed both the expedition and the theft of maps and notes. The police made no progress in their investigation. That did not surprise Willy.

It will be just another 'break and enter' to them. It won't have a high priority, he thought.

Mr Beck assured them that he had purchased more maps and charts and was asking old friends for copies of clues.

Mr Beck also mentioned that the *Pterodactyl* had flown out that day and had not returned. He said the people at the airport had not been able to tell him where it had gone. All they could confirm was that Mr Jemmerling and his man Hobbs had been on board. This news disturbed Willy even more and his impatience gnawed at him so that he felt he had a physical itch.

Surely Mr Jemmerling isn't the thief? he mused. Then he shrugged. *If he is then he will beat us to the wrecks for sure.*

It was like this for the next four days. The only relief was a few cuddling sessions with Marjorie. At school he and his friends discussed every aspect of the proposed expedition and became increasingly excited as Friday drew nearer. The discussions also gave Willy more sober food for thought. Present at many of the meetings were not only people like Carmen and Tina but also Noddy and Luke Karaku and other friends.

So many people know about this expedition it is no secret, Willy thought. Then he worried about which one, if any, might be in the secret pay of rivals. *Our security isn't very good,* he mused.

The other distraction was getting his Christmas shopping done. This he found very difficult. *What on earth can I buy Marjorie?* he wondered. *What do you buy a teenage girl? And who else do I have to buy presents for, and what to get them?*

It at least kept him busy after school and on Thursday evening.

Friday came at last. That evening was the last Air Cadet parade for the year. Willy made sure his uniform was as perfect as he could, polishing and ironing and then, after dressing, studying himself in the mirror until his brother Lloyd teased him. His mother drove him there and he could hardly contain himself. All he wanted to do was tell everyone about the flight in the Catalina, but he was aware it would sound like boasting.

But it was Stick who did that, allowing Willy to put in seemingly modest additions. That was still enough to cause Finlay and others to turn up their noses in jealousy. The training paraded followed its usual course: first parade, an admin session during which he handed in his permission form and medical and Next-of-Kin forms for the January promotion course; and received an explanation of what to expect on the course; then drill and final parade. During the session on the promotion course Willy repeatedly thought about his friends on the Army Cadet Promotion Course.

It finishes in a few days' time. I wonder how they are all going? he thought. He also considered it a pity that the army cadets weren't coming on the expedition the next day. From what Mr Beck had said it was the one needing a bit of bushcraft. *Having expert navigators like Peter and Graham along would make things easier,* he thought.

That night he could hardly sleep for excitement. Willy had never been on a long sea voyage and was just a little anxious that he acquit himself well. *I don't get airsick, so I shouldn't get seasick,* he told himself.

The idea of being seasick in front of the navy cadets was not something he wanted to happen!

It was an early start in the morning. Willy was roused from a restless sleep at 04:30am. After a quick shower and shave he dressed in old dark blue longs and shirt, gym boots and cap. His kitbag was all packed and he had a second bag with hiking and camping gear, plus maps and books.

Before sitting down for breakfast he checked he had his camera, pocket magnetic compass and protractor. His father joined him at the kitchen table. As always, his mother fussed about all the usual perils: falling overboard, sharks, crocodiles and getting sunburnt. Willy took all this with good humour. He was too excited to be annoyed.

By 06:00am a taxi had taken Willy, his father and mother to the Portsmith wharf where the *Wewak* was berthed. They were met by Captain Kirk who was supervising the final loading of a large yellow coloured machine.

"For road making," he explained. "We are taking it to Cooktown."

Another taxi arrived and Mr Beck and Norman got out. Then a car deposited Andrew and Carmen. Mrs Collins got out to speak with Willy's parents. Willy was becoming a bit anxious by then as there was no sign of Marjorie. His anxiety increased when the mate, a tanned and chunky man named Lester Trembath, instructed them to bring their gear and to follow him. The group picked up its bags and walked along the wharf to the gangplank near the stern.

As he walked beside the landing craft, Willy was struck by the nautical smells; the salt, paint, diesel mixture. He had visited ships before and been on short trips on the ferry to Green Island and so on but had never been on a large vessel. He had seen the *Wewak* before but had never really taken notice of its construction and layout but now he was struck by the length and by the chunk of white painted superstructure at the stern. She had been built, he knew, as a navy LCT, a Landing Craft Tank. He was aware there must be room for heavy tanks to be driven on across the bow ramp but because of the high sides he could not see into the well deck.

Going up the gangplank and seeing the dark water below gave him more of a thrill than he expected.

I am afloat, he thought happily. *The adventure has begun!*

They were led onto a small space right at the stern, the deck seemingly covered with a capstan, chains, and an anchor, plus the usual deck clutter of cleats and bollards, and small hatches. A semi-inflatable power boat hung on davits over the stern. From there they were led through a door into the saloon. Just going inside changed everything when a strong draught of hot air and engine smells engulfed them.

Willy saw that one side of the space was taken up by steps

(companionways he was to learn) that led down to the engine room and up to the bridge deck, and by a tiny shower cubicle, a toilet, larder, and galley. The cook, a small bald man named Frank, leaned out to greet them, all the while wiping his hands on his apron. The starboard side of the saloon was a long dining table with bench seats on three sides, the longest against the starboard bulkhead.

Mr Trembath pointed at them and said, "The skipper said that it might be best if Mrs Williams and the two girls bunked down here. It isn't very private, but it is out of the weather and the toilet and shower are right there."

This was agreed to. Mr Trembath then pointed up the companionway on the port side. "Mr Beck, you and your son are to share the small cabin on the port side at the top of the companionway here." He then turned to Andrew and said, "You are Andrew Collins? Good. You share the aft cabin to port up there. Take the top bunk. The other belongs to the deckhand, Spike Hartnett. Now, you others come with me please."

The mate led them forward past the funnel and along a central corridor between the cabins occupied by the cook (to port) and the engineer (to starboard). This brought them to a door which led out onto a steel deck in front of the superstructure. The front end of this small space was a steel bulwark marking the rear of the tank deck. A canvas awning had been rigged across and canvas wind 'dodgers' and safety netting had been lashed along the railings on either side to make a relatively sheltered area.

"Sorry, but this is the best we can do for four of you. I think you had better fight it out among yourselves. There are four army surplus folding stretchers there for you to sleep on. You will need to change in the shower."

Willy looked around with some dismay. It all looked very primitive and open to the weather. Seeing his expression Mr Trembath laughed.

"You'll survive. This is the topics in Summer, not the North Atlantic in Winter. Besides, we just took a mineral exploration team up the cape and they managed okay."

Willy's father laughed and said, "It will be fine."

At that moment, Stick and Marjorie arrived with their parents. Marjorie jiggled with excitement, but Stick swore and said, "Bloody hell!" when shown the camp stretcher out on the deck under the tarpaulin.

Parents then looked through the accommodation and spoke to Capt

Kirk. Willy took himself out of the crush and stood looking forward from his sleeping area. In front of him was the tank deck, a well 3 metres deep with steel sides. Sitting in it were several vehicles including two small 'Four wheelers' and the road making plant. Willy used his imagination to picture it full of tanks and heading for that climatic moment of dropping the front ramp on an enemy held beach.

Have I got the guts to face something like that? he wondered.

From where he stood, he could not see over the front ramp. So he walked forward along a walkway on the outside of the steel walls of the well. Only steel wire handrails provided safety and he thought the water looked uncomfortably close.

Up on the starboard bow next to a huge pulley wheel over which the steel cable for the ramp ran, Willy could see back along the whole length of the vessel. It looked quite large from there, the double story superstructure looking quite substantial.

Andrew joined him, saying, "The skipper is chasing all the parents off now. We will get under way soon."

"Can't be soon enough," Willy replied impatiently.

A wiry looking middle-aged man in grimy overalls came forward and said, "Which one is Andrew? You are? I'm Spike. okay young fella, the skipper says you are my offsider so come with me."

Spike shook hands with Andrew and led him away, leaving Willy feeling quite left out. As the sun was now well up and there was almost no breeze Willy found he was sweating profusely. He made his way aft to the superstructure and joined the others on the deck near his stretcher.

Capt Kirk leaned over the wing of the bridge above them and called, "I'd like you all to stay there while we get underway, and please don't come up to the wheelhouse unless we invite you. The tide has just turned so we will be on our way."

Willy glanced over the side and saw that the murky green water had an obvious current in the direction they were pointing. He watched as Andrew and Carmen, both in blue work clothes and with gloves on, helped cast off and coil the mooring lines under the supervision of a burly man with a pipe stuck in the side of his mouth: Dan Appleyard, the bosun. Andrew and Carmen both seemed to know what they were doing and were given grudging approval at the way they did their work. Watching them at work really made Willy feel like a passenger.

The deck vibrated as the diesel engines increased their revolutions. Willy noted the bow of the vessel swing away from the wharf and experienced a peculiar sensation he did not like to label as fear. A man on the wharf, dressed in bright orange safety vest and plastic safety helmet, unhooked a rope (Which Andrew called a spring) and tossed it free. Andrew, Carmen, and Spike hauled it dripping in through a fairlead and set to work coiling it.

They look like they have been doing that for years, he thought, sensing that he was feeling both a bit useless and a bit jealous.

The vessel began to slide away from the wharf with barely a ripple, the speed increasing every second. Marjorie and Stick went to the rail to farewell to their parents but both Andrew and Carmen only gave their mother a brief wave. Then the engines rumbled faster, and Willy nodded.

"On our way at last!" he muttered.

There was nothing to do but stand at the rail and watch the vessel make its way past the dry dock and ship repair yard and the rows of moored trawlers. The bow swung to starboard, and Willy saw the mouth of Smiths Creek ahead, the wider waters of Trinity Inlet opening up. Once clear of the point, the landing craft turned to port down the main shipping channel past the bulk sugar terminal. There was a huge, slab-sided bulk carrier at the sugar terminal, but Willy saw that Andrew was staring ahead at two grey painted patrol boats at the navy base.

Between the sugar terminal and navy base was the Navy Cadet's depot, TS *Endeavour*. Both Andrew and Carmen stared hard at it but the place looked deserted. Willy had been there several times on visits but to him it was just a big shed and a few other buildings in a fenced-off yard.

Willy had never travelled down that part of the city by water so found it mildly interesting, noting the familiar buildings behind a line of oil wharves and general cargo wharves. Then they slipped past the old city wharves and the more familiar parts of the city waterfront: the Pier, Yacht Club, Tourist jetties, Marina and so on. Beyond them the inlet widened out, the channel marked by two rows of huge steel posts which seemed to march out to the distant horizon.

For a few more minutes Willy stood with the others looking alternately to port at the Esplanade and city and at the mangrove swamps lining the eastern side of the inlet. It was all very familiar and made him feel a sudden strong sense of 'home'.

Marjorie stood beside him, gently touching his arm and obviously happy to be with him. They were left alone for ten minutes, and Willy was quite surprised at how quickly the city seemed to recede. He knew that the *Wewak* could push along at about 12 knots.

That's over twenty kilometres per hour, he thought.

Carmen came and called them in for breakfast and Willy met the cook again and was squeezed in at the end cross bench next to Marjorie for a full breakfast of bacon and greasy fried eggs which he suspected was some sort of practical joke on the part of the cook.

He wants to see if we get seasick easily, he thought.

But he found he was hungry and ate as much as he was given. While he was eating his toast the vessel began to pitch ever so slightly as they began to encounter the small waves in the outer inlet. By the time breakfast was over the vessel had a pronounced movement, both pitching and rolling. It gave Willy a very uneasy feeling to see the whole horizon slide up and down across the port hole.

I hope it doesn't get any rougher than this, Willy thought, sensing that he might not be a very brave sailor.

It was an irritating and worrying idea which he tried to push aside. But when he went out on the aft deck and looked back towards the now distant city and land that was many kilometres away, he felt distinctly uneasy.

Oh well, nothing to do but act brave, he told himself. He was committed. *At least we are on our way at last!*

He leaned on the port rail and stared ahead, willing the LCT to move faster.

Chapter 22

COAST TO COOKTOWN

For the next ten hours, Willy mostly sat on a folding chair in what shade he could find and watched the coast slip by. To help him he had his air navigation charts. From time to time either Andrew or Carmen would stop and talk, looking at his chart and either pointing to places they knew or checking. Both had sailed that section of coast several times and were much more experienced. They were also allowed in the wheelhouse, indeed had to work there, taking turns at steering. That added to Willy's feelings of being a spare wheel. Ruefully he conceded that the weekend before it had been his turn to feel superior.

Luckily the weather, while extremely hot and humid, stayed fine. There was, so he was told by Carmen, only a gentle breeze of about 10 knots and the average wave height was only about 1 metre. The old LCT just slid across these with barely any unpleasant motion. Just the odd larger-than-normal wave threw up a shower of spray.

For most of the day there were almost no clouds but during the afternoon some large cumulus clouds formed over the coastal mountains, all trying to build into cumulonimbus. It was fascinating to watch but they were too far away to affect the voyage.

The first part of the trip was northwards and about 3 nautical miles offshore, the course leading the vessel past the northern beaches of Cairns: Machans Beach, Holloways Beach, Yorkeys Knob, Clifton Beach and Trinity Beach. Willy could clearly see such obvious features as Double Island and then Haycock Island. Buchans Point was easy to identify but after that the course trended slowly away from the coast so that the long stretch of mountains which had their feet in the sea as either rocky headlands or beaches was just too far off to make out details.

That big triangular mountain up on top of the coast range is Black Mountain, Willy observed.

Below it was one of his favourite beaches: Wangetti, but it was all but invisible over the curve of the earth.

Island Point and Port Douglas were easy to identify, and the course went close past the Low Isles. Willy had been there on holiday trips with his family. His parents came out to watch as the flat disks of the two islands slipped past. One was just a flat mass of mangroves which appeared to be sitting on the sea. The other was a ring of pure white sand backed by a belt of vegetation, all topped by the startling white finger of a light house. The sea between the two was a mixture of browns and light greens. Willy knew that the brown meant coral. A dozen tourist launches and yachts lay at anchor, and he could just make out divers in the water.

As the two islands slid astern, Willy was called in to lunch. This was cold meat and salad, so he made himself a corned beef sandwich, adding pickles for extra flavour. An hour later they passed a completely different island: Snapper Island, a 'high' island that was really an extension of the coastal ranges. It was ringed with steep rocks and covered in lush green vegetation. By then the *Wewak* was past the mouth of the Daintree River and the coastline trended back eastwards as the northern limit of Trinity Bay. From then on, the course was close to the shore, within a nautical mile. This allowed a clear view of the big, jungle-covered mountains that backed the coast along there.

It gave Willy a chance to study Thorntons Peak from another perspective and he compared that with the mental images from the previous flights. While he was doing this Andrew came and said that they were now allowed in the wheelhouse. As the afternoon sun was now shining into the area where he was sitting, he was happy to do that.

In the wheelhouse he found Carmen at the wheel and Andrew and the mate bending over the chart table. Capt Kirk was there, sitting in a solid chair bolted to the deck from where he could see the steering and the radar and sonar screens. Willy, Marjorie, and Stick took turns looking at these and then Willy joined Andrew at the chart table.

The mate pointed off to port and said, "That is Cape Tribulation. It was just north of there that Captain Cook ran on the reef."

Willy was offered a pair of binoculars and stared at the low, jungle-covered hump that was Cape Tribulation. On either side were long sandy beaches backed by trees and palms. Jungle-covered mountains towered behind the narrow coastal plain and the rain forest ran right down to the water's edge. The whole scene was a mass of brilliant colours: lush greens and sparkling blues and golden sand.

"It is certainly very beautiful," he commented. "I can see why the tourists come here."

"It is," Andrew agreed. He then moved to the starboard wing of the bridge when Capt Kirk called him over. Capt Kirk pointed and said, "Endeavour Reef is over there, about two miles. See that flattish area amid the waves?"

Willy joined them and tried to focus the binoculars, but the rolling movement of the landing craft made it very difficult and he gave up, peeved that both Capt Kirk and Andrew could apparently stand quite still, yet move in time with the ship to hold their binoculars steady. To prove he could do it Willy tried again, squinting against the glare of the afternoon sun which was sparkling off the waves. Even then he wasn't sure if he could see the reef or not. He knew the story of how the *Endeavour* had struck the reef during the night but found it interesting to listen to Capt Kirk describe the drama from a seaman's point of view, of the dramatic struggle to lighten the ship and to haul her off, then the struggle to keep her afloat while they made their way north to find a place to careen her.

For the next three hours the *Wewak* pushed on northwards. During this time Willy stayed in the wheelhouse, watching the coast and talking. They passed the Hope Islands, Walsh Bay, Archer Point, Walker Bay and the mouth of the Annan River. Ahead quite dramatic isolated mountains began to appear over the horizon; odd, flat-topped, and very rugged. The chart gave their names: Indian Head and Cape Flattery. Willy remembered seeing them from the air.

"That is where all those huge sand dunes start," he said to Andrew.

Andrew nodded and then pointed slightly to port of their course. "Grassy Hill. Cooktown is just around the other side."

"Good," was Willy's comment. The coast he found very interesting but already the novelty of sea travel was beginning to pall. "We could have flown that in half an hour," he grumbled.

It was 4:00pm when the *Wewak* rounded the end of Grassy Hill and entered the mouth of the Endeavour River. Willy stood with Marjorie and Stick at the port rail below the bridge. He studied the river mouth and was surprised how wide it was, and how many sand bars there seemed to be. The far side of the estuary was lined with sand dunes or mangroves. To port he noted that there were a few houses on the end of the point and a white painted lighthouse on top of the hill. Then the wharf came into view and more of the estuary.

Stick suddenly gripped Willy's arm and pointed up the river. "Look! The *Pterodactyl*!" he cried.

Willy looked upriver past a scatter of anchored yachts, motor launches and fishing boats and saw the familiar, black-painted shape of the Catalina sitting at anchor out in the middle of the river.

"Mr Jemmerling! He is here. Oh, I hope he hasn't beaten us to the wrecks," he said.

The *Wewak* slowed as it passed the wharf. There were two vessels berthed alongside: a fishing trawler and a small sailing yacht. A few people stood or sat on the wharf. A couple were fishing and a group of four had 'Council Worker' written on them by their overalls and orange safety vests. The others were just loungers or sightseers. As the *Wewak* began turning slowly to port to bring its bow ramp in to a sloping concrete boat ramp, Willy idly looked at the two vessels. On the small sailing yacht, seated under a small awning at the stern, were a man and two women. The man turned to watch the barge and Willy saw his face, then gasped in surprise.

"Jacob van der Heyden!" he cried.

"Where?" Marjorie asked, pressing against him.

"On that yacht," Willy answered. He could see Jacob looking towards them but there was no hint of recognition. Then he was gone from view as the *Wewak* moved forward and the yacht's cabin blocked the view. "I wonder what he is doing here?" he muttered.

"He might live here," Stick suggested.

"He lives in Sydney, or so he said," replied Willy.

Marjorie answered. "He is obviously looking for whatever it is he was looking for."

"You might be right," Willy answered.

His attention was then taken off Jacob by the bow ramp of the *Wewak* being lowered. The landing craft had swung out across the channel to starboard, then came around to port and crept forward at right angles to the wharf and shore until the steel ramp scraped on the sloping concrete. Mooring ropes were hurled ashore, the port one by Andrew, and within a few minutes the LCT was made fast. Capt Kirk and the mate both came down from the bridge and climbed down into the tank deck and made their way forward. They met the council workers and had a short discussion. The work of unloading the road making machine began.

Capt Kirk made his way aft, leaving the supervision of the unloading to the mate. As he climbed up from the tank deck, he looked at the friends and stopped.

"We will be here a couple of hours. You can go and see the town if you like."

Willy looked ashore and, apart from a nearby shop, could see no sign of a business district. Behind the wharf was a bitumen car park and road which curved off to the right out of sight among trees, squeezed in between the lower slopes of the hill and the beach. None of the scattering of buildings in sight looked like a town centre.

"Where is it sir?" he asked.

"The main street is along there," Capt Kirk replied, gesturing to where rooftops were just visible above the treetops. "Ten minutes' walk. Don't worry, it isn't a very big town, and we won't leave you behind."

"I will just check with Mum and Dad," Willy said. He felt like the walk, if only to get off the vessel. "Anyone else coming?" he asked.

"I will," Marjorie replied at once.

"Me too. I've never seen Cooktown," Stick answered.

Willy found his mother and father and put the idea to them. They both agreed it was a good idea. "We will come too. I see a taxi there on the wharf. That will save walking in this heat."

Willy could only agree with the comment about the heat. Now that they were in the lee of Grassy Hill the afternoon heat was sweltering. Hats were found and the group made their way forward. Carmen and Andrew were asked but both declined.

"Love to," Carmen said, "But we are getting paid to work so we stay here."

"There'll be other times," Andrew added confidently.

The group climbed down the steel ladder into the tank deck. In the heat of the afternoon sun this was like an oven. They hurried forward, climbing carefully over the chains and steel wire ropes that held the machines and Four Wheelers in place. Taking care not to stumble on the steel ramp with its raised steel ridges they made their way ashore.

As they walked up the concrete ramp, Willy said, "I would like to go and say hello to Jacob van der Heyden."

"Good idea," Marjorie agreed.

Willy's father nodded. "You do that. We won't all fit in the taxi anyway. Your mother and I will go first and then send it back for you in a few minutes. Don't keep it waiting because I will have paid for both trips."

Willy nodded and turned left. He headed across the wharf to where the small yacht was tied up. As he got closer, he saw that it was only about 7 metres long, of the 'trailer-sailer' type. He knew he was no expert on boats but to him it had a distinct air of being poorly maintained. The ropes looked grey with age and the paint was faded and peeling. As he reached the edge of the wharf and looked down, Willy saw the name painted on the stern. Picked out in new gold letters was the word *Dyfken.*

That figures, he thought.

Then he saw Jacob looking up at him from under the awning, a slightly puzzled look on his face. Willy realised he had not recognised them so he said, "Hello Jacob. I am Willy Williams, from the Catalina."

Jacob stood up and looked up at them, the deck of the yacht being a metre or so below the level of the wharf. He frowned for a second and then his face cleared.

"Oh hello! I didn't recognise you. I'm sorry."

As he said this a very pretty blonde girl of about 16 came into view from under the awning. She wore a bikini top and faded shorts and Willy could see straight down the front of her top.

Now that is a lovely bosom, he thought, noting her pleasing shape.

A woman also came into view, a larger, older version of the girl. She had on khaki shirt and shorts and her shirt was very well filled. It reminded Willy of a bit of his father's advice of looking at the mother before he decided to marry a girl because that was what the girl might look like in twenty years' time. The woman gave a quizzical and anxious smile.

Jacob said, "These are some of the air cadets who helped rescue me, Mum. This is Willy Williams. He was the one who spotted me in the water as they flew over."

"Oh hello! I'm Hendrika van der Heyden. Thank you for what you did," she said.

The girl, obviously Jacob's sister, introduced herself. "I'm Julia," she said. "Thanks."

Stick, and Marjorie were introduced but neither Jacob nor his sister or mother made any attempt to invite them aboard. They all seemed a bit nervous.

Julia pointed upriver and said, "Did you come off that flying boat?"

Willy shook his head. "The *Pterodactyl*? No. We are travelling on the *Wewak,*" he explained, pointing to the LCT.

"I saw the plane and thought it was the same one," Jacob commented.

"No, this one belongs to Mr Jemmerling," Willy replied. "We had a flight in it last weekend. When did it arrive, do you know?"

"Only about an hour ago," Jacob answered.

"Which way did it fly in from?" Willy enquired.

Jacob pointed northwards. "From that direction."

Willy nodded. "Have you been here long?" he asked.

"Only today to get fuel and water," Jacob replied. He didn't sound very happy.

Marjorie asked, "Are you still looking for whatever it is?"

There was a moment's silence and Willy distinctly saw a look of anxiety cross Jacob's face. His mother's went positively stony. Then Jacob shook his head and said, "Just touring around," at exactly the same moment his sister said, "Just doing some fishing."

There was an embarrassed silence and Willy noted that both brother and sister looked flustered and exchanged anxious glances. To save the situation he said, "I see you've named your yacht the *Duyfken.* We flew over Dyfken Point last Sunday." He went on to describe the flight.

The van der Heydens were polite and chatted, but Willy quickly got the impression that the visit was not welcome. It wasn't helped when Julia asked what they were doing. All three of them then did what Jacob and his sister had just done. Willy said touring, Marjorie said a holiday trip and Stick said fishing, which Willy thought sounded most unlikely if they were passengers on a cargo vessel.

There was another uneasy silence and Willy felt sure that the van der Heydens were staring at them with suspicion. To his relief, the taxi returned and he was able to say, "Oh good! Here's our taxi. Oh well, be seeing you. Have a good trip."

"Same to you," Jacob replied, but in a hard, suspicious sounding tone.

The three friends hurried across to the taxi and climbed in. Willy found he was sweating and knew he was feeling a bit tense. No sooner had they settled in their seats and done their seatbelts up when Marjorie squeaked, "They are looking for a treasure or whatever it is."

Willy glanced at the taxi driver, whose head jerked round at the word treasure. Furious at the slip Willy dug his elbow into Marjorie's side.

"Ow! I... oh!" Marjorie cried, making it worse in Willy's eyes. She gave him a 'sorry' look with big, anxious eyes.

The taxi started up and drove off towards the town. Willy stared out at the passing scene. They passed several buildings including a nice-looking motel, then open bush, followed by a cluster of police buildings on the left. On the right was a grassy footpath with alternating small beaches and clumps of mangroves. Just past the police station they passed a small park on the right.

The taxi driver pointed and said, "That's where Captain Cook beached the *Endeavour* for repairs."

Having heard and read so much about Cook's exploration during the last few weeks Willy stared at the place with interest. The park was right on the edge of the beach and in it sat a stone monument and a genuine old-fashioned muzzle-loading, ship's cannon.

Stick was curious about it and asked the taxi driver who informed them that it was a real cannon, a 24-pounder made in 1803 and sent to Cooktown in the late 19th Century to help defend the port against possible Russian attack.

"Russians!" Stick cried incredulously.

They discussed this while they drove on with a tree lined footpath and beach on the right and then more buildings on the left. Some of these were substantial business premises. The main street opened up ahead of them and Willy was instantly struck by how wide it was and how quaint and old-fashioned the town looked. There was also an impression of how deserted it was. Theirs was the only vehicle moving, although several were parked along the kerbs. There wasn't a single person in sight.

After passing a grand, old, two-storey hotel made of timber which stood on a corner they asked to be let out.

"We will walk thanks," Willy said.

The taxi braked to a halt and the friends climbed out. Willy went to climb up over the kerbing and channelling onto the footpath and stopped.

"Look at this. The gutters are all stone," he exclaimed.

He looked right and left and saw that the old, hand-hewn stone gutters extended right along the street. Similar stonework could be seen across the fifty metres of deserted bitumen.

The trio strolled along, taking in the sights and enjoying the change of scene. Despite the heat Willy found he was enjoying himself. Without even thinking about it he took Marjorie's hand and she smiled happily. Willy now studied the layout more closely and noted that most of the buildings were of 19th Century design. He also noted that almost every second allotment was vacant and was either weeds and sun-browned grass or with a few trees and bushes growing in it.

Halfway along the block they came to a shop and went in. It sold soft drinks and ice-creams, so they all purchased one of each. The soft drinks were placed in a plastic carry bag and the friends walked outside and continued on along the block, licking their ice creams as they sauntered along.

"This is just what I needed in this heat," Willy commented. Even though it was nearly 4:45pm the sun was still high in the sky and the air was stifling. He opened his mouth to comment on the building they were just passing, a grand old bank with a wide, stone staircase and a pillared portico, when he stared in surprise.

Through the door had come Mr Jemmerling. He was dressed all in white and wore a white 'Panama' hat. In his left hand he clutched a large brown envelope. In other circumstances Willy thought Mr Jemmerling's white trousers and shirt would have looked ridiculous anywhere else but somehow they just seemed to suit the place and the wearer.

Mr Jemmerling saw them as he hurried down the steps and his face split into a smile. "Hello again," he said cheerfully. "What brings you lot to Cooktown?"

"Oh, just touring," Willy answered, just as Stick started to say fishing.

"Sightseeing, eh?" Mr Jemmerling said, stopping at the bottom of the steps. He looked both ways along the street. "Did you drive here?" he asked.

Before Willy could answer Stick said, "No, we came by sea on a barge."

"On the *Wewak* eh? That would have been interesting," Mr Jemmerling commented.

His comment flabbergasted Willy, leaving his mind seething with suspicion. *How does he know about the 'Wewak'?* he wondered. That was followed by the suspicion that Mr Jemmerling might be keeping them under surveillance. *Or, worse still, he has a spy among our group,* Willy thought unhappily.

His unhappiness was increased when Mr Jemmerling said, "So you are on you way to retrieve one of your aircraft wrecks are you?"

Willy was aghast. He glanced at Stick and Marjorie, ready to snap at them if they answered. They looked back at him with anxious looks. When they did not reply, Mr Jemmerling gave a short laugh and said, "Sorry. That wasn't a fair question. It is your secret and you must keep it." He smiled and said, "Your ice creams are melting."

Willy saw that Marjorie's ice cream was dripping unnoticed down her front. She squealed and shoved it hastily into her mouth. Willy and Stick both licked at theirs and Willy wracked his brains to try to think of something polite to say.

Mr Jemmerling smiled again, then glanced at his watch and said, "Anyway, I'd love to stay and chat, but I must fly. I need to get this in the mail before the post office closes. So I will wish you all a Merry Christmas and hope we meet again."

He sounded so obviously sincere that Willy blushed with shame and confusion. "Same to you sir, and thanks again for the flight last weekend."

"My pleasure young Willy. Now I really must trot. Goodbye," Mr Jemmerling replied as he set off at a brisk walk along the footpath in the direction the friends had come from.

Willy and his friends stood on the footpath and watched him hurry away, crossing the wide street at a brisk walk. "Well!" he said. "I didn't expect to run into him."

"Do you think he is watching us?" Stick suggested.

"Spying on us you mean?" Willy answered. "I don't know. He is such a nice person and so generous that I can't decide if it all just a cunning front or not."

By this time Mr Jemmerling had vanished into the old wooden post office set under mango trees over on the river side of the road. The friends continued walking, licking their ice creams and commenting on the town but to Willy it was all of no importance. All he could think about was Mr Jemmerling and why he might be in Cooktown.

They passed a second hotel and more shops, grateful for the shade from the awnings they had out over the footpath. At the far end of the block they came to yet another two-story, timber hotel. "This seems to be the end of the business district," Willy commented. He had finished his ice cream by then and opened one of the soft drinks.

"I'm getting a bit hot and tired," Marjorie said. "I'd like to go back to the ship."

"Alright. Along the other footpath for variety," Willy agreed. In the sweltering tropical heat he felt he had seen enough of Cooktown for the moment.

The friends crossed the street, being held up by the first vehicle they had seen apart from the taxi. As they started walking back along the tree-lined footpath towards the wharf Stick said sarcastically, "It's busy!"

They laughed, then laughed again when three vehicles drove past in quick succession and Willy commented that it must be the Five o'clock Rush.

As they walked along, Willy kept looking for Mr Jemmerling but he saw no sign of him, not even at the post office when they reached it. It was a lovely old timber building and he peeked in just as a lady began shutting doors and windows.

Not in there, he noted. *Now where has he gone?* He hadn't seen him recross the street or get into a vehicle.

As they passed the post office, which was the last building on that side of the street, Willy saw that a pathway led towards the river through a belt of scrub and mangroves.

Maybe he went that way to get on a boat? he thought, picturing Mr Jemmerling climbing aboard the *Pterodactyl.*

That got him looking mostly in that direction. For a hundred metres he could only get glimpses of the river through the belt of mangroves, but he managed to spot the flying boat, still lying to a mooring in midstream. After that the mangroves thinned out and patches of mud and small beaches appeared. Small boats lay on the shore or bobbed at anchor just out from the mangroves.

The friends came to Captain Cook's memorial and spent a few minutes looking at it and in studying the old ship's cannon. It was the genuine article and Willy was quite thrilled to see the date 1803 stamped in the end of the trunnions.

Andrew will like this, he thought.

From there they had a good view out over the estuary and Willy spent a few thoughtful minutes staring back at the now distant shape of the Catalina. Then he noted that the tide had begun to make, and he checked his watch.

"Half past five! Come on, we had better get back."

They resumed walking. A few minutes later, Willy's mother and father drove past in the taxi, heading for the wharf. They stopped and asked if they wanted a lift. Willy shook his head. "No thanks. It is only a few hundred metres. We will walk," he said.

The taxi drove on and the trio continued on their way. As they rounded the curve just past the police station Willy noted a man walking quickly towards them, the first pedestrian they had met. The man wore dirty old grey overalls and a greasy cloth hat but had a camera with a very powerful telephoto lens attached to it slung around his neck.

It was the man's odd behaviour that first attracted Willy's attention. The man twice stopped and looked back, then resumed walking. It was then that Willy was struck by the incongruity of the expensive camera and the old clothes.

He doesn't look like a tourist, he thought.

The idea that he might be a birdwatcher or something similar crossed his mind. That thought made Willy look more carefully at the man. The man had seen them but appeared to take no notice, until they were about 25 metres from him and his eyes met Willy's.

Recognition was instant and Willy almost stopped walking as the shock hit him.

That is the man who burgled the Beck's! he thought.

Chapter 23

DARK SUSPICIONS

Willy felt the wave of shock sweep through him as he tried to keep his face normal. He was dimly aware that he had tightened his grip on Marjorie's hand and that she had turned her head to look at him but he was focused on the approaching man. As the distance narrowed Willy's mind raced. What to do?

Should I confront him, or try to catch him? he wondered.

A mix of emotions added to his confusion: excitement, anxiety, even fear as he realised there would be a very strong possibility of a fight if he tried to physically restrain the man.

He watched the man's face. It wore a slightly puzzled look and what Willy imagined might be a guilty expression. What was obvious was that the man had not made the mental connection to who they were.

He knows he's seen me but he doesn't recognise us, Willy thought. But he was in no doubt. Images of the fleeing burglar's face came vividly to his mind, and he was sure this was the same man. *About thirty, brown hair, brown eyes,* he noted.

By then they were only five paces apart and the man moved to the outside of the footpath to pass them. Willy tensed ready for action and tried not to keep looking the man in the eyes. By then the man's expression had changed to one of suspicion and dislike.

He passed within arm's reach of Willy's right side, giving Willy a hostile glare as he did. Willy made himself keep walking, even though every instinct cried out to turn and keep watching lest he be set upon from behind. To keep control Willy counted to ten before glancing back over his shoulder.

As he did, the man did the same and their eyes briefly locked before Willy looked hastily away. It was obvious to Willy that neither Marjorie nor Stick had recognised the man and that both were quite unaware of the tenseness of the situation. Rather than spoil the plan that was rapidly forming in his mind Willy made himself walk another 25 paces before again glancing back.

This showed the man still walking quickly on along the footpath towards town. A fractional movement of the man's head warned Willy and he flicked his own head to the front again.

I don't want him to become suspicious, Willy thought.

He made himself walk another fifty metres, his mind boiling with ideas and suspicions.

By then the *Wewak* and the wharf had come into sight ahead. Willy again glanced back. The man had rounded the bend and was out of sight.

Stopping abruptly Willy said, "Did you see that man?"

"Yeah, so what about him?" Stick answered.

"He was the man who burgled the Beck's," Willy replied.

Stick snorted with disbelief. "Oh bunkum!"

"He was, Stick. I got very close to him when we were chasing him. It is the same man," Willy replied forcefully. He was so sure he did not care whether Stick believed him or not.

Marjorie looked doubtful and said, "Did he recognise you?"

Willy shook his head. "I don't think so. He was puzzled but I don't think he could place where he might have seen me," he said.

Stick was still doubtful. He said, "So what if he is? What are you going to do?"

"I'm going to follow him," Willy said.

Marjorie looked horrified. "Not on your own," she cried.

Willy nodded. "Yes. Marj., you are going to the *Wewak* to tell my parents. Stick, you are going to the police station to report."

Stick looked scared and started to mutter excuses. "Oh, but we aren't sure. We don't have any proof."

"I'm sure," grated Willy. "And I aim to get proof. I'm going to follow that character and try to find out where he lives and who his associates are."

"How do you know he has associates?" Stick challenged.

Willy was now in a fever of anxiety lest he lose the man, so he just snapped, "Because he was picked up by a man on a motorcycle when we chased him. Now get going both of you."

Marjorie did not want to leave them, but she bit her lip and hurried on towards the wharf. Willy thought she would be safe. It was only a couple of hundred metres and the *Wewak* was just visible at the bend. Stick hesitated but then turned and came with Willy as he set off walking quickly back towards town. They had to go together anyway as the police station was a hundred metres in that direction.

Now that he had decided Willy walked as quickly as he could, anxious not to lose the man. Stick hurried along beside him, still muttering that it was silly and that they should both go to the police station.

It took a minute's fast walking to reach the slight bend in the road. As he walked Willy kept looking ahead for the first glimpse of the man. Movement on the footpath about 200 metres away caught his eye and he immediately halted, using his arm to stop Stick. It was the man, and he was still walking towards the town. At that moment he was passing the Captain Cook memorial.

"There he is. Now, we need to wait a bit longer," Willy said. The street from there on was straight and offered little cover. The only other option was for them to try to make their way forward along the beach and through the fringe of the mangroves. Willy rejected this idea but was worried. He and Stick were the only other pedestrians and would be very noticeable if the man looked back.

The man went into the shadows of the line of mango trees lining the footpath. *We will still be visible, but if we leave it much longer he might go into a building or something and we won't know which one,* Willy thought. He decided to take the risk and resumed walking.

Another minute's walk had them opposite the police station. "Off you go, Stick," he ordered.

"What do I do after I have told them?" Stick queried.

"Go back to the ship," Willy replied.

Still Stick hesitated. "What if there is no-one there?" he asked.

"Then go back to the ship. Now go!" Willy snapped.

Stick looked unhappy but did as he was told, angling across the road. Willy kept on walking. To his dismay, he saw the man turn right and vanish from view between the trees.

Did he go into the post office? Willy wondered.

It was the nearest building but he didn't think the man had reached it. He hurried on, sweating heavily from the exertion.

He became so worried that he might lose the man that he began to jog. As he did, he kept his eyes fixed on the place where the man had gone from view, ready to jump under cover if he re-appeared. Along the way he passed the old cannon and the Captain Cook memorial. It took him two minutes to cover the distance, relieved to have the trunks of large mango trees to give some cover. As he reached the place Willy slowed and looked out to his right.

"There he is!" Willy muttered thankfully.

He came to a stop behind the trunk of a large mango tree and watched. Through a fringe of small mangroves he saw that the man was working on a dinghy that was hauled up on a small beach. The man did something to the motor, then pushed the dinghy into the water and sprang aboard. As it slid backwards on the tiny ripples of waves, the man lowered the outboard motor and started it.

"Damn! I can't follow him now. I wonder where he is going?" Willy muttered.

He wiped sweat clear of his eyes and squinted into the reflected sparkles of sunlight to look out into the estuary. Anchored at varying distances from 50 metres to a hundred were five small vessels: two sail yachts and three motor launches.

Is it to one of them? he wondered.

The man turned the dinghy to face the river and increased the revolutions. The dinghy surged out into the river, heading straight for a dirty brown looking motor launch. Then, to Willy's dismay, the dinghy turned to port and headed upriver, vanishing from view behind the mangroves to his left.

Willy swore and started running towards the post office. As he ran, he kept looking to his right but he found no gap in the belt of mangroves. These became thicker and wider, and he realised he would not get a clear view of the river that way. All he got were a couple of glimpses of a sail boat's mast and, away in the distance, the tail fin of the *Pterodactyl.*

"I should have gone the other way, back to Captain Cook's memorial," he told himself.

He turned and sprinted back that way, ignoring the curious stare of a man who drove past in an old blue utility. Willy was healthy but he was no athlete. Within another hundred paces he was puffing badly and had the beginnings of a stitch. Ignoring the growing pain he pushed himself to keep running. His breath started to come in hot gasps and he could feel his heart hammering but he kept on.

Two minutes later he was on the beach at the memorial. *I was right!* he thought.

From there he could see most of the river, but there was no sign of any small boat. He had to shield his eyes against the glare of the afternoon sun as he was looking almost west but he could only shake his head in annoyance. The man had vanished.

Did he go to one of those anchored boats? he wondered.

Then another unpleasant thought crept unasked into his mind, and he stared hard at the distant black shape of the flying boat. *Did he go to the 'Pterodactyl'?* he wondered.

Is he working for Mr Jemmerling? It hurt even to think such thoughts.

Willy waited a couple of minutes, but no boat appeared. Then he turned to make his way back up to the footpath. Once there he turned left and began walking towards the wharf, wiping perspiration from his face. He found that the sweat was literally dripping from him, from his fingertips and his face and even trickling down his back and legs.

Bloody hell, it's humid! he thought.

Seeing from his watch that it was nearly a quarter to six made him shake his head. It seemed that the blazing summer sun would never set and there was no breeze at all.

Even when Willy reached the wharf five minutes later there was only a whisper of wind. He hurried towards the *Wewak.* As he did, he glanced along to his right and got another surprise; the *Dyfken* was no longer there. Climbing quickly aboard the *Wewak,* he hurried aft and climbed quickly up from the tank deck to where his anxious parents, his friends, Mr Beck and Norman, and most of the crew of the ship were gathered under the awning.

"Well?" his father demanded, an anxious look on his face.

"He got away," Willy said. "He got in a dinghy and went up the river."

He gestured in that direction. As he did, one of the *Pterodactyl's* motors spluttered and then burst into life. The sound carried loudly to them over the still water.

"I wonder?" Willy said, moving to the starboard rail and staring up the river.

The flying boat's other engine started and both engines began what was obviously a take-off test.

"Do you think he went to the flying boat?" his father asked.

Willy bit his lip. "I don't think so," he said. "He might have but I didn't see him."

"Oh, I'll bet he did!" Stick blurted out. "That Jemmerling has been spying on us all along. I'll bet that man works for Jemmerling."

Andrew squinted at the flying boat. "There is no sign of any dinghy there. Could they get it on board?"

"Not easily," Willy replied. He felt very guilty at even having hinted that Mr Jemmerling was involved.

The sound of aircraft engines increased in volume, and they all turned to look. The *Pterodactyl* began to move.

"She is taking off," Willy said, quite unnecessarily.

Once again, he shielded his eyes to look upriver. It was almost straight into the setting sun. The sunset reflected off the water in shards that were painful even to squint into. It was a relief when the flying boat moved forward to pass across the stern of the ship. Willy made his way aft along the side of the superstructure until he stood at the stern. From there the sun was side on and his heart skipped a beat at the sheer beauty of the aircraft as it began to surge across the flat water. In spite of everything he still thought it was a great machine.

By the time the *Pterodactyl* was astern of the *Wewak* she was leaving a long, creaming white wake and was lifting onto her chine. With the sun no longer blinding him Willy could admire the whole thing. He found all his emotions in turmoil. Was that black-painted flying boat the carrier of evil? Or was it just coincidence.

To raise his emotions another notch he saw an arm extend from the cockpit of the now skimming flying boat. It waved and Willy could tell it could only be for them.

Or is it a signal to someone on the 'Wewak'? he wondered, hating himself for his dark suspicions.

Mr Beck was annoyed. "He's waving to us. The cheeky bugger!"

"I suppose he thinks he's won," Stick said gloomily.

The flying boat raced on, the sun now on it and behind the watchers. Willy wished he had his camera as it was a beautiful and dramatic scene: the creaming white foam, the black flying boat, the green and blue shades of water and beyond the dramatic landforms of the distant mountains. As the flying boat reached the mouth of the river it began to encounter waves, each one throwing up a shower of spray as it was struck by the racing bow. It made Willy think of the awful take-off when they had rescued Jacob.

That reminded him of the *Dyfken* and he glanced to his right to check that it was no longer berthed at the wharf. Then, as he shifted his gaze back to the flying boat, his eyes detected a tiny dot of white out to sea to the northeast. A thin black line against the sky indicated a mast.

And then the flying boat lifted off. Willy smiled with pleasure to watch the Catalina lift and climb away. As it did, it turned to port.

"Going north," he commented.

"Oh no! He will beat us to the plane," Marjorie cried. She turned to Captain Kirk. "Can't we get going? We don't want them to beat us."

Captain Kirk smiled but shook his head. "Sorry. We will sail when the tide lifts us off and that won't be for another hour or so yet."

Willy suddenly felt depressed. He watched the flying boat continue to climb and turn until it was silhouetted against the reddish tinge of the sunset to the northwest. Seeing the black shape, a sudden, vivid image sprang into Willy's mind, making him think that it really did look like one of the giant flying reptiles of the dinosaur age. The image it conjured up made him give a sudden, involuntary shudder. Once more dark suspicions clouded his mind.

As the Catalina dwindled to vanish in the distance Willy turned and stared at the distant vessel to the northeast. "Is that the *Dyfken*?" he asked.

Captain Kirk answered. "If that is the little yacht that was berthed here, then yes it is. She got under way about an hour ago," he said.

The cook now interrupted, saying that dinner was ready. They made their way into the saloon to get out of the sun, which even as it began to sink below the hills inland was still scorching to the skin. Willy sat beside Marjorie but found he had almost no appetite. He was so irritated by the escape of the man, and of the worries and suspicions that seemed to suddenly surround them that he did not want to eat at all. His mother made him, insisting that he drink plenty of cordial.

As they ate dinner the sun sank below the hills to the west and darkness set in. With dusk came a swarm of sand flies and mosquitoes. Once the meal was over the crew, including Andrew and Carmen, went to work to make ready for sea. Capt Kirk asked the others to stay out of the way.

Willy made his way out to the stern with Marjorie. He actually wanted to be alone to think but could not find it in himself to tell her to go away. A slight breeze had sprung up by then and he leaned on the railings and looked down at the swirling, gurgling water: a murky dark green in the lights near the hull but rippling black further out. Up the river he saw that the anchored vessels had mostly turned on their mooring lights. A single moving light caught his eye, and he knew that at least one boat was heading down river.

Marjorie wanted to snuggle up, but Willy was still perspiring in the humid tropical night and felt all sticky and knew he must smell of sweat. He was actually pleased when his mother came out.

"You had better have your showers you two," she said. "That will keep you out of the way while the ship leaves harbour."

Willy agreed. Underfoot the deck was now trembling as the engines revved and he saw water swirling away along the sides as the propellers were put into reverse. Shouted commands from forward, accompanied by the splash of mooring ropes being cast into the water all told Willy they were backing away from the concrete hard.

After collecting a change of clothes, towel and toilet bag from his kit, Willy made his way up one deck to the male shower. As he reached the door of the shower, he found it closed and a knock revealed that Stick had beaten him too it. With nothing better to do Willy stepped through the door that led aft onto the small deck above the stern and looked out. He saw that the *Wewak* was slowly reversing out into the estuary. This was so wide that they had ample room to turn safely.

As he stood there, Willy noted a light moving seawards. It was over near the far side of the estuary. He presumed it was the boat he had seen moving a few minutes earlier.

A fisherman? he wondered.

But it was too dark, and too far away for him to tell. There was certainly no danger of the *Wewak* going anywhere near it.

Stick came out of the shower, rubbing his wet hair with his towel, just as the *Wewak* stopped moving astern and began to turn. Willy found the manoeuvre interesting, so he leaned out to watch. It took longer than he expected and required the LCT to go slow ahead, back towards the wharf. Willy found it very hard to judge distance in the dark and marvelled at the skill of Captain Kirk and sailors like him as he watched the bow seem to slide sideways well clear of the fishing trawler at the wharf. The many lights, both on shore and also flickering ones on piles on the water all made it even more confusing for Willy.

Once her bow was facing seawards the *Wewak's* engines rumbled to 'full ahead' and she began butting her way out into the smaller waves of the river mouth. Willy watched for a few more minutes as the lights of Cooktown quickly slipped astern, then he made his way into the shower.

Twenty minutes later, he stood next to Andrew and Carmen in the wheelhouse. The mate had the wheel and Captain Kirk stood near him, eyes moving from the radar screen to the dark sea outside. Willy could see several flashing lights and Andrew explained they were automatic warning lights on reefs and rocks.

"It's a dangerous bit of coast," Andrew said, showing him the chart.

Willy looked outside again. In the starlight he could now make out the rugged, flat-topped mountains a few miles to port. He noted that the sea was slightly rougher than earlier but that mostly the landing craft just slid across it with a gentle twist and roll motion. Only occasionally did the flat bow strike a larger than normal wave. When it did, she shuddered slightly and there was an audible *thump!* and a few seconds later droplets of spray would splatter on the windows.

Captain Kirk frowned and bent to look at the radar, tapping the screen a couple of times. Then he picked up his binoculars and made his way out onto the port wing of the bridge and stared ahead. Carmen moved to look at the radar screen, so Andrew and Willy joined her. Carmen pointed.

"I think it is this little blip he is worried about," she explained.

Willy studied the greenish picture with interest. He saw that the shape of the coastline was clearly visible. So were a couple of pinpoints that were small reefs with beacons on them. Andrew pointed to a distinct blip several miles ahead.

"That is a boat," he said.

Suddenly, Captain Kirk came to the door of the wheelhouse. "Bring her round to starboard two points, Lester. There's something ahead there."

The mate did as he was told, spinning the wheel, then steadying the LCT on the new course. No sooner had he done this than Captain Kirk let out an oath and shouted, "Bloody hell! Hard a-starboard."

Willy followed Andrew out onto the starboard wing of the bridge as the *Wewak* began to swing into the waves.

"There!" Andrew cried, gripping his arm and pointing across to port.

Willy glimpsed a dim grey shape which he then realised was a small motor launch without any lights on. For a second he held his breath, fearing there would be a collision. Then he saw that they would miss. The motor launch suddenly rolled violently and turned sharply away. The sound of a frightened ejaculation carried across the waves.

Captain Kirk bellowed at the motor launch through a loudhailer, telling the people on it they were bloody fools and should have their navigation lights on. There was no reply, but Willy saw patches of white which indicated that the launch had increased speed and was powering away, heading inshore.

As the *Wewak* turned to starboard, the launch vanished from Willy's view behind the superstructure. He and Andrew hurried back into the wheelhouse but did not go out onto the other wing of the bridge, where an angry Captain Kirk was fuming.

"Bloody idiots!" he snapped. He turned to look back into the wheelhouse and ordered the LCT to turn back onto her proper course. Then he shook his head and said to the mate, "I wondered what that blip on the radar was. It was so small I thought it might have been a defect on the screen. I couldn't see any lights. Just as well I went out to look or we would have run that silly bastard right over."

"No survivors then," the mate replied as he steadied the landing craft back on course. "If they didn't get killed in the collision, or drowned in the wreckage, they would have been minced up in the screws."

Willy was appalled and winced at the mental image of the ship's propellers slashing and slicing into people. Knowing that the *Wewak* was brightly lit with all the regulation navigation lights, plus lights in the superstructure, he wondered how the near collision could possibly have occurred. He said, "Surely they could see us coming?"

Captain Kirk, who had again stared out to port, lowered his binoculars and gave a sad shake of his head. "You'd be surprised how rarely people in boats keep a lookout astern."

"Still hasn't got any lights on," Andrew commented.

"Can you still see him?" Captain Kirk asked, again raising his glasses.

"No sir," Andrew replied.

Only then, as Willy stared through the window at the dark sea and darker coast beyond, did the thought occur to him.

I wonder if that was the man we followed making his escape from Cooktown?

Chapter 24

BATHURST BAY

Willy turned to Captain Kirk. "Sir, that launch might have the man I was following on board. He might be trying to escape from Cooktown on it. That's why it has no lights."

"Maybe," Captain Kirk answered. He looked around as Willy's parents, the Becks and Stick all crowded up into the wheelhouse to find out what was going on.

Andrew, who had been staring out through binoculars, lowered them, and said, "What if they were keeping tabs on us? Wasn't that what you thought; that Mr Jemmerling was paying them to spy on us?"

Willy thought about that and felt confused. "But why would they have been ahead of us then?" he said.

Stick answered, "Maybe they are slower than us and wanted to get a head start?"

Captain Kirk shook his head. "No, that launch has a good turn of speed. Besides, he wasn't watching us at all."

The mate agreed, adding, "How would he know we were going to steer northeast? For all he knew we might just have been heading back to Cairns."

Willy moved to the radar screen. "Can we still see him?"

The mate pointed to a faint blip. "That's him, about a mile on our port beam."

"Can we try to catch him?" Willy asked.

Captain Kirk snorted and shook his head. "Fair go young fella! He could easily outmanoeuvre us, even if he couldn't outrun us. Besides, we don't know if it is your friend or not."

Andrew laughed. "And even if we did, what would we do, run alongside and board him with cutlasses?"

"But we must do something!" Willy cried.

"We will," Captain Kirk replied. "I will notify the relevant authorities of a breach of marine regulations, and they can investigate."

"You will tell the police?" Willy asked.

"Yes, and the Coastwatch and Customs," Captain Kirk replied. "Now, if all you people wouldn't mind leaving the bridge, please, it is getting a bit too crowded here."

As Captain Kirk began radioing, Willy went down to the saloon with the others. He wanted to go out on deck, but the door was closed and the ship's 'Standing Orders' were no-one out on the deck at night. Instead he sat and drank cold Milo and discussed the situation with the others.

After half an hour he asked if he could go back up onto the bridge again. Captain Kirk said yes, so he went up. A check with Andrew informed him that they were now off Cape Bedford and that the dark cape ahead on the port bow was Cape Flattery. He was also told that Captain Kirk had informed the police, Customs, Coastwatch and Marine Safety Organization. Also the incident had been noted in the ship's log.

Willy looked at the radar but could see no sign of any blip that might be the motor launch. "Where is it?" he asked.

Captain Kirk pointed astern. "We've left him behind. He is too low and over the curve of the earth, so we don't have him on radar any more."

Willy pointed to another blip. "Then what is this thing?"

"Those blips are small islands and that one is a small craft a mile or so ahead of us on the port bow," Capt Kirk answered, adding, "You can see his lights."

Willy looked and could, tiny dots of white light against the dark mass of Cape Flattery. "I wonder if that is the yacht *Dyfken*?" he said.

Capt Kirk shrugged. "Could be. It would be about right. We are overhauling them quite quickly. They must be only doing about seven or eight knots to our twelve."

Willy stared at the tiny lights. *I wonder if that is Jacob and his family?* he thought.

Again he wondered what it was that Jacob was doing off the coast of Cape York. He voiced this to Andrew, adding, "You'd think he'd stay away after his last experience."

"Whatever he is looking for might be very valuable," Andrew said.

That led them to another discussion of the treasure theory but, as on previous occasions, they argued round in circles for lack of information. It was 10:00pm by then and Willy's mother called him down for another cup of Milo.

"It is bedtime for you," she said. "You've had a very long day."

Willy did not want to go to bed. Partly he was too interested but he also wanted to see if anything else developed. Reluctantly he did as he was told. Out on the canvas covered enclosure he found it was very windy and scatters of spray came back from time to time, but the canvas screens kept most of it out. Satisfied that the ropes, netting, and canvas screens would stop him slipping out of his stretcher and over the side in his sleep he lay down and made himself comfortable. The four stretchers were placed facing fore-and-aft, so he actually felt quite comfortable.

Soon afterwards Willy slipped into a deep sleep. By now the throb of the engines was a comforting background noise and the movement of the ship wasn't so marked as to cause any alarm or to tip him out. There were dreams but later he could not remember them, only that he had dreamt.

A squawking noise woke Willy. Feeling tired and bleary eyed he pulled his sleeping bag aside and looked up. To his surprise, it was already getting light. Then the squawking came again and he saw it was coming from a large seagull which was hovering on the wind just forward of the screen.

Bloody hell! Where did that night go? he muttered. A check of his watch told him it was no illusion. It was just after 05:00am.

A glance showed all the others still asleep. For a few minutes Willy lay back and contemplated trying to go back to sleep. But the attempt was a failure and he decided he may as well get up. Slipping quietly to the deck he stood up and looked out.

About a kilometre ahead to starboard he saw a small rocky island with a lighthouse on it, the light now flashing faintly in the dawn. To the left of the island was a rocky headland with flat land inland of it. At least ten kilometres beyond the headland was a much larger feature, a regular range of rugged mountains.

I wonder where we are? Willy thought.

He patted down his tousled hair, found his chart and went to the wheelhouse. Carmen and the mate were on duty, Carmen at the wheel.

"Can I come in?" Willy asked.

"Certainly," the mate replied.

Willy went to the chart table. "Where are we, sir?"

The mate pointed. "Here, about a mile south of Barrow Island. That is Barrow Point off the port bow."

"What are those mountains ahead?" Willy asked.

"Cape Melville. Bathurst Bay is around the other side of it," the mate answered.

That sent Willy's excitement level up. *Nearly there,* he thought.

He said, "How long before we get there?"

"About three hours," the mate said. "Time for more sleep if you want it."

Willy shook his head and moved to look out through the front. He noted that the sea was even calmer, was almost flat with only small waves. For that he was thankful as it meant they could land.

For the next hour and a half he watched the passing coastline and pondered all that had happened during the last few months. He was then called down for breakfast and found all of the others now awake. A big breakfast of sausages, fried eggs, mushrooms, toast, and cereal followed. Willy found he was very hungry.

By the time breakfast was finished Cape Melville was off the *Wewak's* port beam. Willy came on deck after cleaning his teeth and stared at the rugged coastline in something approaching awe. The cape appeared to be made of thousands of giant grey boulders with only small clumps of scrub between them. It was one of the most forbidding landscapes he had ever seen.

At 07:00am the *Wewak* rounded the end of the cape and headed west, slipping between some offshore rocks and Pipon Island. To check that what he was now looking at was actually Bathurst Bay Willy went up to the wheelhouse. He found Mr Beck and Norman leaning over the chart table with Captain Kirk.

Captain Kirk tapped the chart with the end of a pencil and shook his head. "I can't land you exactly there. The water is too shallow offshore and there are a few shoals. It will have to be a kilometre further west I'm afraid."

"Are you sure?" Mr Beck asked.

"Positive," Captain Kirk replied. "I landed a mineral exploration team a bit further along only last Wednesday."

"Can you put us ashore straight away?" Mr Beck asked.

Captain Kirk nodded. "Pretty well. High water is at 10:42, at two point eight metres. We like to go ashore at the start of a rising tide so that we lift off as soon as we unload."

"Are you staying at all?" Norman asked.

Captain Kirk again shook his head. "We are contracted to lift these mining people off tomorrow so we will land you and then pull out and anchor, then come in again to pick them up."

Mr Beck did not look happy, and he and Norman moved aside to talk quietly.

Captain Kirk looked at Willy. "Yes Willy, what is it?"

"Sir, those big islands ahead at the other side of the bay. Is that the Flinders Group?" Willy asked.

Captain Kirk nodded and pointed ahead. "Yes. The one on the left is Denham Island, with Blackwood Island beyond. The big island in the centre is Flinders Island, with Stanley Island behind it to the right. That low island off to seaward of them with the lighthouse on it is King Island," he explained.

Willy remembered seeing them from the air and noted that from sea level they looked even more barren and rugged.

"Thanks sir," he said.

Once again, he anxiously scanned the whole stretch of the bay but what he was looking for, the *Pterodactyl,* was not there. He had half expected to arrive and find the Catalina sitting on the bay. It was a relief to see nothing but calm sea.

Carmen came through and relieved Andrew at the wheel. Andrew came over to look at the chart and then started talking to Willy. While they talked Stick and Marjorie came up to join them.

Captain Kirk frowned and said, "It's getting a bit crowded in here. We are going to be doing some manoeuvring soon. If you kids want to watch then go up onto the monkey island. It's safe enough in daylight."

Willy had not been up to the monkey island, the highest level of the superstructure directly above the wheelhouse, so he was happy enough to follow that suggestion. However his mother insisted he roll his sleeves down and get a hat before he did. The group made their way aft to where a ladder led up through a trapdoor and climbed up to the deck above. Once there, Willy was glad they had because it gave them a very good view in all directions. The only drawback was the lack of protection from wind and sun.

No sooner had Willy settled to leaning on the railings at the forward end than the hum of aero engines made him look around.

Is that the 'Pterodactyl'? he wondered.

The aircraft was easy to locate. It came from behind them and was flying low. His brain instantly noted its details: high-wing, twin-engine, retractable undercarriage. As it flew overhead at about 500 feet, Willy noted the red and white paint scheme and badges of the Custom's Coastwatch Service.

Andrew shielded his eyes to watch it then said, "I hope they have found that launch we nearly ran down."

"I hope so too," Willy replied. As the aircraft flew on westwards his thoughts turned to his suspicions about who might be on that launch.

For the next half hour the group stood and watched the coastline slipping by about a mile to port. The weather was clear, with a gentle breeze from off the land, but very humid and sticky. The sea was calm and there was almost no surf breaking on the beach. Only a distant line of cumulus clouds behind them showed any possibility of any change.

The beach held Willy's attention, for all of its monotony. It stretched almost unbroken for about 20 kilometres, all the way from Cape Melville to the Bathurst Range at the Western end of the bay. Backing the beach was a long line of sand dunes, gleaming white in the tropical sun. Crowning the dunes was a belt of stunted scrub: low, twisted trees and bushes which looked to be quite a thicket. Behind that the tops of a eucalypt forest showed. From his study of the map Willy knew that there was flat land extending inland for several kilometres, right to the base of the Melville Range. Hidden from view were large areas of salt marsh, mudflat, swamp, and more sand dunes running parallel to the beach.

After proceeding several miles from the cape, the *Wewak* turned to port and headed in for the beach. As the LCT nosed slowly in Willy clearly saw areas of shallow water showing up and could soon see the bottom the whole time. As the *Wewak* continued on towards the beach Willy did some daydreaming, imagining that he was on a navy landing craft heading for an enemy held coast during wartime.

Images from movies he had seen of amphibious landings made him shudder. *Guns firing, tracer bullets flying, smoke, fire, dead marines in the surf,* he pictured.

He said to Andrew, "I wouldn't like to be on a landing craft if this was a battle. There is no cover at all."

"It could be pretty grim if there was any real opposition," Andrew replied. Willy then realised that he had been having similar thoughts as Andrew went on to say, "It must have been great when *Wewak* really did her stuff at Makassang. I reckon commanding a landing craft would be a great job."

Stick, who had been listening, snorted and said, "You could end up real dead, real fast. I think I'll stick to a career as Air Force ground crew."

"I'll go for the glory," Andrew said, his eyes sparkling. "If you survived it would be something to be really proud of."

Willy knew that Andrew was very romantic and that made him smile because he also knew that Andrew had proved he was very brave. "I didn't know this ship was at the landing at Makassang," he said, referring to the Australian intervention on that island ten years earlier.

Andrew nodded. "She was. She was one of six landing craft that went in with the first wave."

"So what does *Wewak* mean?" Stick asked. "I mean, it's not Australian, is it?"

Andrew shook his head. "No. It is a town on the north coast of New Guinea. She was named after it because the Australian Army did a landing there back in World War Two. So she is really named after a battle as well. She was later transferred to the PNG Navy and kept her name. They sold her to Mr Kirk two years ago when they got a new LCH."

As he explained this the *Wewak* grounded very gently with a series of slight shudders while still about 50 metres from the shore.

"We will get wet!" Stick wailed.

"You don't have to," Andrew replied. "It is only waist deep at the most and I heard Captain Kirk tell Mr Beck that he would nudge her further in as the tide came in a bit more."

"We need to get ashore and start looking," Willy said.

Now that they were there he was gripped by impatience. At the back of his mind was a niggling worry he could not quite pin down.

Thirty impatient minutes later, during which Carmen exactly plotted their position on the 1:50 000 scale map and she and Willy had twice calculated the magnetic compass course they had to walk to the approximate location of the 'Kittyhawk' wreck, the group made their way down into the tank deck and forward to the ramp. This had now been lowered and only about 10 metres of shallow water lay between them and the dry sand.

"Can we go now?" Willy asked, adjusting the belt with two water bottles on it.

His father shook his head. "No. First we have to unload everything and make sure we are ready," he vetoed.

"Aw Dad! Someone might beat us to the wreck," Willy wailed.

"Who?" his father asked, indicating the empty beach and bush.

Willy had Mr Jemmerling's name on the tip of his tongue but instead he said, "This mining exploration team. They might stumble on it by accident," he suggested.

"Not likely," his father said.

Mr Beck turned to Captain Kirk, who had joined them on the ramp. "These mining people, where did you land them?"

Captain Kirk pointed along the beach. "About half a mile further along, where the water is a bit deeper. You can still see their wheel tracks on the beach."

Willy looked and was just able to make out disturbed sand above the tide line. That got him feeling even more agitated.

Mr Beck next asked, "What are they looking for?"

"They weren't clear about that," Captain Kirk replied, adding, "Not that there is anything unusual about that. Those sort of people keep their cards pretty close to their chests. There can be a lot of money involved."

Willy's mother now made a comment which crystallised the niggling worry Willy felt. She said, "I find it an extraordinary coincidence that two groups should both want to land on this beach by barge in the same week. I would imagine years go by and no-one ever lands here."

"You are right there," Captain Kirk agreed. "I doubt if I have seen more than one person on this beach in twenty odd years of sailing past it every few weeks."

On hearing that Willy's suspicions and anxieties increased. "Mineral exploration people would have instruments to detect metals, wouldn't they?"

"Quite likely," his father agreed.

Mr Beck turned to Captain Kirk. "This mining group Captain, how many people and what gear have they got?"

"Six men, led by a fellow named Jenkins. They have a bulldozer, plus a 'Bobcat' thing with a front-end bucket, a Four Wheel Drive, and two trucks loaded with fuel and stores," Capt Kirk replied.

"Oh well. It may mean nothing," Mr Beck said doubtfully. He then gave instructions to start unloading.

Captain Kirk held up his hand. "I just need to remind you; this is the 'Stinger Season'. There might be deadly jellyfish. Make sure you have long pants on, and strong footwear in case of poisonous seashells or stingrays."

Willy knew all that but had quite forgotten about such perils of the tropical ocean. Now he looked at the sea with a wary eye. Somewhat gingerly he followed Andrew as he stepped off the ramp into thigh deep water. To his surprise, the sea felt warmer than body temperature and he decided he wouldn't be swimming in it anyway. This idea was strengthened when a wave came in and wet him to waist height.

Marjorie refused to get wet. "You carry me," she said.

"No. Wait for the boat," Willy replied. He wasn't going to carry her in his arms with all the crew and his friends grinning at him.

A small, flat-bottomed dinghy was carried down and slid into the water, held steady by Andrew and Willy till two paddles were produced. Willy's mother and father and Marjorie and Stick then climbed in and were pushed right into the ankle-deep shallows. After they were ashore, Andrew instructed Willy to help him push the boat back to collect their bags and camping gear.

As he waded out, Willy said, "Where are we camping?"

Captain Kirk heard this and said, "Not within a hundred paces of the sea. A few years back a huge crocodile that was swimming past one night crawled up and dragged some tourists out of their tents. They were camped along near the western end of the bay there, and had their tents only forty of fifty metres from the water's edge."

"Crocodiles!" Stick cried, looking around anxiously.

"And sharks," Capt Kirk added.

Sharks! Willy thought. That thought made him glance anxiously around, then gasp in fright. Only 20 metres away the triangular fin of a shark was sticking out of the sea!

"Shark!" he cried, splashing to the end of the ramp and scrambling quickly onto it, heedless of grit and scraped knees and knuckles.

"Only a little one," Andrew commented, pushing the boat to the ramp.

Carmen, who stood there ready to pass down kitbags, snapped at him. "It might be, but you can get out of the water, silly brother."

Andrew grinned but did as he was told. Willy stood there dripping and fascinated. The shark swam quite close and he saw it was only about a metre long. It was a brown colour and hard to see in the water which was stirred up with silt. The shark swam around for a few minutes and then vanished under the ramp.

That made it worse. "Where did the bloody thing go?" Willy asked. He stared long and hard at the water.

"Never mind," Andrew answered. "We will travel in the boat. Now help me load it."

The kitbags were loaded in, and Willy joined Andrew and Carmen in the boat and helped propel it to shore. Mr Beck and Norman then carefully drove the two '4 Wheelers' loaded with camp equipment down the ramp and into the shallow water. They spluttered ashore and up the beach. A dozen jerry cans of fresh water were then ferried ashore. Mr Beck then did a communications check with the satellite phone.

As soon as that was done, Captain Kirk began calling orders and the *Wewak* winched up her bow ramp and reversed off. As the LCT backed out into deeper water, Willy experienced a sense of being very isolated.

We are a long way from anywhere, he thought. *I hope nothing goes wrong.*

It was 10:00 by then. Mr Beck directed them to move the stores up to the top of the dunes. Willy carried his kitbag and a rolled-up tent up the sandy slope. It was steeper and higher than he had expected and was puffing and sweating profusely by the time he got there. The location did not impress him as a very nice camp site. It was a thicket of small, wind-twisted trees and bushes and five paces into it there was no breeze at all and the air was stifling.

Mr Beck looked around and said, "This isn't very nice. I think we had better spend some time looking for a more suitable campsite."

Carmen pointed east. "There are some casuarinas a couple of hundred metres that way. That might be a better spot."

"We will look," Mr Beck said.

Willy wiped sweat from his face and felt impatience surge. "Oh sir! Can't we also start looking for the plane? There are enough of us to do both things at once."

Willy's father supported him. "I agree. It is only about two kilometres inland from here. I think four of us should go, taking water and radios, while the others find a suitable camp site."

"Who goes?" Willy asked, very anxious to be included.

"Mr Beck and Norman because they have been there before, and some of you kids," Willy's father answered. "Who wants to go?" he asked.

Willy at once put up his hand. So did Andrew and Carmen. Willy's father nodded and said, "Okay, three of you. I think Andrew and Carmen because they are good navigators, and you Willy."

Once that was decided they made sure that the 40 Channel UHF hand-held radios were working and that they had their pocket compasses, maps and water. Willy's father made sure they had their compass bearings worked out correctly both ways.

"We don't want to have to go searching for lost people," he said. "So stay together and be back in two hours please. This is just a preliminary reconnaissance."

Norman extracted a rifle from his gear and checked it. "Just in case of pigs or crocs," he explained.

Satisfied the reconnaissance party was ready, Dr Williams, who had been unconsciously accepted as the leader of the expedition, allowed them to go.

At last! thought Willy as he checked his small compass and then followed Carmen and Andrew into the thicket.

Chapter 25

TOUGH GOING

Within a couple of minutes Willy realised that walking the two kilometres might be tougher than he had anticipated. The thicket was unpleasant to push through and the plants scratchy. That made him glad he wore his long-sleeved, dark blue shirt and long trousers. He was also quickly glad he wore a pair of old cadet books as the sand underfoot was soft and he noticed that Andrew and Carmen, both of whom wore joggers, frequently grumbled about sand. The thicket did not have thorny vines like the wait-a-while and stinging tree of the rainforest, but it had its own unpleasant little surprises.

The first of these was the stifling heat. The next that became quickly apparent were green ants. A few sharp nips around the neck and wrists got Willy and the others slapping and scratching. Next, both Carmen and Norman got stung by native paper wasps.

After pushing through the dense stands of bushes for a hundred metres or so, the group came out in a more open hollow. This was studded with clumps of spiky grass, the points of which easily pierced the cloth, causing exclamations of surprise and pain. At almost the same time yet another irritating surprise was encountered. Carmen suddenly cried out in pain and slapped at the back of her neck.

"March fly," she explained disgustedly.

Willy then realised another was buzzing close to his head. He swatted at it, loathing the big brown flies with their savage bite. Larger than horse flies they settle quietly and then stick in a proboscis about 4 millimetre long to suck blood. It was not the first time any of them had encountered the annoying insects.

Andrew swatted at one and then said, "Bloody things! What I'd like to know is why they are called March flies when they appear in December!"

Willy had to smile. The blasted things were always around in summer, but were not usually a nuisance in the city or the wet rainforest areas. Keeping a wary eye out for more insects he resumed walking.

Beyond the hollow was another sand dune. This appeared to extend off to both sides, parallel to the beach dune. This dune was covered by quite different vegetation: a mixture of paperbarks and cottonwoods. The paperbarks were no worry and there was little undergrowth, but the cottonwoods grew in thickets with branches growing out almost at ground level. These were awkward to negotiate, and all of the group were hot and sweaty by then.

The sandy ground under the cottonwoods was covered in a thick carpet of dead leaves. These crackled and slipped underfoot and also housed various 'nasties'. There were numerous spiders but twice Carmen sprang back in alarm when snakes were seen. Both of these were yellow-bellied blacks. Watching the repulsive reptiles slither away sent cold chills through Willy.

We are a long way from medical help, he worried. He knew that the medical plan was to use the satellite telephone to call for an Emergency Services helicopter. *That will have to come from Cairns and will take a couple of hours to get cranked up and get here, then another hour or so to get back to a hospital,* he calculated. *You could be dead in that time.*

The cottonwoods and paperbarks extended inland for several hundred metres. On the inland side the group came to a paperbark swamp. This brought them to a halt on the edge of the water. Willy stared at the dark-coloured water with distaste and anxiety. It did not look deep and was only a hundred paces across to the next low dune, but…!

Carmen looked at it anxiously. "Do you think we should cross?" she asked.

"You are worried about crocs?" Mr Beck stated.

Carmen nodded. "I am."

Willy felt another stab of fear. His eyes scanned the swamp, staring suspiciously at several semi-submerged logs. "We could detour around it," he suggested.

"We could," Andrew agreed.

So they did. First, they went to the left, but that brought them to a much larger pool, a hundred metres long and fifty wide, and obviously deep water. So they retraced their steps and went to the west. Mr Beck now became anxious, worried that they might get lost. Carmen and Willy both reassured him.

"All we have to do is walk north and we must come to the sea," Carmen said.

In the end they waded a shallow, 25-metre-wide part of the swamp. On the other side they saw another snake. This was a dark, olive brown and more than a metre long. Seeing the reptile got Willy even more concerned.

That might be a taipan. We might survive the bite of a black snake, but not the bite of a taipan, he thought.

He had read that death from a Taipan bite could occur in minutes. To his relief, the snake slid off into some bushes.

Fear now got him looking very carefully at where he placed his feet. The country they were now moving through was across another low sand dune that was aligned parallel to the others. It was covered in waist high dry grass; blady grass and some sort of prickly grass. Trees and bushes made it fairly close country and also blocked both the view and the wind. Only an occasional glimpse of the distant Melville Range gave some assurance of heading in the right direction.

Norman stopped to have a drink. "Bloody hell Dad, how did you ever find a plane wreck in this stuff?" he asked.

"From the air," Mr Beck answered. "It is on the edge of a big salt marsh, and I was a lot younger and a lot fitter then."

Willy also drank, emptying his first water bottle. That worried him because he had only one more and they still had not covered the distance.

After another few hundred metres they came out on the edge of a salt marsh. Much of this was covered with clumps of spiky saltwater grass but there were flat open patches of dry mud and salt pan. As the group walked out of the relative shade of the trees the heat seemed to engulf them. The sun felt as though it was scorching through the cloth of his shirt.

Suddenly Norman gave a low warning hiss and stopped. "Pig!" he whispered.

He stepped clear of them and raised the rifle, working the bolt to load a round into the breech as he did. Willy looked and then sucked in his breath. About a hundred metres away, on the far side of the salt pan, he saw the wild pig. It was big, black, and terrifyingly fast. To his enormous relief, it was running away from them, not charging.

Andrew also gasped and said, "Boar."

"Yes, and just as well," Norman said. "If we run into a sow with piglets we might be in real trouble."

Willy thought of stories he had heard about wild pigs and shuddered. The adult pigs weighed several hundred kilograms and were very strong. He knew that he had no chance of survival in a hand-to-hand struggle with one of the creatures. They had very sharp teeth and wickedly vicious curved tusks that could slice and rip. The only escape was up a big tree. A hasty look around showed the nearest suitable one to be a good hundred paces away and he doubted if he could cover that distance before a wild pig caught him.

The stinging bite of a march fly took his mind temporarily off pigs. He slapped at it and crushed the insect with a feeling of irritated satisfaction. The group resumed walking, going straight across the salt pan on the compass course. It took three minutes of walking in the sweltering heat before they entered the belt of timber beyond.

The soil changed back to sand and the trees changed to some sort of stunted and twisted tree which grew in dense thickets. A few paperbarks grew amongst them. There were more green ants and then they encountered yet another irritating nuisance: hairy caterpillars. Andrew struck a nest of them and cried out in pain and dismay. Within seconds his skin came up in angry red welts. Luckily this was only on his left wrist and hand.

"Will you be alright Andrew?" Carmen asked anxiously.

Andrew nodded. "I think so. It stings but I've been stung by the little buggers before and don't think I am allergic to them," he replied.

They had another drink and Mr Beck studied an aerial photo he had. "This belt of scrub is only a couple of hundred metres wide," he explained. "The salt pan where the 'Kittyhawk' landed is the one on the other side."

"Landed?" Willy queried. "I thought it crashed."

Mr Beck nodded. "The pilot obviously thought it looked the best place to land in this area and he was lucky, to begin with. He got his wheels down on a patch of dry mud and had almost rolled to a standstill near the trees before his wheels broke through the crust. The plane then pitched up on its nose and slid forward in soft mud till it hit the dry sand and stopped. That pilot was a very lucky man," he explained.

"Did he survive?" Andrew asked.

Mr Beck nodded. "Yes. He made his way to the beach and was picked up by a small coaster and taken to Cooktown," he said.

"Didn't the air force try to salvage the wreck?" Carmen asked.

"Yes, they did," Mr Beck replied. "They hauled it off the mud and took out the guns and radios. But the wreck was obviously too far from the beach to haul out so they left it and the sand and leaves blew over it and trees grew up to hide it."

He described again how he had been lucky enough to find the wreck many years before.

The group pushed on through the scrub, sweating and muttering. It became so thick that Willy began to compare it to the jungle, except that the trees were only four or five metres high, and it was all very dry. Suddenly Andrew, who was leading, stopped and cried out. "Come and look at this!"

They hurried forward, stepping out onto a bulldozed vehicle track. Willy stared at it in concern. It was obviously new. The crushed vegetation piled along the sides still had green leaves on it. Deep wheel ruts in the sand showed that vehicles had been along it recently.

"The mineral exploration people?" he suggested.

"Has to be," Norman agreed.

"It is going almost the way we want," Carmen added, lining her compass up with the track.

Willy looked both ways and saw that the clearing ran diagonally from his right rear to his left front. A sharp sense of unease suddenly gripped him. *It is heading for the plane,* he thought.

He said, "Those mining people might find the wreck."

With that he pushed past Andrew and set off along the track as fast as he could stride it out in the soft sand. In the cleared lane the air was stifling, and the sun reflected up off the white sand with a cruel glare. A heat haze shimmered along it. Willy ignored all this and pushed himself to go as fast as he could, ignoring the dripping sweat and hot, rasping breath. The others followed at their best speed, the group quickly stringing out.

After 200 metres of walking Willy came to the edge of the large salt pan. It was at least a kilometre long and half that wide. Here the heat haze shimmered with a regular mirage effect. The vehicle track curved left along the edge of the sand. Willy paused, chest heaving, to take stock.

For a few seconds his eyes misted and went blurry, and he saw black dots. Then he shook his head and wiped sweat from his eyes.

Heat exhaustion, he thought.

Then he gasped in shock as he realised what he was looking at. About a hundred metres away was a cluster of vehicles and men. A big, yellow bulldozer and two trucks were clearly visible. One of the trucks had a side mounted, folding crane and at that very moment it was using it to hoist aboard the wrecked fuselage of a 'Kittyhawk'!

As the full realisation of what he was seeing burst into Willy's consciousness, he experienced a wave of intense anger.

That's our plane! he thought.

With his emotions boiling he ran towards the truck. But he didn't run very far. He was too winded and hot, and his speed dropped to stumbling trot.

While he ran towards the trucks, Willy saw that the fuselage was being settled into a timber cradle on the back of the truck. The men were so intent on what they were doing that they did not notice him until he was only about ten paces from them. Then one man glanced around and jumped in surprise. He was big man, wearing grey overalls and a white plastic 'hard hat'.

"What the...? Who the bloody hell are you?" the man cried.

"That's our plane," Willy croaked, his breath now coming in hot gasps.

The man laughed. Willy came to a tumbling standstill and was aware that at least four other men were watching. He gulped and tried to recover his breath. Then another person moved from behind the truck, a man dressed all in white, and Willy gasped again.

"Mr Jemmerling!"

Mr Jemmerling frowned and then said, "Hello, young Willy. You look a bit hot."

Boiling anger seethed in Willy. He panted and then shouted, "That's our plane!"

"I think not," Mr Jemmerling replied coolly, his gaze shifting to the others who were now hurrying to join Willy. "Finders-keepers covers it I think."

"But we came all this way to get it!" Willy cried in furious dismay.

"So did I," Mr Jemmerling replied. He then said, "Hello, Mr Beck. Hello, young Norman. And hello to you two also."

Mr Jemmerling's cool manner further infuriated Willy. "You can't take the plane without a permit."

Mr Jemmerling shook his head and flicked open a plastic folder he was carrying. "I have a permit. I think it is a case of 'The early bird catches the worm'."

"You are the worm!" cried Willy. "You have cheated us."

Mr Jemmerling pursed his lips. "There is no need to descend to personal abuse," he said. "I haven't cheated anyone. It was a fair race and I won."

"You deceived us and tricked us, taking us on that flight," Willy retorted.

He was so upset he felt tears prickle in his eyes and he blinked to avoid the humiliation.

"Be careful what you say young Willy," Mr Jemmerling replied calmly. "You knew I was after the information, and you joined us with your eyes open. And you are being a bit ungrateful."

Willy knew he was and that spurred his emotions into a seething mixture. "You spied on us, and you robbed us to get the maps," he accused.

Mr Jemmerling's eyes narrowed, and he said, "I don't like being accused of being a cheat or a thief. I have done none of those things. The only information I was ever lucky enough to get from you people was when your friend put his finger on the map one night at your Air Cadet depot."

Bloody Stick and Noddy! Willy thought angrily.

He was aware that the other members of the group were now standing next to him. The men in Mr Jemmerling's work team were all standing on the truck or beside him. They looked ready to support their employer.

Willy said, "You had that man break into Mr Beck's and steal his notes and charts."

A flush of anger showed on Mr Jemmerling's face, and he snapped. "I haven't paid anyone to burgle anyone. Be careful young man. If you continue to make unfounded allegations, I will take you to court for slander."

Andrew gripped Willy's arm, and muttered, "Steady on Willy. We have no proof."

Willy was still very upset, so he said, "We saw the same man in Cooktown. He was spying on us and then he got in a boat and headed out into the river towards your flying boat."

Mr Jemmerling frowned. "I have no idea what you are talking about.

Now stop making accusations or back them up in court." He then turned to Mr Beck. "Sorry, Mr Beck, but we were here first. This is my plane now."

But Willy wasn't ready to give up. "So how could you possibly find this plane without using Mr Beck's notes and map?" he challenged.

"By doing some research in the historical records, by doing a lot of flying at low altitude and taking hundreds of aerial photographs, and by using all the expertise and equipment of my mineral exploration team," Mr Jemmerling replied, for the first time showing a glint of real anger.

"Mineral exploration!" spat Willy. "You must have lied to Capt Kirk to hire his ship to transport you."

One of the men took a step forward, fists clenched but Mr Jemmerling restrained him. "I will handle this thanks, Mr Jenkins. Now listen here, I don't like being called a liar, particularly by an ignorant and ungrateful boy. You underestimate me. This is a real mineral exploration team. Mine. I own the firm and I employ these men. When this little task is done, they will survey our whole lease here. So I haven't lied to anyone."

The retort really stung Willy, particularly the accusation of being ungrateful. Looking at the tough looking men of the work crew doubt entered his mind and he flushed with embarrassment at possibly having made a real fool of himself.

"Oh but!" Willy cried, frustration, suspicion, and doubt swirling in his mind.

He glanced at Mr Beck and was appalled at what he saw. Mr Beck looked very red in the face and his disappointment was plain on his face. Norman had a bitter twist to his lips and both Andrew and Carmen looked both puzzled and angry.

Norman said, "That's enough, Willy. We have no proof."

"No, you can't have any," Mr Jemmerling said, "Because I haven't done any of those things. Now please move off our work site and let us get on with our work."

Reluctantly Willy allowed himself to be led a few paces to one side. Intense feelings of bitter disappointment and defeat surged through him. He looked around and noted that both wings of the wreck were lying under the trees. They were badly corroded and buckled but were still real wings. Timber packing frames lay nearby. Realising how thirsty and how close to heat exhaustion he was, he took out his water bottle and drank.

Andrew also drank, then held his water bottle upside down to indicate he was out of water. Mr Jemmerling, glancing around, saw this and said, "Would you like some water?"

"Not from you!" Willy cried.

He knew he was being bad-mannered and churlish and that only fuelled his unreasonable anger. Knowing that he was reacting that way did not help much, just made him more angry at himself. Mr Jemmerling glanced at him and turned his back, making Willy feel even worse.

Norman now took charge. He took a couple of photographs and then said, "There is nothing more we can do here. We had better go back to the beach to tell the others. Come on."

He and Mr Beck turned and sadly walk away. Carmen took Willy's sleeve and urged him to follow. Andrew came last. As he plodded along the scorching vehicle track, Willy felt the bitter taste of defeat.

Beaten! he thought. *Too late!*

Chapter 26

HARSH WORDS

As he walked away, Willy was on the verge of tears. He was so disappointed that he felt like lashing out. Seething with bitter resentment he looked back, noting the vehicles, the men working busily, the bulldozed bush, and the aircraft wreck. The sight of Mr Jemmerling watching them go added to his anger.

"It's not fair!" Willy cried.

Norman nodded. "It's a real disappointment, that is for sure," he said.

Willy started to go over all of the angry thoughts that swirled in his head. "How could Jemmerling possibly have a permit when you already have one Mr Beck?" he asked.

Mr Beck, who was puffing along at the rear and looking quite worn out gave a wry smile and replied, "It's called money. He obviously paid the government the required fee and they issued him with one."

"But how could they issue two permits for the one plane?" Willy persisted.

Mr Beck shrugged. "I've had mine for a few years. Maybe they thought I was no longer interested. I should have checked with them."

By then the group had reached the place where the bulldozed track went into the scrub. After one last, bitter look at the aircraft, now being crated up on the back of the truck, Willy followed Andrew and Carmen along it.

"I still say it is unfair," he grumbled.

Norman grunted and then said, "It is, but life is sometimes like that. Anyway, the 'Kittyhawk' doesn't look like it is in very good condition. All the bottom of the fuselage and half the wings have corroded and rotted away, and the engine just looks like a ball of rust."

Mr Beck agreed. "All those years in that salty environment can't have done it much good."

The group trudged along in the blazing heat, each step now seeming to be an effort in the soft sand. When they came to the point where they had entered the track Carmen stopped.

"Do we go back through the scrub on a compass course?" she asked.

"This track goes back to the beach," Norman said.

"Yes, but it will be shorter to walk in a straight line," Andrew said.

"And a lot cooler. At least in the bush there is some shade," Carmen added.

Willy drained the last of his water and held the bottle up. "I'm out of water. I vote we stay in the shade."

Mr Beck agreed. To Willy he looked utterly worn out. A twinge of concern that the old man might collapse in the heat made him bite his lip. He saw Norman giving his father anxious glances as well.

"The track might be easier to follow," he suggested.

Willy glared along the bulldozed lane. To him it looked as raw as the hurt he was feeling. "I'm not walking along Jemmerling's track," he said.

Carmen aimed her compass into the scrub. "Bush it is. Let's go."

That ended the argument. The group plunged back into the scrub, walking quickly. It was still very hot, but Willy was sure that the small amount of shade more than compensated for the effort of weaving around the trees. It only took them a few minutes to reach the smaller salt pan. Carmen walked straight across it.

As they reached the bush on the other side, Norman called from behind, "Slow down a bit, please. Dad's not as young as he used to be."

Carmen slowed down but kept steadily on. Willy blinked perspiration from his eyes but then licked dry lips. His tongue and mouth felt dry and he had a headache. That warned him he was entering the first stages of heat stress.

When I stop sweating is the real danger point, he reminded himself, remembering First Aid lessons at cadets.

Norman again called out, "Carmen, aren't you using your compass?"

Carmen shook her head, but it was Andrew who answered. "We are just following our footprints," he explained.

Willy looked down and felt silly. *I didn't think of that,* he thought.

They plodded on, weaving and pushing through the cottonwoods, eyes alert for snakes and other 'beasties'. Ten minutes sweaty walking brought them to the tea-tree swamp. Here the footprints were not as obvious, but Willy recognised the place and they crossed easily at the narrowest point. They pushed on into the scrub beyond, again following their tracks from the outward journey. By then Willy was no longer worried.

The sea is only a few hundred metres to the north, he thought.

At 01:20pm, the group burst through the last line of the thicket and emerged on top pf the beach dune. Ahead of them the blue tropical ocean filled half the horizon. Willy sighed with relief as a faint breeze cooled his heated skin. Then he eyed the *Wewak.* The LCT was anchored about half a kilometre offshore and lay side on to the beach. At that distance the rust and grime weren't visible so her black hull and white superstructure looked quite impressive. The old phrase: 'A painted ship on a painted ocean' flitted through Willy's mind.

Then what he thought of as 'the betrayal' took over as the main thoughts, fuelling very mixed emotions. Did Captain Kirk know? Was he a party to any deception? Willy found it hurtful even to think such thoughts as he really liked Graham and his father, and they had been very well treated on the ship.

But I need to know, he told himself.

Carmen and Andrew slid down the face of the dune and began walking to the right along the beach. Willy followed, then looked back to check that Mr Beck and Norman were following. They were but Mr Beck looked awful. 'Haggard' was the word that flitted across Willy's mind.

We only walked about five kilometres at most, he calculated, *and it took us about three hours.* He knew from listening to Graham and Peter that a fit soldier could have covered that distance in one hour. *We aren't really ready for this sort of thing,* he thought.

A hundred metres away, under the casuarinas that lined that part of the beach, Willy saw the others waiting. The sight of his parents made him feel simultaneously relieved and depressed.

We failed, he thought.

That was the theme of the conversation for the next few hours. Seated in the shade under a tarpaulin stretched between four trees the group sat around and discussed the situation, and what to do next. It felt particularly bitter to Willy. The holiday adventure of discovery and exploration that he had looked forward to for weeks had ended within hours; and ended in a horrible shock.

"Should we go and watch what Mr Jemmerling is doing?" Stick suggested.

Willy's father shook his head. "No point. We know what they are doing. Besides, it is much too hot now."

Willy could only agree with that. They had shade and there was a faint breeze coming off the land, and he was full of water again, but the heat was fierce. Waves of it could be seen shimmering along the beach. When the mosquitoes, March Flies and irritating high-pitched whine of the cicadas were added to that it was distinctly unpleasant.

"It might at least rain," Willy grumbled, eyeing the distant clouds lining the horizon.

"That's why the tourists come to this part of the world in winter," his mother replied.

"But what will we do now?" Willy cried in exasperation.

"Go home and then try again after Christmas," his mother replied calmly.

Willy pouted. "But Jemmerling might beat us to the other wreck as well," he said.

"He might," his father agreed. "Presuming he knows there is a second wreck and where to look."

"Does he know if there is a second wreck?" Carmen asked.

Willy wasn't sure. He re-ran in his head all the conversations and incidents he could remember, but was left feeling unsure and uneasy.

The group talked themselves out eventually and then lay around in the shade resting or talking about other things. To ward off the attacks of the sandflies, mosquitoes and March Flies Willy's mother insisted they put up mosquito nets. These were ex-army ones that were tied up by four corner strings. Willy lay under his, feeling hot and depressed. From time to time he got up and looked along the beach to the west to see if Mr Jemmerling's party had reached the sea.

On one occasion Andrew joined him. There was no sign of life further along the beach. Andrew gestured at the exposed sand bars and shoals. "It is low water. They can't load the landing craft until high water."

"When is that?" Willy asked, irritated that he hadn't thought of such an obvious fact.

Andrew looked thoughtful for a moment then said, "Be about 10 tonight, but I don't think Captain Kirk will try to beach the *Wewak* in the dark. More likely tomorrow morning at about eleven."

That answer irritated Willy too, condemning them to a long night of waiting. He blinked in the glare of the setting sun and muttered irritably, "Bloody Hell, it's hot!"

It was too. The dry sand of the upper beach felt as though it was scorching the skin. As both Willy and Andrew had removed their boots and socks to cool down, they had to run back up the beach to the shade.

The sun seemed to hang in the sky forever, blazing down, causing sweat to trickle and tempers to flay. At last it slid downwards, going down behind the trees to the West southwest. As it went down, the evening meal was prepared and eaten. Willy did not have any appetite but his mother insisted he eat something. A corned beef sandwich was the best he could manage. Marjorie was no help. She just sat and grumbled, plucking at her sweat soaked shirt and pushing sticky straggles of hair away from her face.

The temperature dropped a few degrees to give relative coolness as the sun went down in a magnificent blaze of red sky. A different species of mosquito began to swarm and bite, causing much application of repellent. Lanterns were lit and Willy's father insisted that they organise a sentry roster.

"We aren't nearly far enough from the sea and there is a swamp inland of us. We need guards awake in case a croc decides it is Christmas," he explained.

It was a long, depressing evening. When it was bedtime Willy lay under his mosquito net but was quite unable to sleep. For hours he lay awake, brooding and feeling bitter. He found it a relief to be out on guard duty ('Watch' as Andrew and Carmen called it.). From 01:00am to 03:00am he stood out on the beach with a big torch, turning it on occasionally to check that no red eyes were gleaming from the water. For the first hour he shared with Andrew and for the second with Norman.

But nothing happened. The sea was calm, with only a faint breeze blowing offshore so that there was no surf, just a gentle lapping. The lights of the *Wewak* shone brightly, reflected on the water. The moon was almost full so there was plenty of light. When Andrew walked off along the beach to do a pee Willy could still see him clearly at a hundred metres. Apart from the occasional squark of some night bird and a few splashes from the ocean there was no sign of life.

When Willy lay down after being relieved by Stick, he again fidgeted and sweated. But this time he dropped into a restless sleep.

It was so hot and humid that Willy slept only fitfully and woke feeling drained out and grimy. Even in the grey before the sun came up he found he was perspiring. He hoped there might be a breeze when the sun rose but there wasn't. The camp came slowly to life. Marjorie sat up and Willy thought she looked a real wreck. Her face was puffy and her hair had its usual morning 'rat's nest' appearance.

Seeing him she said, "I am not enjoying this. I want to go home."

That was how Willy felt. *All that effort for nothing!* he thought bitterly.

Breakfast was eaten almost in silence. Mr Beck looked pale and ill and shook his head. "I'm getting too old for this sort of caper," he grumbled.

"Do we go home?" Willy asked.

"Nothing else to do," his father replied. "No point in hanging around another three days."

"Can we go on the *Wewak*?" Stick asked. "I thought it was contracted to do some other job for a couple of days."

"We can ask," Willy's father answered.

Andrew pointed. "There's a boat coming ashore now," he said.

Willy looked and saw a small dinghy leave the side of the LCT. "It's not heading for us," he observed.

"No. It's making for Mr Jemmerling's landing place," Carmen said.

Norman raised binoculars and studied the small boat. It had three people in it. "Captain Kirk is in that boat."

Willy's father stood up. "Let's go and talk to him then," he said.

Willy stood up with the others, even though he did not feel like seeing Mr Jemmerling again. Just the thought of the previous day made him feel bitter and angry.

Marjorie sensed his mood and slipped her arm through his. "Cheer up Willy. It will be alright," she said.

But Willy wasn't in the mood. Knowing that he was being difficult made him feel even more sulky. He wished Marjorie would let go but she kept on walking with him. As they walked along the beach, his mood got rapidly worse. The catalyst was the appearance on the beach of the big truck carrying the 'Kittyhawk' wreck. It came out of the dunes and stopped halfway down the beach. A white 4WD followed it. Several men got out and stood on the water's edge waiting for the small boat.

As he got closer to the vehicles, Willy saw that Mr Jemmerling was one of the men. Another was Mr Jenkins. By the time Willy and the others arrived the men had finished talking and stood watching the new arrivals. Mr Beck and Norman came from behind on one of the 'Four Wheelers'. They arrived almost at the same time.

Captain Kirk called to Mr Beck as he dismounted. "Hello, Mr Beck. How are things going?"

"No good, Captain. Mr Jemmerling here has beaten us to the aeroplane. We have come to ask if you can take us back to Cooktown or Cairns today."

Captain Kirk nodded. "Yes, he was just telling me that and organising to load the plane on the *Wewak*."

"Our aeroplane!" Willy cried, his anger rising along with his suspicions.

"Willy!" his father called warningly.

"It is ours! He's tricked us out of it," Willy cried. He turned to Captain Kirk and said, "You shouldn't take it sir."

"Why not?" Captain Kirk demanded. "I have been contracted to carry cargo for Mr Jenkins today and his money is as good as yours."

Willy was stunned. Several comments he had heard now fitted into place. "He has contracted you? Or was it Mr Jemmerling?" he demanded.

Captain Kirk looked annoyed and replied, "I am not at liberty to disclose information that is 'Commercial-in-Confidence'. As long as the cargo is legal then I will carry it. I have a business to run."

Mr Jemmerling held out his folder. "We have a permit to remove the wreck, Captain."

Willy felt really betrayed and let down. He cried, "Maybe, but I'll bet you don't have a permit to bulldoze all that bush in the National Park there!"

Mr Jemmerling gave Willy a hostile look but did not reply. Willy turned to Captain Kirk and cried, "Oh sir! You are helping our enemies! You are letting us down."

This time Captain Kirk frowned. "Don't you talk to me like that boy! I am just running a shipping business. As it is, I am going out of my way to help, giving your group special rates. If you speak to me like that, I will charge the full charter cost, even if you go back early."

Once again, Willy's father called on him to be quiet. But Willy was really upset. "But it's not fair!" he shouted.

Captain Kirk scowled and snapped back, "Listen lad, it costs thousands of dollars a day to run a vessel like the *Wewak*. I have a family to feed and a business to look after so I can't do this as a charity. If you keep on like this, you will not be welcome on my ship. Then you can find some other way to get back to Cairns. And you can find another ship for your next trip."

Willy's mother now pushed forward. "Willy! That is enough talk like that! Captain Kirk is right. He is only doing his job and he has employees to pay. So stop this silly talk." She turned to Captain Kirk and said, "I'm sorry, Mr Kirk. It is just that Willy has been looking forward to finding the wreck and is now very disappointed."

Willy was, but he was also appalled at what he had said. The thought that he might be responsible for his parents and the Becks paying many thousands of dollars to hire the *Wewak* for several more days, and that the LCT might not be available for the trip after Christmas, quickly calmed him.

He swallowed and bit back tears, then said to Captain Kirk, "Sorry sir. I'm just a bit upset."

"Humpf! Well, yes. Thank you. Now, let's get things moving. Mr Beck, you said you would like to have your party transported back today?"

"That's right," Mr Beck said.

"You will have to travel with Mr Jemmerling's driver," Captain Kirk said.

"That's alright," Mr Beck replied. He gave Mr Jemmerling a hard look and then turned to check that the others had no problem with that.

Willy wanted to say that he would rather be marooned than travel in the same ship as Mr Jemmerling but he managed to hold his tongue. Instead he turned and walked away, deeply embarrassed and upset. One of the reasons for leaving quickly was that tears had sprung into his eyes and he did not want anyone to see them. Marjorie hurried after him and he quickly wiped his face and tried to pretend he was alright.

The group returned to their camp and packed up. Captain Kirk went back to the *Wewak* and conned the LCT in to the beach on the incoming tide. By 10:00am the barge was ashore and the truck was driven aboard. By then the camping gear had been loaded on the 4 Wheelers and they were driven along the beach and up the ramp onto the LCT. The others walked along, carrying their bags.

By the time they arrived at the landing craft they were all sweating and Willy was getting a headache from the fierce glare off the sea and sand. He saw Mr Jemmerling talking on a radio in the white 4WD and looked away, still feeling deeply angry at the man. He made his way up onto the tank deck and walked aft past the truck. In the tank deck it was like an oven, and he found it a relief to climb up to the main deck level.

As Willy dropped his bag under the canvas awning just forward of the superstructure his ears detected the unmistakeable hum of aero engines. He moved to the rail and looked out. Into view from the south came a dark, twin-engine aircraft. Willy recognised the distinctive silhouette of a Catalina.

The Pterodactyl. *Maybe Jemmerling isn't travelling with us?* he thought.

He wasn't. The Catalina landed, sent a rubber boat crewed by Mr Hobbs ashore and picked Mr Jemmerling up, took him out to the flying boat which then took off. Mr Jenkins drove off in the white 4WD and only one of Mr Jemmerling's men, the truck driver, a solid looking middle-aged man name Al, boarded the *Wewak*.

As soon as the truck was secured by chains and turnbuckles the *Wewak* reversed off the beach. This time Willy noted that the LCT had dropped a stern anchor on the way in and a winch attached to its cable helped haul the barge off the sand. But Willy wasn't really interested. He just stood at the port rail and sulked.

Once well clear of the shallows *Wewak* started moving slow ahead and turned to port. Once she was facing east and parallel to the beach the engines were moved to cruising speed and the homeward journey begun. Willy stood staring out to sea but hardly noted the distant islands and clouds. Only when he was called inside for lunch did he move.

The voyage back was not a happy cruise. Willy brooded and mostly stood at the starboard rail and watched the coastline slide by. He was annoyed that both of his parents quite happily spoke to Mr Jemmerling's man. Willy knew that he was being churlish about the situation and that fuelled his anger. The man was only doing his job and had not even been aware of any rivalry so was blameless. But Willy still thought of him as being a member of the enemy camp and ignored him.

In the evening, as the *Wewak* came south past Cape Flattery, Willy sat outside with Marjorie. She snuggled up and tried to comfort him, but he wasn't in the mood. Not only did he intensely dislike the feel of sticky skin on sticky skin, but he did not want the 'We-know-what-ya-doing!' looks from the others. His rejection put her in a bad mood, and she also began to sulk.

"It's not the end of the world!" she cried, clearly miffed. Then she went off inside, leaving him to his dejection.

What didn't help was being able to look at the truck and its tarpaulin covered cargo. It was almost as though it was being flaunted as a trophy to irritate, although he knew this wasn't so. What was also worrying Willy was the thought that Mr Jemmerling might also beat them to the second wreck, the 'Beaufighter'. He was deeply bothered by the fact that Captain Kirk had said in Mr Jemmerling's hearing that the group planned a second trip.

Now he was sure that Mr Jemmerling knew that there was another wreck.

Chapter 27

ANXIOUS HOLIDAY

For Willy the journey back to Cairns was a time of anxiety and dejection. During the night he slept badly, experiencing dreams of pushing endlessly through scrub and swamps only to always arrive too late. By daylight the *Wewak* was abeam of Cape Tribulation, having by-passed Cooktown. For the next eight hours Willy grouched and brooded until both his mother and his father separately told him to snap out of it.

"But Mr Jemmerling might beat us to the 'Beaufighter' too!" Willy snapped back.

"So what?" his father replied. "Just think of it as a race and enjoy the competition."

Willy knew that was sound advice, but he found it hard to do. At the back of his mind was the constant niggling worry that it would not be a fair competition; that Mr Jemmerling was spying on them.

He may even have a paid spy in our ranks, he thought unhappily, Stick's face flitting across his mind.

At 2:15pm the *Wewak* turned into the main shipping channel at Cairns. Willy stood with his friends at the starboard rail and watched the city grow larger as they got closer. The weather had been building up and the bow of the barge was thumping into waves continually, making her shudder, as well as roll and twist. That got Marjorie feeling woozy and Stick looked unhappy. For Willy it merely meant hanging on. Now he just wanted to get home.

Andrew came past and smiled. "Won't be long now," he said cheerfully.

"Can't be too soon for me," Willy said.

Andrew shrugged. "I think it's great. I'm really looking forward to next week."

"What happens then?"

"We are taking cargo to Thursday Island," Andrew replied. Then he grinned and added, "The mate tells me it will mostly be a load of beer. He says the nickname for T. I. is 'Thirsty Island'."

Willy knew that both Carmen and Andrew were staying on as crew members of the *Wewak*. He asked, "Will you be home for Christmas?"

Andrew nodded. "Just. We are due back on the twenty third. That will give us time to do some Christmas shopping," he said.

"Oh! Christmas shopping!" Willy groaned.

Marjorie squeezed his arm and snuggled against him. "Ooh! I like shopping. What are you giving me for Christmas Willy?" she asked.

Willy felt trapped. He had not yet decided. "What would you like?" he asked.

"You know what I like," she said with an impish grin.

"Apart from that!" Willy cried. Then he blushed when the others all laughed and teased them. "You know what I mean!" he said in exasperation.

"We know alright!" Stick teased, causing Willy to blush some more.

Andrew shook his head and moved on aft. The conversation moved to what else they could do during the holidays seeing they were finishing the expedition five days early. Carmen came past and heard this.

She grinned and said, "You could always go looking for that crashed plane in the jungle up behind Castor."

This suggestion drew cries of mock horror. More sensible suggestions followed: swimming, picnics, parties, shopping. The conversation continued in a desultory way until the *Wewak* had passed the main wharves, navy base and bulk sugar terminal. Off the mouth of Smiths Creek the *Wewak* was met by a tug and manoeuvred so that its bow ramp was placed on a concrete ramp. The tug was necessary as the tidal flow would have otherwise kept swinging the LCT's stern around.

While this was going on the lashings securing the truck carrying the 'Kittyhawk' were cast off. As the driver climbed into his cab Willy's father said, "He is driving it all the way to Mr Jemmerling's museum in New South Wales."

When the bow ramp was lowered the first person Willy saw standing on the shore was Mr Jemmerling. He had several photographers with him and that peeved Willy even more.

He is big-noting himself with the press, he thought sourly.

The 4 Wheelers and the truck were driven off and then the bow ramp winched back up. The tug, which had been pushing sideways against the stern, tooted and backed away, then the LCT reversed back out into

Trinity Inlet. A few minutes later, it was heading up Smiths Creek to Portsmith, proceeding slowly against the outgoing tide. As they came opposite the wharf at Portsmith Willy saw Graham, his sister and mother standing there. Graham waved and he gave a half-hearted wave back. The *Wewak* did some manoeuvring with one screw pushing forward and the other aft until the vessel had done a 180 degree turn and was facing back down the creek. She was then edged in against the wharf and tied up.

As soon as the gangway was in place, farewells were said. Willy now felt so ashamed of how he had spoken to Captain Kirk that he avoided him, but he did thank the other members of the crew. As he made his way down onto the wharf, he hoped his omission had not been noticed but inside he did not feel good.

I should have been brave enough to do the good-mannered thing, he told himself.

Despising himself for being a weakling he made his way back aboard and sought out Captain Kirk. "Thank you, sir, and sorry for my rudeness," he said.

Captain Kirk gave him a hard look, then nodded and accepted the outstretched hand. "Don't be so quick to rush to judgement young man," he said. Then he smiled and said, "See you next voyage."

Feeling much better Willy made his way ashore. "Hello Graham, how are you? How did your promotion course go?" he asked.

"Okay," Graham replied.

Kylie snorted. "Okay indeed! He topped the warrant officers course, Willy."

"Hi Kylie. Well done Graham. How did your mates do?" Willy asked.

"Pete topped the sergeants course; Steve came ninth, and Roger came seventeenth out of two hundred on the corporals course," Graham replied.

Willy really wanted to ask how Barbara had done but Marjorie had now joined him, so he did not dare. Instead he said, "We didn't get the plane. Mr Jemmerling beat us to it."

"I know," Graham answered. "Dad told us."

The reference to Captain Kirk made Willy feel embarrassed. To keep the conversation going he said, "What are you planning to do for the holidays?"

Graham made a face and so did Kylie. Graham gestured to the *Wewak* and said, "Acting as voluntary unpaid crew on the *Bounty* with Captain Bligh," he grumbled.

Mrs Kirk heard this and said, "Graham, don't speak about your father like that. You know it is necessary."

Graham made a wry face. Willy said, "Unpaid?"

Graham nodded. "That's right. The whole family is going to sea. Mum takes over from the cook and us kids become deckhands. Alex is already at sea on the *Malita*."

Willy was surprised. "Is that necessary?" he asked.

Graham's mouth tightened into a grim line. "Yes. It is the only way Dad can afford to allow the crew to take annual leave. It's getting worse every year. As the roads in Cape York Peninsula get better there is less trade for the coastal shipping. So the family have to help out."

"But Andrew and Carmen get paid?" Willy asked.

Graham nodded. "Yes, but as apprentices on junior wages."

"Rather you than me," Willy said. He was about to add more but was interrupted by a teary-eyed Marjorie. "Marj. What's wrong?" he asked.

"M... Mum... and (sniff) Dad, have (sob) have decided we can go to Brisbane to Aunty Ethel's (sob) straight away. They said we can (sniffle) l... l... leave the d... d... day after to... tomorrow. Oh, boo hoo!" she cried.

Willy felt stunned and hurt. *Can nothing go right now?* he thought.

Then he gathered his thoughts and said, "Then I'd better get you your Christmas present tomorrow."

"Thank you," Marjorie wailed. Then she cried, "I want to stay here with you. Oh boo hoo, sniff!"

She flung her arms around Willy and sobbed.

Marjorie's father called, "Come on girlie! You've had a bleedin' week to do all that. Now let's get home."

Willy kissed her on the cheek and gently eased her away. Still sobbing she was led away. Stick gave a wry smile and waved and walked off after them. Willy felt suddenly very lonely. The Becks came and shook hands and wished everyone a Merry Christmas.

"See you on the twenty seventh," Norman said as he left.

After a few more words the Kirks made their way aboard *Wewak*. Willy sighed and bent to pick up his bag. His father called to him, and he followed his parents to where a taxi waited.

He did manage to give Marjorie her Christmas presents the next day, but it was a short meeting. The presents were a silk scarf, a bracelet and some music CDs. All were wrapped in gift paper.

"You are not to open them until after Santa Claus has been," he said.

Marjorie sniffed and said, "Oh poo! And here are yours." She handed him two quite large cardboard boxes wrapped in bright coloured paper. Then her face crumpled, and she dissolved in tears.

"Oh! I won't see you for nearly five weeks!" she wailed.

Willy did not know quite how he felt about that. Part of him felt relieved but he had to admit he liked to be with her. *And I'll miss the cuddles,* he admitted. All he could do was whisper nice things and hope she was satisfied.

Then the meeting was over, and he was whisked away by his mother to do more Christmas shopping. That night he felt quite depressed and more lonely than he cared to admit. It brought home to him that most of his friends at school and Air Cadets were really only acquaintances. The people he really felt more in common with were Andrew, Peter, and Graham.

For three days, Willy did chores at home and went shopping with his mother. He saw almost no friends and got quite lonely. Work on plastic models did not hold his interest and he had bad dreams about dead bodies in the sea. Most of all he fretted about Mr Jemmerling beating them to the second plane.

This last concern was only slightly eased on the fourth day when they visited the Becks to deliver some Christmas presents and Mr Beck told them that Mr Jemmerling had flown south in the *Pterodactyl.* "He's not the only one with spies," Mr Beck added sagely.

At that Norman scoffed and said, "Oh baloney Dad! I was told that by the mechanic at the airport. He said that the Catalina badly needed an overhaul and was being taken to Sydney. He added that the work could take several weeks."

"So we still have a chance!" Willy cried. It was the first good news he had received, and it cheered him up enormously.

From the Becks the Williams family went to Aunty Isabel's farm near Davies Creek. They stayed there for the next four days, only going back to Cairns on Christmas Eve. Aunty Isabel went with them.

Once at home there was a flurry of shopping, putting up of decorations and present wrapping. Willy relaxed a little and made himself enter into the spirit of the occasion. When all his presents to others were wrapped and labelled, he placed them under the tree. He then went to bed feeling some of the excitement of his younger years. It had been some years since his parents had snuck in to his bedroom after he was asleep to place a pillow case full of presents on his bed so he did not try to stay awake.

For once he slept very soundly. When he woke on Christmas morning Willy was both amused and pleased to find a pillowcase full of presents on his bed. It made him feel very valued and loved and he felt quite emotional for a few minutes. Then he explored the pillowcase. The presents were nothing big or expensive, but he enjoyed the thought that people loved him and cared. There were small chocolates, several comic books, a pencil sharpener shaped like an aeroplane, some toy cars, and a small plastic kit of a 'Hurricane'.

His mother looked in and smiled, then came to kiss him. She then told him to get up and moving. After a shower, shave and dressing Willy had a good breakfast and then sat in the lounge room, waiting impatiently for the other members of the household to finish whatever they were doing so that the presents could be opened. Willy then acted as courier and one at a time handed the presents to each person.

For his father, Willy had purchased a tool kit with an electric drill attachment. To his mother he gave a craft kit that had embroidery and also a weaving frame and coloured yarn to thread through it. Lloyd was given golf balls with his name on them and three music CDs. Aunty Isabel got a book on Australian native birds and that caused her face to light up with pleasure. Willy felt he had done well.

In return he got a nice dress shirt from her. Lloyd gave him a 1:72 scale plastic model kit of a PBY 5 Catalina. Marjorie's present was another 1:72 scale plastic kit, of a Dutch Dornier Flying Boat. With it was a note saying 'Sorry. I couldn't find a Catalina'.

This is even better, Willy thought, studying the picture on the front of the box with great interest.

There was better to come. His mother gave him a digital camera and his father gave him a voucher for a 2-hour ultra-light flight from Mareeba.

"These are great!" he cried, smiling happily around at them all.

Then he studied the brochure with the ultra-light voucher and wondered if he could get them to take him to places he wanted to see.

Like Mt Mulligan, he thought.

It was a very happy Christmas and was followed by a huge roast meal: chicken, turkey, roast potato, vegetables, gravy; all followed by cheesecake, ice cream and chocolates. It was a happy boy that slipped between the sheets that night. As he drifted off to sleep the thought uppermost in his mind was that the second expedition, the one to find the 'Beaufighter', started in less than 36 hours.

On Boxing Day Willy became even more anxious and excited.

Nearly time to go, he thought.

He felt driven to try to find the wreck before Mr Jemmerling. During the day he had to go with his parents to visit relations, notably Aunty Mary, who was actually a 92-year-old great aunt. She was a real old dear so Willy didn't mind too much, but he was glad to get home so he could start packing for the trip.

This time the trip was to be longer, at least an extra day each way just travelling, and they were warned to prepare for two weeks away. That led Willy to pack some books and notepaper as well as his normal camping gear. Remembering the thirst problem from the previous trip he added an extra water bottle to his belt and also some packets of glucose lollies. By bedtime he was packed and ready.

That night Willy was very restless. He had frequent and vivid dreams. These were half nightmares and half erotica. The nightmares always had mangled bodies and sharks in them, and he kept seeing grinning skulls under the sea. The erotic dreams always began with some silly problem from Air Cadets. He was on the promotion course and the Passing-Out Parade was forming up and he couldn't find his boots or trousers. Then Barbara appeared and his mind struggled with the fact that she wasn't an air cadet so could not be there. However she was smiling and warm and willing. But when they began to embrace and kiss she somehow changed into Marjorie!

Willy woke on the 27th feeling both tired and excited. He had a tingling feeling of adventure and felt sure that this time they would be successful. This time his mother was not going, which Willy regretted. She had a medical conference to attend. Lloyd was also staying at home. So it was a slightly emotional farewell at the wharf. Willy's mother drove them there but did not stay.

"No tearful farewells on the jetty for me thanks," she said.

But Willy was a bit tearful. He also felt that this trip would be different.

To begin with we have a somewhat different team, he thought as the Becks arrived.

Now he really missed Stick and Marjorie. In their place were Graham and his sister Kylie. Andrew and Carmen were both there and again would be acting as crew on the *Wewak.* The old LCT was at least familiar and Willy half viewed her with affection.

Cargo was still being loaded by mobile crane when they arrived, so Graham, Kylie and Captain Kirk were already hard at work. Andrew and Carmen hurried to join them. Mrs Kirk took charge and ushered the group aboard and allocated bunks. This time Willy and his father were given bunks in the saloon on the dining benches. Mrs Kirk had the cook's cabin and Graham and Andrew had the deckhand's cabin and the Becks the spare cabin on the bridge deck. Kylie and Carmen shared the bosun's cabin. Thus nobody had to bunk out on the open deck.

When all the gear was stowed Willy went out to watch. He found that the tank deck was full of tractors, two trucks, boxes, fuel drums and an assortment of general cargo such as coils of fencing wire, steel pickets, tools, timber, and corrugated iron.

It was not until 11:30am that all the cargo was loaded and made secure, with tarpaulins lashed over most of it. Captain Kirk then called a halt for a wash and then lunch. This was cold meat and salad and was eaten with a great deal of cheerful chatter. As the saloon could not seat them all Willy took a sandwich and moved to sit out under the awning with Graham and Andrew.

During lunch Willy listened to Graham and Andrew tell stories about their voyage to Thursday Island. Andrew described the thousands of cartons of beer that they unloaded.

"Thirsty Island alright!" he said with a laugh. "And I gather half this load is more beer, for New Year celebrations."

"Will we get there that quickly?" Willy asked.

Graham nodded. "Yes, just. We are scheduled to arrive on the afternoon of the thirty first. We will just drop you off on the way and keep going."

"Aren't you coming ashore to help look for the wreck?" Willy asked.

Graham shook his head. "No. Sorry. I'd love to, but Dad is short-handed. I will see it on the way back when we pick you up again."

On learning that neither Carmen nor Andrew would be coming ashore either Willy felt quite put out. The expedition had shrunk to very few and he realised he would have no friends his own age on shore. Somehow it did not seem quite as much to look forward to.

But I still want to help find the wreck, he thought.

At 01:30pm the *Wewak* cast off and slid almost silently down Smiths Creek to Trinity Inlet. Willy stood at the port rail and felt his excitement grow.

We are on our way! he thought happily.

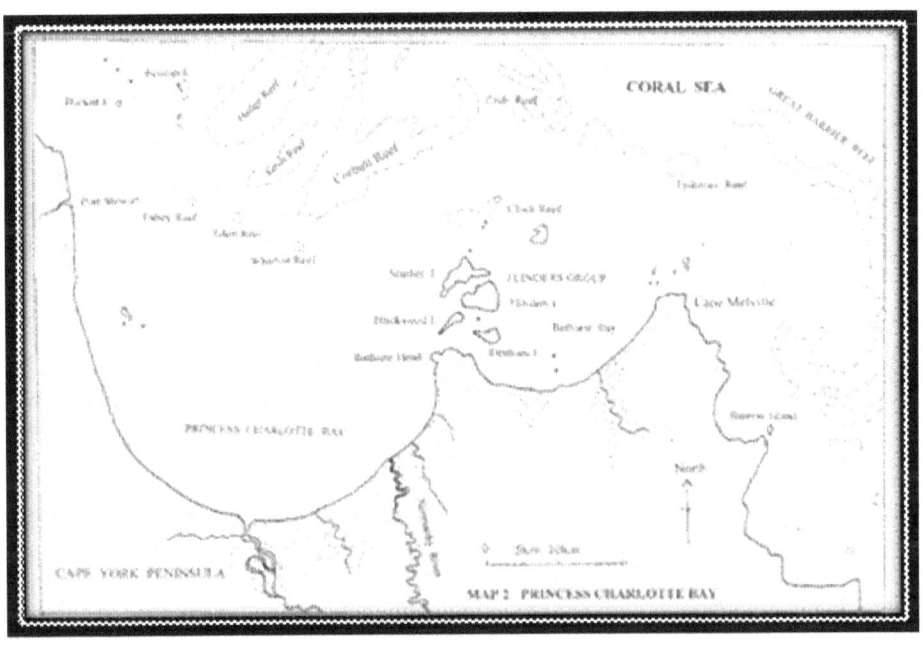

MAP 2 PRINCESS CHARLOTTE BAY

285

Chapter 28

UP THE CAPE

The trip north was mostly uneventful. For most of the time Willy sat on a chair under the awning and either read a book or watched the scenery. From time to time he was joined by his father, or by one of his friends. But Graham, Andrew, and Carmen were mostly busy working so could not spare the time to sit and chat. Willy did not mind as it gave him a chance to sit and think, to take stock of his thoughts and emotions.

The weather was mostly fine: hot and very humid. There were more clouds than on the previous trip and the wind slowly increased as the day went on. Several rainstorms swept over the *Wewak*, the rain pouring down and driving Willy inside. But there were no real squalls associated with the rain and the storms were over in a few minutes. Several other rainstorms passed either side of the LCT as she ploughed her way north. To port the coastal mountains were half-hidden in big clouds and rain and the air was very humid. The conditions were made tolerable by the wind.

The course was further out to sea than on the previous voyage, passing just to the west of the Hope Islands, Egret Reef, and Boulder Reef, aiming just to the east of Cape Bedford. Being so far from the coast meant that Willy had no chance to look into estuary of the Endeavour River. He was able to identify Grassy Hill with its lighthouse, but the town of Cooktown and the river were over the curve of the earth.

"I wonder if the *Pterodactyl* is there?" he muttered, voicing one of his main fears.

His anxiety on this issue was given a sharp jolt when he heard the sound of aero engines coming from astern. Jumping up he dashed to the starboard rail and looked up. But it was not the Catalina. It was one of the Coastwatch aircraft. It flew past at about a thousand feet and Willy was pleased to see it.

They might spot that missing launch, the 'Saurian', he thought.

Cape Bedford was passed at sunset, the rugged cape standing up stark against the red of the sunset. After a well-cooked tea of roast beef and Yorkshire pudding, Willy talked to his father for a while. He then spent an hour up in the wheelhouse talking to Graham and looking out. To begin with the view was pleasant, a setting new moon showing up a sparkle of rippling waves to port and the flashing of an automatic light on Three Islands giving something to look at. But the moon set at 2030hrs as they were passing Low Wooded Isle.

After that it was very dark as clouds came over and hid the stars. Once again, Willy marvelled at how people like Captain Kirk could so calmly navigate through the maze of reefs, rocks and shoals that studded the waters between the coast and the Great Barrier Reef. During this time Graham had the wheel and Willy was impressed by his obvious skill.

When he complimented him on this Graham just shrugged and said, "Been doing it since I was a kid."

After that the only things of interest were a passing rain shower, changing course to round Cape Flattery, and watching the lights of a south bound cargo ship. When Willy commented that this was the first ship they had seen all day, Captain Kirk answered, "I call this the empty ocean. Sometimes we go all day and see only one or two vessels."

Willy thought about that and realised that after leaving the Port Douglas area with its cluster of yachts and tourist launches, he had not seen a single small craft, not even a trawler. He commented on this, and Captain Kirk nodded.

"Yes, once you get up along this part of the coast you only see big, ocean-going freighters that have come through Torres Strait from Asia, a few fishing boats and the odd navy ship or government vessel."

After rounding Cape Flattery, the *Wewak* had the southeast Trade Winds almost directly astern. With a following sea of about 2 metres in height the LCT rode easily, sometimes yawing a little but otherwise riding quite smoothly. Carmen came on duty and relieved Graham at the wheel and Willy went below with him to have supper.

Willy, Graham, and Andrew talked about the expedition over cups of hot, sweet cocoa. Then it was bed for Willy. He stretched out on the cross bench at the aft end of the saloon. Kylie took the long bench near his head. It took Willy a while to get comfortable. His main concern was rolling off the bench when the stern was lifted by a larger than normal wave. He decided that he had been more comfortable on the folding stretcher. Despite that, he drifted into a deep sleep, free of dreams.

Daylight found them just north of Barrow Island. Willy woke to find that Kylie was on duty at the wheel. He looked out, then had a shower and shave before changing into clean clothes. By then they were off Cape Melville. Breakfast was cereal, bacon, fried eggs, toast, and fruit juice. Willy found he felt much refreshed, and he cheerfully looked forward to the day.

By 08:30am the *Wewak* was coasting across Bathurst Bay. The course was directly across the bay, heading for the Flinders Island Group. That meant that they got further and further from the coast and Willy was only just able to see the beach where they had landed on the first expedition. Looking at the scrub-lined shore and remembering those awful minutes when they had come upon Mr Jemmerling's party hoisting the 'Kittyhawk' wreck onto their truck caused Willy a spurt of anger and anxiety.

This anxiety received another boost when a twin-engine aircraft appeared astern. Willy stared at it with concern, but it was only the Coastwatch plane again. He relaxed and went up to the wheelhouse to ask about the course they were following. His air chart showed that the main navigation route for ships was north of the islands, but the most direct route was through the Flinders Island group. However he saw that the bows were pointing between the mainland and Denham Island, the most southerly of the group.

When he commented on this Captain Kirk shook his head. "Yes," he said. "Going north of the islands is more direct but it is also more exposed water and I prefer to stay in sheltered waters as much as possible. Easier on the ship and her cargo usually. We could go through the Fly Channel between Denham Island and Flinders Island, but you will see on the naval chart that there is a small island in that channel and also a blasted rock, Sentry Rock, which may or may not be visible depending on the tide."

"Why is it called the Fly Channel? Are there lots of flies there?" Willy asked.

Captain Kirk laughed and shook his head. "No. It was named after a British gunboat that surveyed the area in the 19th Century, the HMS *Fly*. Her captain was Captain Moresby RN and he also explored the Fly River in New Guinea."

Willy studied the chart and nodded. "So we are going through the Rattlesnake Channel? I didn't know there are rattlesnakes in Australia."

Once again, Captain Kirk laughed. "There aren't. Once again, it was named after a British navy ship, the gunboat HMS *Rattlesnake*. If you study the chart, you will find that almost every cape, bay, island, and reef on the east coast of Australia was named by British sailors, either after famous people or ships or members of their crew."

That was something Willy had never thought about but now he more fully appreciated just how skilled those early navigators must have been to explore the maze of reefs, rocks and islands that studded the entire east coast of Cape York.

And in sailing ships without engines!

It took nearly two hours to cross Bathurst Bay. As the *Wewak* entered the Rattlesnake Channel Willy heard another aeroplane. He at once went out to the starboard bridge wing and looked up. The plane was high up and tracking fast to the northwest. Borrowing binoculars from the mate he managed at last to locate it and then focused.

Only a 'Metroliner' going to Bamaga or Horn Island, he decided.

He lowered the binoculars and went back into the wheelhouse. No sooner had he returned the binoculars than he heard another aircraft. This was lower and coming from astern. Hurrying quickly back out to the bridge wing he looked up. Then his heart skipped. It was the *Pterodactyl*!

The black-painted Catalina flew past at about 2,000 feet, going west. *Damn!* Wily thought. *Now we have competition again. Oh, I hope Jemmerling doesn't know where to look!*

With a growing sense of unease and impatience Willy watched the flying boat fly on to the west, vanishing behind the rugged bulk of Bathurst Head. He at once went in to discuss the situation with the others. This time Willy felt he just had to know.

Turning to Captain Kirk he said, "Excuse me sir, but has Mr Jemmerling hired the *Wewak*?"

Captain Kirk turned from studying the compass. Then he said, "I am not at liberty to divulge whom I may have entered into a commercial contract with, but I can tell you that he has not."

Willy felt some relief. *If he hasn't hired a ship then he can't know exactly where the 'Beaufighter is,* he mused. He now knew that the *Wewak* was the only barge of its type in the region.

But for the rest of the day he was tense. Just knowing that the opposition were in the area added to the anxiety. Willy was very thoughtful and moody as the *Wewak* transited the Rattlesnake Channel and entered the even larger Princess Charlotte Bay. As they slid past Denham Island and

Blackwood Island Willy stared at the rugged islands but barely noticed them.

Course was altered to northwest. This soon took them out of sight of land to the south and west as the very low-lying shores of the big bay trended away from them. Willy went to study the chart.

We are going to pass close to the area where we rescued Jacob from the sea, he thought.

The sea looked almost identical to that awful day. The waves were two or three metres high and sparkled in the sun. Far off to starboard was a long line of huge cumulonimbus clouds but they were over the horizon. Along the track the LCT was following was only clear blue sky. It was all very pretty but to Willy it continually conjured up images of the mangled corpse and the sharks and of fear during the take-off. The memories made him shudder.

They also made him wonder about the search that Jacob had been on. *Is still on,* he corrected. *I wonder what he is looking for?*

That thought got him looking around for signs of the van der Heyden's yacht. To get a clearer view he made his way up to the starboard bridge wing. A check of the chart showed that Corbett Reef was about five miles away. Nearer to them three automatic lights were marked on the chart. Looking out Willy saw them, their location marked by distant black masts sticking out of the sea.

A large bulk carrier came into view, heading south. From astern came a container ship, It looked like a huge block, climbing up over the horizon. The container ship steadily overhauled them.

"Be doing twenty knots to our twelve," Captain Kirk explained as the big ship slowly drew level with them about a mile to starboard.

Then it began to draw ahead. Captain Kirk called the ship on his radio and was told she was heading for Singapore.

As the container ship began to sink below the horizon, a fleck of grey and white appeared, coming rapidly from the other direction.

"Warship," said Andrew. He picked up binoculars and went out to study the approaching naval vessel.

Ten minutes later it was about a mile off. Willy saw that it was a frigate or destroyer type, hurrying south and punching through the waves in showers of white spray. To him it looked very businesslike, the grey shape bristling with guns and radars.

Andrew studied her through his binoculars and then said, "HMAS *Arunta*, one of our newest frigates."

Carmen turned to Captain Kirk and said, "Sir, may we render passing honours?"

"Certainly," Captain Kirk replied, adding, "Though I suspect that lordly fellow is too busy to notice such old-fashioned courtesies from small fry like us."

Andrew and Carmen hurried aft. Willy went to watch. The two navy cadets untied the halliards of the faded and grimy red ensign fluttering on the staff and lowered the flag to deck level, then hauled it back up again. Then they stood with hands shielding their eyes from the glare to stare at the passing frigate. Willy watched as well, faintly amused at the navy's quaint customs. Suddenly he saw the tiny white ensign fluttering from the gaff on the frigate's mast go sliding down. A few seconds later it was hauled up again.

Andrew was jubilant. "He dipped to us!" he cried happily. He and Carmen both waved their caps.

"She," Carmen corrected. "Ships are always she."

The trio happily made their way back to the wheelhouse. Graham gave them a grin, but Willy was very aware that he was looking a bit left out. That reminded him that Graham had first joined the navy cadets; that his life's ambition had been to be a naval officer. Because his eyes weren't good enough that ambition had been dashed and Graham had gone through a very difficult few years while he re-adjusted to that bitter reality. That was when the possibility of suicide had been very real.

I hope I can get to be a pilot and don't get disappointed like Graham, Willy thought, suddenly very aware that life could be a very chancy business.

The voyage continued, on past Corbett Reef, Grub Reef, and tiny Fahey Reef with its beacon. Ahead were more small reefs and a couple of tiny islands. A trawler was passed, heading south. Mrs Kirk called them down to lunch. This was sandwiches. Willy opted for peanut butter and honey.

When he went back up to the wheelhouse the islands were much closer. They were widely scattered and quite varied. A couple were just sand cays which barely showed at high tide. Burkett Island was a flat patch of mangroves and others were just bare rock sticking out of the water. Then a patch of white near Burkett Island caught Willy's eye. He looked and saw that it was a small sail yacht.

Captain Kirk had seen it too. He lifted his binoculars and stared, then muttered, "That fellow looks like he is in trouble."

The course was changed and the *Wewak* headed for the tiny vessel. As they drew closer Willy became suspicious. Then he gasped as he recognised the yacht.

"That is Jacob van der Heyden's boat," he commented.

It was. *Wewak* hove-to a hundred metres upwind of the bobbing, rolling yacht. Her name was now clear: *Dyfken*. Then, to Willy's amazement, a black head appeared in the water near the stern of the yacht.

"There's someone in the water!" he cried.

Andrew stared and then said, "A diver."

Captain Kirk used the loudhailer to bellow, "Ahoy *Dyfken*! Are you alright?"

In reply came a faint hail as the tiny, black clad figure was helped back aboard the yacht. Captain Kirk studied the rolling yacht and then said, "Something wrong alright. Let's send the boat over to check."

He gave a string of orders and the LCT turned into the wind and was allowed to drift. The rigid semi-inflatable was lowered and Graham clambered aboard. He started the engine. Captain Kirk climbed aboard, with Graham as his crewman, and the small boat went bouncing off across the waves.

Willy badly wanted to go, to talk to Jacob, but this was clearly a nautical operation, so he kept out of the way. He saw the boat pull alongside the yacht and then watched impatiently as a long conversation take place. After ten minutes the boat came back, punching across the waves. During this time the mate kept manoeuvring *Wewak* to keep her upwind of the yacht. Captain Kirk climbed back aboard.

"They have wrapped a rope around their propeller," he explained. "And the young fellow over there is trying to unravel it but he isn't a qualified diver so he can't use the gear properly." He then looked at Carmen and Andrew. "Aren't you two divers?" he asked.

Carmen nodded. "Yes sir. We are both qualified Advanced Open Water Divers," she replied.

Willy was watching Andrew at that moment and saw his face go pale and drawn. Through his memory flitted pieces of the story of how Andrew and Carman had discovered their grandfather's remains in a shipwreck, and nearly died in the process.

I think Andrew said he was never going diving again? he thought.

Captain Kirk then said, "Would you mind helping these people? If you can't we will have to tow them to the nearest port."

Carmen at once said, "Of course we will sir, won't we Andrew?"

Andrew nodded, but he did not seem keen. Carmen then asked, "Have they got the right gear sir?"

Capt Kirk shook his head. "I'm not sure. You'd better come over and have a look."

At that Andrew swallowed but he followed Carmen and Captain Kirk down to the boat.

Poor Andrew, Willy thought. *He isn't game to say no!*

Andrew and Carmen joined Captain Kirk and Graham in the boat and they motored across to the yacht. Twenty minutes later Captain Kirk and Graham came back.

"We need to tow the yacht into calmer water," Captain Kirk explained. "It is too dangerous for them to dive with the yacht moving about like that."

The stern anchor was unshackled, and Graham took a light line across to the yacht. This was then used to haul the steel winch rope across. Captain Kirk and the mate organised a towing bridle and then the mate went across in the boat to ensure the tow was correctly secured. Captain Kirk went up to the monkey island and conned the LCT from there. It took twenty minutes to tow the yacht around to the lee side of the island into calm water behind a coral reef. Willy watched all this from the bridge wing with his father. All the while he wished the risk of diving wasn't being taken.

His concern moved to anxiety when Captain Kirk came down and answered the radio, then held out a small hand-held radio.

"Your friends are going diving. The mate wants you and your dad to go up onto the monkey island to keep a lookout for sharks."

Instantly vivid images of the corpse being torn apart by the shark flooded Willy's mind. *Oh hell! I wish they wouldn't go in the water,* he thought.

Filled by a firm desire to do all he could to keep Carmen and Andrew safe he called his father and made his way up to the highest level. Once there he began scanning the waves, seeking any sign of tell-tale, triangular fins or even flitting dark shadows. But he was not happy. Even though he could see the bottom under the LCT the sea was just too rough to allow easy surveillance for sharks.

After half an hour, he saw two figures clad in dark wetsuits and with SCUBA gear jump off the yacht. Willy's sense of apprehension shot right up. He resumed anxiously scanning the waves.

Another worrying half hour went by before he saw the divers being hauled back aboard the sharply rolling yacht. A few minutes later, the radio crackled and informed them that the divers were safe and not going back in. The rope had been removed from the propeller. A few minutes later, the small boat headed back to the *Wewak* with everyone on board.

Willy went down to help them back aboard. As Andrew climbed over the rail Willy said, "Well done. You are braver than me."

Andrew gave him a smile but looked very pale still. "The job was easy," he replied. Then he said, "But your mate Jacob is a terrible sailor. There are ropes tangled everywhere, torn sails, knots in halliards, and he didn't even know where he was. When we told him he was near Burkett Island he was astonished. He said he thought they were just near Clack Island. That is north of the Flinders Group and is at least fifty miles from here."

"I thought that the Dutch were good sailors," Willy's father commented.

Carmen answered him with a snort. "They might be, but Jacob is a Sydneysider, born and bred and makes a living as a builder's labourer. He wouldn't know a barge pole from a mizzen mast. And as for being a diver!"

Words failed her and she shook her head. Curiosity now gnawed at Willy. He asked, "Did they say what they are doing here?"

Graham answered that. "I asked them. They just said touring the coast."

"Nothing about looking for a treasure?" Willy queried.

Graham shook his head. "Nope. And they didn't seem very friendly. It was like they were glad of the help but really wished we weren't there." He then moved aft to help hoist the boat back aboard. Andrew and Carmen went to help him.

Willy stood at the rail staring at the yacht, which was now moving under power, heading southwards. *I wonder what they are really doing?* he wondered. *Are they looking for a treasure?*

As the yacht went past a hundred metres away, he waved and got an answering wave from the sister (Julia?) but it did not seem very enthusiastic. Then they were gone.

As soon as the boat was hoisted and secured the *Wewak* got under way. Willy returned to the wheelhouse. By then it was 3:00pm. The day was very hot and he was sunburnt and starting to feel quite tired. For a few minutes he studied the chart and then turned to scan the coastline. This was again coming into view as a line of low hills amid a haze of smoke and sea spray.

As they motored along, Willy got a chance to ask Carmen on her own, how the dive had gone. Carmen gave a wry smile and said, "It was okay. Andrew didn't want to do it, but when he saw that I was going in he was determined not to let me do it alone."

"He hates diving, doesn't he?" Willy asked.

Carmen nodded. "Yes, but he doesn't want anyone to know, so don't say anything please." Then she sighed and smiled. "He is very brave," she added with obvious affection.

An hour later the east coast of the Peninsula was only a couple of miles away to port and the details were clear. Willy ticked off the landmarks as they passed them, glad that the voyage was nearly over. Suddenly he stiffened. Coming from the north was a tiny black dot against the sky. It was following the coast. Hastily snatching up binoculars he steadied them on the object. By then it was clear to see with the naked eye. As he had suspected, it was an aeroplane, and not just any plane but the *Pterodactyl*!

Willy watched it fly on south, obviously following the coastline. It vanished in the direction of Princess Charlotte Bay.

They must have seen us, he thought. *But does Jemmerling have any idea where to look?*

An hour later, the *Wewak* was nosed into the beach just to the north of a small rocky headland named Cape Frederick. The group at once began unloading, the 4 Wheelers being driven off immediately. The tide was just on the make and the surf just big enough to be a cause of concern to Captain Kirk.

Willy heard him say to Mr Beck and his father, "Now remember that we are due back in five days time, on the third. We will not be able to hang around for more than a few hours, one tide at the most. Also, if the weather gets bad we may not be able to beach the *Wewak*. In that case you will have to make your way overland to Lockhart River. Now check the satellite phone again please."

From his study of the map Willy knew that there was no road within about 50 kilometres of the area. In between was a wilderness of swamps and bush. Knowing how hard it had been to push through 5km of scrub made him feel quite anxious.

We are going to be very isolated, he thought.

Even though they had an aluminium dinghy with an outboard motor this knowledge did little to ease this sense of intense loneliness.

As the *Wewak* backed off on the rising tide the little party stood on the beach and watched. Willy gave a half-hearted wave to Andrew but also felt a sense of quite determination.

We are here now. So we have a chance to find the 'Beaufighter' wreck. We have beaten Mr Jemmerling.

No sooner had he thought this than he heard the distant hum of aero engines. Looking south he saw the aircraft heading towards them. It was just visible above the ridge leading to the headland. After watching it for a few seconds he shook his head in dismay. The silhouette was too distinctive for him to be mistaken.

Oh no! It is the Pterodactyl*!*

Chapter 29

RUN!

It was instantly obvious to Willy that the people in the Catalina had seen them. The plane put its nose down and dived, to roar over at about 500 feet. Then it began to circle them. As it did, Willy felt a growing sense of unease.

He turned to Mr Beck and said, "Can you remember exactly where the wreck of the 'Beaufighter' is Mr Beck?"

Mr Beck had been watching the Catalina, his face a mask of anxiety. He turned to Willy and nodded, then pointed north along the beach.

"Yes, it is about a kilometre north along the beach. I am fairly sure I can locate it easily."

By then the *Pterodactyl* had begun circling further north, over the area Mr Beck had indicated. Little alarm bells began ringing in Willy's mind. "Mr Beck, I think they are searching for the wreck. Is it possible for them to see it from the air?"

Mr Beck bit his lip and then nodded. "Possibly. Depends whether the wind has blown off any of the sand that we covered it with."

"How long ago was that?" Willy asked as he watched the Catalina come even lower and circle even further north along the beach.

"Ten years," Mr Beck replied.

Norman swore and then said, "I don't like the way he is circling there. That is about where the wreck is."

"We had better get there quickly," Willy suggested.

Norman frowned. "But that will give them an even better clue where to look. They will see us searching."

That put Willy into a ferment of doubt. Was it better? Then he saw the *Pterodactyl* do a wide sweep off to the north, before turning and going even lower. As he watched it he felt another flutter of apprehension. Then a movement on the Catalinas' wingtips crystallised the situation for him.

"He is lowering his wing floats. He is going to land," he said.

"That might mean he has seen something," Norman said, his face set.

"I think he has," Willy agreed. "Why else would he risk landing on waves as big as this."

By then it was obvious that the Catalina was doing a landing approach. This would take it diagonally out to sea, facing into the wind and waves.

Willy watched it for a few more seconds and then said, "If Mr Jemmerling has seen the wreck, he might get to it before us. That might mean he can claim it if he has another permit."

Mr Beck nodded. "He is sure to have."

Willy felt a surge of desperation. "Then we must get there before him and stake our claim. Come on, run!"

With that he set off running. As he did, he saw the Catalina strike the waves with its hull. It did this so hard it threw up a huge shower of spray and bounced. The plane smacked down again on the next wave crest.

That looks dangerous, Willy thought as the Catalina bounced again and again, each bounce lower and slower than the previous one. That confirmed Willy in his suspicion that the people in the aircraft had indeed seen the wreck.

By then Willy had run a hundred metres but already he was tiring and puffing hard. He kept his head turned to watch the plane, noting that it was safely down and slowing quickly in the smaller waves outside the surf zone. A few hundred metres further out from it was the *Wewak*. The LCT had now reversed into deeper water and swung her bows to face north and was proceeding on her way. Tiny figures lining her rail and bridge showed that those on board were watching.

I wish Graham was here, Willy thought. *He is a lot fitter than me.*

That fitness was now of crucial importance became quickly apparent as the Catalina slowed and turned, then began taxiing back along its landing run.

Oh no! Willy groaned.

He was now gasping for breath and labouring and had only run about 200 metres. Already a painful stitch was beginning to grab in his right side.

He had no choice but to slow to a panting walk. As he did, he watched the *Pterodactyl* surge back past him, rolling and pitching as it crossed the waves diagonally.

Surely they aren't going to try to drive it in through the surf? Willy thought.

He knew that if that was possible and it could be run up onto the beach then the people in it could just jump out and run into the dunes to the wreck long before he and the others could reach it.

It was only then that he realised that the others were not running with him. He looked back and saw why. They had been busy hastily untying the load from the 4 Wheelers and now both of the tiny vehicles were roaring along the hard sand near the water, Mr Beck and Willy's father on one and Norman on the other.

Willy came to a stop and gulped in great lung fulls of air to get his breath back. *We might have a chance,* he thought, *but only if...*

Even as he thought this, his hopes shot up as he saw the Catalina spin round in a flurry of spray and come to a standstill about 200 metres off the beach. The flying boat was already about 500 metres further along, but Willy was suddenly hopeful.

That must mean they are not game to drive her in through the surf, he thought. *They will have to launch a rubber boat and paddle ashore. We do have a chance!*

Mr Beck's 4-Wheeler went racing past and Willy waved them on. Norman's pulled up and Willy quickly scrambled aboard. Even before he was settled on the small cargo tray Norman had it moving again.

"Go! Go!" Willy shouted excitedly.

They went racing on along the beach. Norman kept right down near the water's edge where the sand was firmer although several times they hit soft patches which threatened to bog them. Each time Willy's heart went into his mouth.

Oh no! Don't bog! he thought. It would be just too cruel to be that close to success and to be beaten again.

Heart in mouth with trepidation he saw the Catalina anchor. A minute later, when the 4-Wheelers were another 300 metres further along the beach, he saw a dark shape appear from the port side where he knew the door was. It was a rubber dinghy and it had three men in it. From that distance he could not identify them, but one was all dressed in long whites and had a white hat.

That might be Mr Jemmerling, he thought.

"How much further?" Willy shouted in Norman's ear.

"Just past this patch of trees," Norman replied.

Willy looked and saw that a straggly clump of spindly looking mangroves extended from the swamp behind the dunes to a wide stretch of dark mud. The mud extended down to the edge of the sea, ending abruptly in a short, vertical drop. The thought that the mud might be their undoing had him praying and tense but then he saw Mr Beck's 4-Wheeler slowly grind across it, wobbling and sinking but not deep enough to bog.

Norman made his own track across the bumpy mass. It was slow going and Willy fretted, aware that the rubber boat now had an outboard engine going and was motoring quickly in towards the beach. He looked down anxiously as the 4-Wheeler suddenly tilted but then it righted itself and churned on across the uneven, spongy surface. Willy now saw that the mud was actually laced with tree roots and was mostly firm.

Then they were across and the engine was whining at high speed, the noise music to Willy's ears. Twice the 4-Wheeler struck soft patches and nearly tipped over, slewing alarmingly. Willy clung on and whooped. By the time they had covered another hundred metres, the rubber boat was in the surf and only a hundred metres from the shore.

Willy saw Mr Beck jump off his 4-Wheeler and run up the beach, pointing to the dunes. Willy's father followed him. Norman tried to drive the 4-Wheeler up across the soft sand but it came to a wheel-spinning standstill as soon as they hit soft, dry sand. Willy didn't wait. He sprang off and dashed up the sand dune ahead of him. A glance over his shoulder showed the rubber boat among the surf and almost at the beach.

"Where is it? Where?" he cried as he reached the crest of the dune. Mr Beck and his father were there, looking around them.

Mr Beck gave a shrug, his face a mask of determination and even desperation. "I'm not sure. Somewhere round here. The pilot tried to land on the salt pan on the landward side of the dunes. The plane is among the dunes nearest the marsh."

Willy looked and saw that this stretch of coast was quite unlike the previous search area. Here there was a jumble of quite small dunes, three to five metres high at most. The dunes were covered with a thin clothing of tufts of grass and some sort of creeper. Beyond the dune line treetops were visible a hundred or so metres inland. The dunes were scattered with dips and hollows among them and were not in long, straight lines. Between the dunes and the trees was a small salt marsh, much of which was covered by clumps of grass. The remainder was white with a dry crust of salt.

Another glance showed the rubber boat sliding onto the beach. Willy's hopes that it might get capsized in the surf had not been realised. Out of it scrambled three men: Mr Jemmerling, Mr Hobbs, and Harvey. That sight sent Willy and the others racing down the far side of the dune and dashing across the next hollow. They scrambled and clawed their way up the second dune.

"Spread out! Willy, you go to the left," his father shouted.

Willy did so, clawing his way up the steep face of the dune, ignoring the dry sand that stuck to his sweaty skin. On top he paused to look. He was gasping for breath but more from anxiety than running. He looked around, shielding his eyes from the glare.

"Where is it?" he muttered.

He was hoping to see some really obvious sign, such as a tail fin sticking up but then he remembered Mr Beck describing how he and Norman had covered the wreck with tarpaulins to protect it.

Now he began looking for a sharp hummock. There were several but they had clumps of spiky bush growing on them. He ran across to one, his feet sinking in the soft sand and his breath labouring. By the time he had clawed his sweaty, gasping way up one sharp little mound he was sure that there was nothing under it.

From there he looked around. Fifty metres to his right he saw his father and the Becks scrambling almost frantically around among the landward edge of the dunes. And there was Harvey! He ran down the far side of a dune and joined the search, right between Mr Beck and Norman. Willy felt so frustrated that he wanted to scream, and he clenched his fists and turned to scan the edge of the salt marsh.

Rasping breathing behind him made him look around and Willy saw Mr Hobbs sliding down the side of the dune on the seaward side of the small hollow Willy had just crossed. The nearness of the opposition sent his heart rate racing, and he began to dance with frustration as he turned and looked again. Hobbs began scrambling up the loose face of the dune Willy was on. Behind him Mr Jemmerling's head appeared as he climbed the seaward side of the first dune.

With Hobbs only twenty metres away Willy looked frantically around. *They must have seen something from the air,* he reasoned. *Something must be exposed.*

And there it was! A flat surface with a curved edge that could only be a wingtip. It was sticking out of the edge of the next dune about fifty paces away, right on the edge of the salt marsh. As Hobbs scrambled up the dune, Willy slithered and dashed down the other side. He resisted the temptation to call out, lest he be wrong.

His haste was almost his undoing. His foot caught in one of the creepers and he went sprawling. Sand coated his hands and face and he tasted salt and grit. But a glance over his shoulder showed Hobbs staring past him. Ignoring the sharp prickles and sand Willy scrambled to his feet and resumed running. Now he was sure. It was a wingtip. Leaping over and through clumps of spiky grass he ran for all he was worth.

As Willy reached the edge of the saltmarsh, Hobbs let out a shout. "Over here!" he yelled.

Then he was running down the side of the dune in a race to catch Willy. Willy cast a frantic glance back at him, and almost tripped again. Then he ran out onto the dry salt, and realised instantly that he was making another error as his boots at once broke through into soft, slimy mud.

"No! No!" Willy gasped, changing direction and dragging himself back onto the sand. The wing was only twenty paces away. A glance behind showed Hobbs only ten metres away.

"I must win!" Willy snarled to himself as he scrambled and slithered along the steep side of the dune.

Hobbs saw him doing this, apparently losing speed, so he ran out onto the salt marsh instead. Instantly he sank to his knees and he came to a swearing, floundering standstill.

By the time Hobbs had dragged himself back to the sand Willy had reached the wing. He nearly jumped on it, stopping just in time. After bending down to touch it, both to check it actually was metal, and to claim the prize, he faced back and shouted.

"Here it is! I've got it!"

To his dismay, it came out as a gasping croak. By then perspiration was trickling into Willy's eyes and he had to blink and wipe his face to see clearly. Through eyes that seemed misted and blurry he saw Hobbs come to a stop only metres from him. Fearing that Hobbs might knock him over or push him aside Willy tried to shout again but he was so winded that it still came out as a rasping croak.

"Mr Beck! Dad! Here it is! I've found it."

But instead of his father or Mr Beck it was Mr Jemmerling who next appeared. *Oh no!* Willy thought, afraid that he might be robbed of his find even at this moment. Mr Jemmerling slithered down the back of the sand dune and stopped near the exposed wingtip. Then he moved to try to touch it. That sparked Willy's anxieties to a new pitch.

Stepping across to block Mr Jemmerling's path he yelled, "Don't touch it! We found it! It is ours."

To Willy's surprise, Mr Jemmerling stepped back but then smiled. He said, "Well done, young William. That was a good race, but you won it fair and square."

Willy could not believe what he was hearing. All he could do was stand, chest heaving, blinking away the sweat. To his relief Norman appeared, followed by his father and then by a red-faced Mr Beck.

As they did, Willy called to them, "I found it Dad. I was here first."

Mr Beck moved past Willy and bent to feel the exposed metal. "This is the wing alright," he said. Then he straightened up and faced Mr Jemmerling, just as Harvey came running across to join them. "This one is ours, Mr Jemmerling. We found it first."

Mr Jemmerling again smiled. He raised both hands in a placatory way and said, "Of course. I am obviously disappointed, but you won this one fair and square. But you still have to recover it. Maybe we can come to some accommodation?"

"What do you mean?" Mr Beck asked warily.

"What if I make you an offer to buy it, as is-where is?" Mr Jemmerling asked.

That bothered Willy. Having found the wreck he did not want Mr Beck to make any arrangements with Mr Jemmerling. He cried, "Don't sell please Mr Beck. This one is yours."

Mr Beck nodded. "Don't fret young Willy. I want to do this restoration." He then faced Mr Jemmerling and said, "Sorry, Mr Jemmerling. Maybe after we have restored it we can talk again."

Mr Jemmerling looked a bit annoyed but then shrugged. "That is a pity. I would have paid well. Never mind. There are still a couple of Airacobras to locate along this coast. We will go and look for them. And you still have to get the wreck back to civilisation. Do you mind if we help dig the wreck out? I would very much like to see what condition it is in."

Willy could see that the question put Mr Beck in a difficult position. He wanted to say no but Mr Beck finally nodded. "Alright, but on the clear understanding that everything found is left with us."

Mr Jemmerling went stiff and stood up straight. "Of course! I am not a thief! I resent the implication."

"Sorry, Mr Jemmerling, but there were suspicions based on the fact that my house was burgled and that the same man was later seen in Cooktown spying on us on the same day you were there," Mr Beck said.

"I know nothing of that," Mr Jemmerling said gruffly.

"So who were those men?" Willy asked. "Who are they working for?"

"I have no idea," Mr Jemmerling replied. "Now, if you want our help then stop making accusations."

"I can't afford to pay you for the work," Mr Beck answered.

Mr Jemmerling made a dismissive gesture. "This is my hobby. It does make me money, nearly enough to cover costs, but I do it for fun. And Mr Hobbs and the plane crew get paid a yearly salary so they will do what I say," he said.

Hearing that, and the confident and arrogant tone in which it was said, made Willy shiver. He was certain that if Mr Hobbs or the plane crew objected they would quickly be looking for other employment!

At that moment Captain Kirk, Graham, Andrew, and Carmen came striding over the dunes.

"We wanted to know what happened," Captain Kirk explained.

The story was told and Willy was glad of that. *The more people who are witnesses to us finding the plane first the better,* he thought. Even now he was anxious that some legal claim might rob them of the prize.

Captain Kirk listened and then said, "And how long do you think it will take to excavate the wreck and then move it to the beach?" he asked.

"At least three or four days," Mr Beck replied.

Captain Kirk nodded. "Good. Then we can stick to our original plan. We will go to Portland Roads and Thursday Island and unload our cargo, then pick you up on the way back in five days' time, on the third of January."

So it was agreed. Both Graham and Andrew wanted to stay but their request was denied as they were needed to crew the *Wewak*.

"The law lays down minimum crew numbers for the safe operation of a vessel," Captain Kirk explained.

Both Graham and Andrew looked disappointed but shrugged and did not argue.

The whole group made its way back to the beach. Willy was merely a spectator while Captain Kirk and his friends returned to the *Wewak*. The LCT then got under way and headed off north. Watching her dwindle into the distance renewed Willy's acute feeling of isolation. Mr Jemmerling sent Harvey and Mr Hobbs out to the *Pterodactyl* to collect clothes, tools, food and camping gear. An hour later Mr Hobbs was ashore with these things and Harvey on his way back to the Catalina.

"I can't risk the flying boat riding at anchor out there on a lee shore," Mr Jemmerling explained. "*Pterodactyl* will have to wait at Lockhart River."

Half an hour later the Catalina took off, a rough, pounding take-off that got Willy worried lest the plane dive into a wave crest and crash. Once airborne the aircraft turned north and flew away. Watching the tiny black shape rapidly shrinking in size reinforced the intense feelings of isolation.

"Now," Mr Jemmerling said. "Let's set up camp and then get to work recovering the 'Beaufighter'."

Chapter 30

SWEAT

For the next four days Willy sweated. The weather was hot and still and it seemed that the sun was sucking the moisture out of everything. High humidity made it even more uncomfortable as his sweat did not evaporate but stayed on the skin as an irritating and sticky fluid.

To make things worse, there was no shade at all at the crash site so the hard physical labour of uncovering and removing the wreck had to be done during the cooler hours: the early morning and late afternoon. In the middle of the day all the group did was sit or lie in the limited shade of their tents and tarpaulins strung between the spindly mangroves.

Even this was only of limited relief because of the reflected glare from the sand and sea and because there was almost no wind. The weather stayed hot and dry. For most of each day there was hardly a cloud in the sky. The sea settled to a flat calm that swashed gently onto the beach but lay almost still at night. Everyone wished for rain and the weather reports on the radio were eagerly listened to. On the second day there was a glimmer of hope when the weather report informed them that a small low-pressure cell had formed in the Gulf of Carpentaria.

"That's what we want," Mr Beck said. "Nothing like a good low in the Gulf to bring the rain onto the east coast."

But that hope faded on Day 3 when the 'low' moved south onto land near Burketown. Rain was reported south of Cairns, around Innisfail and Tully, but not a drop fell north of Cooktown.

The camp was set up among the dunes at the edge of the small clump of spindly mangroves. The site was unpleasant and also unsafe. Concern over the danger from crocodiles meant they mounted a guard all night, every night. This was always two people on duty, for two hours and with one changing every hour. As there were only seven people that meant two stints of guard duty each night.

That there were crocodiles was certain. During the stillness of the night they could be heard grunting and coughing in the mangroves beyond the salt marsh.

"Barking flat dogs!" Norman called them, but the joke had an edge to it. His rifle was kept handy at all times.

Because it got light about 04:30am, the camp was woken at 04:00am. After a quick cup of brew and a snack they set to work as soon as it was light. By 10:30am it was so hot that work became not just very uncomfortable but a threat to health. Work was resumed at 4:30pm. As the sun did not set till 7:15pm and then the light lingered until nearly 7:45pm that meant about 10 hours of work time.

They needed all of that and used it all. Willy had never worked so hard in all his life. For the first two days his muscles complained at the unaccustomed exercise, but by Day 3 he was starting to feel fit and could almost see his muscles developing. Willy was also pleased to see that Mr Jemmerling and Mr Hobbs both pitched in and did their fair share of the work at the 'Beaufighter'. This included some of the hardest and dirtiest jobs.

But Mr Jemmerling did not do any of the domestic chores around the camp. Mr Hobbs did all of this for him, including washing so that he had clean white clothes every day and every evening.

He was able to do this because water was not a problem. Every morning just after sunrise the *Pterodactyl* landed and unloaded fresh supplies. The Catalina also brought Mr Jemmerling his mail and re-charged batteries for his satellite telephone and laptop computer.

As Mr Jemmerling said, "I might be having the best holiday in years but I still have businesses to run."

It all left Willy feeling quite ambivalent about Mr Jemmerling. He could not decide if he believed him and trusted him or not. What he had to admit was that Mr Jemmerling was usually a very nice person, albeit with a streak of ruthlessness.

I suppose you have to be fairly tough to be a real success in business, Willy mused.

Indeed Mr Jemmerling seemed to thrive in the harsh conditions. He certainly became fitter and did a lot of smiling and laughing. Even when covered in the mud of the salt marsh he could still joke.

"It will wash off," he said. "And besides, it is the mud that saved the plane for you."

Mr Beck had to concede that. Apparently the pilot, fearing it might be soft mud, had opted to do a wheels-up 'belly landing'. That had undoubtedly saved his life as the 'Beaufighter' had slid to a standstill the right way up on the edge of the dunes.

"If he'd landed wheels down the aircraft would have flipped and probably killed the lot of them," Mr Beck said.

Willy now learned the interesting fact that metal aircraft propellers that hit land had the tips bent backwards.

"If they hit water while still spinning then they dig in and the pressure forces the tips forward," Mr Beck explained.

This fact was pointed out on the afternoon of Day 2 when they had shovelled most of the sand off and were able to drag the old tarpaulins aside. These were rotten but had definitely served to help preserve the wreck. Much of the paint was still visible and even the RAAF roundels and serial numbers were clear. Most of the Perspex was still intact but to Willy's great disappointment all the guns and electronics had been removed.

"Taken away by RAAF work parties during the war," Norman said.

The 'Beaufighter' was one of Willy's favourite aircraft types and he had seen those famous newsreels of Damien Parer's showing them attacking Japanese ships during the Battle of the Bismarck Sea in 1942. He had read that the Japanese called them 'The whispering death' because they arrived with so little warning and had such devastating firepower.

Four 20-millimetre cannon, eight .303 machineguns, plus rockets and bombs. They were certainly deadly, Willy thought, imagining himself piloting one in to the attack.

But time and salt and the weather had done their worst. The whole underside was corroded, and the aluminium was so brittle in places that it crumbled or snapped. The huge radial engines were just balls of rust. All rubber had perished and the few bits remaining had turned solid. Every stage in the recovery operation was photographed and recorded.

Once the wreck had been dug clear of the sand it had to be moved to the beach. This was a much harder and more delicate task. It was now that Mr Jemmerling was able to help the most. He had a fund of technical knowledge and expertise and was able to make seemingly impossible tasks easy.

First a vehicle path had to be smoothed through the dunes. Then the smaller pieces were lifted onto the 4 Wheelers using a gyn; a tripod of extendable steel pipes from which a block and tackle was suspended.

Thus the propellers, motors and the torn-off port wing were all moved with relative ease, and a lot of anxiety and sweat.

The tail section including the tail fin and tailplanes had almost broken off during the crash. This part of the wreck was cut off and moved to the beach. Then the really hard tasks began: moving the main section of the fuselage and the starboard wing. As the bolts securing it were all rusted or corroded, there was no option but to cut the wing off, very sweaty work with hacksaws. The wing was then levered onto a tarpaulin and hauled by the 4 Wheelers along aluminium skids out to the beach.

Next, they tackled the fuselage. Everything from inside that could be removed was. Then, by doing a lot of digging, aluminium planks were slid under the rotting lower section. These were secured to give rigidity. Air bags were then pumped up to lift the fuselage higher and then rollers used in conjunction with aluminium skids to slide the wreckage out through the dunes.

They finished the task just on sunset on the fourth day. As Willy stood there, wiping sand and sweat off and feeling very pleased with their efforts, Mr Beck said, "I hope all this stuff is safe here on the beach."

"Why shouldn't it be?" Willy's father asked. "Surely the tide won't come that high?"

"No, but I just hear on the radio that there is a new low-pressure system forming. This one is out in the Coral Sea, and I would hate it to whip up big waves. Then the *Wewak* wouldn't be able to beach and we would have to shift all this stuff back into the dunes."

"Where is the low?" Mr Jemmerling asked.

"Just heard it on the radio," Mr Beck said. "It is out near Willis Island, about seven hundred kilometres away."

Norman shook his head. "That's a long way off. It shouldn't bother us."

"I hope not," Mr Beck replied.

Willy did too. He worried about all their hard work being washed away but was relieved that the sea stayed calm and the wind dropped. Even though it meant he sweated a lot more and the mosquitoes attacked in squadrons, he was content. He felt even easier when Mr Jemmerling called Captain Kirk on the satellite phone and confirmed that *Wewak* was on schedule.

"They are leaving Portland Roads tonight and will be ashore here just after daylight. That will give us about two hours to load before high tide," Mr Jemmerling said.

Willy did not sleep very well that night. The heat and humidity made it too uncomfortable for real rest and he was anxious. Twice he was on guard duty. From 08:00pm he shared with Mr Beck and then Mr Hobbs. Then from 02:00am to 04:00am he shared with his father and Mr Jemmerling. Both times he was struck by how still it was. There was not even a light breeze, and the sea was so calm it barely lapped the shore. The plop of fish jumping seemed to be very loud and made him jump. Each time that happened he shone the torch around looking for any sign of a crocodile stalking them.

At 04:00am they woke the camp and drinks were prepared. Then packing began. By the time the sun rose over the calm sea, Willy was already a lather of sweat and all the tents and tarpaulins had been struck and rolled up. The group then sat down to a breakfast cooked by Mr Hobbs. While they ate, they listened to the radio. What they heard was worrying. The low had moved closer by about a hundred kilometres during the night and its pressure had dropped to 993hp.

"Do you think it will form into a cyclone?" Willy asked.

Mr Beck shrugged. "It might, but it is a long way south of here, and even if it does we are right to load."

That made Willy feel easier. He felt even better when the *Wewak* hove in sight at 05:00am. Just seeing the old veteran in the distance made him feel affectionate towards her. It also brought home to him how glad he was that the relative isolation was now over. Picking up his camping gear and bag be made his way along the beach to where the pieces of the 'Beaufighter' lay just above the high tide line. By the time he arrived there *Wewak* had nosed ashore and dropped her bow ramp.

Graham, Andrew and Carmen came hurrying ashore to look at the wreck. "You got it then!" Graham cried happily.

"We did," Willy replied, glowing with perspiration and satisfaction.

Captain Kirk joined them and said, "Let's get this salvage aboard quickly. I don't like the sound of that low out in the Coral Sea."

"Do you think it might turn into a cyclone Captain?" Mr Jemmerling asked.

"I don't like the feel of it," Captain Kirk replied. "Look, you can see the start of a swell beginning."

Willy hadn't noticed that but now he saw that a regular series of gentle waves was rolling in, making the sea look like it was made of red corrugated iron as the sunrise shone across it.

He said, "Do you think it might come here sir?"

Captain Kirk frowned and said, "You never know with cyclones. They rarely come in on this part of the coast, but I don't trust the weather in January. Now, let's get working."

The next two hours were very hard, sweaty work. Luckily the LCT had brought a forklift along and aided by it and rollers, blocks and tackles and a crew of seamen who knew their business, all the big parts were hauled aboard and made secure under tarpaulins within two hours. Another two hours had all the smaller pieces of wreckage aboard, plus the camp equipment and personal kit.

While they were doing this *Pterodactyl* arrived. Willy took time out to watch the flying boat land, thrilling to see how its keel cut the calm water and then bumped across the tiny swell waves. The crew came ashore in the rubber boat to assist.

By 08:30am the work was all done and the ramp ready to raise. Mr Jemmerling then came and shook everyone's hand and wished them well.

"I am happy," he told them. "Now we both have a plane. And it was a lot of fun. Now I had better be off."

"Where are you going now sir?" Willy asked.

"To check on some of my businesses. I need to see how the mineral exploration team are going, and I believe there is an 'Airacobra' somewhere up the coast a bit that might be worth a look at."

"Good luck then sir, and thanks for everything," Willy said.

He still felt unsure whether Mr Jemmerling had told the truth, but he liked the man so much that the thought made him feel guilty.

"Thank you, young Willy. And remember, when you are a pilot, I can help you learn to fly the old 'warbirds' if you are interested."

"Oh yes sir! Thank you!" Willy cried.

Then Mr Jemmerling and his team made their way down the ramp to the beach. As soon as they stepped off, Captain Kirk signalled and the mate began raising the ramp. Andrew and Carmen were sent to start winching at the stern anchor to heave the LCT off the sand.

"And not a minute too bloody soon!" Captain Kirk muttered as the *Wewak* lifted off on the rising tide and then slid astern.

When the bow struck the bottom several times with shuddering bumps Willy understood what he meant. Already the swell waves were getting bigger. But there was still no wind. That made him sweat even more and he found it a relief to leave the sweltering tank deck and retreat into the saloon out of the blistering sun.

As *Wewak* turned to face south, Willy went out to watch Mr Jemmerling and his crew return to the Catalina. As they climbed aboard he waved and saw arms wave back. Then the LCT's engines went to full ahead and the screws began churning water from under her counter. Within minutes the flying boat was left far behind. Willy watched it take off, punching across the swell to lift off half a kilometre out to sea.

The *Pterodactyl* then did a low, slow pass and everyone went out on deck to wave. Arms waved back.

What a great plane! Willy thought, wishing he was on it instead of the slow-moving landing craft.

Then the flying boat banked and headed off south eastwards. A few minutes later, it had dwindled and vanished into the distance.

Willy watched until he could see it no longer. Then he looked down at the tarpaulin covered pieces of the 'Beaufighter'.

"We did it!" he told himself happily. Then he turned and went inside for a well-earned shower to wash off the sweat and sand.

Refreshed and dressed in clean clothes Willy felt much better, at least for a few minutes. Then the oppressive heat caused him to break into a sweat again, even when sitting in the saloon. Morning tea followed, during which the full story of the recovery were retailed to Graham, Andrew and Carmen.

After that there was little for Willy to do. The *Wewak* ploughed south across a glassy sea at about 12 knots. The air remained still and the sea had a flat, oily appearance with the horizon obscured by shimmering heat haze. Captain Kirk kept glancing at the sky and the barometer and muttering. The sky was clear, with no clouds and an odd glare which gave Willy a headache. He lay down and tried to sleep but it was too hot and he just perspired.

"Oh, why isn't this old tub air conditioned?" he grumbled.

He was not pleased to learn that they were not sailing direct back to Cairns. "We have to pull into a place called Port Stewart to pick up a bulldozer that needs repairs," Graham explained.

Willy found Port Stewart on the chart and then learned that they would be there overnight while they waited for the tide.

Port Stewart, when they reached it at about 3:00pm, was something of a shock to Willy. He had imagined a bay and wharves and a town. Instead all he could see was the mouth of a mangrove creek on a flat, sandy coast. The water offshore was full of shoals and sandbars and it took some tricky navigation to get the LCT through them and up the creek. The creek was about a hundred metres wide and very shallow. Then Willy got another shock. There was no wharf and no town. All that indicated it was a settlement was a barren, mudflat with a single sad looking coconut palm and the crumbling remains of some old cattle yards. A sloping gravel ramp comprised the entire port facilities.

Parked on the plain amid shimmering waves of heat was a large yellow painted bulldozer and a white 4WD. Two white miners sat in this and watched. The *Wewak* was conned in to the hard at about 4:00pm and the bow ramp lowered. The bulldozer was then coaxed on board with some difficulty as its engine kept failing and it had some defect in its gears. The machine was then secured by a sweat drenched crew using chains and turnbuckles.

By then it was after 5:00pm and they had missed the tide. All they could do was sit and watch as the water drained away.

"ALL of it!" Willy cried in astonishment as the *Wewak* was left sitting high and dry on the sandy bed of the creek. Apart from a few puddles there was no water at all.

The two miners departed in their vehicle and the only movement ashore was the arrival of a battered utility with half a dozen Aborigines of various ages and both sexes. They appeared to ignore the LCT and walked out on to the sandy bed of the creek. Here they set about collecting worms and shrimps for fishing bait. Then they set up camp some way from the shore, back near some distant trees. At no time did they come near the LCT.

"This is the port for the town of Coen," Captain Kirk explained.

"Can't be much of a town," Willy said, still sweating as the sun set.

"It isn't," he was assured.

Night brought very little relief. It remained stifling, with no wind. The discomfort was increased by swarms of sand flies and mosquitoes. Insect repellent seemed to be quite inadequate in keeping these off. Of further concern was the weather report after the 7:00pm news. This said that the 'low' in the Coral Sea had deepened to 985hp and had moved closer to the coast. It was now about 500 kilometres east of Cape Tribulation. It was still a long way off and well south but Captain Kirk looked anxious.

"I am not just worried about us," he explained. "I've got the *Malita* heading north from Townsville after being slipped for hull cleaning and the *Bonthorpe* is coming down past Lockhart River towing the barge *Oura*. The *Oura* is loaded to the eyeballs with empty forty-four-gallon drums, five thousand of them, and they are only making about seven knots as a tow."

Andrew asked the question Willy wanted to know about. "Sir, if this low becomes a cyclone is it likely to come this way?"

Captain Kirk shook his head. "No. Very few cyclones come in north of Cooktown. Nine out of ten strike the coast between Cairns and the Whitsunday Islands. But it will mean we might have to hang around up here for a few days waiting for one to blow itself out."

With that depressing thought Willy took himself to bed, lying under a mosquito net in a lather of sweat. It was an uncomfortable night and he slept badly. It was almost a relief to be woken at 05:00am the next morning.

Daylight brought no improvement in the weather. It remained hot and still with no clouds in the sky. Nor was there any water in the inlet yet. The tide had turned and was on the make but only a few trickles were visible out between the headlands. An early breakfast was mostly eaten in silence. The main topic of conversation was the 'low'. This had moved very little during the night and was still about 500 kilometres away. But it had deepened, the central pressure dropping to 977hp. The announcer informed them that it had begun to take on some formation and there was a possibility it might develop into a cyclone.

Captain Kirk spent some time on the radio and learned that the *Bonthorpe* and her tow had passed by during the night. They were now crossing Bathurst Bay, heading south.

For the next hour Willy sat in the shade and tried to read a book while watching the tide come in. To his surprise, it really flowed in, the brown water swirling across the sand much faster than he imagined was possible. The wide expanses of sand vanished very quickly. This was to the evident pleasure of the Aborigines who appeared on the bank armed with fishing lines, cast nets and fish spears. By 07:00am the LCT was afloat.

An hour later *Wewak* was under way and nosing carefully out of the entrance. Once safely out past the many sandbars speed was increased and course set of the Flinders Island Group. This was almost directly across the 'chord' of the great curve of Princess Charlotte Bay.

Within another hour the low coast had dropped below the horizon and there was nothing to see but the flat, gently undulating sea. Willy talked, read, and tried to snooze. But it was so hot that all he seemed to do was sweat. Lunch was eaten with no enthusiasm. Willy resigned himself to another boring, sweaty afternoon.

Then at 1:00pm he heard Graham calling his father.

"What is it?" Captain Kirk called from his bunk.

He usually slept during the day because he was awake and on watch at night so was short tempered and not amused at being woken up.

"A small boat ahead Dad, er, sir. It looks like it is in trouble," Graham replied.

Out of idle curiosity Willy made his way up to the bridge to look. A check of the chart showed they were near Wharton Reef, a small reef with a lighthouse on it. Nearby he saw a small, white-hulled sailing yacht. The yacht appeared to be rolling in the gentle swell, and as they got closer he saw that the sails and rigging did not look right.

"Got his mainsail all torn and tangled somehow," Captain Kirk said, observing the yacht through his binoculars. Then he raised them again to study the yacht. "Hmm," he murmured. "I think that is your friend the 'Flying Dutchman' in the *Dyfken*."

That got Willy's interest. *Jacob van der Heyden again!* he thought. *What is he doing?*

Chapter 31

SAURIAN

The *Wewak* hove to fifty metres from the yacht. By then Willy could see what Captain Kirk meant. The yacht's mainsail was only half up and was all in a tangle. Captain Kirk leaned over the wing of the bridge and raised a megaphone.

"*Dyfken* ahoy!"

Willy could clearly see Jacob, his sister, and his mother. They waved back and a faint 'Hello!' was called back.

"Do you need assistance?" Captain Kirk called.

There was a short delay during which Willy could clearly see Jacob arguing with his sister. It was Julia that answered.

"We have a bit of a problem with our sails and the engine has broken down," she called.

Captain Kirk swore under his breath. Then he said, "We can't leave them if there is the possibility of bad weather."

Carmen stepped forward. "Sir, I have been trained on the rigging of yachts like that. I spent a week on one during my coxswains course."

"Good. You and Andrew come across with me and we will take the engineer," Captain Kirk replied.

He went below, calling for Jock Cullen. Ten minutes later the boat was lowered. Willy badly wanted to go, so that he could question Jacob about what he was looking for but there was no room for him. Graham and the mate were left in charge of *Wewak*.

The boat went across and there was then a wait of half an hour. During this time both vessels drifted, rolling gently on the oily swell. Then a few whiffles of breeze ruffled the sea and Willy sighed with relief. The breeze slowly grew in strength until it was a steady breeze. To Willy's surprise, both the mate and Graham frowned and looked anxious.

"What's the matter?" he asked.

The mate answered. "That wind is coming off the land, from the southwest. That could mean that the low has formed into a cyclone and that the whole system has begun to rotate."

Willy had never been in the destructive part of a cyclone, but he knew enough to also be worried. Even if it was 500 kilometres away it was a threat. He knew that cyclones were gigantic revolving storms that could be two or three hundred kilometres across, with an eye that varied from 20 kilometres to 50 kilometres in diameter. The wind speeds would be above 60 knots, about 120kph, and the entire system could move at anything up to 10 to 15kph. Their course was very difficult to predict.

When Captain Kirk returned at 2:00pm he was just as worried. "Don't like this wind direction," he commented. He then sent the mate and Graham aft to prepare a steel wire towing rope. "Their engine is seized, overheated, and Carmen says that she needs calm water to get up the mast to fix the mainsail. It has a steel wire halyard jammed in the groove that the sail slides up. We will have to tow them to a safe anchorage."

It took twenty minutes to attach the towing cable to the bow of the yacht. Andrew, Carmen, and Jock Cullen returned back aboard, and the boat was hoisted up and secured. The *Wewak* then got under way. All Willy could do was stand out of the way and watch. From a slow start to draw the tow line taut gently speed was slowly increased until they were moving at 10 knots, the *Dyfken* following along a hundred metres astern.

From time to time the yacht would veer and sheer off to one side or the other before steadying back on course. Captain Kirk watched this several times and shook his head.

"I wish those landlubbers could steer a straight course. They could break the tow line with that sort of nonsense."

"Would you like me to or Andrew to go aboard as quartermaster, sir?" Carmen asked.

Captain Kirk shook his head. "No. We got a frosty enough reception as it was." He then bent to look at the radar screen and tapped at it. "Odd little blip. Must be a small boat," he muttered.

Willy and Carmen both moved to look. The screen clearly showed the shape of the huge bay and also the mountainous islands of the Flinders Group 20 kilometres ahead. Several other small blips showed.

"That one is the beacon on Wharton Reef," Carmen said, "And the one to the northwest is the lighthouse on Eden Reef. But this little blip just north of there must be a boat."

At 3:00pm Captain Kirk turned on the computer. This was linked by satellite to the Bureau of Meteorology website and gave the latest weather reports and warnings. Looking at the screen and watching the reactions of the sailors caused Willy a spasm of anxiety. The report said that the low had now developed into a tropical cyclone, a hurricane, except that in the southern hemisphere they rotate in a clockwise direction. It was only a Category 1, the weakest, and was still about 500 kilometres away, but it had turned to a more westerly course. The computer predictions were that it would move west and cross the North Queensland coast between Cooktown and Cairns.

"That is not good news," Captain Kirk said. "We had better start looking for a safe place to be, just in case."

He went to the chart and did some calculations. After a few minutes deliberation and a short discussion with the mate, he announced, "We are going to head for the Normanby River. If there is going to be cyclone, I want to be right up a mangrove creek. And we can fix that yacht's rigging there. Damn! I wanted to reach Cooktown tonight and Cairns tomorrow."

Willy now knew enough about the economics of coastal shipping to understand that a day or two's delay cost a lot of money and he felt sorry for Captain Kirk. Captain Kirk next went to the marine radio and called his other ship, the *Bonthorpe*.

"Where are you now Tom, over," he asked.

"Off Murdoch Point, over," came the reply.

"You'd better think about turning back. I don't want you running into this cyclone, over," Captain Kirk said.

"Already thinking about that. We are starting to run into some big seas already. I don't think we can get to Cooktown before it arrives, over," came the reply.

"Better to be safe than sorry. Turn back, over," Captain Kirk ordered.

The *Wewak's* course was now changed to south. Captain Kirk tried calling the *Dyfken* to explain but they apparently did not have their radio on. Carmen shook her head. "They are unbelievable lubbers. They wrecked their engine, then they got their halyard jammed. Worse still they thought they were at Clack Reef. When I looked at their chart and saw that they had a pencil line from Burkitt Island direct to Clack Reef, I could not believe it. The line ran across Hedge Reef, Grubb Reef and Corbett Reef as though they just did not matter."

"So how come they didn't run on one of them?" Willy asked.

"Pure good luck and bad navigation," Carmen answered. "They had not taken any magnetic variation into account and the currents must have helped push them south. So they went southeast instead of East."

"Did they say what they were looking for?" Willy asked.

Carmen shook her head. "No. They didn't say why they were there at all. They weren't very friendly but had to grudgingly admit they needed a bit of help."

"Strange," Willy commented.

Andrew laughed and said, "It just confirms that they have some secret they want to keep."

It was a good mystery for Willy to puzzle over. He went back to watching. The LCT was now heading directly into the wind and waves, but these were only about half a metre in height and caused almost no noticeable effect. The wind however surprised Willy. It was coming off the land and was hot, as though it was coming from a giant fire. The sky remained cloudless, and the sun blazed down so fiercely that metal fittings were painfully hot to the touch.

After an hour and a half of uneventful progress, the low coast of the southern shore of the bay came into sight. By this time the rugged and barren peaks of the Flinders Group and the Bathurst Range were standing clear above the horizon 15 kilometres to port.

As they approached the coast, Captain Kirk brought *Wewak* to the *Dyfken* riding easily at the end of her tow. "The problem now is to get us across the bar. It is an hour past low water. I don't know this river mouth well, have only been up it twice and that was in a dinghy. But I think *Wewak* will be alright. She only draws a metre at the bow and a bit over two metres aft. It is the yacht I am worried about. I don't know how deep her keel is."

Carmen looked at the yacht, on the deck of which the three van der Heydens were standing and staring at them. She said, "I had a look when we were diving to fix her propeller. She is only a seven metre 'trailer-sailer' and has a sliding keel that is wound up and down, like a big centre board. If that is up she should only draw a bit under two metres."

"We will try that," Captain Kirk agreed. He picked up the megaphone and bellowed, "Raise your keel so we can cross the bar."

The response was a lot of gesticulating and barely audible yells. Captain Kirk called again and got the same response. This time they heard the words, 'Don't know how.'

Captain Kirk muttered an oath and shook his head. "People like them shouldn't be allowed out on the water," he grumbled.

"I can do it sir," Carmen offered.

"Okay. Graham and Andrew, launch the boat and take Carmen over. Then stay in the boat and go ahead of us to try to sound out the best channel," Captain Kirk ordered.

Another ten minutes went by before Carmen had been transferred to the yacht. Within a couple of minutes she came on the radio. "Radio was turned off. Ready to proceed sir, over," she reported.

Captain Kirk got the *Wewak* under way again. He then did a quick check of both the echo sounder to check the depth and then the radar.

"Hmm. That small boat is still on the screen. He must be heading the same way as us," he said. Then he turned and said, "Lester, you take the wheel. I will con us from the monkey island. Dr Williams, will you and Willy come up and help act as lookouts please?"

Willy was more than happy to. Even though it meant standing in the blazing sun it was a useful job to do and he pulled on a hat and followed his father and Captain Kirk up to the monkey island. The LCT then got slowly under way and headed inshore.

To begin with Willy could not make out any sign of a river mouth. All he could see was what looked like an unbroken line of beach backed by dark green trees. Offshore the whole area was a litter of shallows, shoals, and even exposed sandbars. But from the higher position a channel of deeper water could clearly be seen, and Captain Kirk took the LCT in, calling instructions to the mate via the old-fashioned speaking tube.

When they were less than a kilometre off the beach Willy noted a break in the dark green line and soon after that saw that the deepwater channel curved left and went in behind a long spit of sand. The tidal current was very obviously flowing in, and Captain Kirk had a few anxious moments as they rounded the curve.

As they straightened up behind the sand spit, Captain Kirk looked back at the yacht, then at the sky and finally at the horizon behind them. Willy saw him frown and then raise his binoculars.

"There's that boat," he said. "Dark coloured thing and right out on the horizon."

Willy looked but in the glare of the sun all he could make out was a speck of some dark object on the rippling horizon.

Captain Kirk then switched his attention back to guiding the LCT around a sharp curve to the right. To Willy it looked like the gap in the mangroves they were aiming at was much too small for such a big vessel but as they got closer it opened out and he saw that it was much larger, at least a hundred metres wide. Better still, unlike the shallow sandy bottom of Port Stewart, the river had deep water in behind the entrance. The riverbanks appeared to be unbroken mangroves with vertical mud banks.

As the LCT slid slowly into the lee of the mangroves, the breeze was shut off and they were enveloped in hot, sticky heat. With it came sandflies and mosquitoes and Willy could barely wait to rush below to smear repellent on.

Captain Kirk took the LCT about a kilometre up the river, rounding two bends before coming to a reach that was about half a kilometre long. Both banks were massive thickets of mangroves and to his great pleasure and concern Willy saw the tail of a big crocodile as it slid into the water.

"Lots of the slimy buggers up this river," Captain Kirk commented. "It is an ideal saurian habitat. So you keep away from the water and if you go in a boat, keep your hands and feet inboard. Now, this is as far as I want to go for the moment. Any further upstream and the river narrows too much for us to turn around."

He then went down to the wheelhouse and took the wheel, sending the mate forward with Willy to assist. Using a radio Captain Kirk called the boat and sent it to the starboard bow to take a line from the mate. This was taken ashore and threaded around a large mangrove growing right on the edge of deep water. The other end was led back and secured.

"This way, if we need to go in a hurry, we can just slip and go," the mate explained.

"Go where?" Willy asked.

"Further up the river, right in among the mangroves," the mate replied.

"But why? What if we got stuck and couldn't get the barge out?" Willy queried.

The mate laughed and replied, "We would only worry about that if we are still alive. Up a mangrove creek is the safest place for us to be if there is a cyclone. If the old barky gets stuck, well she's insured. That's why they call captains of coasters 'Mudskippers'. It is how they stay alive on the coast of Cape York."

That was all a bit worrying to Willy, but he saw the sense of it. He looked anxiously at the dense mangroves and thought, *There must be dry land through there, if we can make it! An ideal habitat for saurian,* Captain Kirk said.

Just the thought of being chased and grabbed by one of the prehistoric lizards made Willy shudder. Once again, he looked anxiously at the murky green water alongside. The mate then called him aft to help shorten the tow line.

The *Dyfken* was cast off and towed back fifty metres by the boat, Graham acting as cox and Andrew doing the rope work. They then boarded the yacht and helped Carmen drop the anchor. When that was done Carmen got into the boat and it returned to the *Wewak.*

"I need some rope and tools," Carmen said.

"Are you going back to the yacht?" Willy asked.

"Yes, to fix the rigging," Carmen replied.

A feeling of intense curiosity seized Willy. "Can I come?" he asked.

"If the skipper says so," Carmen answered.

Willy asked Captain Kirk who said yes. "Be back for tea at six," he added.

When it came time to lower himself over the side into the boat Willy had a few more anxious looks at the water. Graham saw this and said, "Come on Willy. What's the matter?"

"Your dad said this was the ideal habitat for saurians," Willy answered. "I just don't want to give one a chance of making a meal of me."

Both Graham and Andrew laughed but Willy was gratified to note them both cast anxious glances at the river. Carmen then passed down a tool kit and she slid down into the boat. That got Willy wondering if the boat was now overloaded but a label on the side told him it was designed to carry seven.

It still looks awfully close to the water, he thought, eyeing the freeboard of half a metre with anxiety.

In his imagination he pictured the scenes he had often seen on TV documentaries: the great rush of water and grey hide, the gaping jaws, the rows of horrible yellow teeth!

To his relief, it only took a minute or so to travel the hundred metres to the yacht. The yacht, like the LCT, was now lying diagonally across the stream under the influence of both wind and tide. The boat was secured on the yacht's port side. But when he got there, Willy wished he hadn't come. His smile faded as he saw the van der Heyden's faces almost scowling down at them. Trying to brush this off Willy clambered aboard.

"Hello again, Jacob. Hello Julia, Mrs van der Heyden. How are you?"

"Okay," Jacob answered.

His answer wasn't very friendly, and he made no offer of hospitality, standing just under the awning on the small aft deck.

For something to say to ease the embarrassing silence Willy said, "We have just spent a week digging up an old, World War Two aircraft wreck. It is on the *Wewak* now."

"Aircraft wreck?" Jacob replied, his voice full of alarm. As he did, so he exchanged a glance with his sister who also looked anxious. "What type? Where?"

"A Bristol 'Beaufighter', a twin-engine fighter bomber type. It was buried in the sand dunes a couple of hundred kilometres up the coast," Willy explained.

Jacob looked visibly relieved. He nodded and looked as though he didn't know what to say.

His mother then asked, "Why did we come into this stinking, sweaty river?"

"To repair your rigging in calm water and because of the cyclone," Willy answered.

"Cyclone?" Jacob queried, looking foolish as he did.

Willy exchanged a glance with Andrew who rolled his eyes and went back to helping Carmen and Graham untangle ropes.

"It is a long way off," Willy added. "And only Category One." He then related the mate's explanation as to why this was a safe thing to do.

On hearing Willy's comment that the vessels did not matter because they were insured, Mrs van der Heyden said bitterly, "That's alright for some, but our boat isn't insured."

On seeing the surprised look on Willy's face, Julia added, "We used all our money to buy this boat."

Willy nodded and thought, *There must be a treasure for them to do something like that.* He tried to think of something to say.

Suddenly Jacob stared past Willy, a disbelieving look on his face. He cried, "*Saurian!*"

Willy looked around, scanning the mangroves and river for signs of a crocodile. "Where?" he asked.

Jacob went very pale and looked agitated, then pointed down river. "That boat. It is the *Saurian!*"

Willy looked and saw a motor launch coming into view around the bend close to the sea. The hull of the launch was painted a dark grey and its upperworks dark green. Two heads could just be seen looking over the cabin.

Jacob now became very agitated and even grabbed Willy's arm. "Look! There is 'Gator' Smith, and he's got a gun."

Now Willy saw that both the heads that were visible wore balaclavas, but he could also see what might be the barrel of a rifle or shotgun poking up. He was tempted to ask how Jacob knew that the hooded man was 'Gator' but presumed Jacob could tell. Then he saw the launch turn directly towards them.

Now real fear showed on Jacob's face and sounded in his voice. "They are coming here! They want the maps! We must get away!"

Willy saw that Jacob was grabbing at the large wallet on his belt. He looked at the launch, then at Andrew and Carmen, then back at the van der Heydens. There was no doubt that Jacob was now terrified.

Jacob almost gibbered with fear, then looked desperately around. "Oh quick! They killed Karl and now they will kill me! We must get away!"

A surge of fear overran Willy's doubts. Noting that the boat was tied alongside on the side away from the approaching *Saurian* he reasoned that the yacht could provide cover most of the way back to the LCT. He looked around then quickly gave orders.

"We will be safer on the *Wewak*. Quick Graham, get into the boat and start the engine. Andrew, untie the bow line and be ready to push us off. Carmen, get aboard and steady people and seat them. Mrs van der Heyden, Julia, follow Carmen aboard, quick!"

To Willy's relief, nobody argued. Both Graham and Andrew scrambled nimbly into the boat, followed by Carmen. Willy then grabbed Jacob's arm as he went to jump in next.

"Wait, Jacob. Women and children first is the traditional way," he said sarcastically, amazed at how cool he felt.

Mrs van der Heyden jumped into the boat, almost pitching over the side. Carmen grabbed her and forced her to sit. By then Julia had slithered down and sat next to her mother. Willy then let Jacob go. Jacob scrambled down so hastily he almost overturned the boat. Only the combined efforts of Carmen and Andrew prevented this and he was shoved unceremoniously onto another thwart. By then Willy was hanging over the side. As he lowered his feet onto the same thwart, he took a last look over the top of the yacht's deck.

He saw that the *Saurian* was only a hundred metres away and one of the masked men had moved up onto the foredeck. The man was holding what could only be a gun and Willy felt a thrill of fear.

"Shove off! Get us back fast, Graham. Try to keep the yacht between us and them," Willy called.

Graham nodded and opened the throttle. Even as Willy lowered himself onto the thwart, he felt the boat move. Andrew pushed them clear, and Graham shoved the outboard controls hard to starboard. The boat surged around sharply to port, then lifted its nose as Graham straightened up.

By then Willy was in a fever of anxiety. He dimly heard a man yelling at them from the *Saurian* but could not make out the words over the roar of the motor. By this time he wished he had sat facing aft as he had to swivel his head around to look back.

Halfway, he estimated. *Still no sign of the launch.*

Glancing forward Willy saw that Graham was turning them so that they would go around the stern of *Wewak*. He understood before Graham explained that such a manoeuvre would place the hull of the LCT between them and the launch while they climbed aboard. But it also meant they swung out into view of the launch for fifty metres.

And there it was! Willy saw the bow of the *Saurian* appear. He also saw the man on the foredeck pointing at them. Then the launch's bow turned to port and it came out from behind the anchored yacht, a creaming white bow wave indicating it was now going much faster. The man began shouting at them, calling on them to stop.

Crack! Zipp!

Water flew up close alongside. Willy stared at it in disbelief. "They shot at us!" he cried. Graham shoved the tiller over and the boat slewed to port.

Crack! Tiiing!

Willy heard the bullet go past and then strike the steel side of the *Wewak.*

They wouldn't dare! he thought in astonished disbelief. *There are adults there.* To reinforce this belief, he saw the engineer look out the door at the rear of the saloon.

Graham pulled the tiller across and the boat went surging around to starboard. A second later, they shot behind the protection of *Wewak's* steel hull. Willy saw Captain Kirk staring down at them, a surprised look on his face.

Pointing aft, Willy shouted up, "Pirates! Murderers! Get a gun!"

Graham eased the throttle and yelled, "Get aboard!"

But Jacob screamed no. "No! I am not safe there! They will kill me. I am a witness to Karl's murder."

"They wouldn't dare surely," Carmen suggested. Her face was strained and tight-lipped.

Glancing back Willy did a quick calculation. *We will never get aboard in time.*

He looked at Graham. "Graham, we won't make it in time. Take us round the bow before they come into sight."

Graham nodded and Carmen dragged Julia down as the boat surged forward. As they sped along close beside the rusty and weed-encrusted black hull, Willy kept glancing back, hoping they would get out of sight before the launch appeared.

And there it was!

The *Saurian* slid into view seconds before they reached the bow.

Chapter 32

DESPERATE CHOICES

As though in slow motion, Willy saw the masked man on the foredeck of the launch raise his rifle. It appeared to be aimed straight at him. His whole being seemed to freeze and he could only stare in horrified fascination. Then he saw the man twitch and the tiniest puff of smoke was instantly dispersed by the wind.

Tiing! Whheee!

Willy cringed as the bullet smacked into the steel side of the LCT and then ricocheted off across the river.

"Only a '22'," Graham grunted, and Willy marvelled at his calmness.

As they slid under the shelter of the bow ramp, Willy looked around. "Which way should we go?" he asked.

He could see there were three options: try to run upstream to find somewhere to hide; get aboard the LCT and hope the adults could protect them; or run back down the river along the other side of the *Wewak.*

The others had also obviously been assessing the alternate course of action open to them because Jacob pointed upriver.

"That way!" he shouted.

Graham shook his head and slowed the boat as he reached the other side of the ramp. "No. It is half a kilometre to the next bend. They would either catch us or shoot us. The only reason that mongrel missed then was because the launch was bouncing around on our wake. Besides, there is nowhere to go."

"But there must be a town with police," Julia cried. She looked terrified and was crying.

Willy stared at her in disbelief. *Has she not looked at a map of Cape York Peninsula?* he wondered.

"There isn't," Graham snapped shortly.

He didn't wait to debate but turned the boat sharply to starboard. They scraped through under the mooring rope which stretched across to the nearby mangroves. Then Graham opened the throttle and the boat surged along the LCT's starboard side.

As they came level with the gap between the end of the tank deck and the start of the superstructure, Graham called, "Andrew, stand up and have a look."

Andrew did so, but immediately bobbed down again. "Get going!" he hissed. "One of them is climbing aboard with a pistol."

Before anyone could argue Graham opened the throttle and the boat lifted its bow and started off. Willy and the others all stared up at the deck of the *Wewak* as they slipped past the superstructure. To Willy's consternation, he saw Mrs Kirk step out and block the path of the man. The man had an automatic pistol and, as she tried to stop him, he pushed her roughly aside and waved the gun in her face.

Carmen saw this and gasped. "Graham, that man has got your mum!"

Graham glanced back and swore, then his mouth set in a hard line. But he kept the throttle open and the boat pointed down river. A couple of seconds later the boat sped past the stern of the LCT and out onto open water. Willy looked back and saw the hooded gunman shove Mrs Kirk aside. Then the man ran along the deck to the stern and raised his pistol.

"Come back or else!" the man screamed.

Willy cringed and hunched lower, conscious that Graham had no intention of obeying. A glance showed they were now 25 metres away already.

Bang!

The heavier thump of the pistol sounded simultaneous with the crack of the passing bullet. Where it went Willy had no idea. Graham sent the boat into a skidding side slew, then back the other way. Willy cringed and clung on.

Bang!

Missed, Willy thought.

He glanced at the others to see if any were hit. None seemed to be. His eyes met Julia's and he realised that hers were wide with terror. Jacob looked ashen and was trembling, pale and sweating. His mother looked appalled and was sobbing. Carmen and Andrew both just looked tight-lipped and serious and Graham was obviously angry.

50 metres away.

Another glance back showed Mrs Kirk and Kylie struggling with the man. The man rammed Mrs Kirk hard against the bulkhead and swung the gun to point it at Captain Kirk's face as he appeared on deck.

Oh my God! Willy thought, fearing the worst.

75 metres.

100 metres.

The boat surged down river past the yacht. As it did, Willy looked back and saw the *Saurian* alongside the *Wewak*. There was a man on the launch, pointing at them and shouting to his mate.

Carmen pointed to the yacht. "We could use the radio to call for help," she suggested.

A grim-faced Graham shook his head. "We won't have time. We need to get out of the area. I will look for a trawler or ship," he replied.

So they roared on down the river. To Willy's enormous relief he saw that the gunman on the *Wewak* had let go of Mrs Kirk and was shepherding her, Kylie and Captain Kirk into the saloon.

I hope he isn't going to shoot them all, he thought.

The horrible thought crossed his mind that his father might be shot. It made him feel ill. He doubted if the men would really murder the eight people still on the LCT but there was a dreadful feeling of apprehension.

But they might shoot us if they catch us, he decided.

Spurred on by that terrifying prospect Willy felt relief as they rounded the bend in the river and the other vessels vanished from view. After his ordeal of being under a death sentence by some crooks back in June he knew just what real terror was.

Graham did not slow down. All he did was scan the banks for possible landing sites.

"We could land you and you could scatter and hide," he suggested.

Even as he said this Willy saw a huge crocodile slither down the bank and vanish into the murky water off to port in a swirl of foam and bubbles.

Bloody hell! he thought. *Talk about being caught between the devil and the deep blue sea!*

The others saw it too and Julia gave a near hysterical shriek and cried, "I am not going ashore here!"

"Further along the coast on the beach then," Graham replied.

By then they were at the mouth of the river and Willy was amazed at the change an hour could bring. What had been miles of sandy flats and shoals were now just water and the ripples of gentle surf. The open sea spread out to the horizon.

Despite the urgent need to get away Graham slowed down and Andrew stood up to act as lookout in the bows.

"We will look a right pack of clowns if we run aground and get caught," Graham commented.

As far as possible they followed the same deepwater channel out. This curved left and went west for half a kilometre, the sand spit now all but submerged. Because the wind was blowing offshore the waves were tiny and of little help in detecting shoals.

Once they were out past the more obvious shoals and sand banks Graham opened the throttle again and set course northeast, aiming directly across the bay for the tip of the Bathurst Range.

"Where are we going?" Julia asked.

"The Rattlesnake Channel," Graham answered. "That is a shipping route. I am hoping to find a big freighter or a trawler. They will have a radio we can use."

The surface of Princess Charlotte Bay was a mass of tiny waves over which the boat thumped in a hammering *smack-smack-smack-smack*. Each impact threw up a shower of spray, but as the wind was from astern and they were traveling faster than the tiny waves it was not bad going.

Then Willy saw Julia's face go drawn as she looked astern. "Oh no! Here they come!" she cried.

Willy looked astern and saw the far-off shape of the *Saurian*. Because of its colouring the launch was very hard to see against the dark coastline but the little puffs of white at her bows were plain to see.

"About two kilometres astern," Andrew estimated.

Graham frowned. "They didn't go as far west as we did to get through the sand bars," he commented.

Carmen answered that. "They possibly know the river better."

Willy agreed. "If they have been hiding ever since the murder then that might be their hideout?"

"Quite likely," Graham agreed. He kept looking astern and then began biting his lip. "I think she is faster than us," he said. "Andrew, Carmen, can you measure their size and then keep checking? I want to know if she is catching up."

"I know how to do that," Carmen said. "Andrew, use your finger. Note the size of the launch against it, but keep the finger the same distance from your face each time," she explained.

C.R. Cummings

Andrew gave a wry smile. "Aren't you supposed to use a sextant to do that, to measure the height of the other ships masts by exact degrees?"

"Don't be a smart aleck, little brother. Just do it," Carmen replied.

For ten minutes they sped on. Willy did some comparing with the others. By then he was sure, and he felt his heart sinking.

"They are definitely faster," he said.

"They are gaining alright," Andrew agreed, "And also heading closer inshore than us."

Jacob gave a sort of whimper. He looked ashen faced and was visibly trembling. His mother cried, "Oh do something! Get us out of here!"

That really annoyed Willy. "Oh be quiet!" he snapped. "We are doing the best we can."

"But they might catch us!" Mrs van der Heyden wailed.

"Then give them the bloody map to the treasure and maybe they will leave us alone," Willy snapped.

"But they might still kill us," Mrs van der Heyden replied amid sniffles.

"So there is a treasure map?" Willy asked, meeting Jacob's eyes.

Jacob nodded and then sobbed. "Oh they can have it! I'm scared."

Willy curled his lip and then asked sarcastically, "Do you have spare copies of the map?"

Again Jacob nodded. Willy thought about this and then decided that the gunmen might still feel driven to have to cover their tracks by murder. "Too risky. Anyway, we can't negotiate out here in a little boat on the open ocean," he said.

He saw Graham nod. Graham then turned the boat to angle it in towards the shore. But because they had been steering directly across the bay they were nearly five kilometres out and the beach was just visible. Graham said, "I will try to land most of you on the beach and you can hide in the bush while I go on and look for a ship," he said.

That seemed like a good choice to Willy, so he nodded. The others made no reply. For the next fifteen minutes the boat sped on, blatting across the wave tops, the waves now coming in on the starboard quarter and causing some rolling and spray.

At the end of that time the boat was about 3 kilometres offshore. By then the mountains were looming large and looking very rugged. The flat shoreline where the mouth of the river lay had long since dropped out of sight below the horizon. Graham kept studying the launch and then shook his head.

"We aren't going to make it," he said with flat finality. "Those mongrels are gaining, and they are inshore of us."

"Converging course," Andrew commented.

Willy understood. Not only was the larger boat a bit faster but it had a shorter distance to go.

Reluctantly Graham changed course, once more aiming for the tip of the cape. This was now only about 5 kilometres away. Graham scanned the coast and then the horizon, shaking his head in frustration.

"Oh, where are all the ships?" he muttered.

Willy looked around the horizon and remembered Captain Kirk's words. *The empty ocean,* he called it. The strong possibility that they might not meet another vessel at all sent a deep chill of fear through him but he said nothing.

Andrew said, "Maybe we can lose them in the dark?"

Both Carmen and Graham shook their heads. "It is only seventeen thirty. There are another two hours of daylight almost. They will be up with us by then," Carmen said.

That brought another whimper from Julia and sniffles from Mrs van der Heyden. Willy felt sick, and it wasn't only from fear. Forty-five minutes of thumping across waves of ever increasing size and with the following wind wafting the fumes from the motor forward were also having an effect. On top of a splitting headache he felt sick in the stomach and very thirsty. The sight of the blazing sun and the clear blue sky made him heartily sick of the sea.

Then another crisis slowly emerged. The launch crept closer all the time but in doing so moved up until it was nearly abreast of them and in between them and the land. Willy estimated that it was only a kilometre away. There was obviously very little chance of them getting past it to the shore.

"My mistake," Graham commented. "I should have put you all ashore as soon as we left the river mouth. I think he means to force us away from the coast."

Willy looked ahead. The tip of Bathurst Head was now almost abreast of them. In the distance beyond it the rugged shapes of the Flinders Group began to come into view. "What about the islands?" he suggested.

Graham nodded. "Probably our only choice. If we can play hide and seek among them until dark, we should get away."

"That boat has got radar," Carmen pointed out.

Willy looked and saw the small scanner on a short mast. It surprised him that such a small vessel would have such a fitting.

As the minutes went by the sea became rougher as they went further out into open water. Then the Rattlesnake Channel through into Bathurst Bay began to slowly open up. They all kept looking hopefully in all directions, but the horizon remained empty of shipping.

But any chance of turning east to follow the main shipping route was now clearly lost as the *Saurian* was directly abeam of them and only half a kilometre away.

She is creeping closer all the time, Willy noted bitterly.

That only left the option of going to the west of Blackwood Island. Graham turned that way. As they did, *Saurian* was forced to change course to get around Pullen Point, the most southerly point on the island. The boat sped past it only a hundred metres off the shore.

"What about going ashore there?" Andrew suggested.

To Willy that seemed like a good idea. The island looked large enough and rugged enough to provide plenty of hiding places.

Graham shook his head. "No water, not that I know of anyway," he replied. "You might be lucky to find a brackish rockpool. We will try for Denham. I know where there is a spring on it."

So they pounded on along just off the coast. For a few anxious minutes they lost sight of the *Saurian* and Carmen voiced the fear that it might be hurrying along the east coast to cut them off.

"In that case we are up the proverbial creek," Graham commented.

That brought more whimpers from Julia and her mother. Jacob said, "Oh do something!"

Graham eyed him coldly and snapped back, "We are. We are risking our bloody lives for you. If you don't like it, then bloody well jump over the side and swim ashore."

Then the *Saurian* appeared behind them and still at least half a kilometre back. "Good!" Graham hissed. "We have a chance."

For five more anxious minutes the boat roared on northeast along the shore. By then they could clearly see the even larger and more rugged Stanley and Flinders Islands to the north.

"What about them?" Willy suggested.

Graham shook his head. "No. We need water."

So he followed the rugged coast around to the east. Willy saw the mountainous pile of Denham Island come into view about 3 kilometres away.

But will we make it in time? he wondered anxiously as he watched the *Saurian* come into view only five or six hundred metres behind.

Three minutes went by. *One kilometre down. Two to go,* Willy estimated.

But the launch was still gaining, its bow wave creaming foam as it ploughed through the waves that the boat skimmed over.

Carmen sighed. "This is really pretty. I wish we were visiting under more pleasant conditions."

"Doesn't look tropical though," Andrew said. "Looks more like pictures I have seen of Scotland or cold places like that."

"Scotland," Graham agreed. "It reminds me of that place called Scapa Flow in the Orkney Islands; the place where the British based their battle fleet during the world wars. It is a ring of islands like this."

Willy had seen photos of Scapa Flow, and he could only agree it had a similarity. He opened his mouth to suggest it was a bit too rugged to really compare but he left the words unsaid when the motor suddenly gave a cough and began spluttering.

"What's wrong?" Mrs van der Heyden shrieked.

"Not sure," Graham replied.

"Fuel?" Carmen queried.

Graham unscrewed the fuel cap and looked in, then swore. "Fuel," he confirmed. "The tank is nearly dry."

"Bloody hell!" Jacob cried. He stared at the small beach on Denham Island that Graham was aiming for, his face a mask of near despair.

Only a kilometre, Willy estimated. *But will we make it?*

The motor gave another cough and nearly died, then resumed spluttering. The boat noticeably slowed. Looking astern Willy estimated that the *Saurian* was now only between 300 and 400 metres astern. Details on the launch were becoming visible and two dark blobs that were the heads of the two men were just visible in its cockpit.

This is going to be close! Willy thought.

Chapter 33

WILLY DECIDES

For a few more minutes the outboard motor ran smoothly. Willy kept looking forward and then astern.

About a half a kilometre to go, he estimated. But he also noted with concern that the pursuing launch was creeping closer every minute. *Must be only two hundred or three hundred metres behind,* he estimated.

He knew from his cadet training that they were now inside effective rifle range, and the knowledge chilled him. He went even colder when he saw that one of the men now had his head above the cabin roof and was holding the rifle.

The motor suddenly coughed and spluttered again. Blue smoke billowed from it and Graham shook his head, his face a mask of determination. Then the motor fired again and roared steadily. Willy looked ahead and estimated they were now only about 300 or 400 metres from the shore. A glance astern showed that the *Saurian* had narrowed the distance even more.

Movement beside Willy caused him to glance sideways. It was Carmen. She was quietly pounding her clenched fists on her knees. She met Willy's eyes and gave a tight-lipped smile.

"Come on! Go boat, go!" she said.

Less than 200 metres, Willy calculated. *We might make it.*

With every second his hopes crept up. He began studying the island, trying to pick the best place to hide. The end of the island nearest them was a rocky headland on which the waves were breaking. It was obviously unsafe. A hundred metres along to the left was a short length of sandy beach backed by a steep rock and scrub-covered slope.

We can't climb straight up. We will be like ducks in the shooting gallery, he thought.

At the far end of the beach a straggle of mangroves stood in the water. The hillside behind the mangroves was studded with huge boulders.

He said, "Graham, try to put us ashore over near that little patch of mangroves on the left," he said.

Graham nodded and changed course slightly. The distance shortened with every second. Another glance astern.

We will make it, Willy decided, seeing the launch still at least 200 metres behind.

Then the motor began to cough and run rough. At once their speed fell away. Dismay and fear swept through Willy and he could tell the others were equally frightened. They were now only 100 metres off the beach.

We can swim if we have to, Willy thought, but he knew it would be a desperate last resort. Images of them being shot as they struggled in the water or on the beach swirled in his mind.

75 metres.

50 metres

25 metres, the launch still at least a hundred astern.

Yes, we will make it, Willy told himself.

But even as he thought this the engine spluttered to a stop. Andrew twisted the throttle but nothing happened. But the boat's momentum kept them sliding forward on the calm water behind the headland.

Willy glanced astern and then said, "When we hit the beach run to the left behind those mangroves, then scatter and climb up among the rocks."

"Where will we rendezvous?" Carmen asked.

"The top of the hill?" Willy answered.

Graham shook his head. "Too obvious. The spring is just above high tide level in a sort of cave on the south side of the island. We will meet there," he said.

10 metres.

The boat was slowing but Willy could now see the bottom. Carmen dug her hand in the water. "Paddle!" she ordered.

Willy did so, as did Graham and Julia but Jacob seemed mesmerised by the approaching launch. The boat slid forward another five metres. Willy paddled frantically. Then Andrew stood up and sprang over the bow, holding the anchor.

As he did, there was a shout and a shot from the launch. The bullet cracked over Willy's head, the fear almost causing him to lose control of his bowels. He heard the bullet strike the rocks behind the beach. Then he felt the boat grind onto the sand and he stood up, only to be shoved aside by Jacob, who went bounding ashore.

Willy swore and glanced back as Carmen followed. Then he sprang over the side into waist deep water. The water was warm and that sensation came as a shock, but it was the way the bottom dropped steeply away that really alarmed him. As he tried to hurry ashore, his boots slipped repeatedly on sand which slid from under them into deeper water. He went down but managed to keep his head above water and frantically clawed his way back into shallower water.

Andrew, who was holding the boat with one hand, reached down and heaved him right onto the beach. As Willy stood up, Julia and Mrs van der Heyden scrambled over the bow and onto the beach. Graham went over the other side of the boat in a flat dive which took him in to the beach. As Willy started running, he heard more shouting and another shot which caused him to twitch in fear and run even faster.

To his further dismay, the beach was a poor one to run on. It was composed as much of pebbles and seashells as sand and it had a steep profile so that there was no hard, damp sand near the water's edge. Instead his boots sank in and slid back with every step. But terror kept him running. As he ran, he sucked in hot gasps of air and was dimly aware that his vision was all blurry and only the beach ahead was really in focus.

Willy was aware that there were people running with him and he could see both Jacob and Carmen ahead of him. At every second he expected to feel a bullet slam into his back, and he kept tensing and gasping as he ran. The skin on his whole back seemed to crawl in anticipation.

Nearly at the mangroves, he thought.

As he ran, he glanced back, noting with dismay that the launch was nosing in to the beach. Through sweaty, blurred eyes Willy noted that the man on the foredeck was standing ready, but that he was holding his rifle at the point of balance in his left hand and the anchor in his right.

That is why he isn't shooting, he reasoned. *But the moment he is standing on firm ground we are in deadly danger.*

Another glance ahead, then another back. Jacob was sprinting in behind the mangroves along a narrow belt of sand and small rocks. Carmen followed him. Behind were Graham and Andrew and then Julia and Mrs van der Heyden. As though in a nightmare Willy saw the man jump ashore and toss the anchor up the beach.

Run! Willy thought, his skull gripped by goose bumps of terror.

A cry of pain behind Willy made him glance back. It was Mrs van der Heyden. She had stumbled on a small rock and gone sprawling on the beach. Julia turned back and bent to help her mother up. Willy slowed and kept looking back but almost tripped himself.

Then Graham pushed him. "Keep going!" he snarled.

Willy did, but he didn't feel good about it. Leaving someone to the mercy of the enemy went against the grain but another glance back showed Mrs van der Heyden hobbling slowly after them.

But not fast enough! Willy reasoned, seeing the first man start running after them and the second jumping ashore from the launch, pistol in hand.

Another ten seconds of frantic running had Willy in behind the mangroves and big rocks. As he reached the first large boulder he again looked back, causing Andrew to collide with him.

"Keep running Willy," Andrew gasped.

"But the crooks have got Mrs van der Heyden and Julia," Willy croaked, glancing back and seeing the first man reach the badly limping woman.

Julia began to scream as the man raised his rifle. She grabbed at the rifle, spoiling his aim. He smacked her hard with one hand and shouted, "Shut up girl!"

That caused Willy a spurt of deep anger which mixed with his own fear and apprehension to bring his emotions to the boil. But he could not see what was to be gained by going back.

Without a weapon we can't do anything, he thought unhappily.

Another glance showed that the men had stopped running and were standing with weapons pointed at Julia and Mrs van der Heyden. The men appeared to be shouting angry questions at them and threatening them, but no words registered in Willy's consciousness.

By now Jacob was scrambling up the hillside. This was a mixture of granite boulders and numerous small rocks. Growing in tufts between the rocks was a wiry grass and clumps of a prickly bush. The rugged slope was quite easy to climb and offered plenty of cover and hiding places. The problem was one of fitness. Within a minute Willy found his chest heaving, his breath coming in great rasping gasps and dots dancing before his eyes. He came to a standstill about a hundred paces up from the beach.

Jacob was leaning on a rock just above him, his whole body heaving as he sucked in air. Carmen was just the other side of another boulder. Just below was a panting Andrew. Graham, plainly the fittest of them all, was already up level with Willy and off to his left.

Crack! Sreeeeooo!

A bullet struck the rocks near Willy and went shrieking off up the hillside. Willy flinched and ducked down, still gasping to get his breath back. He was aware that his heart was hammering so hard it made it hard to hear.

God, I hope I don't have a heart attack! he thought in dismay.

A quick glance around the side of the rock he was crouched behind showed him that they were about a hundred metres away from the men. Then he noted that both Mrs van der Heyden and Julia were kneeling on the beach near the start of the mangroves and the second man was standing behind them with the pistol aimed at them. Both men still had their balaclavas rolled down, the sight adding an extra chill of evil to their appearance.

The man with the rifle now shouted, "Hey, you kids! Give us the maps and we will let these women go."

"Oh no! They've got hostages!" Carmen cried, her face going pale with shock.

"What will we do?" Jacob croaked, his eyes wide with near panic.

That really annoyed Willy. "They are your mother and sister. You give them the maps of course," he snapped angrily.

Jacob nodded and swallowed, then gasped, "But... but they might kill me."

That much was obvious to Willy. His mind raced, and when the man shouted again, he yelled back, "Okay, but we don't trust you."

"Tough kid! Give us the maps or we will shoot the old duck. Then we will enjoy ourselves with Little Miss Pretty here. And if you still won't give us the maps then we will shoot her as well and then hunt you all down," the man shouted.

"Oh my God!" Jacob croaked, his whole face taking on a ghastly, haunted look. "We must."

"Yes, we must," Willy agreed. "But first we will negotiate."

Seeing Graham, Andrew and Carmen nod agreement Willy turned and called, "Okay, we agree. We will hand over the maps. But we want to be sure we stay safe. If you hurt either of the women, then we destroy the maps and then spend the night fighting you. Do it our way and you get the maps easily."

There was a minute's delay while the two men conferred. While they did Willy noted that the sun was now very low in the west, was already starting to slip behind the bulk of Blackwood Island.

Be dark in about an hour. Can we last that long? he wondered.

The big man with the rifle yelled back up the hill, "What's the deal kid?"

Willy's mind had been racing, trying to come up with a plan that did not allow any more of them become hostages or place them in the power of a double-cross.

To Jacob he said, "Who is that? Is that Gator?"

"Yes, and the other one is Corey," Jacob replied.

Willy saw that he was trembling and licking his lips repeatedly. *I hope I don't look as scared as that,* he thought. *I won't make much of a fighter pilot if I crumple that easily!* But the only plan he could come up with was full of holes.

He called back, "We need a few minutes to sort out Jacob's papers so that he still has his wallet and credit cards and so on. Then I will come down to the beach with the maps. One of you is to leave your gun and bring one of the hostages with you to meet me. The other man stays where he is with Mrs van der Heyden. Got that?"

"I'm listening," Gator called back.

Willy licked dry lips and felt annoyed with himself. He had not meant to consciously choose between the two females, but Julia's age and good looks had influenced him, and he knew it.

He went on, "You can check that the maps are what you want and then we will step apart. I will lay the maps on the ground, and you will walk back to your mate while the girl comes up the hill. I will stay near the maps until you let Mrs van der Heyden go. Once you have let her go, I will walk away as she climbs up the hill."

There was another delay while the men argued this. Then Gator yelled back, "I don't like it. What is to stop you just running off with the maps?"

"Because Mrs van der Heyden will be in full view of you for most of the time," Willy replied, adding, "And because this is the easiest plan for you. It saves you from more murder charges and all those sorts of problems."

Gator thought for a moment, then yelled back, "Yeah, okay. I will meet you at the bottom in five minutes."

"Right," Willy agreed. He turned to Jacob, surprised how calm and determined he felt. "Okay Jacob, dig out the maps."

Jacob looked sick but nodded. Willy led the way a bit further to the left and crouched behind a larger boulder. The others joined him, crowding in close.

Graham touched Willy's arm and said, "You don't have to do this, Willy. I'll go."

Willy shook his head firmly. "I will do it," he insisted, surprised at his own determination.

Impatiently he held out his hand while Jacob fumbled in the zip wallet on his belt. A bundle of papers, bank notes, coins, notebooks, and wallet were dug out and placed on a flat rock. Jacob tried to sort through them, but his hands shook so much that Willy impatiently pushed them aside and picked up the wallet. He placed this aside and then quickly sorted out other papers and objects which were obviously not treasure maps.

There were two newspaper articles, the headlines of which piqued Willy's curiosity. One read: 'Fate of Makassang Crown Jewels?' and the other said, 'Mystery of who took the Makassang Crown Jewels.'

Hmm, crown jewels eh? Willy thought. He held them up. "Are either of these important?"

Jacob shook his head. "They are, but those crooks already have copies. They don't tell you where to look."

"So what does?" Willy growled. He was fast losing patience with Jacob.

Jacob touched a section of chart and two pages of handwritten notes, plus a photocopy of several pages of a book.

"Those are all the clues I have," he said.

"Do the crooks know about them all?" Willy asked.

"Yes."

"Okay, they will do. Now, when I start going down the hill, you all creep up the hill another fifty metres or so, but do it one at a time and slowly so as not to alarm them," Willy said. As he said this, an angry shout from the beach made him stand up and wave. "Keep your hair on! I'm coming," he shouted back.

Carmen grabbed his hand. "Good luck. I think you are very brave."

Willy managed a smile back and wondered if he was. Removing his hand he wiped it on his trousers and then picked up the vital papers. Then he began to climb back down the hill. The first few steps he found hard because his heart was pounding so rapidly he found it hard to concentrate and to focus. But then he saw the Gator lay down his pistol and take Julia by the arm.

As Willy climbed slowly down, he saw Gator and Julia start walking slowly along the beach towards the bottom of the hill. Willy took his time, every nerve alert. He was very conscious that he might be dead in a few minutes, and he paused several times to savour the beauty of the scene, to sniff the fresh breeze, to admire the ruddy glow of the sunset.

Then he continued on down. It took two minutes for him to reach the beach and he arrived at the same time as Gator and Julia. Making sure that there was a big boulder between him and the man with the rifle Willy stood and waited, trying to appear calm.

Gator stopped and shoved Julia behind him. Thrusting out his hand he said, "Okay kid, let's see."

Willy looked back, noting the eyes showing through the holes in the balaclava. With something of a shock he realised he knew the man.

"You are man who burgled the Beck's, the man we saw in Cooktown," he stated.

The mouth twisted into a sardonic grin. "Yeah, I wondered where it was that I'd seen you, but I couldn't place you," Gator answered.

"Do you work for Mr Jemmerling?" Willy asked.

"Nope. I don't work for anyone but myself. Who's Mr Jemmerlink?" Gator answered.

Willy shrugged. He was certain that Gator was speaking the truth and it seemed to lift a heavy cloud from his mind. Instead he said, "You have been stalking the van der Heydens."

Gator gave a harsh laugh. "Sure we have, the schmucks! But it hasn't been easy keeping tabs on them, even with radar. They've been all over the bloody place as though they weren't sure where to look."

Willy could not resist a wry smile. "Yes, I don't think navigation is one of their strong points," he said. That made Julia blush and he felt a tiny surge of guilt. "So why did you burgle the Becks?" he asked. He remained tense, ready to try to fight the man off if he tried to attack him.

Gator shrugged impatiently. "Because these dopes are looking for a plane wreck and we were told that Mr Beck is the local expert on World War Two wrecks. But none of his stuff was any use to us so we had to go back to tailing this crowd. Now give me the maps."

That made sense to Willy, so he held the papers tightly so that Gator could see them clearly. As he did, he was afraid Gator would just reef them out of his grip and run. There were then a couple of anxious minutes while Gator carefully scrutinised them.

To Willy's relief, he shrugged and said, "They seem to be the ones."

"They are," Willy answered. "So you were going to wait till the van der Heydens had found the plane and the treasure and then you were going to move in and take it off them?" he said.

Gator frowned, then grinned, the sight of the cruel mouth showing through the balaclava sending shivers through Willy.

"Sure we were."

"So why didn't you wait?" Willy asked. "Why come into the open now?"

"We thought they had found it and when we saw them go off with that barge we decided to act. Now, let's get on with this," Gator answered.

Willy nodded. "Okay, you let Julia go and back off. Then I will put the papers down," he said.

This was the critical moment and Willy tensed ready. But Gator just grunted and shoved Julia past him, then stepped back and waited. Satisfied that neither he nor Julia was within easy lunging distance, Willy bent down and put the papers down. To prevent the wind from blowing them away, he placed a small stone on them. He then stepped back.

Julia joined him and he pointed up the hill. "Go and join the others," he instructed.

She did not argue but began climbing the slope. Gator took several more steps backward and so did Willy. Their eyes remained locked, neither trusting the other.

Willy gestured, "Go on, you go back and let Mrs van der Heyden go."

To his relief, Gator turned and walked away without argument. This made Willy suspicious, but he did not know what else to do. So he stood and waited, making sure he could not be shot by the rifle. A minute later he breathed out as he saw Mrs van der Heyden start climbing up the hill. Once he saw that Willy turned and also started climbing. For added safety he angled further away.

Every few seconds Willy stopped climbing, partly to get his breath back but mostly to monitor Mrs van der Heyden's progress up the hill. To his relief, she angled over towards him. Satisfied she had a good start Willy started climbing quickly.

It was as well that he did because Gator snatched up his pistol and started running along the beach towards the maps while Corey raised his rifle and went straight up the slope after Mrs van der Heyden.

The mongrels! They are not going to let us go at all. They are going to hunt us down, Willy realised.

Chapter 34

MAROONED!

A spasm of pure fear coursed through Willy. Then he resumed scrambling frantically up the slope, still angling away to his left. He found it a particularly difficult activity. Even without being hunted it required fitness and agility and he was already feeling winded. Added to this was the need to keep looking around to try to keep track of the situation. This meant he several times stumbled or slipped because his whole attention was not focused on the jumble of rocks up which he was climbing.

After a particularly hard fall he slowed down and took more care. *If I break my ankle or leg I won't get away at all,* he thought.

Rubbing a bruised knee he again looked around. Shots, followed by yelling and shouting made him climb over a boulder to where he could see what was causing it.

He saw that it was being done by Graham, Andrew, and Carmen. They were bobbing up and down behind rocks, hurling cricket ball sized stones down the hill towards Corey. This was obviously to cover Mrs van der Heyden while she struggled frantically up to join them. To Willy's delight he saw several stones land close to Corey, bouncing or shattering when they did. Corey cried out in anger and ducked.

That is a good idea, Willy thought, *But bloody risky!*

That gave him an idea. Looking back down the hill he saw that Gator had begun clambering up after him. A quick search provided Willy with a suitable sized stone. After a careful glance to check where his target was Willy stood and flung it as hard as he could. His eyes followed the stone as it flew down the slope.

It is going to hit him! he thought in disbelief and satisfaction.

But at the last second Gator moved. The stone struck the boulder in front of him and then bounced, striking the man hard in the chest. Gator went down, shouting in pain. A moment later he reappeared, swearing and very angry.

"You little bastard! I'll kill you!" he screamed, raising the pistol.

Willy ducked even as the pistol spat. The bullet struck a nearby rock and went shrieking off to ricochet around hillside.

That worked, Willy decided.

He picked up another stone and hurled it, ducking back even as Gator's pistol fired again. This time his aim was not as good but nor was Gator's as he missed. Willy had no idea where the bullet went. Taking advantage of a third stone he scrambled up around another boulder.

Facing back down the slope he hurled two more stones. Off to his left the others were still hurling both taunts and stones. A glance showed Willy that Mrs van der Heyden had reached them and was being urged on up the hill. Julia had joined in the stone throwing, hurling hers towards Gator.

Willy gave her a grateful grin and moved up the hill a bit further. Then he looked around again.

Where is Jacob? he wondered.

Fearing he might have been hit he looked hard but saw no sign of him. Commanded by Graham, who was shouting orders, the others were pulling back one at a time.

Army cadets doing fire and movement, Willy noted.

Thinking it an excellent idea he yelled to Julia, "I'll throw, you go back up the hill a bit and then cover me."

Julia did so and Willy hurled three rocks. Then he looked back up the hill and saw her wave, then throw a stone. Willy scrambled back up the slope until he was level with her. By then his breath was coming in rasping, hot gulps and he was wildly excited. A quick look back down the hill revealed that neither of the crooks had moved much further up.

"We are winning this," Willy cried, as much to cheer himself up as to inform Julia. "Let's do that again."

Julia gave a mischievous giggle and that lifted Willy's spirits even more. He collected four stones then called, "Okay, go!"

As he tossed the stones Julia went uphill fast. Then Willy followed. By then he was at least a hundred and fifty metres from the beach and, he estimated, about halfway up the hill. Crouching under cover he looked through a bush and saw that the crooks were not following. Corey was still shooting occasionally but Willy judged he was well out of the pistol's effective range. Graham, Andrew, and Carmen worked their way back and across to join him.

Graham grinned and wiped sweat off his face. "That showed the mongrels!" he cried jubilantly.

"They've given that plan up," Andrew added.

Carmen looked back down the hill and then said, "They are going back down. I hope they are going to clear out."

The friends crouched among the rocks, puffing and perspiring as the last of the sun went off them. Willy watched with intent interest as Gator walked along the beach to join Corey near the boats. The two men pulled off their balaclavas and wiped sweat from their faces while they talked. Then they moved to the launch, and both used their strength to shove it back into deeper water. Gator scrambled aboard. Corey passed up the anchor and then his rifle. Then he walked to the boat.

"They are going to take our boat!" Graham muttered.

They did. The boat was pushed off and the anchor rope used as a tow rope to attach it to the launch. Corey clambered back into the launch. Then the launch got under way, backing out and turning. The friends watched in silence, although Willy felt like jeering their retreating enemy. As the launch headed northwest across the channel, Julia spoke.

"How will we get help? Is there a town on the island?"

Graham shook his head. "No. What you see is what you get."

"But... but... we might die!" Julia cried.

Graham gave a wry grin. "Hardly likely. We will just play Robinson Crusoe for a while. We might be marooned but we will survive."

Mrs van der Heyden joined them, followed by Jacob. He had apparently been higher up the hill. *Bloody coward!* Willy thought, but he managed to hold his tongue and not say it.

Mrs van der Heyden was also very worried about being left on the island, but Willy snorted. "At least we are all alive," he said, giving Jacob a pointed look.

Mrs van der Heyden looked bewildered. "But what will we do?" she asked.

Graham answered that. "First, we will get drinking water. If we hurry, we might just make it before it gets dark. Then we will wait until tomorrow and see what else can be done."

Willy switched his gaze back to follow the progress of the launch and boat. These went between Blackwood Island and Flinders Island, then turned to starboard and vanished from view behind Flinders Island.

"I wonder where they are going?" Julia asked.

"To find the treasure," Willy replied.

"Come on," Graham snapped impatiently. "We don't want to be struck on top of this bloody rock pile in the dark."

He set off walking diagonally up the slope to his right. The others followed. As they climbed over more rocks, Mrs van der Heyden asked anxiously, "But what if they come back?"

"They won't!" Willy snapped irritably. "If they meant to finish us off, they would have stayed to do it. They are going to get your crown jewels."

Graham paused on a big rock and called back, "And even if they do come back, they won't find us in the dark. Now hurry up and save your breath for climbing."

The group fell silent, save for heavy breathing and panting as they clambered up the slope. Ten minutes more of hard climbing had them at the crest of the hill. As they paused on top, three facts at once made an impression on Willy. The first was the view. From there they had a magnificent panorama of sea, reefs, islands, and the coast. The Rattlesnake Channel lay below them. The second was that the last of the sun was going off the highest peaks on the Bathurst Range and that dusk was swiftly setting in. The third was the wind. As they came up to the crest it began to buffet them.

"Bloody wind is strong," Andrew commented.

"From the South southwest still," Carmen said, adding, "I don't like that. It might mean that cyclone is coming closer."

"It is hundreds of kilometres to the southeast," Graham replied. "Come on, we might have days and days here to do sightseeing." He set off down the other side of the hill.

Going down was nearly as hard as coming up. It was certainly less safe as they had to continually lower themselves down from one rock to another. The growing darkness did not help. Willy noted a thin scatter of clouds moving with the wind.

It is a definite weather change, he decided.

Fifteen minutes of awkward scrambling later the group were about halfway down the slope. Willy was finding it all unpleasant as they were moving down the exposed side of the hill, almost directly into the rising wind. He paused to choose the best way down another rock and then a light caught his eye. It was out to his left on the sea. Shielding his eyes from the wind he looked more carefully.

"There's a ship!" he cried.

"Yes, we see it," Andrew replied.

It was a big ship, a bulk carrier type. In the dusk its details were obscured but the lights on its masts and superstructure blazed out and Willy could even see the endlessly repeated puffs of white as the ship's bows slammed into the waves. It was heading west through the Rattlesnake Channel.

A sense of frustration gripped Willy. It was obvious that no-one on the ship was likely to see them in the gloom and he knew none had a torch.

Julia voiced his thoughts. "Oh, if only we could signal to it!"

Andrew ignored that but said, "That bulk carrier is almost empty. I wouldn't like to be on that in this weather."

"He might be running away from that cyclone," Graham suggested.

"Maybe, or heading for Weipa to load," Carmen said.

They watched the ship pushing along for a few minutes, but it was at least 2 kilometres away and, Willy thought, it might as well have been on the moon for all the help it was to them. Led by Graham, they resumed their climb down the hill. As they did, the ship vanished behind Blackwood Island.

Twenty minutes later, as the last glow of dusk was dying to the west, they reached the lower slopes just above the sea. This section of coast was steep and rugged, almost cliffs, so Graham turned right and led them along the slope. Willy found it even more awkward to make his way along the side of the hill and he was starting to feel tired and cold. The wind was making his eyes water and he blinked continually.

After another ten minutes, Graham led them down to where a clump of trees grew at the base of a cliff.

"Wait here while I do a bit of a recce," he ordered. "I've only been here once and that was by boat in daylight."

He vanished into the gloom. Willy joined the others in the shelter of a boulder. Even just getting out of the wind was a relief. Now he knew he needed water as his mouth felt dry and his eyes were beginning to feel scratchy. There was little conversation. Most looked too worn out. Now that the fear and excitement was over Willy just felt drained.

Five minutes later, Graham came back and beckoned them to follow. Willy found that during the short halt several muscles which he had not been aware of had tightened up. He was not alone in this as there was a good deal of groaning from the others. It was a short distance but difficult because of the steepness of the slope. It took fifteen more minutes of careful detouring and lowering to reach a rocky 'beach' right on the tide level. Small waves were breaking on the 'beach' and spray began to splatter them as they moved cautiously over the wet, slippery rocks.

The spring was in under a cliff overhang and among several large boulders. It was only 20 metres back from the sea and only a few above it. Three large mangrove trees grew among the rocks of the 'beach'. Graham pointed to a white mark on the cliff above the spring.

"Painted by the navy years ago to help ships find water," he explained.

He led them in under the overhang and indicated the water. In the darkness Willy could barely make out what he was looking at but he gathered that there were a couple of small rock pools. Graham knelt and used a cupped hand to scoop some water up to his mouth.

"Tastes okay," he said.

Willy grimaced and was glad he could not see what he was drinking. When it was his turn he sucked in four handfuls and immediately felt better. Andrew and Carmen both drank without comment, but Mrs van der Heyden protested.

"I can't drink such unhygienic water," she complained.

"It's all there is," Graham answered.

"But... but it could have anything in it," Mrs van der Heyden objected.

"It might have a bit of bird poo and some salt and dust," Graham agreed. "But the human race evolved drinking dirty water so I doubt if it will hurt you much. Anyway, the other choice is going thirsty and tomorrow that will mean heat exhaustion and death."

Julia added her encouragement. "Come on Mum. I will go first."

"Don't you dare Julia. It hasn't been treated," Mrs van der Heyden snapped.

"I'm thirsty," Julia replied and knelt to drink. After a few sips she said, "It tastes okay."

Jacob then hesitantly moved up to drink, but his mother still refused.

Carmen then turned to Graham, who had become their acknowledge expert on being cast away. "What do we do now?" she asked.

"Find somewhere to shelter for the night," Graham said. "This place is no good. The wind is blowing straight into it."

He led the way back among the boulders to the west and found a sheltered nook. It even had some sand in it so wasn't too uncomfortable. The group moved out of the wind and settled themselves. Willy sat between Julia and Carmen and stretched out his legs.

Almost at once Mrs van der Heyden began to complain again. "We can't stay here. Where will we sleep?"

"On the sand," Graham replied matter-of-factly.

"Oh that's impossible! We must go somewhere else," Mrs van der Heyden objected.

Graham obviously lost his temper as he snapped back, "Well off you go! I'm staying here. You can go where you bloody like. If you can find a better place, then good luck to you!"

"Oh, there's no need to talk like that," Mrs van der Heyden replied.

Carmen interceded. "We can find somewhere better tomorrow," she said.

"We will get rescued by then surely," Mrs van der Heyden queried.

"By whom?" Graham snorted.

"Your father."

Graham shook his head. "He will have enough trouble getting the *Wewak* back out of the river. Then he won't know where to start looking. But yes, he will find us in a few days."

"Or an aeroplane will," Willy added. "He will radio for help."

"A few days!" Mrs van der Heyden cried in shocked disbelief. "But what will we eat?"

"Nothing much," Graham answered.

"But... but we will die!"

"No you won't," Graham replied. Willy could tell by his voice that he was getting exasperated. He went on, "It takes weeks and weeks to die of starvation."

Carmen agreed. "I read somewhere that people have lived for sixty or seventy days without food."

Mrs van der Heyden continued to grumble. Willy sighed. *This is going to be a long night if this keeps on,* he thought.

To change the subject he said, "Okay Jacob, tell us about the treasure you are looking for."

There was a silence broken by Mrs van der Heyden who said, "That is our business."

That annoyed Willy. He said, "We all just risked our lives to save you. I think that makes it our business too."

"Oh but!"

"Mum!" Julia interjected. "Willy is right. If they hadn't saved us those horrible crooks would have... would have..."

She sobbed and Carmen moved over to hold her from one side while her mother hugged her from the other.

After Julia had been comforted, Willy turned to Jacob who was sitting at the end. "Well Jacob? That is twice we have saved you. I think you owe us."

When Jacob hesitated, Andrew said, "It won't matter. It's not a secret anymore. Besides, the crooks will get to it first now."

That convinced him. In the darkness Willy saw Jacob nod. Jacob then said, "You read the headlines on those magazine articles I had? Well, that got it all going. If we had a light, you could read them but I have read them so often that I can give you the gist of them."

After a short pause, Jacob went on. "The first article appeared in the newspaper in September last year. It is the one titled 'Mystery of Makassang Crown Jewels?' Do you know where Makassang is?"

Willy did but Graham answered first. "It is a little independent island country next to Indonesia. We fought a war to help them stay independent a few years ago. My cadet company commander, Capt Conkey, fought there. He has told us a bit about it."

Jacob nodded. "Well I didn't know until Grandad read the article and showed me on the map. He used to be an officer in the Dutch Navy you know, and back in the Second World War he was based there. The whole region used to be called the Netherlands East Indies. Apparently Makassang was what they called a 'protectorate'. That meant that the local ruler ran the place with Dutch protection and guidance."

"A rajah," Carmen added.

"Yes, that's right," Jacob agreed. "Well, in September last year they crowned a new rajah. The article is about the fact that they had to use imitation jewels and a fake 'Sword of State' for the ceremony because the real ones had gone missing at the time of the Japanese invasion in February 1942."

"The article says that it is a pity that no-one knows what happened to the jewels and asks the question, were they stolen or were they lost? Apparently, the Japanese claim that they did not take them, that the jewels were missing when they occupied the palace. The Japanese ambassador suggested that either they were hidden by a person or persons who later died and took the secret with them, or they went with the royal family when they fled."

Jacob looked around, and saw that he had their full attention so he went on. "That was the bit that got Grandad's attention. He told us that he was the navigator on a Dutch flying boat that evacuated some of the royal party the night that the Japanese invaded."

Willy interrupted. "A 'Dornier' Do 24, a big machine with three motors. The Dutch had about thirty of them in the East Indies."

"Yes, that is right," Jacob agreed. "Well, Grandad said that there were two flying boats. The other one took the Rajah and his family and personal servants, plus some Dutch officials and their families. His plane carried the Vizier, what we would call the 'Prime Minister', the Lord Chamberlain, who was the official in charge of the royal household, various other officials and some Dutch officers and their families. Grandad said they only carried one piece of hand luggage each and he did not remember any mention of crown jewels.

"They flew to Horn Island but were attacked on the way by Japanese 'Zero' fighters. Grandad said that they managed to escape but that both aircraft were damaged. At Horn Island they did some repairs, refuelled, and then flew on, heading for Cairns. But they did not make it. They ran into a bad tropical storm and then found that the battle damage was worse than they had thought. They crashed in the sea. Grandad said it was horrible. He helped get a lot of the passengers into a rubber life raft, but the waves turned it over and then swept them across a coral reef. Everyone else was drowned. He then drifted for five days before being rescued."

Graham interrupted, "Did he know where the plane crashed?"

"Not really," Jacob said. "But somewhere in this area."

"Who rescued him and where?" Willy asked.

"Some Aborigines from the Lockhart River Mission Station," Jacob answered.

"What about the other plane?" asked Carmen.

"The one with the Rajah? It made it safely to Cairns," Jacob said.

Willy was fascinated but puzzled. "If your Grandad was the navigator, how come he didn't know where the crash was?" he asked.

"Because they were flying in cloud in a bad storm," Jacob replied. "He had a good idea, but could not pin it down exactly."

"Is that what the notes and chart were about?" Willy asked.

"Yes."

"So why didn't he go back and look before now?" Willy asked. "Why didn't people look for the wreck before then?"

"Because there was a war on," Jacob replied. "Australia was in a state of crisis. Singapore had surrendered to the Japanese only five days before, the battle for Java was underway. The Japanese had already landed in northern New Guinea and were bombing Port Moresby and they did the first raid on Darwin the day after the crash. He said everyone was just too busy or they didn't have the resources. Later there seemed to be no point because no-body knew the crown jewels were missing."

Jacob paused, then said, "Grandad said they did a couple of flights to look for survivors but did not see any. He said it was his worst memory of his whole life, the little Dutch children trapped in the sinking wreck and drowning, and women screaming, people fighting to get into the raft. He had nightmares about that but never spoke of it until last year."

"But, if it was a flying boat, why did it sink?" Willy asked.

"Apparently it struck a coral reef on landing. The coral ripped the floats off and the bottom out of the hull. He said the only reason he got out was because it crashed in a lagoon inside a reef," Jacob explained.

"And you think that the crown jewels are in the wreck?" Willy asked.

"Yes."

Carmen asked, "What was the second article about?"

"Once my Grandad read about the jewels, he started doing some research. But he was not the only one. He kept bumping into a man named Hobbs. The article was written by him."

"Hobbs! Mr Jemmerling's man!" Willy cried.

"Could be," Carmen agreed.

"So what was in the article?" Willy asked. He itched to read the two documents.

"Much the same as the newspaper report except that it was published in an aircraft magazine and has lots of technical information on the planes. It gives details like the aircraft registration numbers and names of the pilots and so on. Grandad is mentioned as the only survivor. It also mentioned that he flew 'Qantas' Flying boats after the war and that he was still alive and living in Sydney. After that, he got lots of calls from people, some of them cranks."

"It was horrible!" Julia said. "Total strangers would send him letters or telephone, accusing him of having stolen the jewels and murdered everyone else. It… it… it upset him terribly. It… it…" She burst into tears.

While his mother comforted her Jacob finished, "We think the stress brought on the stroke that killed him. Grandad died in October. That's when I got interested."

"Did your Grandad leave the notes and things?" Willy asked.

"Yes, he did," Jacob said.

"So how did Gator Smith and his scaly mate Corey get involved?" Graham asked.

Jacob grunted, then said, "I told my friend Karl about this, and he knew Gator. We needed a boat and Gator had one."

"So why didn't you find the wreck on your first trip?" Willy asked. "Why did they shoot Karl and try to kill you for your maps?"

"Because I wouldn't let any of them see the notes or chart," Jacob said. "We spent a week looking and I suppose they got impatient. I… er… I couldn't find the reef."

"Yes," Graham commented sarcastically, "We've noted that seamanship and navigation aren't your strong points."

"Well so what? I'm a builder, not a sailor!" Jacob retorted, obviously stung by the jibe.

Willy was not impressed. *Coastal navigation isn't that difficult to learn,* he thought. But he said, "So the wreck is on a reef somewhere?"

"If the sea hasn't washed it away," Jacob agreed.

"So that is why you have the diving gear?" Andrew asked.

Graham nodded and said, "Well, maybe there is still a chance. If we can contact a ship or plane tomorrow, we just might beat the crooks to the wreck, if you can show us where to look."

"I can do that," Julia agreed.

Willy felt a surge of interest and hope. *A wrecked 'Dornier' flying boat. That will be really something. But can we get there first to get the crown jewels?* he wondered.

Chapter 35

SEMAPHORE AND STORM

The discussion of details went on far into the night. Willy learned that Jacob's father was the son of Cornelius van der Heyden and that he was a builder. Mrs van der Heyden was a Dutch migrant who had come to Australia as a little girl in the 1970s. The parents had met at a Dutch cultural event. To fund this trip they had scraped together all their funds and gone into debt. Mr van der Heyden had been unable to come for business reasons. It was obvious to Willy that the whole expedition was launched with poor preparation and on a shoestring budget.

It was an uncomfortable night and Willy got very little sleep. Between the sound of the sea, the sand getting into his hair and clothes, and the stones digging into his flesh it was physically unpleasant. There was also the continual nagging anxiety about his father.

If he is alright, he will be really worried about us, Willy thought.

The wind died away to a strong breeze for much of the night. But apart from one light shower of rain which lasted a few minutes, there were no incidents. Graham said there was no point in having any sentries. As he said, the chances of the crooks coming back, and of then finding them on such a large and rocky island in the dark were too small to bother about.

The diminishing wind lifted Willy's hopes that they would be quickly found and that they could then try to beat the crooks to the wrecked 'Dornier'.

As the first flush of dawn showed in the eastern sky Graham stood up and looked around, then woke everyone. "Drink first, then we start a watch roster so we can try to contact any ship that comes past," he said.

Willy sat up, rubbing eyes gummed with sleep. He felt gritty, dirty, and tired. Stubble on his chin both pleased and annoyed him. It made him feel more manly, but it also felt unpleasant.

"How will you do that?" he asked.

That was the problem. Graham shrugged and said, "If we could light a fire that would help. Has anyone got any matches or a cigarette lighter?"

Nobody had. "What about a mirror?" Graham asked.

"I have, but it's only a little one," Julia replied. She dug in the pocket of her jeans and extracted a small compact. Inside the lid was a small, circular mirror.

"That will do," Graham said.

"How will you use it?" Andrew asked.

"I know how," Carmen said.

Willy puzzled over how to use the mirror. "Are you going to send Morse Code or something?" he asked.

Carmen shook her head. "No. I will just use it to attract attention. Then I will use semaphore and hope there are some old navy-trained sailors on the ship."

"Where will we do it from?" Graham asked.

"Top of the hill," Carmen replied. "Come on, I'm thirsty."

She led the way back to the spring. In daylight it looked even smaller and less palatable, but Willy was too thirsty to be particular. He thankfully drank as much as he could, trying to ignore the slicks of bird manure and green slime that ringed the small rock pool. This time Mrs van der Heyden drank some, but with evident disgust.

Carmen then said, "No need for us all to go up. Mrs van der Heyden, you stay here with Jacob and Julia."

She then led the way up the hill. In daylight this was quite easy going and it only took her twenty minutes to reach the summit. Willy went with the group. As soon as he reached the top, he moved across to look down to where they had landed the previous day. To his relief, there was no sign of the *Saurian* or their boat.

He then scanned the sea in all directions, hoping to see a ship. There was none. Graham explained that the main shipping channel was to the north of the island group. That was dispiriting news and made Willy doubtful of a quick rescue. With nothing else to do the friends seated themselves on a big boulder and talked. The main topics were the chance of being rescued, the previous day's chase, and the chances of finding the crown jewels.

The sun slowly came up, but it was a weak and watery sun which shone fitfully through a thin layer of high cloud. Carmen and Andrew both studied that cloud and the wind very hard.

"I don't like the look of that sky," Carmen said.

"The cyclone?" Graham asked.

Carmen nodded. "Yes. I think it is getting closer."

"A ship!" Andrew cried.

Willy looked and saw the distant shape of a big freighter. It was butting its way west across Bathurst Bay, puffs of white spray showing every few seconds. Carmen sprang up. "Quick! We aren't ready. Get two sticks about a metre long, quickly," she ordered.

This was easily done as grasstrees dotted the hillside. Carmen then instructed Andrew to make two flags with shirts. Graham and Andrew at once pulled off their shirts and began tying them to the sticks. Carmen took out Julia's mirror and held it in one hand while extending her other arm and raising a finger vertically. By the time she was ready Willy was surprised to note that the big ship was much closer.

"He's pushing along," he commented.

"Probably trying to outrun the cyclone," Andrew suggested.

Carmen now positioned herself facing towards the ship. Very carefully she moved the mirror until she could see the sun's reflection on her arm. Having done that she moved the reflected light slowly along her arm and onto her upraised finger, all the time keeping stick and ship in line. When the reflected sunlight reached a point where the beam of light, her finger and the ship were all in line-of-sight she gently moved the mirror up and down so that the light would appear to flash.

"You need the finger as an aiming mark," she explained. "Otherwise you can't tell if the flashes are pointed at the observer."

"You learnt that at navy cadets," Graham said.

"Yes, and the semaphore. You and Andrew have those flags ready for me to use for semaphore."

All Willy could do was nod. He felt a bit useless as the other boys tied their shirts to the sticks by their sleeves. He went back to watching. By this time the big ship was level with them and so far showed no sign of responding.

"What's the matter?" he asked.

"A cloud is blocking the sunlight," Carmen said.

It was frustrating but true. Off to the east the sun had gone behind a thicker layer of cloud that had built up on the horizon. By the time the sun rose above that the ship was past. To their dismay it steamed on through the Rattlesnake Channel and behind Blackwood Island and out of sight.

As the stern slipped from view on the ruffled waters Willy felt his hopes dip sharply.

They sat down again, a mood of dejection gripping them all. Graham added to Willy's feelings of anxiety by saying, "I doubt if we will see any more ships. If there really is a cyclone then none will come down from the north and the ones from the south will have all turned back or taken themselves into harbour."

"Wasn't your Dad's ship, the *Bonthorpe*, supposed to be heading this way?"

Graham nodded. "Yes, she was. But she should be well north of here by now."

The sun came out, striking so sharply that Graham untied his shirt and put it back on again. Willy sat and stared southwards, brooding over the events of the last few days. As he sat there with his head in his hands, he fidgeted with the bristles of his unshaven chin and squirmed because of the grit in his clothes.

I should have had a swim, he thought.

Then his eyes noted the tiny puffs of white way out across Bathurst Bay to the east. By now the whole surface of the sea was flecked by whitecaps and a haze was lowering visibility but repeated flecks of white that were larger than the waves caught his attention. *What is that?* he wondered.

Abruptly his eyes seemed to focus, and he saw he was looking at a small ship bow on. It had an orange-coloured hull and white superstructure.

"Is that your dad's ship Graham?" he asked, pointing.

Graham sprang to his feet and shielded his eyes. "Yes, yes, it is!" he cried. "It is the *Bonthorpe*."

Willy's hopes surged. Carmen and Andrew sprang into action with stick and mirror. Within a minute Carmen was flickering reflected sunlight at the approaching ship. But then more minutes went by and the ship seemed to take no notice. In fact it changed course away from them. Willy then saw that it was towing what looked like a big dark block bigger than itself.

"What's that behind it?" he asked.

"The dumb lighter *Oura*," Graham answered. "It is carrying thousands of empty forty-four-gallon drums."

More minutes went by and still there was no response from the ship. Carmen began to mutter in frustration but remained very careful in her handling of the mirror. "Oh, what's wrong with the lubbers!" she grumbled. "Don't they keep watch on your garbage scows Graham?"

Graham sprang to the defence of his father's ship's companies but was cut short. Willy saw a stab of bright light appear at the bridge of the *Bonthorpe.* "A light! They've seen us!" he cried.

The light began to flicker slowly. It meant nothing to Willy, but he saw that both Carmen and Andrew were moving their lips. *Morse Code,* he thought, feeling slightly guilty that he had never bothered to master such an apparently archaic if elementary skill.

"He asked, 'Do you need help?'," Carmen explained. She began replying with the mirror.

"What are you sending, Sis?" Andrew asked.

"S. E. M.," Carmen replied, adding, "Get those flags ready."

Willy stood and watched as they did so. He felt excited and relieved and was even happier when he noted that the ship and its bulky tow had changed course and were heading towards them. Carmen took the flags and moved to stand on the highest rock so that she was sure she was silhouetted against the sky. She then held the flags up and then lowered them abruptly. The light flickered briefly from the ship, and she nodded to herself and then began making the jerky arm movements with the flags that spelled out letters.

When she finished these she crossed the flags and stood still. The light flickered again. Willy saw her nod and smile.

"Good, they got it," she said, her pride and satisfaction very evident.

Willy was filled with admiration. "What did you tell them?" he asked.

"Help. Wrecked," she replied.

The light flickered again, a long message and both Andrew and Carmen spelled it out letter by letter.

"Move to lee of island. Sending boat," read Carmen.

"Hooray!" Willy cried. "Well done the navy cadets!"

"You start down to the beach where we landed," Graham instructed. "I will go and get the van der Heydens." He took his shirt and pulled it on then set off, scrambling down the rocky slope with the agility of a rock wallaby.

Willy didn't argue. He was just feeling intensely relieved. After Andrew had also retrieved his shirt and pulled it on the group set off down the hill, Willy leading, followed by Carmen and Andrew. But he had only gone fifty paces before Carmen called after him.

"Willy! Slow down! They have to launch a boat and it then has to get here. There is plenty of time and we don't want to be trying to get you down if you have a broken back."

Willy flushed with embarrassment. "Just keen to get off this island," he replied.

"Why is that, Willy? Overseas tourists pay big money to stay on tropical islands."

Willy had to laugh. "Yes, in a five-star resort!" he replied.

Twenty minutes later they reached the beach. All the way down Willy had been thinking about the violent incident the previous day and he even cast a few nervous looks around the islands to check that the *Saurian* wasn't lurking somewhere nearby. Down on the beach they were sheltered from the worst of the wind, and it was so hot that sweat poured from him. He became impatient.

Another half hour went by before Graham appeared with the van der Heydens. They came around the end of the island. A few minutes later, a rigid-inflatable lifeboat surged into view from the same direction. It curved out of the waves and into the sheltered water and nosed in to the beach.

There were two men in it, both wearing safety helmets and buoyancy vests. As the boat grounded one of the crew stood up and stared at them. His mouth fell open in evident surprise.

"Well bugger me! Young Kirk and his mates. Oops! Sorry ladies," he said.

"Hello, Mr Marshall," Graham answered.

"What are you lot doing here? I thought you were on the *Wewak*. Where is she?" Mr Marshall asked, looking around the bay with an anxious frown on his face.

"She's alright, Mr Marshall, or at least I think she is. When we left her yesterday afternoon, she was up the Normanby River," Graham explained.

Mr Marshall clambered ashore and held the bow. "So why hasn't she answered her radio? We've been trying all night and all morning to raise her," he said.

On hearing that Willy felt a sharp stab of apprehension. *Oh no! I hope those crooks didn't shoot them all,* he thought. Concern for his father made his eyes prickle.

Mr Marshall turned to Mrs van der Heyden and put out his hand. "Alan Marshall, mate of the *Bonthorpe*," he said.

Introductions were made and Graham then said, "I thought you were on the *Malita* Mr Marshall?"

"I was, but Mick Busuttin is sick. Besides, your dad likes to swap people around from ship to ship every few months," Mr Marshall explained.

"Captain Bligh that is," Graham said. Both he and Mr Marshall burst out laughing. It was obviously an old joke.

Mr Marshall gestured to the boat, "Anyway, that's enough gabbing. Get aboard. You can tell us the story once we are under way. We want to get back to the ship before this wind gets worse or we may not be able to."

"Is the cyclone closer?" Graham asked as he clambered aboard.

"My oath it is! It is only about two hundred kilometres to the southeast and heading straight for us. It is a Category Four now," Mr Marshall said.

"Category Four!" Andrew and Carmen cried simultaneously.

Willy looked at them and noted the drawn faces and lines of anxiety. As he climbed into the boat he said, "What category was the cyclone you got caught in at Bowling Green Bay last January Andrew?"

"Category Five, the worst," Andrew replied.

Willy noted the haunted look in his eyes and decided that Andrew was scared. *Maybe I should be too,* he mused. *At least Andrew knows that it is like.*

When all were aboard and seated the boat was pushed off. It reversed out fifty metres and turned. Mr Marshall spent five minutes making sure everyone had a flotation device correctly fitted. Then he nodded to the man at the wheel, "Okay Dick, take her away," he said.

The coxswain opened the throttle and spun the wheel. The boat got under way with an impressive surge of power. Once again, Willy experienced feelings of anxiety at how small the boat was, how big the sea was, and how close he was to it. Seeing this Mr Marshall said, "Relax. These 'Rigid Raiders' were developed for the Royal Marines and Royal Navy to use in the North Atlantic. She can safely carry twelve in Force Ten weather."

That reassured Willy a bit, but his fear returned as they came out from behind the headland and into the wind and waves. The boat began surging across the waves, taking them diagonally so that there was a continual twisting and rolling motion but not too many hammering bumps. Spray began flying up, ending conversation and sending them all crouching low.

Within minutes they were all soaked. Luckily the water was warm and it felt reasonably cool in the wind. For ten minutes they travelled over into the lee of Denham Island. Then they turned and pointed the bows to the southeast. Willy saw that the *Bonthorpe* and her tow were right over on the far side of the Rattlesnake Channel.

Tucked in behind Bathurst Point to get some shelter, he decided.

Crossing the five kilometres of the Rattlesnake Channel took only fifteen minutes but for Willy it was a quarter of an hour of hair-raising fear.

Give me flying anytime, he told himself.

Out in the open water the waves were two or three metres high and to Willy's eyes quite huge. The progress of the boat, quartering the waves diagonally downwind, resulted in an endless serries of sickening swoops. This soon had Jacob and Mrs van der Heyden going green and spewing over the side. Even Willy felt his stomach heaving and he wondered if he was going to be sick as well. To Willy's shame and jealousy, Graham, Andrew, and Carmen kept looking around and smiling, like tourists on a pleasure trip.

Willy found it a relief when the boat moved into the calmer water in the lee of Bathurst Point. There were then a few anxious minutes while the boat manoeuvred alongside the *Bonthorpe.* They were then hooked onto a crane and lifted onto the deck of the ship.

Close up the *Bonthorpe* was much bigger than Willy had thought. The ship was almost as big as the *Wewak* but with a much higher bow and sides. A two-storey superstructure was set forward, leaving a large working deck aft. They were met by two men who were introduced as the cook and the engineer.

Once the flotation devices had been taken off and re-stowed in the locker on the boat the group were led through a door into the superstructure. They went along a companionway and upstairs to the wheelhouse. A middle-aged man with a pipe in his mouth met them.

"Tom Proctor, skipper," he said. "Now, what's the story?"

While they talked Mr Marshall took the wheel off the skipper and kept the ship heading into the wind. Willy noted that the engine speed was such that they got no closer to the mountain in front of them.

Captain Proctor was amazed at the account of the crooks. He kept shaking his head. "Bloody hell! I'm worried about the people on the *Wewak.* I wish we could check on them."

"Can't you send the boat?" Graham asked.

He looked quite distressed, and Willy felt the same way, fearing that his father might have been murdered.

But poor old Graham might have lost his father, mother, and sister, he thought unhappily.

Captain Proctor shook his head and pointed out the windows with his pipe. "I could, but I won't. I am not risking lives. If they are alive then it is an unjustified risk, and if they aren't then it, well, it doesn't matter. The wind and sea around the other side of the point will be quite unsafe."

The implications of this caused Willy's already upset stomach to feel quite nauseous. *But he is right,* he thought bitterly.

Graham then explained how they had spent the night on the island and then climbed the hill to signal for help.

At that Mr Marshall said, "That was very well done. Where did you kids learn to signal with a mirror and to use semaphore?"

"Navy cadets," Carmen replied. "I am a Leading Seaman and Andrew is an Able Seaman."

"And which one of you did the work?" Capt Proctor asked.

"Me, sir," Carmen admitted, blushing.

"Bloody well done," Capt Proctor said.

Mr Marshall laughed, then said, "You kids are bloody lucky. If I hadn't done twelve years in the RN when I was a lad, then there would have been no-one on this ship who could read semaphore or send Morse. As it was it took us a while to dig out an Aldis lamp."

Graham said, "Sir, can you try again to raise *Wewak* on the radio?"

"Yes, and we need to inform the proper authorities about these pirates," Capt Proctor replied. "I will get onto it as soon as I have checked the tow again."

"I can do it sir," Carmen said. "If you just give me the schedule of frequencies and call signs. I am a qualified marine radio operator."

Capt Proctor raised on eyebrow. "Navy Cadets again, eh? Hmm, you aren't just a pretty face, are you? Alright, I will show you." He led Carmen to a table at the rear of the wheelhouse next to the chart table. After explaining the set-up to her and discussing who to call and the wording Capt Proctor turned to the others, "Now, you can all go down to the saloon if you wish. Cook will look after you."

"Can I stay up here, sir?" Andrew asked.

"Yes, you all can as long as you keep out of the way. I do not want you going out on deck for any reason."

He then went aft. Through windows in the rear of the wheelhouse Willy saw him and the deckhand, both wearing buoyancy vests and safety helmets, doing something to the towrope.

Mr Marshall saw this and said, "You need to be very wary of a towline. If they snap and are clear of the water, they can spring back faster than a striking snake. Steel wire doing that cuts men in half or can decapitate them. Tow ropes are really dangerous. Ours has broken three times since yesterday. That is why we are late."

The images of hissing ropes disembowelling and slicing flesh was too much for Willy. He had to ask where the toilet was and then hurry down to it. To his great shame he then vomited. To further hurt his pride he found he was frightened to be inside the bucking steel structure.

I must be claustrophobic, he thought miserably as he washed his mouth and had a drink.

As quickly as he could, he made his way back up to the wheelhouse. When he got there, it was to find Carmen shaking her head and looking unhappy.

"Can't raise the *Wewak*. Sorry Graham. Sorry Willy." She turned back to the radio and began calling the marine radio control.

While she called the authorities and relayed the information about the *Saurian* and her crew Willy stared anxiously out the front. He found he was trembling and the awful realisation came to him that he was frightened.

Turning to Mr Marshall he said, "Can you take this boat up a mangrove creek like Captain Kirk did?"

Mr Marshall shook his head. "Ship you mean. Nope. *Wewak* only draws a bit over two metres. This is a deep-sea vessel. She draws five metres. Are you worried?"

"Yes, I am," Willy admitted. "I'd like to be ashore."

"Wouldn't we all," Mr Marshall said with a chuckle. "But we can't just leave the barge. Don't worry, the cyclone may turn away. Anyway, if you are going to be at sea in a ship then *Bonthorpe* is the one to do it in. She was built for fishing and oil rig support off Iceland and in the North Sea. It doesn't get any rougher than there, normally."

That was some small comfort to Willy but deep down he knew he was scared, and he turned to stare anxiously through the windows. He found he was praying that his father was safe, and that the cyclone would not come their way.

But the midday weather report shattered that hope. The weather radar images on the computer screen clearly showed the swirling rain bands and the forecast track showed the cyclone to be only 150 kilometres to the southeast and still heading their way. On the nearby chart table was the carefully plotted position of the cyclone, hour by hour and based on satellite photos of its eye, showed a curving track with them directly in front of it. Instruments on the mast informed them that the local wind speed was now up to 50 knots, 100kph, and rising.

"We are really in for it," Capt Proctor said grimly. "Alan, get down there and check every single thing you can secure is as tight as it can be. This is going to be bad."

Willy felt his heart beat faster with anxiety and the fear began to swell towards panic.

Oh no! he thought.

Chapter 36

CYCLONE

Willy looked out through the bridge windows and stared at the sea with growing anxiety. To deepen his concern he saw that the sea to starboard had quite changed in colour and character in a very short time. Now it was a sort of dirty brown or grey, all flecked with angry, tumbling whitecaps. There was a very clear line where the sheltered water in behind the mountains gave way to the open water that was under the influence of much stronger winds. Willy saw that there were sudden swirling eddies which came from either side to buffet the ship and to give the helmsman a few minutes of hard going till the ship's bows were again held steady into the worst of the wind.

After studying the steadily worsening scene for ten minutes, Willy experienced what he recognised as intense fear. He knew enough about cyclones to feel that. But the van der Heydens were obviously quite ignorant of them, other than in the most general terms. When they came up from the saloon Julia joined Willy and Andrew near the chart table and she looked at it with a puzzled expression on her face.

"If this cyclone is so far away, why are we concerned? Can't we just get out of its way?" she asked.

Willy saw a look of baffled incredulity cross Andrew's face. "We are already in it," he said.

"What do you mean?" Julia asked.

Andrew gestured outside and then pointed aft across the port quarter. "This wind, it is part of the cyclone. They are gigantic revolving storms. But they don't just suddenly arrive and then go away. They are not like tornados. A tornado might last a few hours and cause great damage, but it is very small. When a tornado blows through a city it can take out one side of the street and leave the other quite untouched, and it is gone in minutes. I have seen pictures where a tornado has blown a house to bits while the houses on either side were hardly touched. Cyclones are massive. They aren't a hundred metres across, they are hundreds of kilometres across."

He paused to see if Julia understood. But she still looked puzzled so he said, "This wind here just gets stronger towards the centre. Didn't you hear the weather report? They are warning places up to five hundred kilometres south of here. The dangerous winds on this one must be three hundred kilometres wide."

Carmen had been listening and she pointed to the chart. "Cyclones rotate in a clockwise direction in the southern hemisphere. The most dangerous sector is the left forward quadrant, the quarter on its left front as it advances. That is where the strongest winds are and where most of the rain falls. The radio just said they are getting gale force winds and flood rains in Cooktown and all the way south to Cairns."

"But it's not raining here," Julia objected.

Carmen looked exasperated. "No. That's because this wind has already crossed the coast somewhere down near Cairns, dropping most of its rain, then done a big circle inland and then come back. That is why we are facing southwest but the cyclone is approaching us from the port side. We are luckily in the dry quadrant of the cyclone."

"But... but... I mean, how long do they last?" Julia asked anxiously.

"Days," Andrew said. "This started hours ago and could go on till tomorrow afternoon. It just depends on which way the cyclone goes."

That sent Julia below to join her mother and brother looking very thoughtful. Capt Proctor, who had been listening to all this said, "You kids seem well informed about cyclones. Have you been in one before?"

The others nodded and Willy shook his head. Graham said, "Only on land, last January in the Mulgrave Valley."

"Ah! The famous gold mine expedition!" Mr Marshall put in.

Capt Proctor turned to Andrew. "What about you two navy cadets?"

Andrew nodded. "Yes sir. Same cyclone but Carmen and I were on a small boat to begin with and then got marooned on Cape Bowling Green."

"Ah. I think I heard about that. That was when those fishing trawlers were sunk or washed ashore wasn't it?"

"Yes."

Capt Proctor peered closely at Andrew. "Are you scared?" he asked.

Andrew swallowed and nodded. "Yes sir. Terrified!"

"Good! Sensible man! You might survive in that case," Capt Proctor said. He then slapped Andrew on the back in a friendly gesture and said, "You lot had better go below and have a hot meal and a hot drink. It might be your last chance for a good while and you will need all the energy you can get. Off you go."

Willy did as he was told but within minutes knew he was going to find it harder to cope with than he thought. While going down the steps and along the companionway he experienced a wave of fear that he suspected might be some sort of claustrophobia. He broke into a cold sweat and found he badly needed to be able to see out. It took him an effort to seat himself in the saloon.

But I have to. I must eat. I might need the energy, he told himself.

For half an hour he stayed down in the saloon, perspiring and almost screaming with fear. He managed to hide this and tried hard to act normally. As soon as he had eaten, he made his way back up to the wheelhouse. For him just being able to see out and to think that he might have a chance of getting out if the ship rolled over made the fear easier to bear.

The others came up as well and stood looking anxiously out. Once again, the conversation returned to cyclones. Capt Proctor did not help Willy when he gestured aft with his pipe and said, "This is Bathurst Bay we are in. It is the site of the worst cyclone disaster in Australia's history; Cyclone 'Wahine'. Back in the 1890s that was. I don't remember the details, but I seem to remember that about a hundred schooners and luggers were sunk or smashed onto the beaches and hundreds of people drowned."

"Were you there Skipper?" Mr Marshall asked with a grin.

"Humpff! Don't you get cheeky Mister Mate!" Capt Proctor replied, but he then grinned.

Willy managed a sickly grin but then returned to staring out. To his concern the weather was obviously deteriorating. More and more dark clouds came scudding over and the first real showers of rain began blotting out the view.

"Can't we go somewhere safer?" Julia asked.

Capt Proctor shook his head. "Not with the barge in tow. This is as good a spot as we can find. At least here we have some shelter from the mountains."

"But aren't the mountains dangerous to be near?" Julia asked.

Capt Proctor nodded, "Yes, but only when we can't see them. As long as the weather stays clear or the radar works, we know where we are. If we left this area and tried to reach the open ocean we would be in among the coral reefs and that would be deadly. We would not see them until much too late."

Willy saw Andrew shudder. Andrew said, "That's what happened to the *Merinda*, the ship my grandad died diving on. She must have struck the reef with almost no warning and been forced under. She was about the same size as this ship."

"Steady Andrew," Carmen said, touching his arm.

Willy saw that Andrew was sweating and looking very pale. *How I feel,* Willy thought.

Andrew shook his head. "But we are trapped here, embayed."

"Yes, embayed," Capt Proctor agreed, studying Andrew with worried eyes. "But that ain't such a bad thing to my way of thinking. Whichever way the wind blows we run the risk of being blown ashore if we have engine failure. But at least most of the shore is sandy beaches. If we get blown onto one of them we stand a very good chance of surviving. The ship is unlikely to break up. Even on the rocks I reckon we should be safe enough. So relax."

Willy saw Andrew swallow and nod. "Yes sir," he croaked.

But it was still small comfort to Willy. He moved to stare out through the stern windows to try to hide his fear. As he stood there his eyes focused on the barge, which was wallowing at the end of its tow line. Every wave was breaking against the barge, throwing up huge sheets of spray and making it look like a rock in the surf. Then an odd flickering caught his eye.

What is that? he wondered.

He stared and this time distinctly saw a small black object detach itself from the top of the pile of empty oil drums and go flying off onto the sea. Another followed it.

"Captain, something is happening to your barge," he called.

Capt Proctor moved to look, then raised binoculars to study the barge. "Damn and blast!" he swore. "One of the lashings has come adrift. Drums are falling off."

"Can we pick them up?" Willy asked, seeing another three drums topple off the huge stack.

Capt Proctor shook his head. "No chance. Too dangerous and not worth the effort. Damn! This is going to be costly."

"Why sir?"

"Because each drum is worth a few dollars and because under the environmental laws Captain Kirk will have to pay to have them all collected and the environment cleaned up."

That hadn't occurred to Willy, and as he watched another stack of drums slip and tumble into the sea he felt really sorry for Graham and his father.

"Are they insured?" he asked.

"The cargo is, but it will still cost a lot of money because we will be busy here cleaning up instead of carrying paying cargo up and down the coast," Capt Proctor replied.

All they could do was stand and watch as drum after drum fell off. Then the next row came loose and also began falling off. Willy saw that the drums were piled on their sides in a gigantic stack and were held on by steel wire ropes tightened with bottle screws. It was quickly obvious that the entire stack would go over the side. Only the drums actually inside the hull of the barge were likely to remain.

"How many drums are there sir?" he asked.

"Five thousand, and probably four thousand are going to be lost," Capt Proctor answered.

It only took about twenty minutes for all the drums above the hull of the barge to go over the side. By then the surface of the sea for many kilometres was dotted with floating 44-gallon drums. Willy found it an amazing sight. But it only lasted a quarter of an hour as the gale quickly drove the drums downwind and out of sight across Bathurst Bay.

Watching the lightened barge bobbing and yawing on the huge waves made Willy feel sick with fear. The 6:00pm weather report did nothing to ease his anxiety. By then the eye of the cyclone was near Cape Flattery. The wind speed in Bathurst Bay had increased to 70 knots and was now howling so loudly that normal conversation was impossible. There was also a steady shift in wind direction so that it was coming almost from the west. Watching radar images of the monster on the computer was no help. That seemed to just increase the tension.

We are in real trouble alright! Willy thought, swallowing and feeling nauseous.

Darkness began to set in early, the clouds blocking out the sunlight. As it did, driving rain began blotting out the view ahead. Willy moved to look out of the port side windows and also astern. He found he was gripped by chilling, paralysing dread. He also found he was gripping the edge of the chart table so hard that his hands hurt.

White knuckle terror, he chided himself.

Looking through the rear windows of the wheelhouse was no more reassuring. The stern was rising and falling sharply. Water was sloshing around on the aft deck and every time the stern rose it hauled the tow line clear of the water for 50 metres or so, white streamers of spray blowing off it. Then the tow line would snub at the ship and jerk the stern round. The distant barge was just a dimly seen, dark blob barely visible in a welter of spray and driving rain. Willy began to get tired of standing and of bracing his muscles to keep his balance and to hang on.

By 7:00pm it was fully dark and for Willy everything became more terrifying. The wind speed kept increasing until it was 90 knots and howling so hard and at so high a pitch that it set Willy's nerves on edge. Capt Proctor suggested they all just go down to the cabins and go to sleep, but Willy could not do that. The van der Heydens did and so did Carmen, but Andrew remained in the wheelhouse with Willy.

The hours dragged by with no let up. In fact the weather grew worse as the cyclone moved closer. Vicious cross winds buffeted the ship and rain lashed the windows so hard that even the 'clear view' screens were of little use. Outside was just a terrifying maelstrom of white spray and flecks amid the blackness.

After three hours Willy had to go below to the heads. This merely confirmed what he knew, that he could not be cooped up where he felt trapped and where he could not see out.

Even if all I can see is the radar screen, he thought.

The cook offered him hot chocolate from a thermos flask and Willy accepted that. That helped but he made his way back to the bridge as quickly as he could. Even moving about inside the superstructure was now both difficult and dangerous. He had to press his hands against the bulkheads on both side and going up the steps was like climbing a cliff. It was worse than being buffeted by turbulence in an aeroplane. As the ship rose his muscles all tensed and he felt very heavy. Then it would drop away and leave him with a horrible weightless sensation.

Several times Willy lost his balance and was slammed against the bulkheads or objects on them like the coiled fire hoses. Feeling sick at heart from fear he struggled back into the wheelhouse, to find that things were now even worse. The bow was pitching up and down twenty metres every few seconds and waves were breaking onboard. What appeared to be massive deluges of water were constantly dashing against the windows and everyone had to wedge themselves against the fittings and cling on.

The anxious, fixed looks on the faces of Capt Proctor and Mr Marshall did not help. *They are really worried,* Willy thought.

Midnight crept by amid howling wind and crashing waves which deluged the decks so that the after part of the ship looked like a submerged rock. Driving rain lashed the ship and lightning began to flicker and flash. Outside on the deck something began to bang with a metallic 'Ting! Ting! Ting! Ting!'

The weather report for 24:00hrs was even more worrying. The eye of the storm was now over land and estimated to be only 80 kilometres south of them. It had turned towards them, and the wind speed was now reaching 120 knots. Worse still, the wind direction had continued to shift so that it was starting to come in from slightly north of west.

Capt Proctor shook his head and shouted into Mr Marshall's ear. "We will have to shift soon, or we will be right on a lee shore. I think we had better move now."

Mr Marshall agreed but looked grim as he wrestled with the steering. Capt Proctor moved to the chart table to confirm the course he had already worked out. Andrew watched him work and then asked, "What are we going to do sir?"

"Move over behind Blackwood Island," Capt Proctor shouted back.

Willy saw that to do so they had to edge out from behind the protection of Bathurst Point and then push forward against the storm until they were under the lee of the island. "Denham Island is closer," he observed.

"It is," Capt Proctor agreed, "But to get there we would have to move crabwise across the wind and once there we have these shoals and rocks directly downwind of us." He then peered closely at Willy. "Are you alright son?"

Willy shook his head. He felt so sick in the stomach that he had to swallow before answering. "No, sir. I am scared," he croaked.

"I think we all are," Capt Proctor answered.

He then moved to stand where he could see the radar screen and pass orders to Mr Marshall. The engine revolutions were slowly increased, and the ship began to yaw and pitch ever more alarmingly as it moved out of the shelter of the mountain.

By 01:00am the ship was out in the Rattlesnake Channel and was plunging violently. Willy was appalled. The ship pitched so steeply and violently he felt sure it would drive its bow under one of the huge waves that were piling in from Princess Charlotte Bay.

We will just go under, he thought, the anxiety making his heart palpitate and his body tremble.

He had often thought about what it might be like to die when an aircraft suffered structural failure during a storm, those seconds or minutes of terror while he knew he was going to die, but he had reconciled himself to that. But the thought of the ship rolling over and of him being trapped and drowned in the darkness, and of his body then rotting and being eaten by fish and things filled him with a horror that almost reduced him to a trembling wreck.

He gripped the fittings near the radar screen and peered through the front windows, wishing it was all over and praying for them to be safe. Suddenly the whole ship dropped and then slammed into a huge wave with such force that Willy was almost driven to his knees. The whole bow section of the ship vanished under white water and Willy felt sure this was it. He saw Capt Proctor fall and strike his head, then claw his way back up.

Just as Willy was sure the ship would never rise, she began to come up. But too late to avoid the next hammer blows by another huge wave. There was a horrible, heart-stopping crash and wind and water whistled into the wheelhouse. Willy looked up aghast as icy cold water drenched him. He saw that two of the front windows had been smashed. Wind and spray filled the wheelhouse. Papers, pens, and small loose objects flew in all directions.

Mr Marshall wrestled with the wheel as the ship yawed and pitched. Capt Proctor wiped blood off his left temple. The ship gave an awful yaw and then Willy experienced a peculiar sliding sensation. More water poured through the nearest broken window, and swilled back and forth.

Mr Marshall let go of the wheel with one hand to point over his shoulder. "I think we have lost the tow skipper," he shouted.

Capt Proctor struggled over to the wheel. "You go and look, but make sure you have the bosun with you and have a lifeline on. If the tow has broken, then for Christ's sake winch that line in so it doesn't get wrapped around our screw. And get everyone below to put on lifejackets."

"Aye, aye skipper," Mr Marshall replied. Capt Proctor took the wheel and yelled at Willy and Andrew, "You two put on your lifejackets too."

That sent another tremor of terror through Willy. *He must think we are going to sink,* he thought. Then the ship was lifted up and dropped with the speed of a crashing plane. *Oh my God!* Willy thought as the bow slammed into the next wave with a massive shudder.

The ship struck the wave so hard that Willy was almost thrown off his feet. For a moment he thought they had struck a rock and he felt the fear surge and bile rose in his throat. Then he saw that Capt Proctor has fallen, although he was still hanging on to the steering wheel. The bow lifted and then swung to port.

In a flash Andrew sprang into action. He dashed over to the wheel and grabbed it, then began to heave it round. Carmen came from below and grabbed Capt Proctor and hauled him upright. Capt Proctor was ashen faced and obviously shaken.

"The wheel!" he cried. "I must get her under control or we will broach!"

Broach! Willy thought with a stab of terror.

He knew that meant turn side-on to the waves and that the ship could then capsize and be rolled over. The fear of drowning in such horrible circumstances froze him and made him tremble.

Andrew was wrestling with the steering by then and Willy felt the ship turn and rise to the next wave. Andrew called, "I've got her sir. Give me the bearing please."

Capt Proctor tried to shake Carmen off and grabbed at the spokes, but she helped him to get to his feet and held him against the radar screen.

"No, sir. Let Andrew do it. You get your balance," she said.

To Willy's relief, Andrew appeared to have the ship under control. Capt Proctor saw this and steadied himself. "Steer three one five," he croaked.

"Three one five, aye, aye sir," Andrew repeated.

To Willy's intense relief, the ship rode over the next big wave. He could now see through the broken window and in the freeze-frame flash of lightning he had a horrifying glimpse of an apparently endless series of giant waves hurling themselves towards them.

How can we ever survive these? he wondered.

But the ship kept on, pounding and driving into the huge waves. Spray and rain swirled into the wheelhouse, the icy wind chilling Willy. He noted with part of his apparently frozen brain that Andrew had been helped into a lifejacket by Carmen, who then handed him one. With difficulty he slipped it on and did it up.

Andrew seemed much more in control of himself and he managed a sickly grin and yelled, "If we were out in the open ocean we wouldn't have to fight the waves. We could just lie 'a-hull' and let the ship ride with the storm. But we have to keep facing into them to keep from being driven backwards onto the rocks."

"What happens if the engines fail?" Willy asked. He had a pretty good idea and Andrew's answer confirmed his worst thoughts.

"Then we get driven to leeward until we hit something," Andrew replied grimly.

Willy moved so that he could see the radar screen. Shielding his eyes from the rain and spray he squinted at the screen and was relieved that he could clearly see the outline of the mainland and of the islands. Blackwood Island showed clearly dead ahead. Outside it was so dark and so rough that he found it hard to make sense of the glimpses he got.

"How did the sailors get on in the old days?" he wondered aloud to Capt Proctor.

Capt Proctor gave a short harsh laugh. "They didn't!" he replied. "Once the wind got up, they just hung on and committed their souls to God. That's one reason why the square rigger sailors of old were mostly very religious. You've heard of the 'Beaufort Scale'?"

Willy nodded. He had even once tried to memorize it. Capt Proctor explained, "Old Admiral Beaufort was a sailing ship man, and he only worked his scale out up to sixty knots. Sixty knots is the minimum wind speed for a hurricane or typhoon or whatever you want to call it. His logic was that once the wind got above that then trying to calculate it was irrelevant as no sailing ship could reasonably expect to survive."

That thought appalled Willy even more. His gloomy thoughts were diverted by the arrival in the wheelhouse by Mr Marshall, the bosun and Graham. All were clad in 'Souwesters' and oilskins which were dripping water. Lifejackets added to their bulk. They looked cold and shaken and exhausted.

Mr Marshall pointed aft as he clung to the captain's chair. "The tow line had broken Skipper. We got it wound in and secured," he shouted above the whistling howl of the wind.

"Well done. You look like you need a hot drink. Go and see if Cookie has any," Capt Proctor yelled back.

"Done that Skipper. We will just rest for a minute, then I will take over on the wheel again," Mr Marshall replied.

He led the way back down. As Graham turned to go he gave Willy and Carmen a tired grin. He looked blue and shaken but the gesture cheered Willy a tiny bit. *If only it would stop!* Willy told himself. The storm had now gone on so long he felt he could not endure it for even one more minute.

A few minutes later, there was another shuddering crash as yet another larger than normal wave slammed into the ship. For the next few minutes Andrew and Carmen struggled to hold the ship's head into the wind. Water cascaded into the wheelhouse and flowed knee deep around, chilling Willy even more. Just as the situation seemed to be under control and the ship steady on course again Willy heard Capt Proctor swear. He looked towards him in alarm.

"Damn and blast! The radar has gone out," Capt Proctor cried. He turned to Willy, "Quick lad, we are approaching Blackwood Island. I must ask you to stick your head out and try to spot the land so we don't run into it."

Willy was appalled but moved to one of the broken windows and looked out. He could only do this for a few seconds but found the wind so strong that it seemed to peel his eyelids back and stung so much he could hardly see anything. Even when he looked all he could see was blackness flecked with white.

Fear began to grip him as the awful realisation that they were blind and apparently at the mercy of the storm sank in.

Chapter 37

ANXIETY

Willy had to fight down a bout of panic and nerve himself to look through the broken window. Shielding his eyes with his hands and squinting between his fingers he peered into the tempest. Again he could see nothing but flecks of white in the blackness. Then a flash of lightning lit up a horrifying sight. Directly ahead he saw the dark bulk of Blackwood Island.

"Island, dead ahead," he screamed.

"How far?" Capt Proctor shouted.

Willy had to duck into shelter and wipe his eyes before shaking his head. "Not sure. Not too close I think."

"Keep watch and warn us before we run aground," Capt Proctor said.

Willy did so, looking out every minute or so for a few seconds. Each time he prayed for another lightning flash, and it was only by that illumination that he was able to estimate how close they were. But he also noted that the ship was not pitching nearly as violently. For the first time he began to feel some hope.

Graham and Mr Marshall returned to the wheelhouse and joined in as lookouts. By then there was no doubt, they were in the lee of the island and the waves were noticeably smaller. By 02:00am Willy felt almost safe. By then they were only a few hundred metres from the island and safely tucked in behind it. But it was an anxious feeling of insecurity.

If the engines fail, we will drift back across Bathurst Bay and get dashed ashore on the far side, Willy thought.

Mr Marshall now took charge, ordering both Capt Proctor and Willy to go below to warm up. Willy realised he was shivering violently and that his skin was covered in goose bumps. With an effort Willy allowed himself to be persuaded. He struggled below, clinging on all the way. In the saloon he slumped onto a bench and was immediately wrapped in a blanket by the cook, who then handed him a cup of hot chocolate.

Willy gripped the cup thankfully, allowing it to warm his shaking hands. He did not think he would be able to stay down inside the superstructure without a panic attack but realised he was exhausted, so he sat and shivered.

The bosun came in from checking something on the deck and Julia poked a green and sickly face out of a cabin for a minute. To test himself Willy closed his eyes. It was no good. The constant rocking, rolling, and pitching caused him to break into a sweat of fear. He had to open his eyes. To hide his shame he sipped at the warm drink.

He managed to stay there for nearly half an hour before he just knew he had to get up where he could see. The portholes were no use, the steel deadlights had been dropped over them and screwed tight shut. So he put the blanket aside and thanked the cook, then dragged his trembling, tired body back up to the wheelhouse.

As he reached the top of the steps, Willy almost turned back. The place was so wet, windy, and cold it made him flinch. But a sickening lurch made him go on up. Soundlessly he wedged himself in a corner next to the chart table. He noted that Graham and Mr Marshall now had the wheel and Andrew and Carmen were the lookouts.

At 04:00am Carmen moved to the radio but was unable to get it to work. "Water has got into it," she said.

She went below and listened to the weather on a portable radio. When she came back ten minutes later, she reported that the eye of the cyclone was now estimated to be only 50 kilometres to the southwest of them.

"It is moving at about fifteen kilometres per hour, but the weather people claim it is weakening."

Mr Marshall and Capt Proctor both agreed with that. "Wind has shifted too," Mr Marshall added. "It is coming in from the northwest."

"We moved just in time," Capt Proctor said.

Half an hour went by. Willy felt so battered and numb he wanted it all to end. *I don't think I can stand much more,* he thought. But he also felt sure that the wind was not shrieking as loudly and that the ship was not pitching as much.

Capt Proctor confirmed this at about 05:00am. "I think the worst of it is over," he said to Mr Marshall.

Mr Marshall nodded. He looked grey with strain but took the wheel again, relieving Graham. "We are damned lucky the cyclone went to the south of us," he said. "If it had gone to the north I doubt if we would have survived."

This was Capt Proctor's opinion as well. "We would have been goners I reckon. But we are alright now. Cyclones quickly lose their puff when they move over land; and this one has been nearly twelve hours ashore."

"Why is that sir?" Willy asked, as much for something to say as anything.

"Cyclones depend on a continual supply of moisture. They need to be over warm ocean to pick up the evaporation. It is the transfer of energy when the humid air condenses that provides the heat to move the air so rapidly upwards. Once they go over land their fuel supply is cut off."

Mr Marshall added, "The mountains and hills rip the bottom out too and they get disorganised and lose their pure circular air flow."

Willy looked out and suddenly realised that he could see the waves without the aid of lightning. With something of a shock he saw that it was the first grey of dawn.

Daylight! I have survived! he thought. The relief was immense, and he almost collapsed as the tension began to ease out of him.

By 06:00am there was no doubt the worst of the storm was over. The weather report placed the eye of the cyclone 75 kilometres to their southwest and said that the cyclone had been downgraded to a Category 3. The wind had definitely dropped and the rain and lightning all but ceased. With the coming of the pale grey dawn the whole situation appeared altogether different. Willy began to flex his stiff and frozen muscles.

An hour later the first watery rays of sunlight peeked through the rapidly thinning layers of cloud. The wind died even more and the rain stopped completely. Patches of blue began to appear high up to the northwest.

Capt Proctor ordered them all below to have a hot breakfast. This time Willy went without too much concern. He was surprised at himself.

What a weakling and coward I am when things go wrong! he berated himself.

The deckhand and bosun went up to the wheelhouse and the cook was set to work by Mr Marshall. Willy slumped into a corner of the saloon settee next to Carmen and Andrew. Graham and Mr Marshall sat opposite. Then Julia and Jacob appeared from a cabin. Both looked bedraggled and haggard, but Willy could see that they were all looking very dishevelled. The brother and sister joined them.

"Is it over?" Jacob croaked.

"Apparently," Andrew replied.

"I hope my mum and dad are alright," Graham commented.

That gave Willy a jolt and he realised he had been selfishly pre-occupied with his own fears and fate. Only now did he start to think about others. Worry about his father came first.

Then he said to Julia, "I wonder if your yacht is still afloat?"

"Hopefully," Julia answered. She looked exhausted and miserable.

"Cheer up! You are still alive," Carmen said.

"Yes, but we may have lost our boat and all our money and now we won't even get the treasure to compensate us," Julia responded.

That gave Willy another jolt. He had completely forgotten about the two crooks. "My word yes! I wonder what has happened to the *Saurian*," he said.

"I hope they got drowned!" Julia snapped with quite venomous force.

"If they weren't in good shelter they probably have been," Andrew said.

Willy thought about that. The last time he had seen the *Saurian*, the motor launch had been rounding the other side of Flinders Island and heading north. *That is out towards the Great Barrier Reef and the open ocean,* he mused.

He said, "So where is the wreck of the 'Dornier' supposed to be?"

Jacob stared back at him, his face a hostile mask. "That's our secret," he muttered.

That really annoyed Willy. "No it's not!" he cried. "Your mates Gator and Corey know where it is. And we have a right to know. You owe us. We have helped save your life twice. So give."

"No."

"Oh for heaven's sake!" Willy snorted. "Even if you don't give us the exact location, we know the story. We are much more likely to find it before you. We can at least navigate, and we've got the ships. Besides, you can't possibly think you can keep any of this treasure. If it is the crown jewels of Makassang then they are state property and there will be a lot of government officials from both countries very interested. So you may as well tell us and at least share in the discovery."

Jacob still looked stony-faced and defiant, but Julia nodded and said, "Willy's right Jacob. We won't be allowed to keep any treasure."

Willy went on, "Besides, if people died in the wreck of the Dornier, then it is a war grave. We will probably be breaking all sorts of laws if we touch it. This needs to be done the right way."

Carmen now spoke. "Jacob, the only chance you have of making any money out of this now is to be able to sell your story to newspapers and magazines. If we find the plane and the treasure, then you will get some of the credit."

Julia nodded. "Carmen's right Jacob. Tell them please, or I will."

Jacob scowled and then snapped with very bad grace, "Alright. I think the wreck is on a reef named Crab Reef. It is about twenty-five kilometres north of the Clack Islands."

"Thank you," Willy said.

Andrew stood up and put down his hot drink. "I'll get a chart," he said. He hurried up to the wheelhouse. Willy occupied the embarrassing silence by drinking and then wolfing down some toast and scrambled eggs. Two minutes later Andrew was back, carrying a sodden and torn sea chart.

"Sorry, but it got a bit wet," he said. "Capt Proctor said we can have this one."

"Has he got another?" Julia asked.

"Yes. He's securing it to the chart table now," Andrew replied. He spread the torn and soaked chart on the table and they all moved to look at it. It only took a minute for Carman to place her finger on one of a dozen reefs that littered the Coral Sea north of the Flinders Group.

"Here it is," she said.

Andrew studied it and then shook his head. "If those two crooks went that way in that little launch, then I don't like their chances of having survived, not unless they got onto one of the islands before the wind got up."

"Good!" Jacob said.

Having discovered the location the talk shifted to how to get there and how to recover any treasure. Carmen reminded them again that there were serious legal and ethical issues and suggested that the first thing they had to do was inform the relevant authorities.

"We need a radio to do that," Andrew said.

Julia looked aghast. "Don't we have one?"

Carmen shook her head. "Not a transmitter. Water got into it. But I will have a go at fixing it after breakfast. Now, let's eat," she replied.

So they did. Willy sat in silence, reliving the terror and imagining what the cyclone might have been like for the two crooks in a tiny boat in among coral reefs in the dark.

They would have no hope at all, he thought.

After breakfast there was nothing for him to do. Already the seas had dropped, from five metre waves to three metre waves. By then the cyclone's centre was another 30 kilometres away, over 100 kilometres to the southwest. Capt Proctor informed them that he was not moving until the seas had gone down further so they may as well get some rest. They were shown to cabins and given pillows and blankets. Willy lay down on a sofa in Mr Marshall's cabin and was asleep within minutes.

He was woken at midday for lunch. Despite protesting that he was too tired, he was ordered to get up by Mr Marshall.

"You need the energy," he was told. "If the weather worsens again you will be no use if you are weak from hunger. You can sleep again afterwards."

So Willy washed his face and stumbled to the saloon. On the way he noted that the sun was shining and that the waves had gone down even more. Now they looked to be fairly normal one or two metre waves. During lunch he learned that the cyclone was now nearly 200 kilometres inland to the southwest and was weakening further. It surprised him how quickly it all seemed to subside back to normal.

"We were lucky," Capt Proctor told them. "According to the radio some of the places south of the eye have taken a real battering: Hopevale Aboriginal Community, Cooktown, and Laura. There has been heavy rain and severe flooding all the way south to Cairns."

"I thought we didn't have a radio?" Julia queried.

"We don't, not a transmitter. But we have several little receivers. They give us the news and weather forecasts. Young Carmen is working on the transmitter and thinks she will have it going soon."

She did have. By 12:30pm she was able to gain contact with the Marine Radio in Cairns. They all crowded into the wheelhouse to listen while she relayed the news that *Bonthorpe* was safe.

An anxious looking Graham at once asked her, "See if they have any news of *Wewak.*"

Carmen asked but the control had no news. Carmen told them where they had last been seen and was told that the authorities would send search planes as soon as they had dealt with the more urgent situations being caused by flooding down the coast.

Carmen then tried calling both *Wewak* and *Dyfken* but there was no response. Each time she called Willy saw a look of anguish in Graham's eyes and he felt very sorry for him.

He might have lost his mum and his dad and his sister, and the family might have been financially ruined by the cyclone, he thought. That his own father might also be dead he tried to not think about.

After three failed attempts, Graham turned to Capt Proctor. "Sir, can we use your boat to try to go and see what has happened?"

Capt Proctor shook his head. "Sorry son, but the boat is gone. She was torn loose and went overboard sometime during the night. But we can move closer and then try to find a way ashore. We will take ourselves to near the mouth of the Normanby River."

Everyone except Capt Proctor and Mr Marshall were ordered off the bridge. The ship then got under way, shaping a course southwest through the Rattlesnake Channel. This brought them out into more open water and into bigger waves. The wave pattern was very confused and it was rough going, but Willy was so worn out he felt no fear. Instead he went below and lay down again. He was so tired he was asleep within minutes.

The *Bonthorpe* came to anchor about a mile off the mouth of the Normanby River at 1:45pm. The noise of the anchor chain roaring down the hawse pipe woke Willy and snatches of conversation penetrated his fuddled mind. Waking himself and rubbing gummed up and sore eyes he went to look. He was surprised to see that the sea had now subsided to mere ripples. The wind was now just a pleasant breeze from the north.

Between them and the shore was a huge area of shallows and sand bars and he could see why Capt Proctor had not wanted to take such a deep draught vessel closer to the shore. But how to get ashore to check?

Willy joined an anxious and distressed Graham on the deck aft of the superstructure. Carmen and Andrew joined them. They stared glumly at the intervening shoals and water and puzzled over how to get in.

"One thing is for sure, this ship won't be going in," Graham said. "She draws seven metres and it is hours before the tide is up."

Willy puzzled over the problem. He was deeply worried about his own father but could see that not knowing was tearing Graham apart emotionally.

His parents might have been dead before the storm, he thought. *The crooks might have shot them.*

But how to find out? He could see that ideas such as rafts were absurd. Not only was there the danger of crocodiles but the river appeared to be in flood and large quantities of debris: logs, trees and grass, were washing out.

Then a sound reached his ears that sent his hopes soaring. "An aircraft," he said, looking around.

The plane was coming from the north, and he shielded his eyes from the glare and squinted in that direction. After a minute's fruitless search he suddenly spotted a tiny dark shape. Even as he detected it his brain registered the silhouette.

"That is the *Pterodactyl*!" he cried.

It was. The flying boat came straight towards them, flying at about a thousand feet. As it reached them it went into a banking turn circling them. Willy suddenly became agitated. "Carmen, quickly! Radio the *Pterodactyl* and ask them to search up the river. Quick!"

There was a rush for the wheelhouse. Willy emerged on the bridge panting and excited. *A plane is just what we need,* he thought happily.

He arrived to find Capt Proctor already talking to the aircraft. Carmen danced with impatience and then requested politely that she be allowed to use the radio. A puzzled Capt Proctor nodded. Carmen sat down at the table and grabbed the handpiece.

"They are friends of ours," she explained.

She quickly called *Pterodactyl*, using the plane's name rather than its registration call sign. It was Mr Jemmerling who answered.

"Who is that? Over," he replied.

"Carmen, Carmen Collins. I am here with my brother Andrew and with Willy Williams and Graham Kirk. Over," she replied.

"What are you doing on that ship? I thought you were all on the *Wewak*. Over," Mr Jemmerling answered.

"We were on the *Wewak*. It is a long story, one that you will want to hear. Please sir, can you fly south up the Normanby River and see if the *Wewak* is still there, with a yacht. Over," Carmen said.

"South up the Normanby. Roger, over," Mr Jemmerling replied.

Willy saw the flying boat bank sharply and head south.

We will soon know the worst, he thought.

Chapter 38

TEST OF COURAGE

As the *Pterodactyl* flew towards the low-lying coast Willy glanced at Graham. He saw that his face was set in a sort of frozen mask, his eyes filed with anxiety.

Poor bugger! He will know the worst soon; and so will I, he thought.

The flying boat was still quite visible when Willy saw it turn and then go round in a wide circle, low over the distant mangroves.

They must be able to see something, he decided.

But there was then an agonising wait of five minutes while the flying boat went round and round.

Then the radio crackled and he heard Mr Jemmerling's voice calling, "Hello *Wewak. Wewak*, this is flying boat *Pterodactyl*, over."

There was no answer, but the flying boat kept circling and Mr Jemmerling called three more times. There was no response and Willy felt a sensation of sick apprehension churning in his stomach.

Pterodactyl abruptly turned towards the *Bonthorpe*. As she flew towards them Mr Jemmerling called them up. Carmen answered at once.

Mr Jemmerling acknowledged and then said, "The *Wewak* is there, and she looks quite undamaged. There are people on her superstructure waving. I think one of them is Captain Kirk and one is definitely a woman. There must be something wrong with their radio, over."

Willy felt the band around his chest loosen and saw Graham sigh with relief and sag. Mrs van der Heyden then said, "Can you ask them if our yacht is okay?"

Carmen did and Mr Jemmerling confirmed that there was a yacht moored to the bank near the *Wewak*.

"It appears alright," he added.

"Oh thank heavens for that. We might salvage something from this disaster after all," Mrs van der Heyden commented.

Willy now said to Carmen, "Carmen, please ask Mr Jemmerling if he can search for the *Saurian*."

Mr Jemmerling came back after she had made this request, saying,

"Yes, but I want to make sure the people on *Wewak* are alright first. Do you have a boat? Over."

"Negative. It was washed overboard during the cyclone. Over," Carmen answered.

"Alright, we will use our rubber boat. We will land and you can tell me this story while we get organised. Over," Mr Jemmerling replied.

Willy was pleased and surprised at that. He also became anxious. *There is a lot of floating debris coming out of the river,* he thought. *If the flying boat hits a floating log it will sink.*

But it was obvious that the people in the aircraft could clearly see the problem as they flew up and down a couple of times, then came in to a landing approach well to the east. By then the sea had subsided to ripples only a few centimetres high and the flying boat kissed the water with barely a bump. For a couple of minutes she slowed, showing a lovely curl of white bow wave. Then she turned and taxied over, anchoring a hundred metres from the *Bonthorpe.*

Ten minutes later Mr Jemmerling was helped aboard from the *Pterodactyl's* rubber boat, which was crewed by Mr Hobbs and Harvey. Willy felt very pleased to see him and hurried over to help him aboard. Mr Jemmerling shook his hand and gestured to the ship.

"Looks like you took a bit of a battering."

"We did," Willy agreed. "It was bloody horrible. Give me flying any day."

Mr Jemmerling laughed and turned to greet Capt Proctor. Willy then introduced the van der Heydens. That really got Mr Jemmerling's interest. "You are the chap Willy helped to rescue, the one who was floating in the sea with a shark?"

Jacob nodded. He looked exhausted and somehow defeated and Willy felt sorry for him. Mr Jemmerling next shook hands with Mrs van der Heyden and Julia. Then he looked at Carmen and said, "And there is an interesting story you said Carmen?"

"Yes sir, but it can wait. Can we please check to see if the people on the *Wewak* are alright?" Carmen answered.

Mr Jemmerling nodded. "Of course. I will send our boat into the Normanby River with a radio to check on the *Wewak* and her people. While that is done, we will fly around and see if we can locate anyone else who might need help."

"It will be dangerous going up that flooded river in a rubber boat," Capt Proctor warned.

Mr Jemmerling gave a thin smile. "You are right. That is why I will send Mr Hobbs here and a couple of volunteers."

Graham at once put up his hand. "Please sir. I have to go. My mum and dad and sister are on *Wewak*."

"It will be dangerous."

"Oh poo!" Graham snapped. "I have spent my whole life in little boats in these waters."

Andrew said, "Besides, even the crocodiles must have some sense of what is worth eating."

That caused a laugh and eased the tension. Mr Jemmerling said, "Yes, alright. Who else?"

Willy at once put up his hand. "Me sir. I want to find out if my dad is alright."

"Of course. Now, it is only a small boat. Room for one more," Mr Jemmerling said.

Mr Marshall at once volunteered. "I can help with any ship work," he added.

The relief expedition was quickly organised. Mr Jemmerling was ferried back to the Catalina and the rubber boat returned. Somewhat anxiously Willy joined the small party in the rubber boat. That short step was a small test of courage for Willy as the boat looked so small and so close to the water and he was acutely conscious it was only an inflatable. As he lowered himself to a sitting position, he eyed the muddy waters around them with anxiety.

From the sitting position Willy felt even more anxious. The water was lapping at the inflated rubber sides and seemed to be only a few centimetres from him. He had the impression he was already sinking, and thoughts of the rubber being punctured by floating logs caused his fear to shoot up. But he determined not to show it and tried to focus on the task.

The boat set off, pushed along by its small outboard motor at about 5 knots. As it made its way into the shallows the Catalina took off and then came back low overhead. Willy watched it with interest. "I wish I was up there instead of down here in this crocodile soup," he commented.

The others laughed but Willy did note them cast a few anxious glances at the murky, muddy water that surrounded them.

The Catalina circled twice over the *Wewak* and then turned to head west, following the coast of Princess Charlotte Bay. At the next river mouth it went inland and did some more circling. Then it continued on, following the coastline.

Willy watched till the Catalina was out of sight, then transferred his attention back to his own predicament. He was secretly appalled at the speed of the muddy current and by the amount of floating debris that it carried. The rubber boat was continually dodging trees and logs and frequently pushed through floating muck. To get up the river they had to hug the banks to keep out of the strongest flow.

It took about twenty minutes to cover the distance, but at 3:05pm they rounded a curve and the yacht and the *Wewak* came into sight. From that distance they both looked quite undamaged. To Willy's relief, there were people visible working on deck and these soon saw them and began waving. He waved back and found himself all choked up and in danger of blubbering in front of his friend. Then he saw his father and tears did come and he didn't care. Weeping with joy he waved.

A couple of minutes later he was helped aboard. His father was also overcome with happiness, and for the first time in his life Willy saw him cry.

"Oh Willy!" he croaked, then hugged him tight.

Willy clung to his dad for several minutes, uncaring what his friends thought. They obviously thought it was perfectly natural for Willy noted tears on the faces of all the Kirk family when Graham was embraced by them. Even tough Captain Kirk looked to have watery eyes and Graham certainly was crying.

Willy's father eased him away and looked him up and down. "Oh I am glad to see you! I was afraid you were a goner when that cyclone hit," he said.

"So did we!" Willy answered.

"What happened?"

"It's a long story," Willy replied.

At that Captain Kirk interrupted. "Then let's save it for later. I want to get these vessels out of this river while we can. If we waste time yakking we will lose the tide."

He at once gave orders and sent people to carry out various tasks. Willy was sent with Graham to tend the mooring lines at the bow and

Mr Hobbs and Mr Marshall to take over the yacht. They climbed back into the boat and went across to the yacht with a towrope. The *Wewak* was then untied from the mangroves and turned itself to face downriver. That done the towrope was brought across by the rubber boat. Once the tow line was secure Mr Hobbs returned to the yacht and fastened the rubber boat to the yacht by its painter, then climbed aboard. After coiling and stowing the mooring lines Willy and Graham made their way to the monkey island to act as lookouts.

The voyage downriver to the open sea was then begun. The first part was easy, the river being deep and the current of flood run-off hurrying them along. The tricky part was navigating the sandbars at the river mouth but by staying in the main flow they made it without incident.

As they moved out into the open sea near the *Bonthorpe* the Catalina reappeared, flying in from the north. The *Wewak* was manoeuvred alongside the *Bonthorpe*, fenders being placed over the side by Graham, Kylie, and Willy. The two ships were then lashed together. The yacht was tied up astern. Mr Hobbs motored over to the Catalina and returned a few minutes later with Mr Jemmerling.

There were greetings and much chatter and Captain Kirk called them all to the saloon of the *Wewak*. Everyone crowded in and Mrs Kirk, helped by Kylie and the cook from the *Bonthorpe* produced afternoon tea. Willy noted that it was 3:45pm by then and he began to fret. Now that he knew his father and Graham's family were safe, he had begun to think about the *Saurian* and its possible fate.

Carmen then told the story, starting with when they had taken the *Dyfken* in tow. As the story of the arrival of the crooks and the subsequent chase and handing over of the maps unfolded Mr Jemmerling looked more and more interested and incredulous. Captain Kirk told how the crooks had boarded the *Wewak* and explained that they smashed the radios in both vessels and also took the satellite phone before leaving.

Willy, Andrew, and Graham added some details of the chase and about the fight on the island and Willy explained how he had negotiated the release of Mrs van der Heyden in exchange for the maps. At that point he experienced a surge of shame and turned to Mr Jemmerling.

"That was when I spoke to this Gator character, and he said he had never heard of you. It seems I was wrong, sir. I jumped to conclusions that you were paying him to spy on us and to steal Mr Beck's maps and so on, but they were doing that all on their own. I'm sorry, sir. I apologise for all those horrible things I said."

Mr Jemmerling nodded and looked grave. "Thank you, Willy. I appreciate your honesty and your courage in saying sorry. Now Carmen, this launch the *Saurian,* you last saw it heading north behind Flinders Island the evening before the cyclone arrived?"

"Yes. I am sure the crooks wanted to find the Dornier and get the treasure before we could warn the authorities," Carmen said.

The details of the Makassang crown jewels and of Jacob's grandfather had to be covered again and then Willy provided details of the Dornier. Mr Jemmerling nodded.

"Yes, I've seen pictures of the Dornier flying boats, but a real wreck! Now that would be something."

"It must be a war grave sir," Willy put in, concerned that Mr Jemmerling's desire to own vintage aircraft might over-ride his sense of what was right.

"Yes Willy. Give me some credit for decency please. Now, you think the crooks headed off out towards this Crab Reef out on the outer Barrier Reef?"

"Yes sir."

"But didn't these crooks know that there was a cyclone out there?" Mr Jemmerling queried.

No-one could answer that. The best that Carmen could suggest was that the last weather warnings they had heard had all put the cyclone well out to sea and heading southwest towards Cairns.

"It changed track the next day and came this way," she added.

Willy now voiced his concerns. "We must go and look Sir. Could we use your plane to do that?"

"Yes, we could," Mr Jemmerling said. He looked at his watch. "Hmm. Just after four o'clock. We have about three hours of daylight. That gives plenty of time. okay, we will fly around for a couple of hours and see if we can locate this launch, and anyone else who might need help."

As soon as Mr Jemmerling agreed Willy was gripped by an intense desire to be in the search plane. He said, "Please Mr Jemmerling, may I come with you?"

Mr Jemmerling frowned. "If your dad agrees."

Willy turned to his father. "Please Dad," he begged.

Willy's father nodded and looked at Mr Jemmerling. "Yes, he can go. It is obviously very important to him."

Mr Jemmerling looked doubtful, then nodded. "Yes, I see. Alright, and also young Jacob here, if he wants."

Jacob looked unhappy but nodded. So it was agreed. There were a few more minutes spent in making quick preparations and then Willy, Jacob and Mr Jemmerling were ferried across to the flying boat in the rubber dinghy.

The short trip in the rubber boat was another small test of courage for Willy but he was so determined to fly in the Catalina that he clenched his jaw and made himself act calm. But all the way across he eyed the muddy waters anxiously.

A croc could just lunge up and drag me in, he thought.

Once in the flying boat Willy felt safe and relaxed. He was told to take a seat behind the pilot. As soon as the rubber boat was lifted from the water and dragged through the door was closed and the engines started. After a few minutes warming up the engines and a lot of careful study of the take-off area, the throttles were opened and the Catalina began her take off run.

As the aircraft unstuck and lifted clear of the water, Willy relaxed. Now he felt much happier. Mr Jemmerling, who was seated in the co-pilot's seat, now turned to Willy and asked him for advice on their course. Willy suggested that they first search around the Flinders Group and other islands in that area. This suggestion was accepted and the Catalina set course for Flinders Island.

Five minutes later they were over Blackwood Island. Willy looked down at the calm blue sea and the gentle surf washing the island's rocky shore and could only marvel at the change ten hours had brought. Already the night of terror seemed to be an unreal nightmare. They circled the island at 500 feet, then went over to Denham Island. As they circled it, Willy pointed out where they had been marooned and where the spring was on the south side.

As they circled around over Bathurst Bay the pilot pointed off to starboard. "What is that black object on the shore over there?"

"Looks like a ship. We had better investigate," Mr Jemmerling said.

The plane came around to starboard and Willy saw the tiny dark shape they were referring to. It was on the beach near the eastern end of the bay.

Near where we went ashore to try to get the 'Kittyhawk', he decided.

Then it came to him what he was looking at. "That is the barge the *Bonthorpe* was towing," he said.

"What the devil are all those black things?" the co-pilot commented.

Willy could see them now and he laughed. "They are forty-four-gallon oil drums," he said. "The barge was carrying five thousand of thcm and about four thousand went over the side in the storm."

He had a vivid image of the drums toppling overboard and of the entire surface of the sea being dotted with bobbing fuel drums.

As the Catalina flew over the area, Willy saw that the black object was indeed the barge *Oura*. It was stranded in the sandy shallows and appeared undamaged. Scattered along the beach, sometimes singly but more often in clusters, were hundreds and hundreds of drums. Most were right up on the edge of the trees at the back of the beach, but hundreds of others were still floating around on the sea. In places they had gathered in huge clusters.

"That will take a bit of cleaning up," the pilot observed.

"Yes, poor old Captain Kirk will have to foot that bill," Mr Jemmerling agreed.

That made Willy feel sorry for the Kirk's again and he became anxious that Graham might have his lifestyle changed dramatically because of it.

By then the Catalina was almost at Cape Melville. At his suggestion they turned to port and headed northeast to check around Pipon Island. There was no sign of any wreckage or boats there, so they turned to port and hcaded west. Ten minutes later they were circling King Island. That was also devoid of wreckage or people, so they went on west to the Clack Islands. Here again they drew a blank.

"We should go out to look for this Crab Reef," he suggested.

There was a short discussion about fuel, and it was revealed they had enough for another five hours flying. The plane was turned to starboard and went north. Willy stared out, feeling unreasonably anxious. He decided that this was because they were heading away from the land and out towards the deep ocean and the outer Barrier Reef. He was surprised that the sea was now so calm he could see down to quite a depth. The coral reefs began to appear and their shapes were so obvious he could easily identify them on the chart.

That is Corbett Reef off to port, he told himself.

He nudged Jacob and pointed to the left. "That is the reef where we first picked you up. Over on the other side of it."

Jacob nodded. "Yeah. I should have got one of those GPS things. It might have helped us find places."

All Willy could do was keep his face neutral to hide his contempt. He went back to studying the sea and the chart. At five miles to the minute it was not very long before a great scatter of reefs appeared ahead.

The outer Barrier Reef, Willy thought. He was struck by the line of surf on the eastern side and by how the ocean colour changed dramatically to a dark blue on the ocean side. *Really deep water,* he thought.

With competent navigators and electronic navigation aids it took only a matter of minutes to locate the correct reef. The pilot pointed down and said, "There it is, Crab Reef."

Willy looked down and felt a surge of excitement. The shape corresponded exactly with the chart. He could see that Crab Reef was in among a real jumble of small reefs.

That might account for why the Dornier wreck hasn't been found before this, he thought. It was certainly well off the normal air routes and would be a very dangerous place to take a ship.

Crab Reef had a lagoon several kilometres long inside a wide fringe of coral. The water in the lagoon appeared to vary in depth but was mostly clear of coral outcrops and had a sandy bottom. Willy stared down, searching for anything that might resemble an aeroplane in shape. But his gaze almost immediately fixed on a more obvious shape. It was dark in colour but lighter than the brown and black looking coral. Seeing it caused him to suck in his breath as he recognised what he was looking at.

"That is a boat down there," he croaked.

"You are right," Mr Jemmerling said. "Upside down and submerged."

Oh my God! Willy thought in horror.

As the Catalina went into a sharp bank to port to circle the place, he saw quite clearly that what he was looking at was an upturned motor launch. It lay about fifty metres from the edge of the lagoon, near a sort of outcrop that protruded into the lagoon and was silhouetted against the sandy bottom. Then his eyes focused on the coral outcrop, and he gasped again.

"That is the plane wreck down there. It is stuck right against the reef and has lost a wing," he cried.

As they circled around again, Willy stared at the shape and was even more convinced. *That is definitely it,* he thought. He could see why any casual observer flying over would not suspect the shape was anything other than just more coral. *And it would be invisible from a boat. Only a diver would notice it,* he decided.

But was the treasure still in it?

Then Willy shifted his attention back to the capsized launch. It looked battered and damaged but much of the bottom was intact. To add to his concern, he saw that part of the hull was actually breaking the surface.

It must have air trapped in it, or the water is every shallow, he thought.

But even as these thoughts crossed his mind another horrible possibility came to him. "There might be people still alive trapped in that launch," he said.

The plane went around again, slower and lower. They all stared at the upturned boat.

Mr Jemmerling said, "Is that the *Saurian*?"

Neither Jacob nor Willy could answer. Upside down as she was and with the superstructure obviously smashed it was impossible to tell.

"It doesn't matter," he said. "We have to go down and check."

"Serves the buggers right," the pilot said.

Jacob stared wild-eyed at the launch and then cried, "I hope they are dead!"

Willy was horrified. "We have to look. We can't just fly away," he cried.

Mr Jemmerling looked at him and said, "What can we do? You would need diving equipment to look inside safely, and we haven't got any."

"Can't we at least land and tap on the hull to see if anyone answers?" Willy asked. He was now feeling awful. The thought of leaving without checking appalled him. "Please! I will never sleep again if we go away and then later learn that there were people trapped inside."

The plane circled and Willy could see that Mr Jemmerling was studying the situation. After a couple of minutes he shook his head. "We can land easily enough on that lagoon, but I think it is too risky. And even if we did find there is someone alive how would we get them out? If we knock a hole in the hull that will let the air out and it will sink. No, it is a job for divers. We will radio the authorities."

As he said this, Willy felt a surge of desperation. Then it came to him and he said, "We can get divers and diving equipment. Carmen and Andrew are both qualified divers and there is diving gear on Jacob's yacht."

Mr Jemmerling sucked his teeth and said, "We would have to ask them. It will be dangerous, and they may not want to do it. I don't like the idea of them risking their lives for a couple of murderers. And they might find dead bodies. That will give them nightmares for the rest of their lives."

"We can at least ask," Willy pleaded.

"Yes, alright. Mr Johnson, take us back to the *Bonthorpe*," Mr Jemmerling ordered.

The Catalina swung round to a southwesterly course. As it settled on this, Willy was gripped by an intense feeling of urgency. He said, "Sir, can we please radio and ask to have the diving gear ready when we get there?"

Mr Jemmerling looked irritated but nodded. "Yes, alright. By Jove, you can be a persistent blighter, Williams!"

He then radioed Captain Kirk. Captain Kirk answered almost immediately and agreed to have the diving gear ready.

Ten minutes later the *Pterodactyl* was over the Flinders Group, skimming past the highest peaks at only 1000 feet. Once again, Willy marvelled that they had survived the chase and the cyclone.

I will never forget being marooned here, he thought.

Another ten minutes had them circling at 500 feet over the mouth of the Normanby River. Looking down from above Willy could clearly see the *Bonthorpe, Wewak, Dyfken* and the small rubber boat all moored side by side. To Willy's eyes the *Wewak* looked much too large to have fitted into such a small river, but he now appreciated just what a useful craft she was.

She looks just like a model, he thought as he studied the LCT.

It confirmed his opinion that flying was the only way to go. He even laughed when he realised that the Catalina was bouncing more in the afternoon turbulence than the *Bonthorpe* had been that morning and he barely noticed it.

Mr Johnston did two slow circuits to check the landing area for obstructions and debris before he brought the flying boat down. It was a text-book landing on an almost calm sea. The Catalina was then taxied over to near the ships and anchored. By then it was nearly 5:00pm and Willy was starting to fret.

If we don't hurry it will get dark and we will have to wait till tomorrow, he thought anxiously.

But it was another 5 minutes before the rubber boat was alongside and ten more before Willy was able to climb up the side of *Wewak* to put his proposal to Carmen and Andrew. As he did, Willy saw Carmen nod and Andrew go pale and look anxious.

Mr Jemmerling then explained the situation regarding the *Saurian.* Gesturing to Willy he said, "Young William here insists that we send divers in to check that there is no-one still alive and trapped in the hull."

Captain Kirk looked aghast. "My word yes! That would be too awful. I made a mistake once when we found the wreck of a yacht on a reef. We flew over in a light plane and I saw the yacht was upside down with what appeared to be the stump of the mast driven up through the hull. But there was no movement and no sign of life so we flew on, looking for a fishing trawler. Later I learned that there had been a man on board, an Islander, and he had died. It hadn't been the mast I had seen. It was a naked black man standing upright but apparently too exhausted to raise his arms. I found that out when someone went to the wreck and reported the hull was still sound and the mast hadn't been driven through it. It haunts me to this day."

Mr Jemmerling looked grim. "No doubt, but whoever looks inside this launch might also be haunted all their life if they find a dead body. I don't want to be responsible for traumatising these kids. And we must remember that these men are murderers. They might become violent or take hostages."

Later, when he thought about it, Willy was sure it was that 'kids' that tipped the balance.

Andrew at once said. "I am willing. If we don't go and there is someone in that launch I will be haunted with guilt anyway."

Carmen shook her head. "You don't have to go Andrew. I will."

Andrew's face set in a stubborn mask. "We will both go. Divers should work in pairs." He then turned to Captain Kirk, "Sir, we want to go. We will be careful. We are trained at wreck diving and have… have some experience. You may not know but I found my grandfather's body in the wreck of the *Merinda*."

Captain Kirk nodded. "I did know. But you are both minors in my care. You are my responsibility."

"Please, sir!" Andrew cried.

Both Captain Kirk and Mr Jemmerling were obviously unhappy with the idea and continued to discuss it. While the adults debated Willy fretted, went to the toilet, and became even more anxious as the minutes slipped away. With every minute the sun seemed to slip lower in the west, and he became more tense.

Finally he interrupted, pointing at his watch and saying, "Please Captain Kirk. It will be dark if we waste any more time."

Captain Kirk frowned but then nodded. He turned to Andrew and Carmen and said, "Okay, you have my permission. But promise me you won't take any risks."

Both Andrew and Carmen promised. Willy watched admiringly, knowing that Andrew was scared but trying not to show it. He said, "Can we please hurry. We need to look before it gets dark. The weather might change during the night or the air trapped in the pocket might leak out."

Mrs van der Heyden now spoke for the first time. "Are you going to use our diving gear?" she asked.

Andrew nodded and explained that they had already laid it out and checked it. She pursed her lips. "It would have been nice to be asked."

Andrew just grunted, then went to the side and began climbing into the rubber boat. "Come on Sis, pass down that diving gear. We've only got about an hour of daylight left."

Willy now moved. He was determined not to be left behind, so he climbed down into the boat.

Carmen said, "Where are you going Willy?"

"You are taking Mr Jemmerling and me to the Catalina first," he said. "Come on Mr Jemmerling."

To Willy's relief, Mr Jemmerling did as he was told. Five minutes later Willy clambered into the Catalina and sat himself in the small saloon, feeling very anxious but also very pleased. Mr Jemmerling joined him and called Harvey to get them some coffee and biscuits.

Then he laughed and said, "You are a pretty determined chap aren't you, young William?"

Willy could only nod and smile. *I am,* he told himself. *When I think it matters.*

Chapter 39

WILLY IS BRAVE

By 5:45pm Andrew, Carmen, Mr Hobbs, the diving gear, and the rubber boat were all on board the Catalina. As soon as the door was locked the engines were started and the plane took off. Willy again sat behind the pilot with Mr Jemmerling beside him. Jacob sat with Andrew, Carmen, Hobbs, and Harvey in the cabin.

The Catalina flew low and fast, not bothering to climb above 1000 feet. Once again, they sped across Princess Charlotte Bay and then over the Flinders Group and out to sea. As they flew northwards Mr Jemmerling sent several long radio messages to the authorities, describing the situation and what they were doing about it. He also checked the latest weather warnings. To Willy's relief, the weather forecast for their area was for light northerly winds. The cyclone was now right across near the western side of Cape York Peninsula and was likely to go out into the Gulf of Carpentaria.

It won't bother us anymore at least, he thought.

By 6:10pm they were over Crab Reef. Five minutes were spent circling, to allow Andrew and Carmen a chance to see the wrecks and also to check the lagoon for obstructions. Willy also had a good look for sharks but did not see any. The pilot then put the aircraft down.

Inside the lagoon the water was almost flat calm and the landing was very smooth. The Catalina taxied to near where the bow of the *Saurian* was just visible. It was awash, with only a few centimetres sticking out. *Pterodactyl* was anchored as close as they dared to the wreck of the launch but well clear of the coral.

Down in the cabin Andrew and Carmen prepared to dive. Willy went down but kept out of their way by sitting in the cabin. Mr Hobbs inflated the rubber boat and launched it, then went aboard and held it ready. Jacob peered out of the saloon door, looking miserable. Mr Jemmerling stood at the bottom of the flight deck steps and fussed.

"Don't you children get caught up by something and drown," he said.

Carmen looked at him with a look of annoyance. "We won't! We do have a good idea of what we are doing. If there is any possibility of getting snagged, we won't go in." She returned to testing the pressure gauges on the tanks. "Hmm. We only have enough air for about fifteen minutes anyway."

"Twenty minutes," Andrew said.

As they sorted out weight belts and ropes, Willy noted that they were still wearing their clothes. "Aren't you going to wear wetsuits?" he asked.

Andrew shook his head. "They were a poor fit. We will be alright. The water won't be that cold. But we do need some gloves," he explained.

Harvey found them some gloves, gardening gloves from the look of them, that had been used when digging out the 'Kittyhawk'. Two waterproof torches were dug out of a locker and tied to their weight belts. It was obvious to Willy that Andrew was having to force himself and he felt sorry for him and also a bit guilty.

I hope I am not placing them at risk, he thought. He also felt guilty at the possibility they might see horrible sights that would haunt them.

Carmen obviously felt the same way as she said to Andrew, "You don't have to come Andrew."

"I do! I am not going to let my sister take risks without me there to help," he muttered fiercely. Picking up his gear he passed it down to Mr Hobbs, then climbed down into the rubber boat. Carmen followed. The motor was started and the boat puttered off out of view around the tail of the Catalina.

To be able to watch the dive, Willy moved to one of the cabin portholes. The others did likewise, or went up to the flight deck. The rubber boat was soon beside the wreck and a shot line was thrown in. Willy saw Carmen and Andrew each struggle into a buoyancy control device with its attached air tank, then test their regulators again. Face masks were rinsed and fins adjusted. Then, with both hands holding their face masks on, they rolled backwards out of the boat into the water.

As the two heads bobbed in the water while final adjustments and checks were made, Willy felt really anxious. He looked around the surface of the lagoon for any sign of a shark fin and saw none. He hoped there weren't any. The image of the shark tearing the corpse to shreds filled his mind and he began to breathe very fast from apprehension.

Mr Jemmerling looked at his watch and muttered, "Half past six. It will be dark in half an hour. They had better get a wriggle on."

Even as he said this the two heads sank below the surface amid a flurry of bubbles. Then all Willy could do was watch and hope. Minutes ticked by and apart from the tiny stream of bubbles from beside the upturned launch there was no clue as to what was happening. Willy tried to imagine them groping their way into the shattered structure and had images of horrible things lurking there: dead bodies, moray eels, an octopus. Just thinking of such things gave him goose bumps and he realised he was breathing so fast he was almost hyperventilating. With a conscious effort he slowed his breathing and tried to act calm.

A head broke the surface and Willy sighed with relief. One safe! Then a second head appeared. He saw the diver's face masks pulled down around their necks. Both spoke to Mr Hobbs for a minute. Willy saw Mr Hobbs nod and then the two swimmers moved away and clung to the hull of the launch.

What is going on now? Willy wondered, as he saw the boat start moving and then turn towards the flying boat, leaving the divers behind.

A minute later Mr Hobbs was at the door. Mr Jemmerling leaned out to talk to him and Willy and Jacob crowded in behind. "What is it?"

"They've found one dead body. Gator Smith, they think it is. There is no-one alive in the wreck, but Carmen wants another rope and a net or bag. And Andrew said Willy is to come over to look."

"Willy?" Mr Jemmerling queried. "Okay, get in Willy while we find a rope and a bag."

Willy was both puzzled and scared, but he was also curious. *What do they want me to see?* he wondered.

Gingerly he lowered himself into the tiny boat, clinging tightly to the door frame as long as he could to counteract the slithering and bobbing motions of the rubber boat. Once he was seated, he looked anxiously around the lagoon, very conscious that he was now almost at water level. No triangular fins were visible but that did nothing to calm him.

Mr Jemmerling passed down a coil of rope and then a canvas kitbag. "The sun is nearly down. Tell them to hurry please," he said.

Willy nodded and glanced around, noting that Mr Jemmerling was right. The sun was now a huge orange disc sitting on the western horizon. Mr Hobbs shoved off and opened the throttle. As the boat surged and seemed to flow over the small waves Willy found he was fascinated by the close-up sight of the flying boat sitting on the sea.

I should have brought my camera, he thought.

As they approached the launch and the two divers Willy's curiosity overcame his fear. "What is it?" he called as they surged to a stop at the floating buoy secured to the shot line.

"You'll see," Andrew said. "Now, wait while we do this. Tie one end of that rope to the bag and the other end to the dinghy, then give it to me."

Mr Hobbs did this. By then Carmen had submerged and Andrew followed her. This time Willy was able to look down into the water and watch. He could see the bottom and also the dark figures that were the two divers. There were a couple of anxious minutes while both vanished in under the upturned hull and then one reappeared and began ascending.

It was Andrew. As his head broke surface he removed his regulator and said, "Pull up the bag, but do it carefully."

He then clung to the side of the boat while Willy and Mr Hobbs hauled in the rope. This led to Willy getting splashed, but he was too interested to care. Looking down he saw the bag coming up, held by Carmen. The bag contained a soggy, rotten case that looked like it was an old suitcase of the brass-bound, metal steamer trunk variety. The case was too big for the bag and half protruded from the top. It was covered in marine growths and was very heavy and leaked water. As soon as they tried to lift it aboard, it split and more water cascaded out of the cracks.

Carmen took out her regulator and said, "Don't try to lift it into the boat. Mr Hobbs, tie it so it hangs underneath and take it back to the *Pterodactyl*. Tell them to lift it aboard very carefully. Willy, you get in the water and come with us." She then retied the rope to the boat so that the bag and case were just under the water.

Willy had all his attention focused on the mysterious case. It took several seconds for Carmen's request to sink in.

"Get in? In the water?" he asked disbelievingly.

Andrew grinned. "Yes Willy, in the water."

"But... but why?" Willy asked. He felt a sudden surge of fear and doubt.

"You will see. Now be brave and get in. Quickly please, we are running out of time and this is a once in a lifetime moment," Andrew said.

It will be if I get eaten by a shark, Willy thought. He was a good swimmer but did not like the ocean at all.

"But I'll get wet," he mumbled in a feeble attempt to avoid their request.

Mr Hobbs said, "What's going on? Why do you want him in the water?"

Andrew pointed at the Catalina and said, "Mr Hobbs, please take the case to the flying boat and then come back to get us. Oh come on Willy! You'll regret it if you don't. Wet clothes don't matter. You will like this, now be brave and get in. Stop worrying about sharks."

Willy had an inkling of why they wanted him in the water, but it still took a conscious act of suppressing his fears to make himself move. Very cautiously he lowered his legs in, gasping with surprise at how cold the water felt. Then he slid down until only his head was sticking out. Carmen and Andrew moved in, one on either side.

"Let go Willy, we've got you. We've got buoyancy control devices on. We won't sink," Andrew explained.

Reluctantly Willy let go of the rope looped around the outside of the rubber boat. Breathing fast from fear he allowed himself to be towed away from the boat. Mr Hobbs looked doubtful and shook his head but then started the boat moving towards the Catalina.

As he watched that boat go away, Willy experienced a real spasm of terror. All he could see in any direction were rippling waves and the half-sunk red disc of the sun. For the first time he really appreciated the awful situation that Graham and Andrew had been in when they had survived a floatplane crash and were left floating in the sea for eighteen hours. He had to control a spasmodic urge to draw his legs up. They seemed to tingle as they dangled there. At every second he expected a shark to rip them off and he tensed in anticipation.

Be brave! he told himself as the two divers towed him backwards across the lagoon.

They swam for fifty metres past the barnacle and weed-encrusted hull of the launch and then stopped. Carmen then took off her face mask and handed it to Willy.

"Here Willy, put this on," she ordered.

"You aren't going to take me under, are you?" Willy cried.

Then he swallowed a mouthful of water as a wave struck him in the face. Coughing and spluttering and stinging eyes kept him busy for the next couple of minutes.

"Trust us. Just do it please," Andrew said.

He spat in the face mask and rinsed it, then half pulled it on to Willy's head. The strap tangled in Willy's hair, pulling and hurting but his cry of pain was ignored. Willy helped and managed to get the face mask on.

Andrew then pointed down and said, "Now put your face in the water and look down."

Cautiously Willy did so. Then he mentally gasped. With the face mask he could see quite clearly and there it was, the wreck of the Dornier!

Fascination at once drove out the fear. Willy stared in wonder. The wrecked aircraft lay on the bottom with its tail stuck on the coral reef and the nose lying out in the lagoon. He could not really tell how deep it was but guessed at about ten metres. One wing was completely missing and all the vertical fins were also gone but the other wing was there and so were two of the three engines. Much of the surfaces were thickly encrusted with coral and weed growths but to Willy's delight there were still several pieces of Perspex in the cockpit windows.

He lifted his head to breathe and cried, "This is amazing!"

Taking another big breath he again put his head down. This time he could focus on detail, on the bent propeller blades, the small fish flitting in and out of the missing cockpit window, the glimpse of the rusting seats for pilot and co-pilot, the open side door.

Seeing that door and the crumpled, torn hull half buried in sand, caused him to experience vivid images of the crash. He remembered Jacob's grandfather's story, the screaming women, terrified young Dutch children drowning. The horror of it caused him to shudder. For a few anxious seconds he looked around, half expecting to see white skulls amid the wreckage. Then he shook his head.

Don't be silly. The sea creatures would have consumed them long ago, he told himself.

Once again, he came up for air. This time he wanted to talk but Mr Hobbs was returning so all he did was take another long look before the boat arrived. Mr Hobbs was terse.

"Get aboard!" he yelled. "The boss isn't happy."

I am! Willy thought.

Feeling very pleased he allowed himself to be dragged and pushed into the boat. He then helped hoist in the diving gear and then Andrew and Carmen. As soon as they were aboard, Mr Hobbs opened the throttle and headed back towards the Catalina. Willy noted with a shock that the sun had almost set and the whole sea now had a purple look.

"That was fantastic!" he enthused.

"It was, wasn't it?" Andrew agreed.

Then more sober thought s came to Willy, and he said, "Was it horrible in the launch?"

Carmen nodded. "Bit gruesome. Gator was all battered about and tangled in ropes and clothing."

"Sorry, but I had to know," Willy said.

"So did I," Carmen agreed.

They arrived at the door of the Catalina to find an angry Mr Jemmerling. "What the devil were you bloody kids playing at? It's nearly dark."

"We were looking at the 'Dornier'," Willy explained.

Mr Jemmerling's face at once transformed. "Ah!" he said. "Yes, well, we can always come back and look at it tomorrow. Now get aboard."

They passed the gear up and climbed aboard. The boat was hauled through the door and deflated. As they stowed the gear and then stood there in their dripping clothes, Mr Jemmerling said, "I hope you didn't touch anything or go inside the wreck? We could be in trouble with the law if you did."

"We didn't," Carmen assured him. "And we didn't need to. But I think Gator or Corey did. Where's the case?"

"In the saloon," Mr Jemmerling said.

He led the way to where Jacob and Harvey were already seated. Mr Hobbs, the pilot and the co-pilot crowded in behind them until there was barely room to move in the small compartment.

For a minute they all just stood and stared at the slimy, battered case. Mr Jemmerling then gestured to Jacob and said, "You open it young van de Heyden. This was all your idea."

Very gingerly Jacob reached forward and touched the trunk. But it had already been forced open before so all he had to do was prise up the lid. This caused something to snap, and more water trickled out but the lid was able to be swung back. Willy leaned forward to look in and was disappointed. Inside was just a mush of black, rotting material of some sort and a collection of seashells and weed.

Even more gingerly Jacob reached in and grasped a long object that was just visible. He lifted this up, slime and ooze slithering and trickling off it unheeded onto the table. Willy stared with fascination. It was a sword. As Jacob brushed at it, he saw that it was a curved sword with a brass or copper scabbard. Set in the brass were dull coloured objects of blue, green and red which he then realised were precious stones. The haft, he noted, appeared to be made of gold and was also studded with jewels.

"The sword of state!" Jacob breathed in awe.

"They will be glad to get that back," Carmen observed. She gently took it from Jacob and wrapped it in a cloth, then began to rub at it very gently.

Jacob dug into the slush and extracted a metal box the size of a shoebox. It was very rusty and the old steel crumbled in his hands. Onto the table cascaded dirty water, mud and a trickle of diamonds. It was a necklace. Then a huge ruby with a pin fastener dropped out, followed by a dark green, emerald brooch, the jewel the size of a hen's egg.

As the jewels were laid out on a towel. Willy could only gasp in aware and shake his head.

The Makassang crown jewels! We have found them!

There were pearl necklaces and earrings, diamond clasps, a starburst arrangement of diamonds that Willy later learned was a Turkish 'Chelingk'; rings, gold ornaments and gold and silver buckles and buttons. These were all emblazoned with the Komodo dragon emblem of Makassang.

By the time they had finished looking at the jewels, darkness had all but set in. Mr Jemmerling was the first to notice this and set things in motion. The jewels were wrapped in cloth and the aircraft took off. They lifted off and climbed into a sky, which showed only the last glow of the sunset to the west.

"We are not going to try to land on the sea in the dark," Mr Jemmerling said. "We will go to Cairns."

So they did. Along the way the teenagers dried themselves and the jewels were all cleaned and then they were photographed holding them. Mr Jemmerling sent several long radio messages and made a couple of phone calls on his satellite phone. He was very careful not to mention where the wrecked 'Dornier' was except that it had crashed in the sea.

"We must protect it from looters," he explained.

Carmen and Willy were allowed to phone their parents to warn them they were coming. Mr Jemmerling then radioed *Wewak* and *Bonthorpe* with the news.

By then Willy felt utterly drained. He slumped in a seat and felt overwhelmed by the experiences of the previous week. But it was not over. When the *Pterodactyl* rolled to a standstill on the tarmac at Cairns Airport Willy saw that there was a crowd of TV camera men and media reporters, plus police, and various official looking persons.

Mr Jemmerling getting publicity, he thought with a wry smile.

But he had underestimated Mr Jemmerling again. Mr Jemmerling certainly took some of the publicity but it was Jacob that he thrust to the front to tell his story and he helped him negotiate to sell it to several newspapers and magazines. Willy was just glad to see his mother and to watch.

The crown jewels were taken off by several armed Commonwealth Police and a couple of officials. There were questions for Andrew and Carmen about what they had seen in the capsized *Saurian*, and then they were allowed to go with their parents. Mr Jemmerling again cautioned them not to tell where the wreck was and then asked them to keep in touch.

Willy was whisked away by his mother. At home he found he was shaking and could barely stand. Shock and exhaustion had worn him out. After a hot bath his mother gave him a sedative and bundled him into his own bed. Just being in the familiar surroundings of his own room was extremely comforting to Willy, even though it felt unreal. He closed his scratchy, tired eyes and slipped into a deep sleep.

He slept for twelve hours.

* * *

When Willy woke he found that his father was home. Mr Jemmerling had sent the *Pterodactyl* to pick him and the Becks up. "The plane took some police divers and officials up to look at the *Saurian* and the 'Dornier; wreck. They recovered Gator Smith's body," he added.

Hearing that made Willy have vivid flashbacks to the terrifying waves during the cyclone and he shivered as he imagined Corey's body being tumbled in the surf on the reef and then drifting in the sea, rotting and being torn apart by the fish. It was very morbid and depressing stuff and he wished he had Marjorie there to help take his mind off it. The best he could do was talk to her on the phone.

Willy also found that the discovery of the 'Dornier' wreck and the Makassang crown jewels were headline news. Because of his involvement in the chase by the murderers he was also named and the local news media wanted to interview him. His parents allowed this but sat with him to protect him.

The hardest thing Willy found was to keep his mouth shut when the reporters asked him where the 'Dornier' wreck was located.

The next day, at Mr Jemmerling's invitation, the family was flown to Crab Reef. Andrew and Carmen came with them. Mr Jemmerling had hired diving gear and his own diver and underwater cameras and the two wrecks were explored and extensively photographed. This time Willy was happy to go snorkelling and he even dived down to touch the tip of the sunken flying boat's middle propeller blade.

Pterodactyl then flew them to Bathurst Bay where Captain Kirk was just completing the salvage of the barge *Oura*. The barge was dragged off the beach at high water and the tow secured. Andrew, Carmen and Mr Jemmerling's diver then did a survey of the barge's bottom to check for damage. Luckily the barge had not been holed. Once that was done *Bonthorpe* set off, towing it south to Cairns.

Graham was quite jealous that he had missed out on being there when the treasure was discovered and more so at not having seen the wrecks. As he was still required to work on the *Wewak*, which was remaining to try to collect as many of the 44-gallon drums as possible, Willy felt sorry for him. When both Carmen and Andrew volunteered to stay and help with the work Willy felt he should as well.

He asked his parents and they looked doubtful. "You have your cadet promotion course in six days," his mother reminded him.

"I know. I will be alright Mum. I will feel bad if I don't help," Willy replied.

When Captain Kirk assured his parents that they would be back in Cairns in time for that, they said yes. So Willy spent four hot, sweaty days helping to roll empty drums down the beach, tie them into rafts so they could be towed by a boat to the *Wewak*, then helping to roll them up the LCT's ramp and stack them in the oven like heat of the tank deck. But he became fitter and stronger and was glad he was helping his friends.

The promotion course at Garbutt RAAF Base in Townsville came next and after that promotion to the rank of corporal. With the start of school he was, along with his friends, a minor celebrity. This was reinforced from time to time by articles in aircraft magazines about the aircraft wrecks, particularly that of the 'Dornier'.

But the biggest event to climax the adventure was being flown to Makassang in February. Mr Jemmerling took him and his father, plus Andrew and Carmen and their mother, Graham and his father, and the van der Heydens. They flew there in *Pterodactyl* for a dedication ceremony for the crown jewels by the Rajah. They were only there four days but as it was Willy's first overseas trip he was very excited. They were the guests of the Rajah in the famous pink coral 'Sun Palace' atop the equally famous five hundred 'Steps of Heaven'.

The Rajah was a young man, dressed in a western suit and a Malay kopiah. He had been educated in England and greeted them warmly. The people also welcomed them as heroes and saviours. It was brought home to Willy that the crown jewels had a sacred and mystical significance that greatly strengthened the legitimacy of the Rajah's rule and the tenuous independence of the tiny country. The Indonesians, who claimed it as part of their territories, were not pleased.

When Willy had watched the elaborate public processions and ceremonies and seen the Buddhist culture that set the island apart from Moslem Indonesia, he was also pleased to have helped. The fact that he had to sit through several hours of entertainment by bare-breasted dancing girls helped.

Before they left to return to Australia there was a final audience at the palace. At this the Rajah pinned on each of them a tiny replica of the sword of state. These were made of gold and with an inlay of tiny diamonds. On the back of each badge was a Sanskrit inscription that said they were the friends of Makassang and honorary citizens.

"You have made my throne secure. I number you among my friends," said the Rajah, shaking Willy's hand. "If you ever need help, just ask."

ACKNOWLEDGEMENTS

For their help in the preparation of this book the author would like to thank the following:

The Beck Family of the Beck Collection, Kennedy Highway, Mareeba, for their advice, encouragement and technical information, and in particular the late Mr Sid Beck. Note, since the 1st edition of this book was published the Beck's museum has closed but in respectful memory the story has been kept unchanged.

Craig Justo for permission to use his splendid photo of a Catalina in flight.

Mr Graham Orphan, Editor of *Classic Wings*

Sqn Ldr John Leroy and the staff of the RAAF Museum, Townsville.

Sqn Ldr Mel Dundas-Taylor
For his encouragement and information on aircraft wrecks in NQ

My late father, Captain H. W. Cummings, Master Mariner, and the ship's companies of the *Wewak* and *Bonthorpe*.

I would also like to acknowledge Bob Piper whose article 'The Secret Airfields – Iron Range' in *Flightpath* Vol 16- No 2 Nov-Jan 2005 provided details included in Chap 17.

Torres Strait Heritage Museum and Art Gallery
Mr A. L. SeeKeee and Ms V. SeeKee
Wasaga, Horn Island

'Savannah Aviation'
For information on the B24 'Liberator' crash at Moonlight Creek.

Enjoy more C.R. Cummings stories

The Air Cadets

The Navy Cadets

The Army Cadets